Mary E. Braddon

Under the Red Flag

and other tales

Mary E. Braddon

Under the Red Flag
and other tales

ISBN/EAN: 9783337103934

Printed in Europe, USA, Canada, Australia, Japan

Cover: Foto ©Andreas Hilbeck / pixelio.de

More available books at **www.hansebooks.com**

UNDER THE RED FLAG

And Other Tales

BY THE AUTHOR OF

"LADY AUDLEY'S SECRET," "VIXEN," "ISHMAEL,"
"WYLLARD'S WEIRD" ETC. ETC.

LONDON

JOHN AND ROBERT MAXWELL

MILTON HOUSE, ST. BRIDE STREET, LUDGATE CIRCUS

AND

SHOE LANE, FLEET STREET, E.C.

CONTENTS

Contents

UNDER THE RED FLAG

CHAPTER I.

GRETCHEN IN THE GARDEN

STARS shining in the deep purple of a summer sky ; June roses blooming and breathing sweetness on the soft, cool night ; leaves whispering ; low faint sounds of falling waters from a fountain hidden in the foliage ; and across the dim shadowy night the flaring lights and gaudy colours of a painted and gilded temple, in which the band is playing one of Strauss's tenderest waltzes.

The melodious strain is drawing to its close. The players attack the coda with crash and hurry, the pace intensifying as they near the end. All the waltzers have fallen out of the ranks, except one couple, and those two waltz as if it were impossible to tire—as if they were the very spirit of dance and melody, creatures of fire and air, motion incarnate.

The girl's golden head reclines against her partner's shoulder, but not with an air of weariness ; the attitude expresses only repose ; the graceful gliding step, the harmonious flowing movements, are as natural as the fall of waters or the waving of forest boughs. The rosy lips are slightly parted, the sweet eyes look starwards with a dreamy gaze. There is far more of spirit than of gross earthliness in the slim willowy form, the fair and radiant face, which the stars and the lamps shine upon alternately, as those revolving figures circle—now in the glare of the orchestra, and then under those solemn worlds of light which are soon to look upon stranger, sadder, darker, crueller sights than this Sunday evening dance at the Closerie des Lilas.

There are some who think it is a wicked thing to dance on a

Sunday evening, even after one has worshipped at one's parish church faithfully and reverently on Sunday morning ; some there are who think it is wicked to dance at all ; and there are others who adore their God in dances, and are moved to wild leapings and whfrlings by the spirit of piety ; others, again, who are devil-dancers, and worship the principle of evil in their demoniac gyrations. But assuredly, of all who ever danced upon this earth, none ever danced on the edge of a more terrible volcano than that which trembled and throbbed under the feet of these light-hearted revellers to-night— happy, unforeseeing, rejoicing in the balmy breath of summer, the starlit sky, the warmth and the flowers, with no thought that this fair Paris, whitely beautiful in the sheen of star- light and moonlight, was like a phantasmal or fairy city—a city of palaces which were soon to sink in dust and ashes, beauty that was to be changed for burning, while joy and love fled shrieking from a carnival of blood and fire.

Even to-night there were bystanders in the lamp-lit garden who shook their heads solemnly as they talked of the pro- bability of war with Prussia. The battle of Sadowa had been the beginning of evil. France had played into the hands of her most dangerous rival, and had been swindled out of the price of her neutrality. To have allowed Austria to be crushed by Bismarck was worse than a crime, it was a blunder. And now all the signs and tokens of the time pointed to the likelihood of war. The day had come when the overweening ambition of the house of Brandenburg must be checked, and in the opinion of the Bonapartists the onus to fight was upon France. Opinion among the people was divided ; and there were many who were friends of peace. A campaign would be a triumph for French arms, of course ; but such triumphs however certain, are never won without loss. For France as a people there must needs be profit and fame ; but for in- dividuals—well, even in a succession of victories some French blood must be shed, some French corpses must lie scattered on distant battlefields—there must be cypress as well as laurel.

Yet the idea of impending war was not unpleasant. It revivified the intellectual atmosphere, set the hearts of men and women throbbing with new hopes, new fears. To elderly people it seemed only the other day that the army was coming home in triumph after the Italian War, and France was crowning the liberators of a sister land ; but to the young people that Italian campaign seemed to have happened a long while ago. It was time that France should arise in her might and strike a great blow.

So the middle-aged folks, mere spectators of the evening's amusement, put their heads together and discussed the political situation—some arguing from one point of view, some from another ; and those two waltzers circled faster and faster with the closing bars of the coda. With the last chord they stopped. The dark-haired young man withdrew his arm reluctantly from his partner's slim waist, and then they went off arm-in-arm towards the shadow of the trees—dark-haired youth and fair-haired youth, all the world to each other, and infinitely happy.

'Faust and Marguerite,' said a corpulent citizen, who had been watching the dancers while he talked of Bismarck and the Duc de Gramont.

'Happily I see no Mephistopheles,' replied his companion 'If the young people go to perdition it will be their own doing.'

'The girl is very pretty,' said the other, 'and I think I have seen her lover's face before to-night.'

'He is to be seen any day at the Café Malmus. He is a journalist—a sprig of nobility, I believe, but as poor as Job. He writes for the papers. He ranks as an *esprit fort* and something of a wit."

'And the girl—do you know who she is ? She has hardly the air of a grisette.'

'She is like Nilsson in Marguerite. No, I'll swear she is no grisette—nothing of the Mimi Pinson there, my friend. I never saw her till to-night. Look yonder, just emerging from the trees : do you see ? '

'Is it Mephistopheles ? '

'No, but the spirit of evil in a woman's shape—envy, hatred, revenge, all incarnate in a jealous woman. Great Heaven, such a face—see, see ! '

His friend looked in the direction indicated. Yes ; there, creeping from the covert of the trees, stealthily, serpent-like, stole forth a woman—young, handsome, smartly dressed in a black silk gown, and a bonnet all roses and lace—a shopkeeper in holiday attire. The face was dark with hatred and malice, the eyes were bright with angry fires. Slowly, stealthily, the footsteps followed in the path the lovers had taken—following as the shadow follows the sun, as night follows day.

But now the band struck up a quadrille composed of the

liveliest airs from the *Princesse de Trebizonde*, which had lately enchanted the boulevards ; and then began those wild choric measures in which Parisian youth excels all other nations. The *habitués* of the garden—the clerks and the shopmen and the commercial travellers, industrial and intellectual youth of every grade—began their diversions, to the delight of the spectators. Legs were flung in the air, wild leapings and convulsive evolutions diversified the humdrum figures of the legitimate quadrille ; each dancer tried to surpass his *vis-à-vis*. Now the right had it ; anon, by a still wilder bound, the left triumphed ; while the lookers-on laughed and applauded. But there was no offence in this outbreak of muscular activity and high spirits. Sunday dances at these gardens are sacred to the people. There is very little admixture of the *demi-monde* on a Sunday evening ; the clerk and the counter-jumper, the little industries of Paris, have the field to themselves.

The journalist and his fair-haired sweetheart did not reappear in the quadrille. They were sauntering side by side in a shadowy alley, hearing the joyous music vaguely ; for the lowest whisper of a lover's voice has more power on the listening ear of love than the loudest orchestra that ever crashed and jingled in the music of *Orphée aux Enfers* or the *Grande Duchesse*.

'Why should Rose doom us to wait ?' pleaded the journalist, bending his dark ardent eyes on the fair sweet face beside him. 'What does poverty matter, if we are true to each other and strong to conquer fortune, as we are, Kathleen ? We can bear a few privations in the present, knowing that Fate will be kinder in the future. I have won a shred of reputation already, though I write for such a wretched rag of a paper that I can earn very little money ; but fame will come and money will follow before we are ten years older. At my age Balzac was no richer than I am.'

'I am not afraid of poverty,' answered the girl gently. 'Why should I fear what I have known all my life ? Rose and I have always been poor ; but we have always been happy ; except once when she had the fever. Ah, that was heart-breaking ! No money to pay a doctor, no money for wine or fruit or fuel, no money for the rent, and the deadly fear of being turned out of our lodging while she lay helpless and unconscious on her bed. No prospect but the hospital. Yes, those were dark days. I almost envied the rich.'

'Almost envied, my angel! I am made of a different stuff, and I hate and envy them at all times. That hatred gives bitterness to my pen—rancour, acidity, all the qualities our Parisians love. It is my chief stock-in-trade. I could not live without it.'

'Ah, you feel the sting of poverty more than I do, because you come of a race that was once rich, a family that was once noble.'

'Yes; I come of a decayed race—worn out, effete, passed by in the press and hurry of a commercial age. That is why I hate the insolent *roturier* brood that have battened in the sunshine of imperial favour; the stock-jobbers and gamblers, corrupt to the core, and swelling with pride in their dirty gold. My grandfather was a gentleman and a soldier; he fought for his king till the last ray of hope had faded. And when his faithful little band of Chouans were scattered or slain, and he had escaped by the skin of his teeth from being shot down by the Blues, he shut himself up in the old stone tower of his château, and lived among peasants, as peasants live, and let his son and daughter run wild. My father was very little in advance of his father's farm-labourers in education or manners, when he entered the army, a lad of fifteen, soon after the restoration of the Bourbons. But he was one of the handsomest men of his day. He had good blood in his veins; and it seems somehow that race will tell, for twenty years later he was one of the finest soldiers in the French army. He married a rich wife, loved her passionately, spent all her money, ruined her life, and died broken-hearted and a pauper within a year of her death, leaving me to face the world, penniless, and with very few friends, at twelve years of age. The Empire was then in its golden dawn. One of my first memories is of the Coup d'Etat, that awful night of the second of December, when the bullets whistled along the Boulevard Poissonnière, like the hailstones in a summer storm, and the terrified wondering bourgeois were mown down like ears of corn. My father was at the head of his regiment that night; and my mother and I were looking down upon the scene from our apartment at a corner of the boulevard. Two years later I was an orphan.'

'Oh, what a hard childhood and youth you must have had!' said Kathleen, full of pity.

'Not harder than yours, little one. You and the sister have not had too much of the sunshine of life, I take it.'

'No; but we have always been together. We have faced

the storm side by side ; or perhaps I ought to say that Rose
has faced it bravely by herself and sheltered me. But you
have been quite alone—no brother, no sister.'

'Not a creature of my own flesh and blood,' answered
Mortemar. 'If it had not been for a bluff old brother-officer
of my father's I must have starved, or been brought up on
state charity. He got me a pension, just enough to pay my
schooling in a humble way, from the Emperor, in consideration of my father's services on the second of December, but
this allowance was to cease when I was eighteen. The
influence of my father's old friend got me accepted at one of
the finest schools near Paris, the school kept by the Dominican
Fathers at Arcueil, where I was educated at a third of the
pension paid for the other pupils, by the benevolence of the
Prior, who pitied by desolate position. Here I remained till
my eighteenth birthday ; and I ought to be a better man than
I am after the care and kindness those good monks lavished
upon me. When I left school the good old friend was dead,
and from that time I have had to live—somehow--by my
own labour of head or hands. I believe it is considered
the finest training for youth; but it is hard, and it hardens
the heart and the mind of a man.'

'Has it hardened your heart, Gaston ?' asked the girl,
drawing a little closer to him in the dim starlit avenue.

'To all the world—except to you.'

And now, at a turn of the leafy path, they came suddenly
face to face with another couple—a stalwart, broad shouldered
man of about thirty, with a tall good-looking young woman
upon his arm—at sight of whom Kathleen exclaimed
lovingly,

'Rose, where have Philip and you been hiding all the
evening ?'

'We have been looking on at the dancers, Kathleen,'
answered Rose ; 'and now I think it is time we all went
home.'

'So soon ?' cried Kathleen.

'It has struck the three-quarters after ten. Did you see
Madame Michel in her fine bonnet and gown ?'

'What, Suzon Michel of the *crémerie?*' asked Mortemar.
'Is she here to-night ?'

'She is here every Sunday night, I believe, and at the
theatre three times a week,' said Rose's companion, Philip
Durand, as devoted to the elder sister as Gaston Mortemar
was to the younger. 'That young woman has a pleasant

life of it.　She has saved money in that snug little shop of hers.'

'She is a vulgar coquette, and I hate the sight of her,' said Rose sharply.

This was a very ill-natured speech for Rose, who was usually the soul of kindness.

'Pray what has the poor little Suzon done to offend you?' asked Gaston, laughing at Rose's impetuosity.

'It is not what she has done, but what she is.　I hate bold bad women ; and she is both bold and bad.'

'This from you, Rose, who believe that the Gospel was something more than an epitome of the floating wisdom of the East !　Have you forgotten the text, "Judge not, that ye be not judged?"'

'When I think or speak of Suzon Michel I forget that I am a Christian,' answered Rose gravely.　'There is something venomous about that woman.　I loathe her instinctively, as I loathe a snake.　And now, Kathleen, we must really go home.'

'One more round, just one more.　Hark ! there is the waltz from *La Grande Duchesse*,' pleaded Gaston ; and, without waiting for permission, he drew his arm round Kathleen's waist, and led her into the circle in front of the flaring orchestra, under the summer stars.

CHAPTER II.

WAYSIDE FLOWERS

THE Rue Gît le Cœur is not one of the fashionable streets of
Paris. It does not belong to the English quarter, or the
American quarter, or the Legitimist quarter, or the Diplo-
matic quarter ; the quarter of Art, or Learning, or Science,
or the *demi-monde*. Beauty and fashion never visit the spot.
It has hardly a place on the map of Paris. And yet, like many
another such street, it is a little world in itself, and human
beings are born and die in it, and passions pure and holy,
and base and wicked, are nourished and fostered there ; and
comedies and tragedies are acted there, turn by turn, as the
wedding feast is spread, or the funeral drapery hung out,
black and limp and dismal, against the dingy door-posts.

Gît le Cœur is a narrow shabby little street, hidden somewhere in the densely-populated district between the Boulevard St. Michel and the Rue des Saints Pères. It is near the
Quai des Augustins, which makes a pleasant promenade for
its inhabitants on summer evenings, near the river, within
sight of the mighty towers of Notre Dame, within sound of
her deep-toned bells. It is near the Morgue, and not very
far from the hospitals ; near the flower-market ; near much
that is central and busy, closely hemmed round with the
teeming life of the workaday world of Paris ; but very far
from the haunts of pleasure, from the famous restaurants,
from clubs and cafés, from parks and parterres, from opera-
house and aristocratic hotel.

It is a narrow street—crooked too—and the houses are of
the shabbiest. In one of these houses, a house which lay
back from the street, and, with three others, formed a stony
quadrangle, enclosing a little yard, dwelt Rose and Kathleen
O'Hara, two sisters of Irish parentage, the daughters of a
poor Irish gentleman, who had come here from the good city
of Bruges in Flanders, just twelve years ago, and had occupied the same little apartment on the third story ever since.
Just nineteen years ago Captain O'Hara was living with a
young second wife and a seven-year-old daughter, the issue

of his first marriage, in the city of Brussels. He had been in the army, in the 87th Irish Fusiliers, had run through his little patrimony, and had sold his commission, and thrown himself almost penniless on the world, after the manner of many other gentlemen, English as well as Irish. Twice had he married in ten years, and twice for love. Nothing could have been more honourable or less prudent than ether marriage ; and now he was living from hand to mouth in furnished lodgings in Brussels, writing a little for the English newspapers, getting a little help now and then from his own family, and now and then a ten-pound note from a wealthy maiden aunt of his wife's—the aunt from whose handsome house in the Circus, Bath, pretty Kathleen Reilly had run away with her handsome captain. The aunt had not forgiven or taken her back to favour ; but she sent a little help occasionally, out of sheer charity, and always accompanied by a lecture which gave a flavour of bitterness to the boon.

Captain O'Hara and his wife were not unhappy, in spite of their precarious fortunes. It was summer, and the scent of the lime-blossom was in the air of the park and the boulevards ; the lamplit streets and cafés were full of brightness and music in the balmy eventides of July. The young wife was looking forward tremblingly, yet hopefully, to the cares and joys of maternity. The dark-eyed step-daughter adored her. Too young to remember her own mother, who had died in Bengal, where the girl was born, the child idolised the Captain's fair-haired wife, and was fondly loved by her in return. Never was there a happier family group than these three, and when the expected baby should come, it was to be a boy, the Captain declared in the pride of his heart ; a son and heir—heir to empty pockets, wasted opportunities, bankruptcy, and gaol. He was pining for a son to perpetuate the noble race of O'Hara. The baby was to be christened Patrick, after some famous Patrick O'Hara of days gone by, the age of war and chivalry, and poetry and pride, when Ireland had not yet yielded to the proud invader.

Alas for the unborn child on whom such hopes had been founded, about whom such dreams had been dreamt ! The fatal day of birth came, and the child was a girl ; and before the wailing infant was six days old the young fair mother, with the rippling golden hair and innocent blue eyes, was lying in her coffin, strewn with white lilies and roses, and all the purest flowers of summer-tide. The brave young heart, which had never flinched or faltered at poverty or trouble, was stilled for ever. The wife who had been content to bear Fate's worst ills with the husband of her choice was gone to the shadowy home where his love could not follow her.

Captain O'Hara never looked the world or his difficulties bravely in the face after that day. He lived to see Kathleen a lovely child of five years old ; but he was a broken man from the day of his wife's death. He roamed from foreign town to town, living anywhere for convenience or cheapness. He spent six months at Brest, a year in Jersey, the two girls with him everywhere, nursed and cared for by Bridget Ryan, the faithful Irish maid-servant who had taken Rose from the arms of her Indian ayah, and had followed the Captain's fortunes ever since. He led a wretched out-at-elbows life, getting a little money by hook or by crook, and leaving a little train of debts behind him, like the trail of the serpent, in every town he left.

In Jersey, where cognac was conveniently cheap, the Captain took to drinking a good deal—not in dreadful drink-ing bouts, which would have frightened his poor children out of their senses, but in a gentle homœopathic sort of sottishness which kept his brain in a feeble state all day long, and gradually sapped his strength and his manhood. While the Captain was dawdling away his day—strolling down to the tavern or the club, lounging on the esplanade, gossiping with the goers and comers, meeting old acquaintance, and sometimes getting an invitation to dinner, with a cigarette always between his lips—the two children, of whom the elder was not eleven, and the younger only four, used to play together all day upon the golden sands in front of their shabby lodgings, while the Irish nurse gossiped with the landlady, or sat in the sun darning and patching the children's well-worn frocks or the Captain's decaying shirts.

The two girls were happy in those sunny summer days by the sea, in spite of their poor lodgings and scanty fare. Fruit was cheap, and flowers were abundant everywhere, and there was no stint of bread and butter, and milk and eggs. The children wanted nothing better. But it was a dismal change for them when their father carried them back to Belgium, and established them in a stony street in Bruges, where the peaked roofs of the opposite houses seemed to shut out the sun, and where, instead of the sweet fresh odours of sea and seaweed, there was an everlasting stench of dried fish and sewage.

It was winter by this time, and it seemed to be the winter

of their lives. Kathleen cried for the sea and the flowers of sunny Jersey. She could hardly be made to understand that summer was only a happy interval in the year, and that flowers do not grow in the stony streets of a city. The days in Bruges were cold and dismal, the evenings long and gloomy. If it had not been for Biddy Ryan the poor children might have pined to death in their solitude. Captain O'Hara was never at home in the evening, rarely at home in the afternoon, and he never left his bed till the carillon at the cathedral had played that lovely melody of Beethoven's, 'Hope told a flattering tale,' which the bells rang out every day at noontide. The Captain found the café indispensable to his comfort, the *petit verre d'absinthe suisse* a necessity of his being, a game at dominoes or draughts the only distraction for the canker at his heart : thus the children, whom he loved fondly enough after his manner, were dependent on Biddy Ryan for happiness ; and the faithful soul did her utmost to cheer and amuse them in their loneliness. She told them her fairy stories, the legends of her native Kerry ; she described the green hills and purple mountains, the lakes, the glens and gorges, the islands and groves and abbeys, of that romantic county ; until Rose, who had seen but little of the grandeur and glory of this earth, longed with a passionate longing for that land of lake and mountain, which was in somewise her own land, inasmuch as her father had been born and bred within a few miles of Killarney.

'And ye'll both go there some day, my darlints,' said tender-hearted Biddy, 'and it's ladies ye'll be, and never a poor day ye'll know in ould Ireland ; for by the Lord's grace the Captain's rich cousins may all die off like ratten sheep, and his honour may come in for the estate ! There's quarer things have happened than that in my knowledge, and sure it's great hunters the gentlemen are, and may ride home with broken necks any day.'

Rose said she hoped her cousins would not die ; but she wished they would ask her father and all of them to go and live at the great white house near the lakes, which Biddy described as a grander palace than the king's château at Lacken, which she and Rose had been taken to see one day with the Captain and his young wife, before Kathleen's birth.

The children were never tired of hearing Biddy talk of the lakes and mountains, the Druids' Circle, MacGillycuddy's Reeks, and the great house in which their father was born.

It was their ideal of paradise, a home where sorrow or care could never enter, gardens always full of flowers, a land of everlasting summer, woods and glens peopled with fairies, skies without a cloud, gladness without alloy.

One gray hopeless afternoon, when there had not been a rift in the slate-coloured sky since daybreak, Kathleen suddenly turned from the window, against which she had been flattening her pretty little nose, in the hopeless attempt to find amusement in looking into the empty street, and asked :

' Does it ever rain in Ireland, Biddy ? '

' Yes, love, it does rain sometimes ; and sure, darlint, that's why the hills and the valleys are all so soft and green.   You wouldn't have it always dhry : the flowers wouldn't grow without any rain.'

' Must there be rain ? ' inquired Kathleen simply.   ' Papa says I mustn't cry.   Why should the sky cry ?   The sky is good, isn't it ? '

' Yes, dear, it is God's sky.'

' But papa says it's naughty to cry.'

The time came only too soon when very real tears, tears of passionate grief and wild despair, were shed in that dingy Belgian lodging ; and when the two children and their faithful servant found themselves alone in the bleak strange world, face to face with starvation.

The captain caught cold one bitter February night, coming home, in the teeth of the east wind, from his favourite café ; and although devotedly nursed by Biddy and Rose, who was sensible and womanly beyond her years, the cold developed into acute bronchitis, under which James O'Hara succumbed, a few days after his thirty-seventh birthday, leaving his children penniless and alone in the world.   There were only a few francs in the Captain's purse at the time of his death ; for the short sharp illness had been expensive, albeit the English doctor, a retired navy surgeon, had been most modest in his charges.   The captain's watch and signet ring were pledged to pay for the funeral ; and while the coffin was being carried to the cemetery, a letter, ill-spelt and ill-written, but full of tender womanly feeling, was on its way to the wealthy Miss Fitzpatrick of Bath, pleading for her orphaned great-niece Kathleen, and Kathleen's penniless half-sister.

Miss Fitzpatrick of Bath was a staunch Roman Catholic, and a conscientious woman; but she was not a warm-hearted woman, and she was not deeply moved by the thought of the Captain's untimely death, or of his desolate children. She had been very angry with him for running away with her niece, who was also her companion and slave ; and she had never left off being angry ; yet she had given him money from time to time, considering it her duty, as a rich woman, to help her poor relations. And now she was not inclined to ignore that duty, or to deny the orphans' claim.

She went over to Bruges, saw the children, and in Kathleen beheld the image of her own dead sister's little girl as she had first seen her twenty years ago, when the orphan was sent to her rich aunt, as the legacy of a dying sister, the sole issue of a foolish marriage. And behold, here was another golden-haired child, sole issue of another foolish marriage, looking up at Theresa Fitzpatrick with just the same heaven-blue eyes, and the same scared, shrinking look, as doubting whether to find a friend or a foe in the richly-clad stately dame.

If Miss Fitzpatrick had been of the melting mood, she would assuredly have taken the child to her heart and her home, and the child's dark-eyed, frank-browed, lovable step-sister with her. There was ample room for both girls in the big handsome house at Bath—empty rooms which no one ever visited save the housemaid with her brooms and brushes ; luxuriously-furnished rooms, swept and garnished, and kept in spotless order for nobody.

Although there was ample room in Miss Fitzpatrick's house, there was no room in Miss Fitzpatrick's heart for two orphans.

'I shall do my duty to you, my dears,' she said, 'and I shall make no distinctions, although you, Rose, are no relation of mine, and have no claim upon me.'

'You won't take Rose away ?' cried Kathleen, pale with terror, the blue eyes filling with tears.

'No, my dear, I shall not separate you while you are so young,' answered Miss Fitzpatrick, complacently settling herself in her sable-bordered mantle. ' By-and-by, when you are young women, you will have to make your way in the world, and then you may be parted. But for the next few years you shall be together. How have they been educated ?' she asked, appealing to Biddy, who stood by, curtsying every time the lady looked her way.

'Sure, ma'am, my lady, the captain was very careful with them : he'd never have let the dear childer out of his sight, only he wanted a little gentlemen's society now and then, blessed soul, and he liked to spend half an hour or so at a caffy. But many's the day I've heard um reading poethry to the two childer, beautiful—Hamlick and the Ghost, and King Leerd, and Romulet and Julio. There never was a better father, if the Lord had been pleased to spare him,' concluded Biddy, with her apron at her eyes.

'My good woman, you do not understand my question,' said Miss Fitzpatrick impatiently. 'I want to know what these children have been taught. I begin to fear they have been sorely neglected by that foolish man. Can they read and write and cipher?'

Biddy, hard pushed, was fain to confess that Kathleen did not even know her letters, and that Rose was very backward with her pen, though she could read beautifully.

'I thought as much,' said Miss Fitzpatrick. 'And now, Bridget Ryan, I'll tell you what I mean to do : you seem to have been a faithful servant, so I shall not allow you to be a loser by Captain O'Hara's death. I shall pay you your wages in full, and send you home to Ireland.'

'With the young ladies?' asked Biddy, beaming.

'What should the young ladies do in Ireland?' exclaimed Miss Fitzpatrick ;' they haven't a friend in that wretched country. No, you can go back to your home, for I suppose you have some kind of home to go to. But I shall place the two young ladies in a convent I have been told about, three miles from this city, where they will be carefully educated and kindly looked after by the good nuns. I shall pay for their schooling and provide their wardrobes till they are grown up ; but when they come to nineteen or twenty, they will have to earn their own living. The better they are educated the easier they will find it to earn their bread.'

Biddy could but confess that Miss Fitzpatrick, upon whom the elder sister had no shadow of claim, was acting very generously ; yet she was in despair at the thought of being separated from the children she had nursed, and who were to her as her own flesh and blood. If Miss Fitzpatrick had sent them all three to Ireland, and given her a cottage, a potato field, and a pig, she felt she could have worked for the two children, and brought them up in comfort, and been as happy as the days were long. They would have run about the fields barefoot, and with wild uncovered hair, and made a friend and companion of the pig, but they would have grown up strong and beautiful in that free life; and it seemed to her that such a life would be ever so much happier for them than the enclosed convent in the flat arid country outside Bruges, the grim white house within high walls, the tall slated roof of which she and her charges had seen many a day frowning upon them from afar off in their afternoon walks.

She accepted her wages from Miss Fitzpatrick, but she declined the fare home to Ireland.

'It may be long days before I see that blessed counthry,' she said, 'for, with all submission to your ladyship, I shall try to get a place in Bruges, so that I may be near these darling childer, and gladden my eyes with the sight of them now and then, whin the good nuns give lave.'

Miss Fitzpatrick had no objection to this plan. She was a good woman according to her lights, but as hard as a stone. She wanted to do her duty in a prompt and business-like manner, and to provide for these orphans; not because she cared a straw for them, but because they were orphans, and to feed the widow and the orphan is the business of a good Catholic.

She put the two girls into a fly next morning, after spending an uncomfortable night at the best hotel in Bruges, where the foreign arrangements and the all-pervading odours of garlic and sour cabbage-water afflicted her sorely, and drove straight off to the Sisters of Sainte Marie.

Here, in a rambling, chilly-looking house, with large whitewashed carpetless rooms, and corridors smelling of plaster, Miss Fitzpatrick handed the orphans over to the Reverend Mother, a stout, comfortable-looking Belgian, who, for a payment in all of ninety pounds a year, was to lodge, feed, clothe, and educate the two children from January to December. There were to be no vacations. The school year was to be really a year. Children who had parents might go home for a summer holiday; but for these orphans the white-walled convent, in its flat sandy garden, was to be the only home.

And now there began for those orphan sisters a new life— very strange, very cold and formal, after the life they had led with the careless yet loving father and the devoted nurse. It was a life of rule and routine, of work and deprivation. The convent school was a cheap school, and though the Sisters were conscientious in their dealings with their pupils, the fare was of the poorest, the beds were hard and narrow, the coverlets were thin, dormitories draughty and carpetless, everything bleak and bare. The children rose at unnatural

hours in the cold dark mornings, and were sent to bed early
to save fire and candle. It was a hard life, with scarcely a
ray of sunshine. Some of the nuns were kind and some of
the nuns were cross, just as women are outside convent-walls.
There were no pleasures, there was very little to hope for:
the nuns were too poor to afford pleasure for their pupils.
Chapel and lessons, lessons and chapel; chapel twice a day,
lessons all day long ; that was the round of life. Half an
hour's recreation at stated intervals—just one brief half-hour
of leisure and play, if the children had strength to play, after
two long hours bending over books, puzzling over sums.

Rose bore her trials like a heroine. Kathleen fretted a
good deal at first, and then when she grew older and stronger,
she became a little inclined to occasional outbreaks of
rebellion. She had a sweet loving nature, and could be ruled
easily by love—by threats or hard usage not at all. The
nuns, happily, were fond of her, and petted her for her
beauty and brightness and graceful ways. While dark,
proud Rose, earnest, thoughtful, laborious, plodded on at her
studies, always obedient, always conscientious, Kathleen
learnt by fits and starts, was sometimes attentive, sometimes
neglectful, sometimes industrious to fever-point, sometimes
incorrigibly idle. She had all the freaks of genius.

Life went on thus with a dismal monotony for five long
years ; till it seemed to the sisters as if they could never have
known any world outside those convent-walls, any horizon
beyond that western line of level marsh and meadow, where
they used to watch the sun going down in a golden bed
behind the tall black poplars. To Kathleen it seemed as if
the old sweet life, with father and nurse, must have been a
dream. One bitter grief had come to them in the last year.
The good faithful Biddy was dead. It had been her custom
to visit them on the last Saturday in every month for an hour
in the afternoon, by special permission of the Superior ; and
neither storm nor rain, snow nor hail, had ever kept Biddy
away. Her visit was a bright spot in the lives of the girls.
They clung to her and loved her in that too brief hour as if
she had been verily their mother. The vulgar Irish face, the
hands hardened by toil, the coarse common clothes, were, to
them, as dear as if she had been the finest lady in the land.
She came to them laden with fruit and cakes, and she brought
them bright-coloured neck ribbons to enliven their sombre
black uniform. She told them her scraps of news about the
outside world. She walked with them in the garden, or sat

with them in the visitors' parlour, and they were utterly happy so long as she stayed.

At last, after they had been four years and a-half in the convent, there came one never-to-be-forgotten Saturday on which there was no visitor for the Demoiselles O'Hara. It was a peerless June day, and the girls had pictured Biddy as she walked along the sandy road from Bruges, where she had a hardish place as maid-of-all-work in a Flemish tradesman's family. They fancied how she would enjoy the sunshine, and the hedges all in flower, and the song of the lark. If they could but be with her, thought Kathleen, dancing along beside her, gathering the wild flowers ! But hark'! there was the convent clock striking three. In another moment the bell would ring, the loud harsh bell, which sounded so sweet upon that one particular afternoon. Biddy was the soul of punctuality. The clock had seldom finished striking before the bell rang. The girls were sitting in the garden, as near the gateway and the porter's lodge as they were allowed to go. They waited and waited, listening for the bell, which never rang ; which never was again to be rung by that honest hand. At last the clock struck four, and they knew that all hope was over for that day. From three to four was the hour appointed by authority for Biddy's visit. She would not presume to come after that hour.

'There will be a letter to-morrow, perhaps,' said Rose, with a sigh. 'Poor dear Biddy ! It is such an effort for her to write.'

But the days went by, and there was no letter. The last Saturday in July came, and there had been no sign or token from Biddy. The rules of the convent school were strict, and the girls were allowed to write to no one except relations.

That last Saturday in July was a dull stormy day, a sullen sultry day, with heavy thunder showers. Again the two girls pictured their friend upon the sandy road, this time wrapped in her Irish frieze cloak, the countrywoman's cloak which she had worn ever since Rose could remember, and struggling against the storm with her stout Belgian umbrella of dark-red cotton. But the clock struck three, and the clock struck four, the girls waiting through the hour with listening ears and beating hearts, and there was no touch of Bridget Ryan's hand upon the convent bell.

Then Rose grew desperate, and went straight to the Reverend Mother, and asked permission to write to Bridget, who must be ill, or surely she would have come. The Superior hesitated a little ; rules were strict, and if once broken—and so on and so on. But the pale anxious face and tearful eyes touched her, and she gave the required permission and the necessary postage stamp.

Three days Rose and Kathleen waited anxiously for the reply to their letter, and then came a formal epistle from a lawyer in Bruges, who had the honour to acquaint the young ladies that their late father's old servant, Madame Ryan, had died at midnight on the last Saturday in June, after a very short illness, and that she had bequeathed the whole of her savings to Mademoiselle Rose O'Hara, said savings amounting, after payment of funeral expenses, to five hundred and fifty francs.

Deep and bitter was the grief of the sisters at the loss of this faithful friend—the only woman friend whose warm motherly love Kathleen had ever known. Rose gave a hundred francs to the Reverend Mother to be spent in masses for the beloved dead. Kathleen wanted her to devote all the money to that sacred purpose.

'What do we want with the poor darling's money?' she asked.

'Nothing now, dear,' answered the more experienced elder sister ; ' but the day may come when a little money will save us from a great deal of misery.'

The day came when those few gold pieces, which Rose kept under lock and key with all her little treasures in a small japanned box that had belonged to her father, made the two girls independent of tyranny, or of that which seemed to them as tyranny of an altogether unbearable kind.

The good Reverend Mother, under whose firm but friendly rule Rose and Kathleen had grown up, one to a tall, well-developed girl of eighteen, the other to a slim sapling of eleven, was transferred to a larger and wealthier convent, and was replaced by a sour-visaged nun whose piety was of the gloomy order, and who wanted to rule the community with a rod of iron. Everything was changed under her dominion, every rule was made more severe, every little innocent pleasure was curtailed or forbidden. A dark pall came down upon the convent, and discontent brooded like an evil presence by the hearth.

Kathleen, in high health, active, full of life and spirits, was one of the first to break the new rules. Her gaiety was misconduct, her fresh ringing laugh an offence. She was continually getting into disgrace ; and Rose, who saw her punished by all sorts of small privations and by the burden of extra tasks, rebelled in her heart against the tyrant, although she urged her young sister to submission and obedience.

There came a day—a bright summer day—when the punishment lesson was heavier than usual, although Kathleen's offence had been of the slightest kind.

'Kathleen O'Hara has an obstinate disposition, and it must be conquered,' said the Reverend Mother, when she was told of a blotted exercise or a little outbreak of temper.

To-day Kathleen had a headache. She was flushed and feverish, overcome by the midsummer heat. Just a year had gone since Bridget's death, and it seemed to both girls as if that year had been the longest in their lives—the longest and most unhappy. The child made a feeble effort to write the German exercise which had been given her as a punishment task: but she soon gave up altogether, and sat crying, with the book open before her, and the sun pouring its fierce light upon her flushed, tear-stained face.

This was taken as rank contumacy, and when the Reverend Mother came upon her round of inspection from a superior class, she ordered Kathleen off to a room at the top of the house, a bare garret under the thin hot roof, which was used only for solitary confinement in very bad cases. It was the Black Hole of the convent.

Kathleen was marched up to this place of durance vile, and kept there till evening prayers, with the refreshment of a slice of black bread—such bread as the coachmen give their horses in that country—and a cup of water. In the cool eventide she was let out of her prison, which had been like an oven all day, and she and Rose lay down together side by side in their narrow beds at the end of the long dormitory, nearest the door.

When all the others were asleep Rose knelt by her sister's bed, and kissed and comforted her; but the child was broken-hearted. She said she would die in that miserable house. Lessons were given to her which she could not learn, and then she was punished for not learning them. She had been frightened in that dreadful room. She had heard things—awful things—running about behind the walls, squeaking and screaming. She thought they were demons.

'They were rats, darling,' said Rose, caressing and soothing her. 'You shall never, never be put in that room again, if you will be brave, and trust me.'

Rose shuddered at the thought of that stifling garret, under the burning roof, and the rats running about behind the wainscot. She had heard of children having been eaten alive by rats.

'Shall we steal out of the house to-morrow morning as soon as it is light, and go away and live by ourselves somewhere?' she asked, in a whisper.

It was an hour after bed-time; the other children were all sleeping on their hard little bolsters. There was no one to overhear the sisters as they whispered and plotted. It was no new thought with Rose O'Hara. She had been meditating upon it for a long time, ever since the new rule had begun and had made Kathleen unhappy. She had never forgotten those words of Miss Fitzpatrick's: 'When you are grown up you will have to get your own living, and then you may have to be parted.' The very thought of severance from Kathleen, this only beloved of her heart, was despair. Rose made up her mind that there should be no such parting. Why should they not work and live together? Rose felt herself strong and brave, and able to work for both. She had wasted no opportunity that the convent afforded her. She had learnt all that her teachers had given her to learn, and now felt herself able to teach as she had been taught. If Miss Fitzpatrick were left free to plan their lives, she and her sister would be parted; but if she took their fate into her own hands, they could spend their lives together— stand or fall together, prosper or fail together; and, in her young hopefulness, it seemed to her that failure was hardly possible.

She whispered the plan to Kathleen. They were to get up at daybreak—at the first glimmer of light—dress themselves, and creep out of the dormitory and down the stairs, with their shoes in their hands. The door opening into the garden was bolted only. They had nothing to do but draw back the heavy bolts noiselessly. The garden was guarded by high walls, except in one weak point which the girls knew well. An older wall, only eight feet high—a ponderous old wall, with heavy buttresses of crumbling brick—divided the western side of the garden from an extensive orchard sloping down to the river.

This wall had been scaled by many a young rebel, in quest of plums and pears, and it would be no obstacle to the sisters' escape. Rose would take a change of linen in a little bundle, and her fortune of fifteen gold pieces, Biddy's legacy, in her pocket; and with this stock of worldly wealth they would make their way to Paris, that wonderful, beautiful city, of which they had heard so much from some of their school-fellows, the daughters of small Parisian tradesmen, who had been sent to the Belgian convent for economical reasons.

'Are we going to walk all the way?' asked Kathleen.

'Not all the way, darling. We can go by rail. But if we find the journey would cost us too much we might walk part of the way.'

'I will walk as far as you like; I am not afraid,' said Kathleen.

Their scheme prospered. In the dewy morning they climbed the crumbling orchard-wall, where there was plenty of foothold on the broken bricks, and ran across the wet grass to the edge of the river, following which they came to the high-road. They avoided Bruges, the city of church towers, and steep roofs, and many bridges, and made for the road to Courtrai. Their first day's journey of fifteen miles was over a dusty road—flat, dreary, monotonous—a long and weary walk; but they rested on the way at a cottage, where they enjoyed a meal of bread and fruit which cost them only a few pence. Not for years had they so relished any feast as they enjoyed this dinner of black bread and black cherries, which they ate in a little arbour covered with a hop-vine, in a corner of the cottage garden. They were three days on the road to Courtrai, sleeping in humble cottages, and living on the humblest fare. At the railway station at Courtrai Rose found that the price of railway tickets to Paris, even the cheapest they could buy, would make a great hole in their little fortune; so she and Kathleen decided that they would walk all the way. It was a long journey, but not so long as that of the Scotch girl whom Rose had read about in Sir Walter Scott's story.

'I should like to walk,' said Kathleen. 'I have been so happy to-day—no lessons, no one to scold us. It is so nice to have the sky, and the flowers, and the fields all to ourselves.'

Rose found a decent lodging for the night in a weaver's cottage, and they started next morning on the road to Paris, Kathleen as merry as a lark, Rose happy, but with a grave sense of responsibility.

They were weeks upon the road, in the balmy summer weather, walking and walking, on and on, under a cloudless blue sky; for the heavens favoured them, and the peerless

July weather lasted all through their journey, save on one
day when they were caught in a thunderstorm, and had to
take refuge in a deserted stable, where they sat crouched
together in a dark corner, while the thunder rolled over
the broken thatch, and the lightning sent lances of fire zig-
zagging across the dusky gloom.

They were often very tired ; they were often half choked
and half blinded by the chalky dust of the long level roads ;
but they were happy ; for they were together, and they were
free.   It was the first real holiday they had known since they
had entered at the convent gate.   No lessons, no burdens of
any kind.   Every day they knelt in the cool shade of some
strange church to pray.   They heard the mass sung by strange
priests before village altars.   They found friends at the
cottages where they lodged.   The women all admired
Kathleen's golden hair and blue eyes, and sympathised with
the sisters when told that they were orphans beginning
the world together.   No one overcharged or robbed them.
They were treated generously everywhere.   Their very
defencelessness was their shield and breastplate.

And thus through toil, that had none of the bitterness of
toil, they slowly approached the great city, which to their
young imaginations was like a fairy city.   They did not
quite believe that the streets were paved with gold :   but they
fancied life would be very easy there, and that their hearts
would be always light enough to enjoy the sparkle of the
fountains, the glory of the broad strong river, the perfume of
flowers, the beautiful churches and beautiful theatres, and
shining lamp-lit boulevards, about which their schoolfellows
had told them so much.

CHAPTER III.

KATHLEEN'S LOVER

THE first sensation with both sisters, when they came within view of the mighty city, was disappointment. Rose felt her heart sink within her. The houses were so high, the streets so long and dreary ; the city seemed a wilderness of stone and plaster. All the trees on the boulevards—those long new boulevards by which they entered Paris—were white with dust, and had a withered look. The houses had a poverty-stricken air, despite their size and newness. They looked liked big white gaols. As for flowers or fountains, parks or gardens, there was no sign of any such thing.

'What an ugly place !' cried Kathleen piteously. 'Those girls at the convent must have been wicked storytellers.'

They tramped on and on, till at last they came to the heart of the town, to the place of fountains, and palaces, and gardens, and flowers. It was in the summer sunset. All things were gilded by that western radiance. Soldiers were marching along the Rue de Rivoli, drums beating, trumpets blaring. Lamps were lit in all the cafés, crowds of people were sitting about in the open streets, the concerts in the Champs Elysées were beginning their music and song, myriad little lampions shining and twinkling in the last rays of the sun. Cleopatra's Needle, fountains, palace, soldiers, statues, trees, flowers, all fused themselves into one dazzling picture before the eyes of the two young travellers.

'O Rose, how beautiful ! how beautiful !' gasped Kathleen, breathless with rapture. 'How happy we shall be here !'

But while they stood admiring the fountains, listening to the martial music, the shades of evening were descending, and they had still to find a shelter for the night. Useless to look for such a shelter in this region of palaces. Rose took her sister by the hand and walked on, trusting to Fate to carry them to some humble district, where they might find friends and economical fare, as they had done everywhere on the way, thanks to Rose's instinct for discovering the fittest places, the right people.

Stars were beginning to flash and tremble upon the blue river as the orphans went over the bridge beyond the Louvre into that poorer Paris on the left bank of the Seine. Here they roamed about in the twilight till they drifted somehow into the Rue Gît le Cœur; and at the door of one of the shabby old houses Rose saw a fat, middle-aged matron, with a good-natured face, of whom she asked for advice as to a lodging.

The matron heard her story, and at once spread her motherly wing over both girls. There was a *garni*, a furnished third floor in the middle house in the yard. The rooms were small: just two little rooms and a tiny closet for kitchen; quite big enough for two girls. She led the way, introduced Rose to the *concierge*—whose husband was a shoemaker, occupying the basement of the house—and who went panting up the narrow stair, key in hand, to show the lodging.

It was very small, very shabby; and cheap although it was, the rent seemed a great deal to Rose, after her experience of village lodgings on the way; but her new friend told her she might walk miles and get nothing so cheap in all Paris; so she took heart, and hired the apartment for a month certain, paying the fifth of her golden pieces, of which she had spent just four upon the road, as an instalment of the rent. And then, still directed by her stout friend, she went to a *crémerie* round the corner and bought some milk and rolls and a little cheese for supper; and the sisters sat down in their new home, so bare of many things essential for comfort, and laughed and cried over their first meal in Paris. Kathleen was almost hysterical with fatigue and excitement. All the way they had come, even in the midst of her girlish gladness, she had been haunted by fears of pursuit. The Reverend Mother would send the gardener after her, and have her taken back and shut up in the sun-baked room where the rats lived.

'But now we are safe,' she said, with her head on her sister's shoulder, and Rose's arm round her, 'we are safe in Paris; and if Reverend Mother sends after us, we'll go to the Emperor and ask him to take care of us. We are his subjects now.' This was in '62, when the Empire was in its glory, and there was a sense of power and splendour in the third Napoleon's dominion over this beautiful modern Babylon, such as must have been felt in Rome under the politic sway of Augustus. These girls felt as if they were in a fortress, now they were within the charmed circle of imperial magnificence.

Years of struggle, and poverty, and industry, and self-denial came after that happy evening when the girls sat in the twilight, dreaming of a bright future ; but though the training was severe, it was, perhaps, the best and noblest school in which humanity can be educated. The sisters were never unhappy, for they were together, and they were free. Rose was sister, mother, guardian, all the world of love and shelter for Kathleen, who bloomed into exquisite loveliness in that humble Parisian lodging, a fair flower blossoming unseen, with, happily, few to note her beauty.

Rose found only too soon that education was a drug in the Parisian markets. After heroic efforts to get employment as a morning governess in a tradesman's family, she fell back upon the only industry which offered itself, and, by the help of her first Parisian friend, Madame Schubert, the stout matron who had found her a lodging, she got employment as an artificial flower-maker, in which art she progressed rapidly, and, in a couple of years, attained a perfection which insured her liberal wages—wages which enabled her to maintain the little lodging, and feed and clothe herself and her sister. The fare was of the simplest, and there was a good deal of pinching needed to make both ends meet in that luxurious expensive city of Paris ; especially in winter, when fuel made such an inroad upon the slender purse ; but somehow the girls never knew actual privation, never went to bed hungry, or were haunted in their slumber by the night-mare of debt. The little rooms on the third story were the pink of neatness. Kathleen was housekeeper, and her busy hands swept and dusted and polished, and kept all things bright. The modest gray or brown merino gowns were never shabby or dilapidated. Collars and cuffs were always spotless, and the little feet neatly shod. There were always a few halfpence for the bag at Notre Dame, and there was always a loaf to divide with a poor neighbour, or a cup of soup for a sick child.

On the other hand, the pleasures of the sisters were of the rarest, and, perhaps, that is why they were so sweet. A steamboat excursion once or twice in the long summer to some suburban village that was almost the country ; a visit to a cheap boulevard theatre once or twice in the long winter. But O, how heavenly was the scent of lime blossoms, how exquisite the verdure of summer meadows, to those who tasted

the luxury so seldom ! And how vivid and real was that
sham world of the stage to those who so seldom saw the
curtain rise upon that paint and tinsel paradise !

Rose and Kathleen lived as humbly as grisettes live, and
dressed as grisettes dress ; but they preserved the secluded
habits of English ladies—knew no one, and spoke to no one,
outside the narrow enclosure of that little stone-paved yard
in the Rue Gît le Cœur, with its three houses divided into
about twenty domiciles. Among these dwellings the sisters
had made a few respectable acquaintances, including Madame
Schubert, the stout matron who grew more and more obese
as the years went by, who was described somewhat vaguely
as a *petit rentier*, and whose only business in life was to know
the business of her neighbours, and to attend upon an ancient
coffee-coloured pug almost as obese as herself.

As she was their first, so was Madame Schubert their best
and most intimate friend, and, indeed, the one only person
whom the Demoiselles O'Hara visited and received in this
vast city of Paris. She was always their companion and
protectress in those happy excursions to the country, those
fairylike nights at the theatre. It was she who supplied the
secluded damsels with news of the outside world. She knew,
or pretended to know, everything that was going on in Paris;
and she certainly did know everything that went on in the
Rue Gît le Cœur.

It was Madame, or in familiar parlance Maman, Schubert
who gave Rose and Kathleen the first information about a
new lodger who had taken up his abode in the two little
garrets over their own apartment—a young man with a
handsome face, and *gentil*—ah, but how *gentil! tout-à-fait
talon rouge.* He would bear comparison with any *gandin* on
the boulevard, although his coat looked as if it had been well
worn, and all his worldly goods consisted of one battered
portmanteau and an old egg-box full of books.

'He writes for the papers—for the *Drapeau Rouge*,' said
Maman Schubert. 'I have seen the printer's devil going
up stairs with proofs. But he is not rich, this youth, for he
breakfasts at Suzon Michel's *crémerie*, and he often buys a
slice of Lyons sausage and a loaf as he goes home in the
afternoon, when other young men are going to their favourite
restaurant.'

'Dear maman, how is it that you know everything about
everybody ?' exclaimed Rose.

She had met the new lodger on the stairs that morning

and could not deny his good looks. He was tall and slim.
He had dark eyes—eagle eyes—and a black moustache, and
features as clearly cut as a profile on a Roman cameo.

'I have eyes and ears, and a heart to sympathise with my
neighbours in their joys and sorrows,' said Madame Schubert
'One might as well be the statue of King Henry on the
Pont Neuf as go through the world caring for nobody but
oneself.'

This was a clever way of making a feminine vice seem a
virtue; but Maman Schubert was really a good soul, and
always ready to help a poor neighbour. She was very fond of
the O'Hara girls, and already she had begun to build her
little castles in the air for their benefit. Rose was to marry
Philip, that honest young mechanic from the far south,
beyond Carcassonne, who was doing so well as a journeyman
cabinet-maker, and who was something of an artist in his
way, and thus a little above the average mechanic. And
now here had there dropped from the sky, as it were, the
very lover of lovers for Kathleen—young, handsome, refined,
as charming as a lover in a play.

Maman Schubert told herself it was high time Kathleen
should have a lover, whose duty it would be to protect and
cherish her, and to marry her so soon as ever they were rich
enough to marry. She was much too pretty to remain un-
guarded by a strong man's love. For such fresh and innocent
loveliness Paris was full of snares; she could not go
the length of a street alone without encountering perils.
The wolf was always on the watch for this lamb. Rose
O'Hara's avocations compelled her to be absent all day long,
and she was obliged to mew her young sister in the little
sitting-room, forbidding her to go a step beyond her daily
marketing, which all had to be done within a narrow radius
of the Rue Git le Cœur.

The wolf, as represented by the *gandin* or *petit crevé*, was
not often on the prowl in this humble locality. The pave-
ments were too rough for his dainty boots, the region
altogether too shabby for his magnificence. But from the
Sorbonne, from the Luxembourg, and from the Hôtel Dieu
issued wolves of another and rougher species—students of all
kinds; and Rose lived in ever-present fear lest one of these
should assail her cherished lamb. Maman Schubert was
often too lazy to go marketing; and then Kathleen must
needs go alone on her little errands to the greengrocer, or
the pork-butcher, or the *crémerie*.

The *crémerie* was just round the corner—one of the neatest daintiest little shops in Paris; or at least it was so thought by the inhabitants of Gît le Cœur, who patronised it liberally. It was a tiny shop in a narrow street, and one descended to it by two stone steps, trodden hollow and sloping by pilgrims in past ages ; for the shop was an old shop, coeval with the departed glories of the Faubourg St. Germain.   It was cellar-like and dark, but that was an advantage on a hot summer day.   It was cool and shadowy, like a rustic dairy, and it was clean—ah, how it was clean !   You might have offered a napoleon for every cobweb to be found in Suzon Michel's shop, without fear of being out of pocket by your offer.   The little tables at which Suzon's customers breakfasted were of spotless marble.   Her thick white crockery had never a stain or a smear.   Her brass milk-cans and tin coffee-pots were as bright as silver in a silversmith's shop.

It was in this half-underground apartment that Gaston Mortemar, the young journalist, took his breakfast every day—coffee and eggs, roll and butter, occasionally diversified by a plate of radishes.

This simple and wholesome fare was enlivened by the society of Madame Michel, a buxom black-eyed widow of six-and-twenty, who had always the last news of the quarter, and a cheery word for every comer, and who found a great deal to say to this particular customer.   She stood behind her bright little counter, flashing her knitting needles, or moved deftly about the shop, polishing and arranging her pots and pans, while Gaston Mortemar breakfasted, and that hour seemed to her always the brightest in the day.   By the time he had lived six months in the Rue Gît le Cœur, they were on very intimate terms.   She used to upbraid him if he were five minutes later than his usual hour, and she would pout and look sorrowful if he seemed in haste to depart. Once she served him a better breakfast than he had ordered, and wanted to supply him with a dainty dish gratis ; but Monsieur Mortemar drew the line here.   His angry flush and haughty frown told the little widow that she had gone too far.

'Please to remember that I am a gentleman, and not a *pique-assiette*,' he said, ' and that I eat nothing I cannot pay for.'

Madame shrugged her shoulders, and said it was hard she could not offer an *omelette aux points d'asperges* to a friend if she liked,

' When I visit my friends I take what they choose to give me,' answered Gaston coldly; ' but I have no friends in this part of Paris.'

Suzon Michel looked as black as thunder, and took the journalist's money in sulky silence. She broke a jug before dinner-time, and was snappish to her customers all the rest of the day.

' What Satan-like pride !' she exclaimed, thinking of her favourite patron ; and then she muttered a remark which might have found a place later in the columns of the *Père Duchêne*.

She cried when she went to bed that night, cried and sobbed, and swore an oath or two by way of solace, before she laid her head on her pillow, thinking that Gaston Mortemar would come no more to the little table at the end of the shop. But at the usual time he walked into her shop, and sat himself down with an imperturbable visage. She served his coffee as carefully as ever, but said never a word. He read a newspaper while he breakfasted, paid, and went, without a word on his part.

Next morning there was a bunch of daffodils on the little table, a bunch of yellow bloom lighting up the shadowy corner. Suzon had trudged to the flower-market before she opened her shop, to buy these spring flowers for the man she loved. Yes, she loved him, and meant to marry him if she could. He was a gentleman, and she *canaille de canaille*. But what of that ? Did not the gutter throne it yonder on the other side of the Seine, in the Bois, in the Parc Monceau —daughters of the gutter made glorious in silks and satins, driving thoroughbred horses, scattering their lovers' substance in waves of gold ? Did not all that was noblest in the land lay itself down and grovel at the feet of the gutter ? And her gentleman was poor and friendless ; he lived in a garret, and toiled for a pittance. Surely he would be willing and glad to marry her, when he knew that she had saved money, and had her little investments in the public funds.

He smiled at sight of the first flowers of spring, and, looking up at the widow, saw that she was smiling too. All her sullen gloom had melted at sight of him. She was so glad he had not forsaken her shop. Perhaps it would have hurt her even more than his desertion to have known how insignificant a figure she made in his life, and how little he had thought about the day before yesterday's dispute.

He asked her the news, and her whole face beamed at the

sound of his voice. She prattled away gaily for the rest of the hour, and considered every other customer an intruder while Gaston sat at his little table.

'You ought to put up a placard in your window, with "Relâche" upon it, when Monsieur is here,' said a grumpy porter, to whom she had served a pat of butter with scant civility, and whose keen eye saw the state of affairs.

This kind of thing went on for more than a year. Now and again, when Gaston was in luck and had made a few francs more than his ordinary earnings from the newspapers, he rewarded the little widow's attentions by taking her to a theatre, and giving her an ice or a supper in the Passage Jouffroy before he escorted her home. He treated her *en grand seigneur* on these occasions, and these evenings were to Suzon Michel as nights spent in paradise; hours to dream about for weeks after they were gone, to long for with a passionate longing. Yet they brought her no nearer to the man she loved or to the realisation of her hopes. Not a word was ever spoken of love or marriage. When they parted on the steps of the *crémerie,* while the bells of Notre Dame were chiming one of the quarters after midnight, they were as far apart as ever. If she was ever to be Madame Mortemar the offer of marriage must come from her own lips, Suzon thought; and she would not have shrunk from telling the man of her choice of those snug little investments, and her willingness to share her economies with him. Feminine delicacy would not have hindered such an avowal ; but there was something in the man himself which sealed her lips.

Gaston was as cold as ice, as calm as marble. He had that placid languor of speech and manner which clever young men are apt to affect, until it becomes a second nature. He talked like a man who had lived through every experience that life could offer to reprobate youth, who had grown old in evil before Time had written a wrinkle on his brow.

'Ah, but he has lived, that youth ! ' said the knowing ones of the quarter. 'He has squandered the paternal fortune on actresses and cocottes, and now he has to write for his bread.'

The fact was that Gaston Mortemar had never had a napoleon to bestow upon anybody, for good or evil. He had worked for his daily bread ever since he left the school of Albert the Great, where he had been one of the brightest pupils of the good Dominicans. He had never been rich enough to be profligate in a grand way ; and he was too proud, too refined to stoop to cheap vice. He was like Alfred

de Musset, a dandy born, created with refined tastes and lofty
aspirations ; but poverty had embittered him. He had fed
his mind with the writings of Villon and Voltaire and Rousseau, Théophile Gautier, Musset, Baudelaire, and Flaubert.
He was a cynic to the marrow of his bones. He tried to
surpass Voltaire in acrimony, Rousseau in discontent, and
lashed himself into fury when he wrote about the great ones
of the earth.

One day he met Kathleen O'Hara in the morning sunshine,
coming in from her marketing, just as he was going out to
breakfast. She wore a neat gray gown and a pale-blue neck-
ribbon, and carried a basket of lettuce and radishes on her
arm ; and he thought he saw a Greuze that had suddenly
become flesh and blood, and had walked out of its frame in
the Louvre yonder, across the shining river. He forgot his
good manners, and turned to look after her as she crossed the
yard and tripped up the steps of that house which he had
just left. He knew that two girls occupied one half of the
third story, but they had kept themselves so close that he had
only seen the elder sister, once in a way, on the staircase.
Madame Schubert was standing in her doorway, scenting the
morning air, and watching the goings and comings of her
neighbours. She and Gaston had long been on friendly
terms, so she gave him a little nod, and laughed as he passed
her door.

' *Gentille, n'est-ce pas, mon garçon ?* ' she screamed, in her
shrill treble, with the Boulevard St. Michel twang.

' *Gentille !* ' She is adorable,' answered Gaston. ' Is it
possible that such an angel inhabits the same dull walls that
shelter me ? '

' Dangerous, is it not ? But she is as good as she is pretty.
A gentleman's daughter too, though she and her sister have
to work for their bread, poor orphans ! The father was an
Irish captain.'

' Irish ! ' exclaimed Gaston, with a touch of surprise.

He had a vague idea that Irish men and women were a
kind of savages who inhabited a barren island on the wild
Atlantic, and ran about half-naked among the rocks.

' Yes, but these girls have never been in Ireland. They
were educated in a convent near Bruges. They are young
ladies, pious, well-conducted, although they work for their
daily bread. Durand, my neighbour, the young cabinet-
maker, is over head and ears in love with the elder sister, and
I think there will be a marriage before long.'

'Durand ! What, the sturdy broad-shouldered youth at No. 7, who whistles and sings so loud as he goes in and out ? '

'Yes ; a fine frank nature.'

'Noisy enough, in all conscience,' said Gaston ; and he went on to get his breakfast.

He was in no humour for conversation this morning, and Suzon Michel's prattle bored him. He read, or seemed to be reading, the *Figaro* while she was talking—a rudeness which galled the widow.

'Do you know those two young ladies in the Rue Gît le Cœur, the house I live in ?' he asked presently, without looking up from his paper.

'Young ladies !' echoed Suzon contemptuously. 'A gentleman may live in the Rue Gît le Cœur, a gentleman may live anywhere, that is understood ; but young ladies—that is too much ! I know two girls who work for the artificial flower-maker on the Boulevard St. Germain.'

'They are ladies by birth and education, I am told.'

'They are stuck-up minxes ; and although that young one has come to my shop every day for the last six years she does not think me worthy of five minutes' conversation ; a little nod and " *Bon-jour*, madame," and she's out of my shop as if she thought the place polluted her.'

'She is shy, perhaps,' said Gaston. 'I should not think she could be proud.'

Suzon looked at him sharply with those flashing eyes of hers—fine eyes, full, black, luminous, but not altogether beautiful.

'What does monsieur know of this young person that he is so ready to answer for her ?' she asked, with a mocking air.

'Very little. I passed her in the street just now. I doubt if I ever saw her till that moment, though we live in the same house. Some faces can be read at a glance. In hers I saw purity, sweetness, truth, simplicity.'

'My faith ! You are skilful at reading faces,' retorted Madame Michel ; 'but it is easy to see virtues of that kind in a pretty woman. Had Ma'mselle Hara been ugly you would not have discovered half these qualities in her face.'

'They might have been there, perhaps ; but I own I should not have looked so keenly. She is the image of a Greuze in the Louvre. You know the pictures in the Louvre ?'

'Not much,' said Suzon, with a careless shrug.

'Why, you go there nearly every Sunday afternoon.'

'True ; but I go to look at the people, not the pictures.'

Gaston paid for his breakfast, and strolled on to his news-paper-office, thinking that Suzon grew more vulgar every day. He was vexed with himself for having allowed her to establish a kind of friendship with him. She ! the keeper of a milk shop !

'And to think that I come from one of the best families in Brittany,' he said to himself. ' Well, I have thrown my lot in with the people. I have made myself their advocate ; I have asserted the equal rights of man. Ought I to feel offended if a milk woman treats me as her friend ? A hand-some woman, too ; bright, agreeable, not without intelligence, and full of strong feeling. Poor little Suzon ! '

Poor little Suzon ! Gaston began to lessen his visits to the *crémerie*. He took a cup of coffee in his garret, and went straight to his day's work. He was too busy to breakfast in the old leisurely manner, he told Madame Michel, when she reproached him with this falling off from the old ways.

' Have I done anything to offend you ? ' she asked, looking at him with eyes which took a new beauty, softened by sadness.

' Offend me, dear Madame Michel ! But assuredly not. You are all that is good. But I am working hard just now. It does not do for a man to saunter through life, to be always a trifler. I have a good deal to do for the paper ; and I spend an hour or two every day at the Imperial Library.'

' If you are getting a learned man I shall see no more of you,' sighed the widow. ' You will not be able to endure my ignorant chatter.'

'Gaiety of heart is delightful at all times,' said Gaston.

'I begin to think that monsieur must be writing verses, he has grown so grave and silent,' remarked Suzon.

And then they parted, with ceremonious politeness on his side, with keen scrutiny and suspicion on hers.

Monsieur was not writing verses, but he was living a poem. Maman Schubert, the good-natured busybody of the Rue Gît le Cœur, had planned a little tea-party—*un thé à l'Anglaise*—and had invited the two O'Hara girls—known in their little circle as the Demoiselles Hara, since the O was too much for a Parisian mouth—and Philip Durand, the cabinet-maker, an honest young fellow, a thorough workman and artist, in a very artistic trade, and a prominent member of the work-men's syndicate : and the cabinet-makers' syndicate ranks high among the societies of French workmen. So far the party consisted of old friends, since good Madame Schubert had been almost as a mother to the girls whom she had seen arrive in the Rue Gît le Cœur, dusty and bewildered-looking, on the evening of their entry into Paris ; and Philip had been Rose's devoted lover for the last three years, haunting her like her shadow as she went to and fro her work, in the early mornings when Paris was being swept and garnished, in the dusky evenings when its million lamps were being lighted. Never was there a more unselfish, a more patient wooer. Rose had been hard with him. Rose had kept him at arm's length. She never meant to marry. She had her mission in life ; and that mission was to take care of Kathleen.

'Will you be less able to guard her when you have a strong man to help you ?' asked Philip. 'Do you suppose I shall grudge her a room in our lodgings, a place at our table ! She will be my sister as much as yours, and as dear to me as to you.'

'That cannot be. She is more than a sister to me. She is the one love and care of my life. Work would lose all its sweetness if I did not know I was working for her as well as for myself. I am sure you are good and generous. I daresay you would be kind to her ; but you might grow weary of her ; bad times might come, and you might think her a burden. I will run no risks. I should feel as if I were giving her a stepfather.'

'And have you made up your mind never to marry ?'

'Never, while Kathleen is single. If *she* were well married it might be different.'

'Then it shall be my business to find her a good husband,' said Philip. 'With such a pretty girl there can be no difficulty.'

But Philip Durand was a poor hand at matchmaking. While he was thinking about the business, and wondering which of the men he rubbed shoulders with at the workmen's chamber was worthy to mate with Rose O'Hara's sister, Madame Schubert, who was an incorrigible schemer in the matrimonial line, had brought Kathleen face to face with the man whom Fate meant for her husband.

The fourth guest and only stranger at Madame Schubert's English tea was Gaston Mortemar ; and that evening completed Kathleen's conquest. He was her adorer and her slave from that hour. It seemed to him as if all life took new colours after that evening. The leopard cannot change his spots all at once ; but the leopard's ways and

manners may be considerably influenced ; and although
Gaston was still Voltairian in his way of thinking, still a
leveller in politics, he worked more earnestly and more
honestly than he had ever done before ; for he had assumed
the responsibility of winning a bright future for Kathleen
O'Hara.

The wooing and winning were easily done, for the girl's
young heart went out to him as Gretchen's to Faust. A
little walk on the bridge in the summer twilight, a flower
or two—bought in the flower-market, but cherished as if it
were a blossom of supernal growth—a chance meeting in the
sunny morning, when Kathleen was marketing, and these
two were pledged to each other for life. But Rose was
terribly wise. She seemed the very spirit of worldliness,
and she refused her assent to an imprudent marriage. When
Gaston had saved a little money, and could earn, say, three
napoleons a week—which was less than the skilled cabinet-
maker earned—Kathleen should be his wife ; not sooner.
Gaston was earning on an average two napoleons weekly,
and there was not much margin for saving out of that.

Hitherto he had found himself just able to live, clothe
himself like a gentleman, and keep out of debt. And to do
even this he had been thrifty and self-denying. But what
will not love do ? He became as sparing as Père Grandet ;
except when he wanted to offer a little pleasure, a theatre
or a café chantant, to the sisters.

Such offers were but rarely accepted. Rose watched
Kathleen like a lynx, and allowed few *tête-à-têtes* between the
lovers. Never was girlish simplicity guarded more closely
from all peril of pollution. But, once in a way, this severe
damsel relented so far as to allow the two lovers to organise
an evening's dissipation ; and it was on one of these occasions,
almost immediately after Kathleen's engagement, that Suzon
Michel saw Gaston and his sweetheart together for the first
time.

It was a sultry August evening, the Seine shining in the
golden light of the western sky, the air heavy with heat.
Durand and Gaston had bought tickets for the side boxes at
the Ambigu, where a new play, by Dumas the younger, was
being acted, to the delight of all Paris—or, at least, that
inferior and second-rate Paris which had not migrated to
fashionable watering-places and mountain springs. Kathleen
and Gaston walked arm-in-arm along the quay, so engrossed
in each other as to be quite unconscious of passers-by. Faces

came and went beside them, voices sounded ; but all things
were dim as the sounds and faces in a dream. They lived,
they saw, they heard, they breathed only for each other.

Close behind them came Rose and her faithful swain ; and
Rose, even in her tenderest moments, was mindful of her
sister. She was fond and proud of her stalwart, good-looking
workman-lover, who was so fine a specimen of his rank and
race, as much a gentleman by nature as Gaston Mortemar
was a gentleman by hereditary instinct ; but she was not
lifted off this dull earth by her love.

As they walked towards the Pont Neuf, with their faces
to the west and the sun shining on them, Suzon Michel met
them. She saw them ever so far off : the tall slight figure
of the man, whose look and bearing she knew so well ; the
golden-haired girl at his side, radiant and lovely in her plain
alpaca gown, and neat little black lace bonnet, with clusters
of violets nestling between the lace and her sunny hair—
those violets which the auburn-haired Empress loved so well.

Suzon slackened her pace as they drew near her. He
would recognise her, of course—the false-hearted one : and
speak her fair, albeit he had broken her heart by his coldness
and ingratitude. He would stop, the audacious one, and
brazen out his treachery, and make light of his heartlessness.

But Gaston walked on without seeing her. He passed
her by, unconscious of her presence, his eyes bent with
impassioned love upon the pure pale face beside him, his lips
breathing softest words. Suzon drew aside. and stood upon
the pavement, looking after them with diabolical hatred in
her face. Rose saw that look, and clutched Philip Durand's
arm.

'Did you see that woman looking after my sister—the
woman at the *crémerie ?*' she asked.

But Philip had been too much absorbed in his betrothed to
have eyes for the divers expressions of the passers-by. He
was full of gladness, thankfulness for his lot. He had been
eminently successful as a craftsman, had won a medal for
a piece of fine workmanship in the Exhibition of '67 ; he
was looked upon as a leading light in the syndicate, and the
dearest woman in the world had promised to be his wife.
Now that Kathleen was engaged there was no more difficulty. So soon as Gaston was in a fair way to maintain a
wife, the two couples would be united.

The evening at the Ambigu was enchantment ; but both

girls refused the luxury of ices at Tortoni's. How were lovers to be thrifty if their betrothed were ready to accept costly attentions? Besides, as they passed the famous confectioner's, Rose caught sight of a couple of carriages setting down some ladies and their cavaliers at a side door, and those painted faces and rustling silks belonged to a world from which Rose O'Hara recoiled as from a pestilence. So they all walked home in the August moonlight, talking of the play, and were safe in the Rue Gît le Cœur before midnight.

Rose did not forget that look of Madame Michel's. Her intense affection for Kathleen made her suspicious of Kathleen's lover. Such a look as that in a young woman's face could have but one meaning. It meant jealousy; and there could hardly be jealously without cause. The look suggested a history; and Rose set herself to find out that history. She consulted Madame Schubert, the one friend whom she could trust in so delicate a matter; and the good Schubert was not long in enlightening her. One does not live in such a place as the Rue Gît le Cœur for five-and-twenty years without knowing a good deal about one's neighbours.

'Yes, my dear, there is no doubt this dear Mortemar had once a tenderness for M'me Michel. He used to breakfast at her shop every morning—a leisurely breakfast, during which those two talked—ah, great Heaven, how they talked! one could hardly get properly served while he was there. And he danced with her in the winter at the Bullier balls, and he used to take her to the theatre. Friends of mine saw them there, as happy as turtledoves. But what of that? A man must sow his wild oats; and Gaston is not the less fond of your sister because he has played fast and loose with M'me Michel.'

'My sister shall not marry a man who has played fast and loose with any woman,' said Rose.

'That is rank nonsense,' answered Maman Schubert. 'Mark my words, Rose: if you try to part those two, you will break Kathleen's heart.'

'Better her heart should be so broken than by a bad husband,' said Rose.

'He will not make a bad husband. Do you think a man is any the worse for a flirtation or two in his bachelor days? That is the way he learns the meaning of real love.'

Rose was not easily appeased. She saw Gaston next day,

and taxed him with his dishonourable conduct to the widow. He was indignant at the charge, and declared that there had never been anything serious between them. She had been attentive to him as a customer at her *crémerie ;* he had been civil to her—that was all. The visits to the theatre meant no more than civility.

'There was something more than civility on her part, and I think you must have known it,' answered Rose, intensely in earnest. 'If you knew it and fooled her, you are not a good and true man ; and you shall not marry my sister.'

Gaston protested against this absurd decree ; but finally admitted that he had been to blame. Yes, perhaps he had known that Madame Michel was just a little taken with him, inclined to like his society, and to be jealous and angry when he deserted her shop. The shop was convenient ; the woman was handsome and amusing. Why should not a man who was heart-whole, who had not one real woman-friend in the world, talk and laugh with a pretty shopkeeper ? It could do no harm.

'It has done harm. I saw as much in Madame Michel's face the other evening.' And then she told Gaston the story of that encounter on the quay.

'Mademoiselle Rose, you exaggerate the situation. Madame Michel has a spice of the devil in her, and can give black looks on very slight provocation. For the rest, she and I have seen the last of each other. I have never crossed her threshold since I was betrothed to Kathleen. I never shall cross it again.'

'Promise me that,' said Rose.

'I promise, from my heart.'

This happened in the year '69 ; and now it was midsummer in the fateful year '70, and France was treading daily, step by step, nearer the edge of the abyss.

CHAPTER IV

THE SONG OF VICTORY

IT was at the beginning of August, just after the victory of Sarrebrück, and while Paris was stirred and thrilled with dreams of conquest, and all a-flutter with warlike feeling, that the two sisters were married in the cathedral of Notre Dame, on a sunshiny Saturday morning.

There was no finery at this wedding, no train of friends. Madame Schubert; a young journalist and playwright who wrote for Mortemar's paper; a middle-aged gray-bearded artist, who had painted plaques for some of Durand's cabinet-work—these were the only guests. The little procession walked across the bridge in the morning sunlight, the sisters dressed alike in gray cashmere, with white bonnets, and each wearing a cluster of white roses at her throat. Nothing could be simpler or less costly than this wedding toilet, yet both brides were charming; neatness, purity, modest contentment with humble fortunes, were all expressed in their bearing and costume.

The ceremony was to be at ten. They were a quarter of an hour too soon; and Philip Durand, who loved the grand old pile with the artist's ardent love of fine artistic work, walked in the shadowy aisles with his painter friend, and expatiated upon the beauties of the building, while Rose walked by his side, proud of her lover's learning and enthusiasm.

Kathleen and Gaston waited nearer the altar, the girl kneeling with bent head and hidden face, deep in prayer; the lover sitting near, dreamily watching the graceful figure in soft gray drapery, touched with glintings of coloured light from the old stained windows.

There were no other weddings at that particular hour on that particular morning. These two couples and their friends had that magnificent temple all to themselves. As the clock struck ten the organ began to peal, and the priests came slowly towards the altar in their rich vestments—for the vestments worn upon the humblest occasions at Notre Dame are splendid—and the ceremonial began.

All was over in less than half an hour, and Kathleen and her sister went back into the sunshine, out of the gray shadows, the magical lights from painted glass, the glory of gold, and splendour of chromatic colour.

'Is that all?' asked Kathleen, looking up at her lover-husband. 'Am I really and truly your wife?'

'Really and truly; and you would have been just as truly my wife if we had never gone further than the mairie.'

'No, no, Gaston; for then Heaven would have had no part in our marriage.'

'My sweetest, I am content that you should be content. Women love old-world fancies,' answered this light-hearted infidel gaily.

There was a stand of carriages in front of the church. Philip Durand hailed two of them, and the wedding party got in. The two bridegrooms had planned the day between them. They were to breakfast at the restaurant in the Place de la Bourse, chosen for the sake of its winter-garden, which gave an air of prettiness to the sordid fact of dinner. And just now, too, in this time of anxiety and ferment, the Bourse was the central point of Paris, where one could always hear the latest news. Just now Paris lived on tip-toe, as it were, palpitating, thrilling with the expectation of great victors—an Austerlitz, a Jena; the news might be flashed along the wires at any moment of day or night. The telegraph clerks were waiting, fingers itching to record the triumph of Gallic arms. No one thought of Waterloo.

The bridal party drove across the river, past the Louvre, into the Rue de Rivoli. What meant this new life and movement in the streets—men running to and fro, women standing in little groups, laughing, crying, hats waved in the air—the wild excitement of a racecourse when the favourite is winning a great race?

'One would think our happiness had driven all the world out of their wits,' said Gaston, with his arm round his wife's waist.

There was only Madame Schubert with them in the carriage. She had insisted on taking the back seat, and sat smiling benignly on the happy lovers, passing proud of their happiness as being in some measure her own work.

The coachman turned round and shouted to them as he rattled his horse over the broad space in front of the Théâtre Français. The pavement before the cafés was crowded with the usual loungers, smoking, talking, drinking; only the talk and the laughter were louder than usual, the crowd was denser, the air was full of electricity.

'A victory!' shouted the driver, looking round at his fare, and cracking his whip ferociously; 'a great victory! MacMahon has made mincemeat of those Prussian dogs!'

'A victory, and on our wedding-day!' exclaimed Kathleen joyously; and then the sweet sensitive face clouded suddenly, and she said, 'There can be no victory without soldiers slain. Many hearts of wives and mothers will be mourning to-day amidst all this joyousness. Oh, Gaston, how thankful I ought to be that you were past the age for service!'

'True, dearest, I am better off here than with the Moblots; but if the National Guard were called out I should have to shoulder my musket.'

'But not to leave Paris,' said Kathleen, nestling closer to him; 'and there can be no fighting in Paris.'

'Heaven forbid! No, love; one or two victories, and Prussia will give us whatever terms we ask. What can a herd of Huns and Vandals do against the fine flower of our army, the stalwart heroes of Magenta and Solferino, the graybeards of Alma and Algiers?'

They drove along the Rue Vivienne. The narrow street was all in commotion; people at the shop-doors, people at the upper windows; a Babel of voices, a shrill uproar of laughter and exclamation. But in the Place de la Bourse, and on the boulevard beyond, the excitement culminated. It was the fever of Epsom when the Derby has just been won —the stir and tumult of Doncaster at the crowning moment of the Leger; and yet a deeper and stronger fever, for this had the awfulness of life and death.

Victory, yes; but where? Which of the armies was it—MacMahon's or Bazaine's? Or was it the two armies which had crushed the Prussian forces between them—which had met and joined, like two living walls, deadly, invincible, squeezing out the life of the enemy?

Every one was asking questions, every one answering, stating, counter-stating, asserting, denying; but in this tumult of statement and counter-statement there was a difficulty in arriving at anything positive, except the one all-inspiring fact that there had been a tremendous victory on the French side. Flags were flying at all the windows—flags produced as if by enchantment; and here came an open carriage slowly through the mob—the carriage of a famous opera-singer. In an instant it was stopped, surrounded by that surging sea of humanity; and the Diva stood up in her carriage at the entreaty—nay, almost the command—of the public, to sing the 'Marseillaise.'

The glorious finely-trained voice rolled out the soul-stirring words, the notes rising bird-like and clear in the summer air, floating up to the summer sky; and then fifty thousand voices, the deep rough tones of an excited populace, burst forth in the chorus, like human thunder. Impossible to resist the magnetism of that passionate patriotism. The eyes of strong men grew dim, women sobbed hysterically. France, la belle France—she had been in peril perhaps; yes, strong though she was, there was never war without peril; but she was safe—safe, triumphant, glorious, with her foot upon the enemy's neck. Alas! to think how the Gallic cock crew and flapped his wings during that one wild hour!

The bridal party pushed their way into the Restaurant Champeaux. Under the glass roof, in the covered flower-garden, there was such a mob that it was very difficult to get a small table in a corner, and a waiter who would cease from hurrying to and fro to take an order from the new-comers. Every one was celebrating the victory with good cheer of some kind. Champagne corks were flying, plates clattering, spoons and forks jingling, and everywhere rose the same din of voices.

Durand and Mortemar contrived, by strenuous exertions, to secure a bottle of champagne and another of Bordeaux, a *poulet gras* and a *Chateaubriand*, some fruit, cheese, salad; and the wedding-party breakfasted merrily amidst the din, squeezed together in their corner, stiflingly hot under the burning glass roof and in the crowded atmosphere! But who would not be happy on a wedding-day, and in the hour of victory? They sat at the little table for more than an hour, nearly half of which time had been wasted in waiting; and when they went out again it seemed to Durand's keen eye as if a change had come over the spirit of the crowd outside. There were only about half the people, and faces were graver—some faces of business men looking even perplexed and troubled: voices were less loud; no more hats were thrown into the air, nor was there any more laughter.

The rest of the bridal party were too much absorbed in each other to note this change in the public temper. The carriages were waiting to take them to the Buttes Chaumont, where it had been decided to spend the afternoon. They were to go back to a dinner which Madame Schubert and Rose had planned between them, in Madame Schubert's apartment, which was spacious and splendid in the eyes of the dwellers in Gît la Cœur.   Durand and Mortemar had wished to give a dinner at some popular restaurant—au Moulin Rouge, for instance ; but the women had set their faces against such extravagance.   Rose argued that it was a sin to squander money on eating and drinking.   She had heard that at such places a napoleon was charged for a single dish, a franc for a pear or a peach ; yes, when peaches were to be had for three or four sous at the street-corners.   So Maman Schubert and Rose had held grave consultations, and had gone marketing together on the eve of the wedding, and now, while they were driving merrily towards the Place de la Bastille, the *daube à la Provençale* was simmering slowly on the little charcoal stove in la Schubert's tiny kitchen.   The *petits fours* from the confectioner's in the Rue du Bac were ready in the doll's-house larder, and the dinner-table was set out with its fruit and flowers and golden-crusted loaves of finest bread, and bottles of innocent Médoc, ready for the feast.

The excitement of the good news pervaded Paris.   The Rue St. Antoine, the Place de la Bastille, were alive with idlers.   They drove by the long dreary Rue de la Roquette, past the prison-walls, away to Ménilmontant and Belleville, where the honest harmless working population, the blue blouses and white muslin caps, were all astir in the sun-shine—a seething crowd.   There was a kind of fair on the Boulevard, a Saturday and Sunday fair—swings and round-abouts, and a juggler or two—all merry in the white August dust, under the hot blue sky.

They drove through narrow old streets on the top of the hill—dusty, crowded, unwholesome, wretched dwellings ; a truculent rabble, blue blouses, white night caps, everywhere ; queer little wine-shops, queer little eating-houses, an intoler-able odour of *petit bleue* and *absinthe suisse*, a tumult of harsh, voices—and so to the wonderful gardens, the green valleys and Alpine crags, the blue lakes and Swiss summer-houses, and Grecian temples of the Buttes Chaumont, those old, disused quarries that have been made into a pleasure-ground for the people of Paris ; surely the prettiest, gayest, most picturesque playground that ever a tyrant gave to his slaves. Let us call him a tyrant, now that he lies at rest in his Eng-lish grave, and all the good he did for the Paris he loved so well is appropriated by new masters, his name obliterated from all things which his brain devised, and his enterprise created.

The wedding-party drove in by the gate that has admitted so many brides and bridegrooms, smart and smiling, in their new clothes, their new bliss. They drove a little way into the grounds and then alighted, and climbed one of the Alpine promontories, and looked down upon the varied scene beneath. Never was a more joyous crowd beneath a brighter sky, amidst a fairer landscape. It scemed as if all Paris were taking holiday. The verdant valley was a palpitating mass of blue blouses, white caps, particoloured raiment, brightened here and there by the uniform of a *sergent de ville*. One could hardly see the greensward, so dense was the throng of humanity. The châlets were crowded with customers ; lemonade, syrups, coffee, ices, Bavarian beer, were being consumed wholesale. Mothers and children, fathers, sweethearts : Paris was all here *en famille*, all elated at the great news, somewhat vague at present. But Gaston and his young wife went higher and higher, seeking some solitary spot beyond this holiday throng, and at last found a hill upon which vegetation was wilder and more romantic, and where they were alone for a little while, looking down upon Paris lying in an oval basin at their feet, a city of white houses and church towers, domes and statues, girdled with gardens, flashing with fountains, thc beautiful river cleaving the white streets and quays like a bright steel falchion touched with gleams of gold.

'Is it not a noble city?' asked Gaston, proud of his birthplace, the only home he had ever known.

Yonder to their left, on the slope of the hill, lay the cemetery, crosses and columns, Egyptian sepulchres, Roman temples, glittering whitely in the sun, amidst a tangle of summer foliage.

'Shall we be there, among the limes, when our life is over, I wonder?' mused Kathleen. 'Perhaps you will have a tomb like Balzac's or Musset's. Who knows?'

'Who knows, indeed, dearest? I have been earning my bread by my pen for the last ten years, and do not find myself any nearer the fame of a Balzac than when I began. Yet who knows what I may do now I have you to work for? Balzac had a long time to wait. Fame comes in an hour sometimes. And of late, inspired by thoughts of you, I have nursed the dim idea of a novel, as I tramped backwards and forwards to the office. Yes, I believe I have a fancy which, worked out faithfully, might hit the Parisians. But a journalist is the drudge of literature. All his faculties are the slaves of a tyrannical master whose name is To-day. He must think only of the present, write only for the present. He must harbour neither memories of the past nor dreams of the future. If Shakespeare and Goethe had written for the papers we should have neither *Faust* nor *Hamlet*."

'But you will not always have to work for the papers?'

'Who can tell? I must be at work early to-morrow to write a description of that scene on the Bourse for the Monday number.'

'If I could only help you!' sighed Kathleen.

'You do help me, dearest. You have helped me to nobler ambitions, to purer hopes. You have made me work with higher purpose, with steadier aim. You are the good spirit of my life.'

'Tell me about your story,' she said, 'the story you have in your mind.'

'It is all about love—and you. I will tell you nothing. But some day I shall contrive to write it, between whiles, between paragraph and paragraph, leader and leader, and I shall get a publisher to produce it, under a *nom de plume*, and the book shall be the talk of Paris ; and you shall read it with smiles and tears, and you shall say, " Oh, Gaston, what a painter, what a poet, what an inspired dreamer this man must be ! I only wish I knew who he is, that I might worship him." And I shall say, " Worship me, love. I am the poet and the dreamer ; and you are my only Egeria." '

He looked like a poet, as he lay at her feet on the sunburnt sward, his eyes gazing dreamily over the city in the valley—dreamily away towards Mount Valerian and the fortifications on the other side of Paris.

They loitered away the long summer afternoon in serenest contentment, in deep inexpressible bliss. It seemed to them as if life were henceforward perfect. They had nothing left to desire—except, perhaps, on Gaston's side, fame and wealth, in a remote dream-like future. Kathleen had no desire to be rich. Poverty had never hurt her ; except in that one sad time, when her sister was ill. And now she had a little money, put away in a secret place, against any such evil hour. Poverty had no flavour of bitterness for this easily satisfied nature. She rose as gaily as a lark ; she went about her little duties singing for very joyousness. Her humble fare was sweetened by her contented spirit. Her humble home was beautified by all those little arts which endear lowly rooms to the dweller. And now, to begin life anew, on the same third floor in the Rue Gît le Cœur, with her lover-husband, was like the crowning bliss on the last page of a fairy tale.

The streets were very quiet, and had a somewhat gloomy look as the wedding-party drove back to Gît le Cœur; but they were all too happy, too much engrossed by their own bliss, to remark the change that had come over the aspect of the city.   No more flags, no more cheering, no more songs of triumph.

'I wonder they did not illuminate some of the public buildings,' said Durand, as they passed the Palais de Justice.

Not a festival lamp twinkled in the August sundown; not a star of coloured light sparkled on all the length of the quays; not a rocket shot up above the chestnuts in the Gardens of the Tuileries.   Paris wore her everyday aspect. However elated the city had been this morning, she was taking her triumph soberly to-night.

The little dinner in the Rue Gît le Cœur was a great success.   The feast was held in Madame Schubert's apartment, and that kindly matron presided at the banquet.   Never was there a merrier meal; voices all mingling now and then in a joyous tumult of speech—voices low and sweet, deep and resonant—and ripples of happy laughter; a frequent clinking of glasses, and anecdotes and *calembours*.   Gaston's friend the journalist turned out a wit of the first water; and the gray-bearded, grave artist proved wonderfully good company: he was loaded with anecdotes, like a six-chambered revolver, and before his audience had done laughing at one story he had begun another, still funnier, and then another, funnier again, a perpetual crescendo of mirth.

Just as a crowning feature, with the dessert, came a bottle of champagne, whose cork exploded with the force of a cannon.

'Listen there!' cried the journalist. 'How that thunders! It is the true wine of war.'

And at this a burst of gaiety. It is such a droll game, *la guerre*, when one's own country is winning.

'Just one little glass more, *un polichinelle*, my friend,' said Gaston, filling his fellow-scribbler's glass, 'to fête our arms.'

After the champagne, Gaston slipped out quietly with just a whispered explanation to his wife.   He had to go round to the newspaper office, in the Rue St. André des Arts, to arrange about his descriptive article for Monday, or, in point of fact, to write his paper on the spot.

He was gone about an hour and a half, and although the anecdotes and *calembours* went on, and the fun was fast and furious all the time, that hour and a half seemed passing long to his bride.

When he came back the gloom of his countenance scared the revellers.

'Why, Gaston, thou lookest as dolorous as the statue of the Commandante! What ails thee, Trouble-feast?'

'It was all a hoax,' cried Mortemar, flinging down his hat savagely, 'a trick of that black-hearted devil Bismarck. There has been no French victory—defeat, if anything. And our shouts, our songs, our flags—all madness and folly.'

'Oh, but come, now, that is a little too strong on the part of *ce coquin* Bismarck.'

'Yes, it is too strong. He is strong and we are weak—weaker than water. A nation that has no prudence, no caution, no coolness of brain, can never be a great nation. We are children, always ready to take a will-o'-the-wisp for a comet.'

'We are Celts, my friend, that is all. And we have the strength and the weakness of the Celtic nature,' quietly answered the gray-bearded painter. 'I am afraid these slow square-headed Saxons will get the better of us. It is the old race of the hare and the tortoise over again.'

CHAPTER V

THE COMING OF THE SQUARE-HEADS

No, there had been no victory. That outburst of patriotic fervour had wasted itself upon an idle dream. Paris awoke in a very savage humour on Sunday morning : and then came laughter and cynical jests. Everybody accused his neighbour of having eagerly swallowed the lie. Everybody declared that he, for his own part, had never believed the news so greedily accepted by the mob.

But in those two new homes in the Rue Gît le Cœur there was bliss, whether the arms of France were victorious or otherwise far away in those unknown lands, which the Parisians were picking out with pins upon gaily-coloured maps, sticking up tiny flags here and there on the map to show where the French troops were, the very spot where great battles might be expected momently, great victories— a new Auerstadt, a second Jena.

What do little birds in their nests on St. Valentine's Day care what battles the big eagles, the hawks, and the vultures are fighting far away among Scottish mountains, on Alpine summits ? The birds have their nests, and each to each is the world in little.

'Let the world slide, we shall never be younger,' said Gaston, who knew Shakespeare, in the translation of Charles Hugo.

He and his young wife were utterly happy. If there were dark clouds impending they could not see them. Is not love blind—blind to all things except the beloved ? The faintest shadow on Gaston's brow troubled Kathleen, but not those signs of tempest which were gathering round France.

The new home was full of smiles. Kathleen and Gaston had smartened the old furniture by some modest additions bought before their marriage—a writting-table, a cabinet, a bookcase filled with Gaston's books, the accumulation of the last ten years, a few old mezzo-tints picked up from time to time at the print-shops on the quay. Kathleen and Rose had toiled for months to make both homes complete and pretty. Curtains and chair-covers were all the work of those two pairs of industrious hands.

Durand, who was richer than Mortemar, had taken the lower floor for his own *ménage*. In the Rue Gît le Cœur that second floor ranked as a rather important suite of rooms.

The apartment consisted of *salon*, fifteen feet by twelve, with two casement windows commanding the shabby little courtyard ; a bedroom somewhat smaller ; a little room which would serve as a workshop for Durand, who did a good deal of artistic cabinet-work on his own account after business hours ; and a tiny kitchen. Durand's skilful hands had made all the best of the furniture in the dead watches of the night, when other men where sleeping or dissipating ; so the home of Rose and Philip was furnished in a style worthy of a man who stood high in the syndicate of cabinet-makers.

But while life was so full of happiness for the newly-married, the sky was darkening outside. An army of undeniable valour, but in number terribly inferior to the foe, and led by generals of scandalous incapacity, was brought face to face with the whole of Germany, in arms as one man, burning to avenge the agony and shame of sixty years ago. On the 4th of August came the defeat of General Douay, beaten and slain at Wissembourg ; and on the 6th the still more deplorable reverses of MacMahon at Wœrth, at Freichwiller, and at Reichsoffen. By the breach thus opened the enemy poured into France like a torrent. They came, the *têtes carrées* ! There was no longer room for self-deception. This was invasion.

And now far off, dimly as in a dream, Paris beheld the pale spectre of siege and famine. The Parisians knew hardly anything of the truth, which came to them only in garbled fragments. They knew not that upon the heels of these three or four hundred thousand men let lose upon France would follow hundreds of thousands more ; yes, nearly all the male population of the old German Empire.

Dark rumours of evil without the walls drew those two households nearer to each other, making home joys sweeter, love closer. But now Kathleen learnt the meaning of fear. She was full of morbid terrors when her husband was away from her. She pictured an advanced guard of Prussians falling upon him in the street ; a shell from the enemy's artillery bursting at his feet. And Gaston went every day to the office of the *Drapeau Rouge*. He had leaders to write, *tartines*, letters, patriotic articles breathing warlike fire, every full stop seeming like a shell. France beaten, France invaded? Ah, but there was nothing in this world so unlikely, so near the impossible; and yet, while he wrote, French arms were being flung down, French soldiers were flying—a wild rabble—from before the face of the foe; and the invader's foot was on the soil, tramping onwards, steadily, steadily, steadily; gigantic, invincible, like some mighty force of Nature; slow, cumulative, pitiless. But say that the soldiers of France had fled; say that Achilles himself had flung down his sword and shield, and taken to his heels; whose was the fault? Why, naturally, it was the government that was to blame, shrieked the *Red Flag*. Down with the Ministers! Give us new Ministers, and our arms will be victorious. MacMahon and Bazaine will unite their forces, and the tide of victory will roll backward across those advancing herds of Huns and Pandours, and sweep the savages back to their native pine-woods, their desert wastes beside the Danube.

There was a sudden shuffle of cards in the political game. Gramont and Ollivier retired, driven out by a vote of censure, and General Montauban, Comte de Palikao, took the helm.

'A military Mercadet with a touch of Robert Macaire,' said the *Red Flag*. 'What good could be expected from such *canaille?*'

The month of August wore on—a month of anxiety, of wavering hopes, of ever growing fears. History records no bloodier battles than Rezonville and Gravelotte, fought in in the middle of that anxious month; and although Bazaine claimed the first as a victory, he was steadily retreating; every day brought him nearer Metz, where he finally retired, abandoning his communications with MacMahon and the rest of France.

Then came the rumour that Metz was blocaked: Bazaine and his hundred and eighty thousand men were bound round with bonds of iron, useless, helpless. MacMahon was encamped at Chalons, recreating his army, and thither regiment after regiment of undisciplined youth was sent to him; and undisciplined youth made the country round ring with the noise of its follies, made France blush for her sons. And still the flood of invasion rolled on steadily as the rising tide. A week, a fortnight at most, and the Crown Prince with his victorious army would debouch upon the plain of Genevilliers. And how, in earnest this time, seeing the enemy so near, Paris awakened to the possibility of a seige; but even yet fear was not so serious as to stimulate the city to prompt and decisive action. The people waited—expectant, hopeful still : something would happen, something unforeseen —a miracle, perhaps.

Something unforeseen did happen ; but the unforeseen wore the shape of shame, defeat, humiliation—an empire overthrown in one bloody day ; Emperor a state prisoner ; Empress a fugitive ; army prisoners of war.

First came the tidings that MacMahon, instead of trying to block the passage of the Germans, instead of falling back upon the capital to fight one of the world's decisive battles under the walls of Paris, was moving northwards, obviously intent upon joining and releasing Bazaine.

What might not be hoped from a coalition between two such generals—one who had risen with every defeat, the other as famous for indomitable energy as for military skill ? What might not be hoped for from Bazaine's hundred and eighty thousand men, the flower of the French army ?

For two days, the first balmy days of September, a restless, feverish, over-excited populace lived upon the boulevards and in the streets. Questions, statements, counter-statements flew from lip to lip. False reports and monstrous exaggerations were in the very air men breathed. Then, on a Saturday, came the news of a great calamity ; a terrible battle had been fought, was still being fought, with fluctuating fortunes, in the environs of Sedan. But the ultimate result ? For this Paris waited with inexpressible agitation. The newsvendors' kiosques were besieged by tumultuous crowds ; hands were stretched forth, tremulous with excitement, clutching at the papers ; men stood upon the boulevard benches, reading the news aloud, above a sea of heads.

Nothing was certain in the news thus devoured, nothing authentic, nothing precise. The crowd, deprived of official information, was consumed by a nervous irritability, a fever of hopes and fears. Men were impatient, captious, quarrelsome. At the first word of doubt they were ready to treat each other as Prussians or traitors ; for a mere nothing they would have challenged each other to mortal combat. Voices were sharp; strangers glared at one another with angry eyes.

Lamps began to shimmer in the summer twilight ; cafés and wine-shops shone out upon the night ; and gradually, imperceptibly, the knowledge of a great catastrophe spread and circulated on every side. Details were wanting ; but France had suffered some terrible defeat. *That* was seen in every face. No one in Paris slept that night. The Corps

Legislatif called a midnight sitting ; and the Second Empire sank through the stage of this world to the realm of chaos and night, evanescent as a scene in a fairy play : and the curtain rose upon the New Republic.

The next day was Sunday, September the 4th, and the new-born Republic began in the glory of a cloudless summer sky. O strange people, children of smiles and tears ! Last night Paris had been plunged to the bottom of a black abyss, steeped in the horror of calamity, brought face to face with the certainty of an imminent siege, her army annihilated, her Empire fallen. Paris had laid herself down in dust and ashes, with weeping and wailing for the splendour that had perished, the glory that was gone.

To-day, Sunday, and a holiday, Paris awoke radiant. Again the excited populace filled the boulevards, poured along the streets, a strong current of humanity trending towards the Champs Elysées and the Bois. But to-day the note is changed. It is no longer the harsh minor of Rachel's wail for her lost sons, but the glad psalm of Deborah. The Empire has fallen, has fallen. Long live the Republic ! Let them come, the *têtes carrées* ! We are more than a match for them *now*. Joy beams on every face. The crowd wears its holiday clothes, the whole city its holiday aspect.

Every now and then a battalion of the National Guard tramps singing along the roadway. They stop their song to cry, 'Long live the Republic ! ' and thunderous acclamations reply, 'Long live the Republic ! '

And now came a time of preparation, expectation, anticipation. The days of uncertainty were over, and William and his conquering hosts were pouring steadily on towards this beautiful city of Paris. Bismarck had declared that he bore no grudge against France : he made war only upon the Empire. And lo, the Empire was ended like a morning dream, the eagles were draggled in the blood-stained dust of disastrous battlefields : and still Germany pressed onward, laughing with a sardonic laughter at the impediments France set in her way. Here a bridge blown to the four winds ; there a viaduct shattered ; railway-lines cut, destruction everywhere ; and yet the barbarous hordes tramped on over the ruins that strewed the way, pouring, pouring, pouring onward, fatal, invincible, innumerable, as the army of locusts in Holy Writ.

The Parisians expected an assault, a great battle, victory or speedy doom. They waited boldly, strong in their faith that Bellona was on their side. The Goddess of Battle had hidden her face from them hitherto, but it must be that she loved her France, laurel-crowned Victrix of so many glorious fields mother of so many heroes.

Yet, although expectant of short and sharp strife, Paris prudently prepared against the hazard of a blockade. She gathered in her flocks and herds, she heaped up corn and coal. The Grand Opéra, that palatial pile which was to have been a crowning glory of the Empire, was converted into a storehouse, half reservoir, half granary. She set to work to complete her unfinished fortifications, but passing slowly. She armed all her citizens. Chassepots and Remingtons were your only wear. And honest shopkeepers, who had never pulled a trigger, swaggered and strutted in warlike gear. Every head wore the képi ; every man told himself that come what might, let trade or family perish, he must be *there*, on the walls, ready to receive William and his Pandours. With some there was an idea that those advancing hordes were fresh from their native pine-forests, half-naked savages, with long hair, and wolf-skins slung across their brawny shoulders—such men as destroyed Varus and his legions—such men as fought and died for Vercingetorix.

'Let them come,' said the sleek grocers and bakers of Paris. 'We are getting ready for them.'

She cut down her wood, her beautiful Bois de Boulogne, the happy holiday ground of high and low. Those leafy arcades were given over to the woodman's axe, those trees were mutilated or hewn down. The swans upon the silvery lake, the fauna of those shadowy groves, were abandoned to the guns of the Moblots. Everywhere the creak and crash of falling timber, the scream of dying beast or bird. There, where the gay procession of carriages used to circulate in the afternoon sunlight, were now loneliness and ruin ; here and there a few scattered plumes, white on the greensward, showed where death had been ; here and there the thick black smoke, and fitful flame, marked a newly-fired thicket.

Paris was a camp, and every citizen a soldier. But the soldier's duties were neither onerous nor varied at this period. There was the morning rendezvous from seven to eight, the day and night watch on the ramparts, short slumbers under canvas, for the casemates which were to shelter these heroes later on were not yet built.

Among these soldiers of the National Guard Philip Durand and Gaston Mortemar were both numbered. The charmed life of the newly wedded was over. The domestic hearth was lonely. The husband could only return to his home in the intervals of his service as a defender of his city. And the wife was full of fear in her lonely home, or prowling in the neighbouring streets on some small household errand, loitering with other wives on doorsteps or at street corners, devouring the last news from the ramparts.

Trade was at a standstill. Each National Guard had his allowance of a franc and a half a day, with a small sum for wife or family ; but it was almost impossible for him to carry on any handicraft during this reign of Chassepot and Remington. Some there were—the few, the elect among workers—who contrived to accomplish something in their brief respite from soldiering ; and among these was Durand. His employer had shut up his factory. What good was there in creating articles of luxury—artistic cabinets *à la Renaissance,* writing-tables *à la Dubarry,* commodes *à la Maintenon,* what use in imitating the finest works of Buhl and Reisnier, when the city was girt with iron, and might ere long be girt with fire ? when at any evil hour, as yet unmarked upon the calendar, a bomb might explode in the middle of the factory, and send Buhl and Reisnier, delicate inlaid work, ormolu and cherry-wood, peartree and ebony, in a shower of splinters through the shattered roof ? The proprietor stowed away his choicest woods in his cellars, and locked up his warehouses and workshops. No goods could be exported from a blockaded city ; and in the city there were no purchasers of art furniture.

But this did not constrain Durand to lay aside his gouges and chisels. Before his marriage he had brought home to his little workshop some fine pieces of old wood, collected in various nooks and corners of Paris—an oak panel from the wreckage of a church, an old walnut sideboard, thick, heavy, clumsy, but oh, so well seasoned and richly coloured, from a sixteenth century house in the Marais—and with treasures such as these to his hand Philip Durand had no lack of work. He had undertaken a *magnum opus* in the shape of a sideboard, which in design and workmanship was to surpass anything that had yet been done in the factory where he was chief workman. All his knowledge of the master-pieces in carved oak, all his taste and skill were brought to bear upon this piece of furniture. His long Sunday afternoons in the

Louvre, his study of the art-books in the Imperial Library, all helped him in his handicraft. Jacques Mollin, his friend the painter, was at his elbow to make suggestions while the drawings for the sideboard were in progress. The mighty dead had their part in the work. This tangle of fruit and flowers on the cornice owed something to Van Huysum. This heap of wild fowl and hares, flung as it were haphazard against a lower panel, was a *souvenir* of Snyders. Everywhere the mind of the artist informed the hand of the craftsman. And the sideboard was as the apple of Philip Durand's eye. It was sure to bring him money, which he cared for only for the sake of his wife and his home. It might bring him fame, which he valued for his own sake, and still more for Rose, who would be proud by-and-by to say, 'I did not marry a common workman.'

She was a gentleman's daughter, the daughter of an officer in the English army, a man of good birth and refined surroundings. This man of the people never ignored that fact when he thought of his wife. He wanted to atone to her for the sacrifice she had made ; he never thought of her as the grisette, earning her living by the labour of her hands ; but as Captain O'Hara's daughter, born and bred as a lady, stooping from her high estate to become a mechanic's wife.

How happy were those brief glimpses of home, those brief hours with gouge and chisel, beside the hearth, while Rose stood by and watched the slow careful work—the chiselling of a feather, the rounding of a peach, the minute touches that marked the scales of a fish !

Yes, even while fear and uncertainty ruled without, while earnings were nil, and the strictest economy was needed lest these days of scarcity should exhaust the little capital amassed with such miracles of prudence and self-denial ; even now, with the enemy within sight of the walls, with the future of France wrapped in gloom, there was gladness in this humble home on the second floor in the Rue Gît le Cœur, and the little dinner or supper of bread and salad, the morsel of Lyons sausage, or small tureen of wine-soup was as a feast at this board, where love ever sat as the chief guest, smiling, blind to misfortune, careless of days to come.

Above-stairs, in the journalist's home, Love also reigned, and here, too, was the deep happiness of perfect union : but with Gaston and Kathleen life was less calm than in the Durand household. Gaston was steeped to the lips in the

fever of politics, was blown hither and thither, his soul tossed
and agitated by every breath of the public whirlwind. He
had friends here, there, and everywhere among the extreme
Republican party ; he believed in Rochefort, he worshipped
Flourens, that hot-headed enthusiast who just at this time
was in command of five battalions of the National Guard, the
beloved of Belleville and Ménilmontant, a leader at whose
beat of drum that seething populace were ready to rise as one
man.

The *Red Flag* was loud in its reproaches against existing
authorities. The *Red Flag* lauded Blanqui and the Blanquists, and was just now at the height of popularity, rivalling
Félix Pyat's paper, *Le Combat* and Blanqui's *Patrie en Danger;*
and yet the day was to come when the *Patrie en Danger* would
cease to charm, and the *Red Flag* would not be half red
enough—would perish as an effete rag, too tame, too conciliative
for the age of anarchy and death. The day was to come when
every colour would be too pale for Paris, save the deep dark
hue of blood.

But at this time Paris had not yet begun to suppress
its newspapers. The *Red Flag* was popular, and Gaston
Mortemar was the most popular among its contributors. He
was paid liberally for his work ; for in this day of doubt and
uncertainty the poorest could spare a couple of sous for a
paper that told how France was being misgoverned, and
called upon the supreme sovereign people—the Mirabeaus
and Robespierres, and Dantons and Marats of Ménilmontant,
to arise in their might, and steer the tempest-driven ship to
a safe harbour—the smooth roadstead of Communism, Collectivism, Karl Marxism, what you will ; every man his own
master, no hereditary nobility, no landowners, no millionaires,
a universal level of blue blouses and cheap wines.

And as weeks and months wore on, and autumn began to
have a wintry aspect, and party rose against party, faction
against faction, and agitation and fever were in the very air
men breathed, Kathleen's breast was fluttered by many fears.
In Gaston's absence she was never free from nevous apprehensions, from morbid imaginings. It was only in those brief
intervals when he was at home, sitting at his desk, writing
passionate, vehement protests against this or that, prophesies
of evil, wild suggestions for wilder action, bending over his
paper with pale, nervous face and flashing eyes, dipping his
pen into the ink as if it were a stiletto stuck in the heart of
the foe, writing as if Satan himself guided his pen, or

snatching some hurried meal while the printer's devil ran off with the copy, to return an hour after with the proof—it was only then, when he was *there*, and she could stand beside him as he wrote, and twine her arms round his neck, or smooth his disordered hair, stooping now and then to kiss the troubled brow, that Kathleen felt her husband was safe. At all other times she thought of him as a mark for Prussian bullets or for private vengeance. She had visions of every kind of catastrophe that might befall him.

'Oh, how I pity the poor rich wives, the great ladies of Paris;' she said to Gaston one day as she sat on his knee, after their scanty meal, brushing back the rumpled hair from his forehead with two loving hands, looking down into the dark eyes which gave back her look of love; 'how I pity them, poor things, sent away to Dieppe or to Etretat, to Arcachon or Trouville, parted from their husbands, languishing yonder in fear and trembling! Don't you think it was cruel of the husbands to send them away, Gaston?'

'No, dearest; unselfish rather than cruel. The women and children have been sent away from scarcity and danger, from trouble and fear. I wish you had let me send you to your old friends at the convent near Bruges, whose charity would have forgiven your flight, and who might have sheltered you in peace and security till this tempest should be overpast.'

'Peace and security away from you? I should have broken my heart in a week. You could never have been cruel enough to send me away!'

'Do you suppose I would not rather have you here, pet?' he asked, looking up at her, drawing down the pale, fair face to meet his own, and covering it with kisses; 'the light of my home, the guardian angel of my life. The brief half hours that we can spend together thus and thus and thus,' with a kiss after each word, 'are better than a year of commonplace comfort; our meal of bread and haricots is better than a dinner at Bignon's in the golden days of the Empire that i dead, when dining ranked among the fine arts. Did you read my last article in the *Drapeau*, Kathleen?' he asked in conclusion, with a little look which betrayed the vanity of the successful journalist—the man who believes that he moulds and makes public opinion.

'Did I read it?' cried Kathleen; 'why, I read every word you write! There is no one so eloquent, no one else whose prose is so full of poetry—except, perhaps, Victor Hugo—but

I like your style better than his,' she added quickly, lest he should be offended ; 'only, Gaston, sometimes as I read I fear that you are not wise, that those grand, glowing words of yours—words that burn like vitriol sometimes—may fire a train which will lead to an explosion, an explosion in which we all may perish. Think of all those people at Belleville and Ménilmontant, and Montmartre and Clignancourt—many and many of them honest, industrious souls, desiring only right and justice, but others, steeped in crime, misery, hatred —a seething mass, fermenting in the corruption of idleness and sin—ready to arise like a poison cloud, and spread death and ruin over the city. Do you remember last Sunday, when we went for a long walk in those streets beyond the Boulevard Richard Lenoir? There were faces in the crowd, Gaston, that made me shudder, that made me cold with horror ; faces of women as well as of men—yes, I think the women were worst—faces which haunted me afterwards.'

'There are blouses and blouses, Kathleen,' said Gaston, smiling at her earnestness. 'You cannot expect that men and women who have toiled and grovelled for two-thirds of a lifetime in semi-starvation—who have seen all the splendours, and pleasures, and comforts of this world pass by, afar in the distance, no more to them than pictures in a magic-lantern— you can hardly expect that kind of clay to dress itself up in smiles on a Sunday afternoon, and to sing hymns of thankfulness to the Creator.'

'I should not have been surprised that they look discontented,' said Kathleen, 'but they all looked so wicked.'

'Discontent and wickedness are very near akin,' answered her husband. 'When there is work for all, and food for all, you will see very few of those wicked faces. I am one of the Apostles of the Religion of Collectivism, and when that is the creed of France there shall be no more starvation, no more discontent, no great masses of wealth locked up in foreign loans or distant railways ; no millionaires' palaces, with a million or so sunk in pictures and *bric-à-brac:* but the money won by the labourer shall be in the pocket of the labourer, and there shall be no such thing as stagnant capital. We have seen enough of Dives, in his purple and fine linen, Kathleen ; it is time that Lazarus should have his turn. Dives means the individual : Lazarus means the nation.'

'But if, when the Prussians have gone, you are going to do away with millionaires, who is to buy Philip's sideboard ?'

demanded Kathleen, perceiving that this paradise of Collectivism was not without its drawbacks.

'No one,' answered Gaston lightly. 'Philip is a fool to create such a white elephant. The age of personal luxury, pomp, and show, and wild expenditure was an outcome of the Empire; it meant rottenness and corruption, bribery, falsehood, debauchery, an age of courtiers and cocodettes, stock-jobbers and card-sharpers. In the age that is coming there will be no carved oak sideboards worth twenty thousand francs, no Gobelins tapestries, no Sèvres porcelain. There will be a bit of beef in every man's *pot-au-feu,* a roof over every man's head, food and shelter, light and air, and cleanliness and comfort, and a free education for all.'

'And it is towards *this* all your articles in the *Drapeau* tend?' asked Kathleen naïvely.

'To this, and to this only.'

'I am so glad. I was afraid sometimes that you were urging the peple to act as they acted in '93, when King and Queen, patriots and priests, and helpless innocent people weltered in their blood, yonder, on the Place de la Concorde.

'My dearest, I preach Communism, not Revolution,' answered Gaston, in all good faith. 'We have no princes to slay. We have got rid of Badinguet and all that *canaille;* we have a clear stage and no favour; and it will be our own fault if France does not rise regenerated, purified, chastened by her misfortune, a veritable Phœnix, from the ashes of ruined towns and villages, from the dry bones of a slaughtered army.'

'And there will be nobody to buy poor Philip's sideboard,' concluded Kathleen sorrowfully, full of regret for the enthusiast in the little workshop below stairs.

It seemed to Kathleen as if a world, in which there were no rich people to buy works of art, no beautiful women clad in satin and velvet, no splendid carriages drawn by thoroughbred horses, no palace windows shining across the dusk with the golden light of myriad wax candles, no gardens seen by fitful glimpses athwart shrubbery and iron railing, would be rather a dreary world to live in; albeit there might be daily bread for all, and a kind of holy poverty, as of some severe monastic order, reigning everywhere.

CHAPTER VI.

ON THE RAMPARTS

Paris was a camp ; but so far it was but playing at soldiers, after all, for those within the walls ; though there was plenty of hard fighting outside ; and many a wounded Moblot was carried to the ambulance on a litter, never to leave it alive ; and many a mother's heart was tortured with fear for her sons ; and many a Rachel wept for those that were not. But though the roar of cannon thundered, or grumbled sullenly in the distance, the National Guard within the walls had what their American friends called a good time. The watch upon the ramparts was the most onerous duty, and it was only the night watch—the cold shelter of a tent, where the sentinel, returning from duty, generally found an intruder snoring upon his own particular knapsack, and under his own particular rug—which the honest citizen soldier found in somewise hardship. For Gaston Mortemar, young, vigorous, full of enthusiasm, ready, like Flourens, to lead five battalions to the fray, if need were, the cold nights of October and the canvas quarters were as nothing. His mind was charged with enthusiasm as with electricity. That bitter defeat, that day of humiliation yonder, on the Belgian frontier, seemed to him the justice of the gods, the salvation of France. The Man of December and Sedan—it was thus Blanquists and Internationals spoke of the late Emperor— was dethroned. That Empire of *clinquant* and *flouérie* had crumbled into dust. *L'Infâme fut écrasé*, and France was free to achieve her glorious destiny, as the liberator of the world, and to establish the millennium of Communism, the peaceful reign of blouses, blue and white, the apotheosis of Belleville and Ménilmontant.

In many a fervid speech Gaston depicted the glories of that coming age, yonder at the club of the Folies Bergères, at two steps from the Boulevard Montmartre, where the talk ranged ever from grave to gay, from the passionate oratory of the fanatic to the lowest deep of *blague* and buffoonery. There, and in the Salle Favre, and in many other such places,

Gaston preached his gospel of free labour, every man his own master, every workman his own capitalist, no concentration of profits, no man permitted to grow rich by the sweat of another man's brow.

'The civilised world has outlived black slavery,' he cried ; ' but so long as we still have white slavery—the slavery of the journeyman under the heel of the capitalist—there is no meaning in the word civilisation ; there is no such thing on earth as justice.'

He paced the ramparts, chassepot in hand, full of such thoughts, ready to repulse the Prussians, who had not the least idea of attacking bastion or curtain while the gradual work of exhaustion was going on within the charmed circle ; and it was only a question of so many months, so many weeks, so many days, when starving Paris must surrender. Already there had been talk of an armistice, and already that heroic cry of Jules Favre, hurled like a gauntlet in the teeth of the enemy, ' Not an inch of our territory, not a stone of our fortresses,' sounded like bitterest mockery.

Gaston's belief in the power of France against Germany was growing feebler every day ; but his faith in the great French people, as represented by the blouses of Paris, and in the Commune, as the perfection of government, strengthened day by day. Were not the people showing every hour of what noble stuff they were made ? See how steadily they faced the terrors of a beleaguered city, the deprivations of a state of siege. Behold their courage, their patience, their gay good temper. Drunk occasionally, perhaps ; but what of that ? Quarrelsome now and again, but in mere exuberance of an enthusiastic temperament. See how little the knife had been used in these occasional brawls—a *coup de savate*, a nose tweaked here and there, sufficed. The people showed themselves a nation of heroes.

It did not occur to Gaston Mortemar that Belleville and Ménilmontant, Clignancourt and Montmartre, were getting a good time ; that it was as if Bermondsey and Bethnal Green, Whitechapel and Clerkenwell, were having a universal holiday, while every man got fifteen-pence a day, and an allowance for his family for doing nothing. At every street-corner there was a cluster of the National Guard, drinking, laughing, orating, playing the game of *bouchon*, an innocent little game of chance with the corks of their wine bottles everywhere, even on the boulevards, dim with the half-light of alternate lamps, there were sounds of laughter and gaiety ;

while day by day came tidings of some skirmish outside the walls, which had ended disastrously for those poor Moblots, who had a knack of running away helter-skelter when they found themselves the focus of a circle of artillery.

It was early in October, and as yet there was no actual scarcity of food. Hardship and famine, the bitter cold of winter, were yet in the future. Luxuries were things to be remembered in the dreams of the epicure or the sensualist ; but frugal Spartan fare was within reach of all who had a little money in the stocking, who had kept their *poire pour la soif.* The little children were not yet pining, sickening, fading off the earth for lack of a cup of milk, and the *crémerie* in the street round the corner was in full swing.

Suzon Michel's *crémerie* was something more than a *crémerie* in these days. It was almost a club. Communists, Internationalists, Collectivists, had their rendezvous in the little shop where Gaston Mortemar used to eat his breakfast in days gone by. The more temperate and respectable of the revolutionary party loved to assemble here. The fare was frugal, but there was a debauch of oratory : and, in the midst of all the talk, the gesticulations, the prophecies, the threatenings and denunciations, Suzon was as the Goddess of Liberty, the Muse of Revolution, the Egeria of the gutter. She had read of Théroigne de Méricourt, of Madame Roland, and she fancied herself something between the two. She talked as boldly, as loudly as the loudest of her customers. She felt that she could mount the scaffold, and lay her neck under the fatal knife without flinching.

Never had she looked handsomer than in these days of fever and commotion. Sometimes she twisted a scarlet handkerchief round her raven hair, and those black eyes of hers flashed and danced and sparkled under the Phrygian cap of Liberty. Her neat black gown fitted her *svelte* figure to perfection. Her energy, her vivacity, her industry were inexhaustible. Her hands were as the hands of Briareus for serving the patriots with their coffee, their rolls and butter. Her gay voice sounded above the other voices in the *mêlée* of wit and patriotism. She sang as she went to and fro among the little tables, waiting upon her patrons ; and her song was always the newest ballad with which the ballad-mongers were undermining the government, the 'Lillibullero' of the hour.

'Je sais le plan de Trochu,
Plan, plan, plan, plan, plan !'

Sometimes, in a moment of exaltation, her customers would call for a stave of the 'Marseillaise' or the 'Ça ira,' and then the clink of cups and saucers and knives and forks upon the tables was like the clash of swords.

But tempting as these morning assemblies of the patriotic and the idle might be to a man of Gaston's temperament, he never crossed the threshold of Suzon Michel's shop. He passed her door twice a day, or oftener, on his way to and fro the newspaper office ; he heard the chorus of voices inside, but he never entered the shop. He had a feeling that loyalty to Kathleen forbade him to hold any commune with Suzon. And what need had he to take his cup of coffee from a shopkeeper's hand when the faithful wife was waiting for him in her bower on the third story, watching the little brass coffee-pot simmering upon a handful of charcoal ? One could not be too sparing of fire in these days, though one were ever so sure that the Prussians must retire from the enemy's soil before winter began in real earnest. The elements would fight upon the side of the besieged. That vast army, shivering yonder under canvas, must beat a retreat at double-quick time before Jack Frost.

It was on one of the clear gray afternoons of October that Gaston stood resting upon his gun, at his post on the rampart of the fort, gazing with dreamy eyes upon a landscape of poetic beauty, the deep rich colouring of autumn subdued into perfect harmony by the tender mists which shadowed without concealing wood and river, vineyard and field, while far off in the dimness of the horizon his fancy conjured up the dark swarm of Prussian helmets, blackening the edge of the landscape. The atmosphere was full of peace, and the silence of this lonely outpost was broken only by the *qui vive* of the sentries and the chime of distant church clocks. A good place for a poet to brood upon the creations of his fancy, or for a journalist to hatch a leading article.

While Gaston stood at ease, with his eyes wandering far afield towards the distant foe, and his fancies straying still further in a day-dream of universal peace, liberty, art for art's sake, and all the impossibilities of the socialist's Utopia, a sound of strident laughter, of deep bass voices and nasal trebles, broke like a volley of musketry through the stillness of the soft gray atmosphere, and presently half a dozen képis, or comrades of the National Guard, considerably the worse for *le petit bleu*, came swaggering along the rampart, escorting a young woman, whose scarlet headgear shone in the distance like a spot of flame.

It was Madame Michel, with the little red kerchief twisted coquettishly round her sleek black hair. She wore a tight cloth jacket, frogged *à la militaire*, over her black gown, the skirt of which was short enough to show an arched instep and a neat ankle. She had put on a half-virile, half-soldierly air, in honour of the times ; and her walk, her look, her manner, were already prophetic of the coming *pétroleuse*.

She came along the rampart with her patriots, who were pointing out the merits and faults of the fortifications, explaining, showing her this and that, swaggering, bragging, abusing Bismarck and his Pandours, singing snatches of patriotic verse. She was close to Gaston before she recognised him.

Then their eyes met, suddenly, his returning from the far distance, hers staring intently. Recognition came in a flash, and the rich carnation of her cheek faded to an almost deadly pallor.

'What, is it you, Citoyen Mortemar, so far from the Rue Gît le Cœur? What, are you too in the National Guard? I thought so devoted a husband would have found an excuse from service. I thought you would be lying at the feet of your English-Irish wife all day, like Paul and Virginia in their far-off island.'

'The nation cannot spare even lovers,' answered Gaston, lightly. 'Hector had to leave Andromache ; and my Andromache would despise a husband who did less than his duty. So far our duties have been light enough, and give no ground for boasting.'

'But let them come on, those Uhlans, those *grédins*, those—' here came a string of double-barrelled substantive-adjectives and adjective-substantives, too familiar afterwards in *Le Père Duchêne*—'let them come !' growled the wine-soaked patriot, 'and we will give them—'cré nom ! what is there which we will not give them ?'

And then the tipsy patriots retired to an angle of the fortification, and began to play the intellectual game of *bouchon*, forgetful of the lady whom they had escorted so far, for an afternoon on the walls of Paris.

Gaston shouldered his chassepot, and began to walk slowly up and down. Suzon followed him, came close to his side, and hissed in his ear,

'And so you are happy with your child-wife ?'

'I am as happy as Fate ever allowed a man to be in this world. Fate gave me the fairest and best for my companion, and then said, "Thou shalt find thou hast filled thy cup of joy in a day of trouble and war. Thou shalt drink only a drop at a time—a drop now and then—as the miser spends his gold."'

'Lucky for you, lucky for her that it is so,' retorted Suzon fiercely, 'for you may so much the less soon grow weary of your waxwork wife.'

'I shall never weary of her,' said Gaston. 'Every day draws us nearer. We may tire of life and its troubles, never of each other.'

'So you think now, while this fancy of yours has all the gloss of freshness. But you will weary of her. She is pretty enough, I grant you ; lovely, if you like ; but her face has no more expression than a June lily ; and you, who have a mind full of force and fire, must weary of such placid inanity. Do you think I do not know you—I who have heard you talk in the days gone by—I who was your *confidante* when you were penniless and unknown? You are beginning to be famous now. You sign your articles, and men talk about them and about the writer. You are pointed at in the street. But I admired you when none other admired you. I believed in you when you were nobody.'

'You were always very amiable, citoyenne, and I hope I did not prove myself unworthy of your esteem,' said Gaston, with a ceremonious bow.

He had an idea that a storm was coming, and he wanted to ward off the lightning if possible, by taking things easily.

'You proved yourself a seducer and a liar !' she answered savagely, her splendid eyes flaming as she looked at him, one red spot on either cheek, like a burning coal, her white lips quivering.

She had given herself over to the rule of her passionate nature in this new period of tumult and uncertainty, a time when all the old boundaries seemed to be swept away, the floodgates of passion opened. A queen, a goddess, in her chosen circle, she had come to think herself a being bound by no law, possessing the divine right of beauty and wit, free to pour out her love or her venom upon whom she would ; and to-day Fate had brought her face to face with the man to whom she had given the impassioned love of her too fervid nature, for whose sake she had been, and must ever be, marble to every other lover.

'You are mad,' he said quietly, 'and your words are the words of a madwoman.'

'They are true words. Seducer—for you seduced me into loving you—yes, as few men have ever been loved, as few women know how to love. Seducer! yes. Your every word, your every look, meant seduction, in those dear days when you and I wandered homewards in the midnight and moonlight, and loitered on the bridge or on the quay, and drank each other's whispers, and looked into each other's eyes, and our hands trembled as they touched. Liar! for though you never declared yourself my lover, all your words were steeped in love. When we have sat together, side by side in the theatre, my head leaning against your shoulder, our hands clasped as we drew nearer to each other, feeling as if we were alone in the darkened house—what need of words then to promise love! Your every look, your every touch, was a promise; and all those promises you broke when you deserted me for your new fancy; and by every touch of your hand, by every look in your eyes, I charge you with having promised me your lifelong love, I charge you with having lied to me!'

There was no doubt as to the reality of her feeling, the intensity of her sense of wrong done to her in those days of the past. Gaston stood before her, downcast and conscience-stricken.

Yes, if passionate looks and tender claspings of tremulous hands meant anything, he had so far pledged his faith—he was in so much a liar. His boyish fancy had been caught by this southern beauty, by this passionate nature, which made an atmosphere of warmth around it, and gave to the calm moonbeams of a Parisian midnight the seducing softness of the torrid zone. He had been drawn to her in those moonlit hours as young hearts are drawn together under the southern cross; and then came morning, and worldly wisdom and the sense of his own dignity; and he told himself with a half-guilty feeling, that those looks and whispers on the moonlit quay meant nothing. A pretty woman who kept a popular *crémerie* must have admirers by the score; and when she was not being escorted to the Porte St. Martin by him, she was doubtless tripping as lightly to the Chateau d'Eau with somebody else.

These were the *amours passagères* of youth, which count for nothing in the sum of a man's life.

Then came the new and better love. Kathleen's fair young face became the pole-star of his destiny; and from that hour he held himself aloof from Suzon Michel. And now she came upon him like a guilty conscience, and charged him with having lied to her.

'I am very sorry that you should have taken our friendship so seriously,' he said quietly. 'I thought that I was only one among your many admirers—that you had such lovers as I by the score. So pretty a woman could not fail to attract suitors.'

'I had admirers, as you say, by the score ; but not one for whom I cared, not one upon whose breast my head ever rested as it lay on yours that night at the street-corner, when you kissed me for the first—last—time. It was within a week of that kiss you abandoned me for ever.'

'A foolish kiss,' said Gaston, again trying to take things lightly ; 'but those eyes of yours had a magical influence in the lamplight. My dear soul, we were only children, straying a little way along a flowery path which leads to a wood full of wild beasts and all manner of horrors. Why make a fuss about it ; since we stopped in good time, and never went into the wood ?'

This was a kind of argument hardly calculated to pacify a jealous woman. Suzon took no notice of it.

'What was she better than I—that fair haired Irish girl— that you should forsake me to marry her ?'

'Why make unflattering comparisons? I only know that from the hour I first saw her I lived a new life. You were charming, but you belonged to the old life ; and so I was obliged to sing the old song :

"Adieu, paniers, vendanges sont faites ! "'

'*C'est ça.* You threw me aside as if I had been an empty basket after the vintage. But the vintage is not over yet, or at least the wine has still to be made, and I know what colour it will be.'

'Indeed !' he said gaily, rolling up a cigarette.

His watch was just expiring ; and even if it were not, the discipline on the walls was not severe.

'It will be red, red, red—the colour of blood.'

The game of *bouchon* had just ended in a tempest of oaths and squabbling, and the patriots came swaggering and staggering towards the spot where Suzon stood with gloomy brow and eyes fixed upon the ground.

'Come, Citoyenne Michel, come to the canteen, and empty a bottle of *petit bleu* with us. *'Faut rincer le bec avant de partir.* Let it not be said that the National Guard are without hospitality.'

CHAPTER VII.

'HEADSTRONG LIBERTY IS LASHED WITH WOE'

NEW YEAR'S DAY had come and gone—a dark and dreary New Year for many a severed household : the mother and her children afar, the father lonely in Paris, not knowing if the letter which he writes daily to the wife he loves may not be written to the dead—for it is months since he has had tidings of wife or child ; and who can tell where the angel of death may have visited ? A change had come over the great city and the spirits of the people—brave still, bearing their burden gallantly, still crying their cry of 'No surrender !' but gay and light of heart no longer, bowed down by the weight of ever-increasing wretchedness, pinched by the sharp pangs of hunger, enfeebled by disease, tortured by the bitter cold of a severe winter, which just now is the hardest trial of all. And now, in these dark days after Christmas, the ice is broken, the siege, for which Paris has been waiting patiently three months, begins in bitter earnest, and the thunder of the guns shakes earth and sky. The Line, the Mobile, the National Guard, all do their duty ; but at best they can only die bravely for a cause that has long been lost. The bombardment ceases not day or night—now on this side, now on that. In the trenches the men suffer horribly. The snow falls on the living and the dead. Every sortie results in heavy loss. The ambulances are all full to overflowing. Trochu, the irresolute, the man of proclamations and manifestoes, has given place to Vinoy ; but what generalship can hold a beleaguered city against those grim conquerors Famine and Death ?

The women bear their burden with a quiet resignation, which is among the most heroic things in history. Day after day, in the early winter dawn, they stand in the dismal train of householders waiting for the allotted portion of meat—a portion so scanty that it seems bitterest irony to carry it home to a hungry family. There they stand—ladies, servants, workwomen, from the highest to the lowest—buffeted by the savage north-easter, snowed upon, hailed upon, shivering, pale, exhausted, but divinely patient, each feeling that in this silent suffering she contributes her infinitesimal share of heroism to the defence of her country. So long as her rulers will hold out, so long as her soldiers will fight and die, so long will the women of France submit and suffer. Their voices will never be joined in the cry, 'Surrender for our sakes.'

The little children are fading off the face of this troubled scene. That is the worst martyrdom of all for the mothers. The little faces are growing pinched and haggard, the fragile forms are drooping, drooping day by day. The mothers and fathers hope against hope. In a day or two, they tell each other, the siege will be raised; milk and bread, fuel, comfort, luxury, the joy and light of life, will return to those desolate households; and the drooping children will revive and grow strong again. And, while the mothers hope, the little ones are dying, and the little coffins are seen, in mournful processions, day by day and hour by hour, in the cold cheerless streets.

At the butchers' shops, at the bakeries, there is the same dismal train waiting day after day. Everything is scarce. Butter is forty-five francs a pound; the coarsest grease, rank fat, which the servants would throw into the grease-tub in times of plenty, is sold for eighteen francs a pound. Gruyère cheese is a thing beyond all price, and is only bought by the rich, who wish to offer a costly present, like a basket of strawberries in February or peaches in March. Potatoes are twenty-five francs a bushel; a cabbage six francs; and garden-stuff, which last year one would have hardly offered to the rabbits, is now the luxurious accompaniment of the *pot-au-feu de cheval*. There is no more gas for the street-lamps, and the once brilliant Lutetia is a city of Cimmerian darkness. Bitterest scarcity of all, fuel has become prodigiously dear; and the poor are shivering, dying in their desolate garrets, pinched and blue with the cold of a severe winter.

Even among the well-to-do classes funds are running low. Provisions at siege prices have exhausted the purses of middle-class citizens. Stocks have been sold at a terrible loss, capital has been exhausted. Ruin and hunger stare in at the windows, and haunt the snowy night like spectres.

For the poor the struggle is still sharper; but the poor are familiar with the pinch of poverty, with the pangs of self-denial. And then, perhaps, there is more done for the indigent in this day of national calamity than was done for them in the golden years of prosperity ; albeit the Empire, whatever its shortcomings, was not neglectful of the houseless and the hungry.

In all these troubled days—with surrender and shame far away yonder at Metz, with defeat on this side and on that, here a General slain and there a gallant leader sacrificed, a little gain one day only to be counterbalanced by a greater loss the next, a threatened revolution, Flourens and his crew strutting, booted and spurred, on the tables in the Hôtel de Ville, little explosions of popular feeling at Belleville, semi-revolt at Montmartre—through all this time of wild fears and wilder hopes the *Red Flag* has been boldly unfurled in the face of Paris, and has managed to pay its contributors. When bread and meat are so dear, who would stint himself of his favourite newspaper, in which for two sous, he may read words that burn like vitriol, sentences that sound like the hissing of vinegar flung upon white-hot iron ? The *Red Flag* finds some pretty strong language for the expression of its opinions about William, and Bismarck, and Moltke, and the hordes of black helmets yonder ; but this language is mild as compared with the venom which it spits upon the Empire that is vanished—the Man of Sedan, the Man of Metz, the Emperor who surrendered Empire and army—all that could be surrendered—in the first hour of reverse ; the general who kept the flower of the French army locked up within the walls of a beleaguered city, tied hand and foot, when they were pining to be up and doing, hungering for the fray, eager to fling themselves into the teeth of the foe, to cut their way to liberty or to death ; only to hand them over to the enemy like a flock of sheep when he found that his game of treason was played out, and the stakes lost irretrievably.

At last came that which seemed the crowning humiliation, a capitulation which, to the soul of the patriot, was more shameful than that of Sedan, more irreparable than Strasburg, more fatal than Metz. Paris surrendered her forts, and opened her gates to the invader ; France gave up her provinces, and pledged herself to the payment of a monstrous indemnity. The flag of the Germanic Confederation floated above Mont Valérien ; and the Guard of the Emperor of Germany defiled along the Avenue of the Grand Armée to encamp in the Champs Elysées.

Dark and mournful was the aspect of Paris on that never-to-be-forgotten day. The populace held themselves aloof from the region occupied by the invaders, as from the scene of a pestilence. Those who came as captors were as prisoners in the conquered city. The theatres were closed, and Paris mourned in gloom and silence for the ruin of France. And on the morning of departure, when, after an occupation of only twenty-four hours, the barbarous flood swept back, the Parisian *gamin* was seen pursuing the rear-guard of William's soldiery, burning disinfectants on red-hot shovels, as if to purify the air after the passage of some loathsome beast.

Unhappily for Paris there were worse enemies than William and his square-heads lurking in the background, enemies long suspected and feared, and now to be revealed in all their power for evil.

With the opening of the gates began an emigration of the respectable classes. Husbands and fathers hastened to rejoin their families, provincials returned to their provinces—one hundred thousand of the National Guard, good citizens, brave, loyal, devoted to the cause of order, are said to have left Paris at this time. Those who remained behind were for the most part an armed mob, demoralised by idleness, by drink, by the teaching of a handful of rabid Republicans, the master-spirits of Belleville and Montmartre.

Too soon the storm burst. There is no darker day in the history of France than this 18th of March, 1871, on which Paris found itself given over to a horde of which it knew neither the strength nor the malignity, but from which it feared the worst. Hideous faces, which in peaceful times lurk in the hidden depths of a city, showed themselves in the open day, at every street corner, irony on the lip and menace in the eye. A day which began with the seizure of the cannon at Chaumont and Montmartre by the Commu-nards, and the desertion of the troops of the Line to the insurgents, ended with the murder of Generals Lecomte and Clément Thomas, and the withdrawal of the government and the loyal troops to Versailles.

When night fell Paris was abandoned to a new power, which called itself The Central Committee of the Federation; and it seemed that two hundred and fifty battalions of the National Guard had become Federals. They were for the most part Federals without knowing why or wherefore. They knew as little of the chiefs who were to command them

as that doomed city upon which they were too soon to establish
a reign of ignominy and terror.   But the Central Committee,
sustained by the International and its powerful organisation,
was strong enough to command in a disorganised and abandoned city ; and on the 19th of March began the great orgy of
the Commune, the rule of blood and fire.   The offal of
journalism, the scum of the gaols, sat in the seat of judgment.
Rigault, Ferré, Eudes, Sérizier—Blanquistes, Hébertistes—
these were now the masters of Paris. They held the prisons ;
they commanded the National Guard.   They made laws and
unmade them ; they drank and smoked and rioted in the
Hôtel de Ville ; they held their obscene orgies in palaces, in
churches, in the public offices, and in the gaols, where the innocent and the noble were languishing in a shameful bondage,
waiting for a too probable death.   There were those who
asked whether William and Bismarck would not have been
better than these.

For Gaston Mortemar, an enthusiastic believer in Communism and the International, it seemed as if this new reign
meant regeneration.   He was revolted by the murder of the
two generals ; but he saw in that crime the work of a military
mob.   He knew but little of the men who were now at the
helm.   Assy, one of the best of them, had protested against
the violence of his colleagues, and had been flung into prison.
Flourens, the beloved of Belleville, was killed in a skirmish
with the Versaillais, while the Commune was still young.
Hard for a man of intellect and honour to believe in the
scum of humanity which now ruled at the Hôtel de Ville,
and strutted in tinsel and feathers, like mountebanks at a
fair.   But Gaston had faith in the cause if he doubted the
men.   That red rag flying from the pinnacles, where the
tricolour had so lately hung, was, to his mind, a symbol of
Man's equal rights.   It signified the up-rising of a down-
trodden people, the divine right of every man to be his
own master.   For this cause he wrote with all the fervour
and force of his pen.

The arrest of the Archbishop and his fellow-sufferers, on
the 6th of April, was the first shock which disturbed Gaston
Mortemar's faith in the men who ruled Paris. That act
appeared unjustifiable even in the eyes of one who held the
sanctity of the priesthood somewhat lightly. The spotless
reputation and noble character of the chief victim made the
deed sacrilege. Gaston did not measure the words in which
he denounced this arrest. He had expressed himself strongly

also upon the imprisonment of Citoyen Bonjean, the good President. From that hour the *Red Flag* was a suspected paper. The man who was not with the Commune, heart and hand, in its worst follies, its bloodiest crimes, was a marked man.

The denunciation of Gustave Chaudey, the journalist, by Vermesch, the editor of the infamous *Père Duchêne*, followed within twenty-four hours by his arrest and imprisonment, was the next rude blow. Again Gaston denounced the tyrants of the Hôtel de Ville : and this time retaliation was immediate. The *Red Flag* was suppressed, and proprietor and contributors were threatened with arrest. Gaston's occupation was gone. His economies of the past had been exhausted by the evil days of the siege ; and he found himself penniless.

He was not altogether disheartened. He sat himself down to write satirical ballads, which were printed secretly at the old office, and sold by the hawkers in the streets ; and in these days of fever-heat and perpetual agitation, the public pence flowed freely for the purchase of squibs which hit right or left, Versailles or Paris, Republic or Commune. The little household in the Rue Gît le Cœur, a fragile bark to be tossed on such a tempestuous sea, managed thus to breast the waves gallantly for a little while longer, and Durand's kindly offer of help was refused, as not yet needed.

Soon after hearing of the arrest of the Archbishop and the other priests, Gaston made a pilgrimage a little way out of Paris. He went to visit his old friends, the Dominican monks, at the school of Albert the Great, and to ascertain for himself whether any storm-cloud was darkening over those defenceless heads. Who could tell where those in power might look for their next victims ? Priests and *sergents de ville* were the *bêtes noires* of the Communards.

All was tranquil at the Dominican School. The house had been turned into an ambulance by the fathers during the siege ; and it was still used for the same purpose under the Commune. The Dominicans could have no affection for a government which turned churches into clubs, forbade public worship, and imprisoned priests ; but they were ready to give shelter to the wounded Federals, and to attend them with that divine charity which asks no questions as to the creed of the sufferer. They had a right to suppose that the Geneva Cross would protect their house.

Out of doors they did not pass without insults. The house

had the reputation of being rich, and the Communards began to talk of hidden treasures, and of a reactionary spirit among the fathers. The Dominicans let them say their say, turned a deaf ear to opprobrious epithets, appeared in public as little as possible, and confided themselves to the mercy of God. Gaston saw Father Captier, the good prior, offered to serve him in any way within his power, which, unhappily, was of the smallest, thanked him for all his goodness in the past, and talked with him of the future, which was not full of promise. And so they parted, each trying to cheer the other with hopeful speech, each oppressed by the dread of impending troubles.

Sérizier, the colonel of the 13th legion, had established his headquarters in a nobleman's château adjoining the Dominican School, and he looked with no friendly eye upon the fathers, whose garden lay within sight of his drawing-room windows. The seizure of the fort at Issy aggravated the already dangerous position of the monks. The Federals, forced to evacuate their position, fell back upon Arcueil and Cachan, and the 13th legion encamped in the environs of the Dominican School. The fathers began to fear that the Geneva Cross would not protect them for ever.

On May 17th a fire broke out in the roof of the château occupied by Sérizier. The Dominicans hurried to the rescue, tucked up their robes, and succeeded in extinguishing the flames. Sérizier sent for them, and they appeared before him, expecting to be thanked and praised.

To their surprise, they were treated as spies, *sergents de ville* in disguise ; they were accused of having themselves set fire to the roof, which was to serve as a signal to the Versaillais. They protested, but in vain.

'We shall make a quick finish of the shaven-polls,' said Sérizier.

On the 19th of May, Léo Meillet, commander of the fort at Bicêtre, was ordered to arrest the Dominicans, with all their subordinates. To accomplish this perilous expedition he required no less than two battalions of Federals, one of which was the notorious 101st, commanded by Sérizier.

Gaston Mortemar heard of the intended arrest on the evening of the 18th. He spent the greater part of the night going from place to place, interviewing those delegates of whom he knew something, and from whose influence he might hope something. He urged each of these to strike a blow in defence of those guiltless monks, to interfere to pre-

vent an arrest which might end in murder. But in vain.
The chiefs of the Commune had grander schemes in hand
than the rescue of a handful of harmless monks.

Gaston was at the school early on the 19th. If he could
do nothing to help his old friends, he could at least be near
them in their day of peril. He was with them when the 101st
battalion invested their house, and he shared their danger.
Sérizier recognised him as the orator of the Folies Bergères,
the editor of the suppressed *Red Flag*—a paper which had
published some hard things about the colonel of the 101st.
He ordered Mortemar to be arrested with the monks.

‘ So you are a pupil of the Dominicans,’ he exclaimed—‘ a
worthy pupil of such masters. We know now where you
learnt to spit venom at honest patriots. You and your
friends the magpies shall stew together in the same sauce ! ’

The capture was made, after but little resistance. Father
Captier, feeling the responsibility of his office as Prior,
entreated to be allowed to put his seal on the outer doors of
the house. This grace was accorded without difficulty.
Those who granted the boon well knew the futility of such
a precaution.

At seven o’clock in the evening the prisoners arrived at the
fort of Bicêtre, after having endured every kind of outrage
on the way there. They were flung into a yard, huddled
together like frightened sheep, standing bareheaded under
frequent showers, stared at like wild beasts by the National
Guard. At one o’clock in the morning they were thrown
into a casemate, where they could lie on the ground and rest
their heads against the stone wall. In vain they asserted
their innocence, and demanded to be set at liberty. The
only answers to their prayers were the obscene songs of
their custodians.

CHAPTER VIII.

GIRT WITH FIRE

ON the 21st, Father Captier was taken before a magistrate in a room in the Fort, and submitted to an informal examination. Then followed two weary days, the 22nd and 23rd, during which the prisoners were left without food ; and while the monks languished and hungered in the gloom of their prison the good people of the Commune were busy with the work of spoliation. Upon an order given by Léo Meillet, two battalions of Federal soldiers entered the school at Arcueil, violated seals, broke open doors, and carried off every object of value, including even fifteen thousand francs in railway shares, the savings of the servants attached to the establishment. These were impounded as national property, and passed by a kind of communistic legerdemain into pockets which were never known to disgorge their contents. A dozen ammunition-waggons and eight hired vehicles were needed to carry off the spoil.

The school only escaped being burnt to the ground by reason of its well-filled cellars. Once having descended to these lower depths, the Federals had no desire to return to the surface, until they had done justice to the Dominican wines. They drank and wallowed there side by side, like swine in the mire, till the hour for burning was past, and thus the School of Albert the Great escaped the flames.

On the following day Léo Meillet and the officers began to feel themselves in danger at the Fort of Bicêtre. The army was drawing near. They resolved to evacuate the fort and fall back upon Paris, where numerous barricades, well provided with artillery, made resistance possible, and where the steep and narrow streets, the labyrinthine windings and twisting of courts and alleys, in the old quarter of the city made flight and concealment easy.

Carriages, carts, waggons, were hurriedly requisitioned on every hand : and then came a flight so eager that the prisoners in their casemate were forgotten.

'Thank God !' cried Gaston, with a wild throbbing at his

heart, forgetting for the moment, that he was an infidel. 'The Versaillais will be here in time to save us.' And the good Dominicans, the men who had turned their house into an ambulance during the siege and the Commune, and who had nursed the wounded Federals without a question as to their belief or their impiety, began to offer up their thanks-givings, and murmur psalms of triumph and rejoicing—those versicles which Jewish captives of old had sung beside the waters of Babylon.

Alas for those pious hearts uplifted in gratitude to the great Deliverer! not thus, not by Versailles, was their deliverance to come. They were to pass to paradise by a rougher road. Their joy had been premature, for they had reckoned without Sérizier.

And yet this Sérizier was one of the master fiends in the Parisian pandemonium. A currier by trade, he had been in early manhood the tyrant and the terror of a great currier's factory at Belleville, and in the revolution of '48 he had been leader of the mob which hanged the proprietor of the factory at his own door. He had been condemned for some political offence during the Empire, and had taken refuge in Belgium. He reappeared in Paris soon after the 4th of September, and played an important part in the siege.

After March 18th he became secretary to Léo Meillet, and later chief of the 13th legion. He commanded twelve battalions, which fought well at Issy, at Châtillon, and at the Hautes-Bruyères. Amongst these battalions there was one which he favoured above all the others, the 101st, his own particular battalion, composed of his friends and com-panions.

A man of fiery temperament, a great talker, a deep drinker, a workman without industry, living upon money extorted from the public purse, Sérizier exercised a strong influence upon the ignorant and brutal beings who surrounded him. He was feared and obeyed by all the 13th Arrondissement, which trembled before him. His hatred against the priests was a passion that almost touched on lunacy. He had profaned the churches by his foul orgies: and it was only the entry of the troops from Versailles which stopped him from selling saintly relics and sacramental plate by auction. Assassin and incendiary, insatiable in his thirst for mischief and destruction, it was his hand which fired the famous manufactory of Gobelins tapestry.

He was a man of medium height, square-shouldered, eyes

shifty and restless, forehead low, lips thick and heavy, receding chin, the head of a bulldog. His voice was harsh and hoarse, his breath exhaled cognac. When he was angry, that rough voice broke out in cursings and fury, more like the howling of a savage dog than the accents of humanity.

Sérizier had his own particular prison as well as his own particular battalion. A house in the Avenue d'Italie had been transformed into a gaol ; and here this man kept those victims who were known as his prisoners. At the final day he cleared his prison by a massacre.

Sérizier had not forgotten the Dominicans and their companions. At his bidding a detachment of soldiers came in search of them, and they were marched into Paris by the Barrière Fontainebleau, amidst hootings and insults and curses from the crowd, a little company of twenty hostages, five of whom wore the flowing black and white robes of the order.

No help from the French army. All yesterday they had been held at bay by the Federal artillery at Montrouge, and were only able to cross the ravines of La Bièvre on the morning of the 25th.

The prisoners were hurried along, almost at a run, to the gaol in the Avenue d'Italie. Embarrassed by the voluminous folds of their robes they did not always walk fast enough ; whereupon the soldiers struck them with the butt-end of their guns, calling out, 'Quick, magpie !' in mockery of their black and white raiment : and so to the prison, which was already full to the brim, containing ninety-seven prisoners, arrested in that district, and detained at Citoyen Sérizier's good pleasure. Bobèche, the gaoler, fatigued by having to write such a list of names, had gone out to refresh himself with a drink. While he was away the Communards came to the prison to ask the Dominicans to help in making the barricades ; but the deputy-gaoler having some respect for the religious character sent fourteen National Guards, imprisoned for some military irregularity, instead of the priests. Bobèche, returning immediately after, was furious with his subordinate, and accused him of shedding the blood of patriots in order to spare the monks. He had a detachment of the 101st battalion at his heels, and he ordered those tonsured scoundrels to be brought out.

Bertrand, the subordinate, yielded after some opposition, and opened the door of the gaol.

'Come, magpies,' cried Bobèche, 'off with you to the barricade !'

The Dominicans came out into the avenue, where they saw the detachment of the 101st, with Sérizier at their head. This time they believed that all was over; but they were deceived, for their agony was to last a little longer.

Father Cotrault, the purveyor, stopped on the threshold of the prison.

'We will go no further,' he said; 'we are men of peace. Our religion forbids us to shed blood; we cannot fight, and we will not go to the barricade; but even under fire we will search for your wounded, and succour them.'

This compromise would not have been accepted by Sérizier, but the Communist soldiers were wavering, they were crying out that it would soon be impossible to hold the barricade against the hail of bullets from the Versaillais.

'Enough,' said Sérizier to Father Cotrault; 'promise to look after our wounded.'

'Yes, we promise,' answered the monk; 'and you know it is what we have always done.'

Sérizier made a sign to Bobèche, and the prisoners were bundled back into the gaol. But they no longer deceived themselves with false hopes. They knew the respite was but brief. They prayed together, and made confession to each other. They might have been spared, perhaps; but the news brought to Sérizier was exasperating and alarming. Some men flying from the Quartier Latin to fight again in the Avenue d'Italie told how the Panthéon, the great citadel of the insurrection, had been taken by the Versaillais before there had been time to fire the mine which would have shattered dome and walls, arches and columns, in one vast heap of ruin. They told how Millière, the chief of the insurgents in this quarter, had been shot, and that the French troops occupied the prison of La Santé. The circle which was soon to enclose the Communards of the 13th arrondissement was narrowing.

What should they do? Fly, or stand their ground to the death?

A great many of the National Guard made off.

Sérizier gathered himself together for a final effort.

'Burn!' he gasped; 'we must burn everything!

He rushed into a wine shop and drank glass after glass of brandy. His wolfish soul, excited by alcohol, by fighting, by defeat, by the sight of the blood which reddened the road and the pavement, appeared in all its hideousness.

'Ah, has the end come so soon!' he cried, striking his

clenched fist upon the pewter counter. 'So be it! Everybody must die!'

He ran back to the avenue.

'Come, come,' he roared, 'I want men of the right metal, to smash the skulls of those magpies!'

A little crowd of Communards answered to his call, and, in advance of the band, two women presented themselves.

They were both furies—both had streaming locks of tangled hair, which were hideously suggestive of Medusa's snaky tresses; but one of the furies was young, and would have been handsome if her face had not been smeared and spattered with blood, and blackened by gunpowder. She wore the costume of a *vivandière*, and had once been smart; but the gold-lace on her jacket hung in shreds, the blue cloth was stained with blood and mire. She carried a gun, which, in her exhaustion, she handed to Sérizier, signing to him to reload it for her. She had hardly breath enough left for speech.

'The priests,' she murmured hoarsely, as Sérizier gave her back the loaded gun; 'are they to be finished—at once?'

'At once,' he answered; 'there is no time for ceremony with those scoundrels. They have had their day, and have made fools of you all long enough, with their mummeries— men, women, and children.'

'They have never fooled me,' answered the woman; 'I am a Voltairian.'

'Ah, *ce bon* Voltaire; if he had lasted till our time we should have shown him some pretty farces,' said Sérizier, turning away from her to give his orders.

While he ranged his men along the avenue, and talked apart with Bobèche the gaoler, the woman in the *vivandière* dress stood leaning on her gun, looking along the road, through dim smoke-clouds and dust and fire.

It was four o'clock in the warm May afternoon—May on the edge of June. The western horizon of Paris was hidden behind the smoke of incendiary fires; the ground trembled with the force of the cannonade. The woman wiped the sweat and mire from her face with the sleeve of her jacket, and looked across the scene of ruin and desolation with fiery eyes. She looked yonder towards the towers of Notre Dame, towards the Quai des Augustins, and the labyrinth of little streets behind those old roofs.

'Not much chance of wedded bliss for those two now,' she said to herself. 'Their honeymoon was short; but her misery shall be long. She and her sister are shut in their lodgings, expecting to be burnt alive every hour ; and he is in prison. What prison, I wonder ?'

The woman was Suzon Michel, and the man of whom she was thinking as she stood at ease by her gun, waiting to do her part, as a strong-minded woman and a patriot, in the slaughter of the priests, was Gaston Mortemar.

Since his arrest she had been able to learn nothing about him. She had been told by her friends the Communards that he had been arrested on account of something he had written in his paper. More than this they would not or could not tell her. There were so many prisons in Paris, all teeming with life, like beehives ; there were such innumerable arrests. People hardly cared to inquire why their neighbours were carried off, or whither. Human feelings, friendship, brotherly love were apt to become deadened in that pandemonium.

Since the week of fighting and fires began, Suzon had been in the thick of all the strife. She had carried her can of petroleum as bravely as any of those bearded ruffians who pretended to make light of her services. She had helped in the fires, she had helped in the carnage, like the very spirit of evil. It was not arson, it was not murder. It was only justice, an eye for an eye.

' They are killing our brothers and friends yonder,' said the assassins, as they shot down new victims.

Mercy at such a time would be cowardice. Only a craven would hold his hand when there was such a grand chance of avenging the wrongs of nobody in particular.

Suzon was drunk with blood, half-blinded by fire. Those flashing eyes of hers, bright as they were, saw all things dimly, through a fiery haze.

The priests—yes, she would help to slaughter them ; not because she knew anything about this particular brood of *calotins*, but because she hated all priests. They had done her no wrong : but her pious neighbours had despised her for keeping away from church : they had thrown their religion in her face : they had scorned her for her infidelity.

' Beware of that woman !' said an old man whom she had offended. ' The woman who never crosses the threshold of a church belongs to a venomous species.'

Yes, she would help in the good work. How the earth shivered under that awful cannonade ! The enemy was at the door ; nearer and nearer came the thunder of the guns. The deadly rain from the mitrailleuses came fast as the heavy drops of a thunder shower. The afternoon sun looked redder than blood yonder, as its lurid rays pierced the smoke. The circle was narrowing, narrowing, narrowing, closing in upon them like a ring of fire. Whom would they spare, those Versaillais devils ? Not one. Universal carnage would change the streets of Paris to rivers of blood, lit by a city in flames. Not a life, not a house would be spared.

'Let us begin ! shrieked Suzon, beside herself; 'let us work with such a good will that there shall be nothing left for those others to do.'

'Are you ready ?' asked Sérizier, facing the door of the prison, with his assassins ranged on either side of him.

'Not one of them shall escape, my General,' answered Suzon, grasping her gun.

Her voice was hoarse and rough, like his own. From head to heel, mind, soul, body, the creature had unsexed herself : and these men-women were even more savage than the devil-men of those days, for they thought their infamy heroism and their cruelty courage. Not one of these furies, waving her petroleum-can, shouldering her chassepot, but fancied herself a Maid of Orleans.

And now the victims were driven into the street, like sheep to the slaughter-house.

'Pass, one by one,' cried Bobèche the gaoler, who held his six-year-old son by the hand.

Was it not well for the boy to see the tonsured heads laid low ? It is thus France rears her patriots—young Romans suckled by the she-wolf Revolution.

The Dominicans, the school-servants, the journalist crossed the fatal threshold. The first to pass was Father Cotrault, and, at the third step, he fell, struck by a bullet.

The Prior turned to his companions.

'Come, my friends, for the love of God,' he said, in his mild voice ; and he and his little train rushed into the open, and ran their fastest athwart the rain of bullets.

Suzon flung herself into the midst of the road, at the risk of being shot down in the *mêlée*. She loaded and reloaded her chassepot, crying, 'Cowards, cowards ! they are running away !'

It was not a butchery, but a *battue*. The poor human game tried to flee, hid itself behind the trees, slipped along under the lee of the houses. Women at open windows clapped their hands and shrieked with joy as they watched the sport ; in the street men shook their fists at the victims ; the scene

was alive with insult and laughter, voices that sounded like
the howling of furious beasts. It was a new carnival of
flowers and sugar-plums ; only the flowers were insult and
outrage, the sugar plums were bullets.

Some of the more active gained the side streets, and
escaped the leaden shower. Five of the priests, seven of
the school-servants, were shot down in a heap before the
Chapelle Bréa.

'Fire, fire upon them !' cried Sérizier, when a convulsive
movement showed that life still throbbed amidst this mass
of death : and thereupon one poor bleeding form that had
faintly stirred received a volley of bullets.

' See,' cried Suzon, as Mortemar, slender, active, lithe,
with youth and vigour on his side, sped lightly along the
boulevard and vanished at a distant turning, ' there goes one
that will cheat us !'

She rushed off in pursuit of him, breathless, panting, mad
with rage. Two of Sérizier's lambs ran with her, pleasantly
excited by the chase. The hunters reached the turning, and
there, a few paces down the narrow street, leaning against a
lamp-post, exhausted by the rapidity of his flight, stood
their quarry.

The men fired instantly. Suzon lifted her gun to her
shoulder, and then suddenly let it fall to her side. She
dashed her hand across her eyes. Was it a dream ? Was
she for ever haunted, waking as well as sleeping, by that one
face ? Through the haze of blood and fire she saw the face
of the man she loved—loved and hated, and hated and loved.
She scarce knew which feeling was dominant in a breast
where both fires burned so fiercely. She saw him, pale as
ashes, his livid lips parted, his eyes staring wildly, as men
look into the face of sudden violent death ; hunted humanity
at bay, the hounds closing round, the huntsman ready with
his knife. A thin stream of blood trickled down the pale
face. One of the bullets had grazed his temple.

' Hold, hold !' shrieked Suzon, throwing aside her gun, and
stretching her arms wide in passionate entreaty; ' do not fire !'

Too late ; another volley whistled past her, as she sank on
her knees, screaming, pleading, blaspheming. She did not
know how to pray.

Gaston Mortemar fell without a groan.

Suzon sprang to her feet, picked up her gun, and struck at
the Communards with the butt-end, flinging about her like a
devil. ·

Sérizier's lambs burst out laughing. They thought she was drunk. In those days, when the very atmosphere breathed cognac and absinthe, it was only natural that a woman should be drunk. They laughed, and left her, having done all there was to do here ; left her grovelling on the ground by the lamp-post, alone with her dead, the warm May sun shining on her through the smoke of the battle, the air smelling of blood and burning.

While she hung over the prostrate figure, lying face downwards on the bloody dust, the rhythmical trot of the cavalry sounded in the distance, and the French troops were entering the Avenue d'Italie. Sérizier had retired into the prison when the carnage was over, and was occupied in revising a list of victims who were to be despatched with something more of formality than he had deemed necessary in the case of the Dominicans : but at the moment when he was about to order out the first prisoner upon his list, his lieutenant rushed in, and whispered in his ear.

All was over. The column of cavalry was seen advancing. The colonel of the 13th legion flung aside his papers, dashed into the avenue, threw himself into one of the houses communicating with the Avenue de Choisy, and disappeared.

When the French troops arrived they found nothing but mutilated corpses.

CHAPTER IX.

THE NIGHT WATCH OF DEATH

FEARFUL was the night that followed that hideous day. Burning, burning, burning ; burning and bloodshed everywhere. The battle had become a massacre, the conflagration a sea of fire. Never had been seen such destruction. The public granaries on the quay, the vast storehouses of Villette, eight hundred burning houses, and as many more newly set on fire, the D'Orsay barracks, the Tuileries, the Palais Royal, the Palace of the Legion of Honour, the Court of Archives, the Hôtel de Ville, theatres, manufactories, libraries, the Rue de Lille, the Rue du Bac, were all blazing and falling into ruin. Paris seemed one mighty brazier, through which wound the Seine, like a river of molten brass.

During the earlier part of the struggle the regular troops had obeyed the orders of their leaders with calm submission, doing their duty bravely in that worst of all combats— street warfare. But as the conflict went on, the sight of those flaming ruins, the savagery of the insurgents, exasperated them, and it was no longer possible to restrain their fury. Their hearts were hardened by many a bitter memory of past sufferings—of wasted heroism, of captivity, sickness, hunger, long stages upon inhospitable roads, the shame of undeserved defeat—sufferings for which their sole recompense had been injury and insult. And these, who had fired the most glorious monuments of France, assassinated her bravest and best, what had *they* done during the war ! They had drunk and swaggered, and held forth in wine shops ; they had strengthened the hands of the foe by their squabbles and revolts, and had garnered their strength for the work of bloodshed and universal destruction.

The soldiers, who had been accused of cowardice, who had been hooted as ' capitulards,' felt that in striking a terrible blow they were not only obeying the law, but avenging their country. The revolt had been pitiless ; the punishment was untempered by mercy. The sanguinary laws which the Commune had promulgated recoiled upon herself. She, who had murdered her priests and soldiers, her justices and senators, perished in her turn by slaughter as merciless as her own.

All through that night of horror Philip Durand watched by the bedside of his wife and her new-born infant in the Rue Gît le Cœur. The little street was safe in its obscurity, safe from the malice of the incendiaries, who had bigger game for their sport ; but the conflagration was terribly near. All the sky was lurid with reflected fire, and the thunder of the cannonade and the rush and roar of the flames were heard in every gust of wind which blew this way, while every now and then came the sharp sudden sound of an explosion—another roof blown up, another wall falling.

The atmosphere was poisoned by the odours of petroleum, and the thick rank smoke from the Granaries of Abundance, where the stores of wine, oil, and dried fish fed the fierceness of the flames and intensified the stench of burning. Everywhere the work of destruction was being hurried on. The Commune was at the last gasp ; these explosions and burnings were the death-rattle.

The little courtyard below Durand's windows was alive with people, going out and coming in, restless, anxious, alarmed, talking to each other in doorways or at open windows, bringing in the last news, which was as likely to be false as true.

Durand opened a window of the little *salon*, softly, while Rose slept, and looked out.

'They are burning Notre Dame,' said a man in the court, seeing him at the window, and eager to impart his information. 'They have piled barrels of petroleum all the length of the nave, half-way to the roof, and they are going to set it on fire. The grand old roof will fly into the air presently, like a pack of cards. It will be a sight worth seeing,' he added, hurrying out as if to a play.

'St. Eustache is on fire,' said another man, ' and they are going to burn the Prefecture of Police. Rigault and his chums have been having a great supper there—seas of wine, mountains of provision—and now they know their day is over, and they are going to blow up the building.'

Durand shut the window. A palace more or less, a church more or less ! What did it matter amidst this universal ruin ?—the Prussians at the door ; the government weak, vacillating, the sport of circumstances ; France in tatters, unable to save her bishops, her generals, her counsellors, her soldiers ; given over as a prey to a sanguinary populace.

This strong, clear-headed man sat down crushed by the weight of his country's desolation. He whose brain was usually quick to plan, cool to execute his plans, now felt powerless to look beyond the horror of the hour ; but the ruin which overwhelmed him was not the destruction that reigned without his dwelling. It was the blank within, that empty home upstairs, which filled him with horror, which was ever in his mind as a haunting fear.

It was three days since Gaston had disappeared, and now Kathleen was gone. She had slipped out unseen by the porter or by any of the neighbours. She had vanished like a ghost at break of day. When he went up to her rooms this morning to carry her the last news of her sister, to cheer and comfort her, and buoy up her sinking hopes, as he had done all through the two previous days of her trouble, he found the nest deserted.

There was no doubt as to her flight, or its purpose. The inner room was locked, and the key taken away ; the outer room was neatly swept and garnished ; everything was in its place. Gaston's bureau was locked ; the glazed cabinet in which he kept his cherished collection of books—not large but so carefully chosen : chosen as poverty chooses it treasures, one by one, deliberately, anxiously—this, too, was locked, and every book on its shelf ; and on the table lay a letter addressed to Durand :—

'Dear Philip, dear Brother,—I am going to look for my husband. Have no fear for me. Heaven will pity and protect my wretchedness. I shall be about all day and every day seeking for my beloved ; but I shall come back here at night for shelter and rest, if possible. If I do not come back after dark you may know that my wanderings have taken me too far afield. But you need have no fear. Of one thing you may be sure—while my reason remains I will not destroy myself. I will be true to the teaching of my childhood, and God will give me grace to bear my troubles.

' Do not let one thought of me distract you from your duty of protecting Rose and her baby. If she asks about me, tell her that I am safe, in good hands, well cared for. Is not that the truth, when I am in the keeping of the Holy Mother and her blessed angels ?—Ever lovingly, your sister,
'KATHLEEN.'

It was midnight ; the long dreary day was over, and she had not returned. Philip had crept upstairs, and looked into the empty room several times in the course of the day ; but there had been no sign of Kathleen's return. He had questioned the landlord, who kept the hall-door locked

and bolted in this time of panic; but the man had seen
nothing of Kathleen.

It had been altogether a trying day. Rose was weak and
somewhat feverish, and inquired anxiously every hour about
Kathleen. Why did not her sister come to see her? Where
was Gaston? Philip was sorely perplexed how to reply. Gaston
was at the newspaper office, he faltered on one occasion.

'But the newspaper was suppressed six weeks ago,'said Rose.

'Yes, but they are beginning again, now that times are
better; and the government will be restored. That's what
makes Gaston so busy.'

'But Kathleen—why does she desert me?'

'She is not very well, dear. It is only a cold; but it is
better for her to keep her room.'

'Yes, yes, let her nurse herself. Oh, I wish that I were well,
and could go to her,' said Rose, with a troubled look.

She was devoured by anxiety about Kathleen; and in spite
of her husband's tenderness, in spite of fussy Maman
Schubert's kindness, in spite even of that new and wonderful
love, the maternal instinct, awakened in her mind by the
infant that nestled at her side, like a bird under the parent
wing, she could not overcome that feeling of fear and restlessness caused by her sister's absence.

'Are you sure that she is not seriously ill?' she asked
Philip, looking at him with fever-bright eyes. 'It is so un-
like Kathleen to make much of a slight illness. And she
must know that I am pining for her.'

'Shall I go and fetch her?' asked Philip, making a movement towards the door. 'It is better for her health that she
should stay in bed; but if you want her so badly—'

'No, no, not for the world. Give her my fondest love.
Tell her to nurse herself. Give her baby's love, too, Philip:
I know this little creature is all love, though he was born in
an evil time.'

'Poor little storm-bird!' murmured Philip, bending over
the bed to kiss the little pink face, so soft, like something
very sweet and lovable, but not quite human.

He was ashamed of himself for the lies he told so glibly.
Yet he knew that it would be dangerous to tell his wife the
truth—dangerous while her cheeks were flushed and her eyes
glassy with fever. Maman Schubert had warned him that
he must wade chin-deep in falsehood rather than allow his
wife's mind to become troubled. He must do anything in
the world to soothe and comfort her. La Schubert herself

was glib and inventive, and her presence had always a soothing effect. She brought Rose imaginary messages from her sister ; and pretended to convey Rose's replies. She dandled the baby, and cooked Philip's dinner, and made the invalid's broth, all with the liveliest air, and made light of conflagration and ruin, although with every hour the roar of cannon, the hiss of mitrailleuse, grew louder, fort answering to fort with sullen thunder, the sound of musketry close at hand.

At midday a hideous noise resounded throughout the quarter. The houses rocked ; fragments of plaster fell from the ceiling.

What was that? The explosion was too loud for any shell, however formidable. It was only the powder magazine at the Luxembourg, which had just been blown up. The Panthéon was expected momentarily.

And still Maman Schubert, with nods and friendly smiles assured her dearest Madame Durand, 'cette pauvre chérie, that the Versailles troops were carrying everything before them. The Commune was surrendering without a blow. Order would be restored, Paris at peace, by Sunday morning.

'And we shall hear all the church-bells ringing for mass, and see the people in their Sunday clothes,' concluded Maman Schubert cheerily.

So the long day and the evening wore through, and it was midnight, and there was no sign of Kathleen.

She whose return was so eagerly awaited in the Rue Gît le Cœur was not very far afield when the clocks chimed midnight. She had wandered about Paris all day, haunting the gates of the prisons, inquiring for her missing husband of every one who seemed in the least likely to be able to answer. Had there been any new arrests made within the last three days, and amongst the new arrests was there a young man, tall, slim, with dark-gray eyes and marked brows, handsome, a journalist? At the gates of Mazas, at the Great and the Little Roquette, at Sainte Pélagie, at La Santé, the patient pilgrim appeared, weary, with garments whitened by the chalky dust of the hard dry roads which scorched her tired feet, drooping in body, yet brave of soul, questioning, seeking, watching, imploring, but finding no trace of the lost one.

Night was falling before she turned away from the gates of La Santé, the model prison of Paris, where General Chanzy had been imprisoned for seven weary days at the beginning of the Commune—night had fallen as she walked slowly and wearily back to that part of the city which she knew best, where the Pont Neuf spans the Seine, and the dark towers of Notre Dame stand out strong and stern against the sky-line.   Night had come, but not darkness.   The crescent moon shed her pale silvery light in the east, and the stars were golden in the deep calm azure of a cloudless sky.   But all at once that azure vault grew dark, and the stars vanished. Gigantic clouds of black smoke mounted to the sky, and then descended earthward, covering the city with an impenetrable dome.   Beneath this inky vault all was lurid.   An awful light glared and glowed on the quays, on the bridges, in the broad space in front of the Hôtel de Ville.   Left bank and right bank blazed and glared ; here some stately public office, there a millionaire's mansion, sent up its tribute of flame to swell the funeral pyre of the doomed city.   ' Chassepot and torch, shoot and burn ! ' was the order of the night.   Yonder in the Rue de Rivoli they were fighting desperately.   Kath-leen ran across the street amidst a rain of bullets, stumbling over scattered corpses, deafened by the roar of the cannonade. Slowly, despairingly, she wandered up and down those dread-ful streets, perpetually in danger, yet passing scathless through every peril.   Now and then a savage scowling face looked at her interrogatively, and then passed by.   Sentinels questioned, and let her pass.   There was no harm in her. She had a distracted look—a pétroleuse who had proved of too weak a mind for that patriotic work, perhaps.   Women are feeble creatures.   This one's head had been turned.   Only an inmate the more for the Maison des Fous.

Amidst blood and fire she wandered to and fro, pausing whenever there was a knot of idlers at a corner, to listen to their talk, or repeat her old inquiries.   Had there been any new arrests within the last three days ?

Arrests ?   There were arrests every hour, a man told her. The gentlemen in power were getting rabid.   Shoot and burn, that was the word.   Murder and fire were their only notion for taking their revenge upon Versailles.   Arrests, forsooth ! What was the use of talking about arrests ?   The prisons were teeming with hostages, there was neither space nor pro-vision for the herd of unfortunates ; and now the word had gone forth to shoot them down in the prison-yards, or to roast them alive in their cells.   Rigault and Ferré, Sérizier, Mégy, these were not men to surrender tamely.   If these fiery stars were to be quenched, they would go down in a sea of blood.

' Anything new ? ' repeated a man in a group that stood

on the bridge watching the burning of the Lyric Theatre, as
if it had been a free representation, waiting for the Châtelet
to take fire on the other side of the wide lurid street,
momentarily expecting the dark towers of Notre Dame to
vomit flames—'anything new? Yes, we live in stirring
times. There is always something new. The Versaillais
have taken the Panthéon, the stronghold of the Commune,
just as the Federals were going to blow it up. Millière has
been shot. That is new. Have you heard of the massacre
of the Dominicans? That is new. And Sérizier has taken
to his heels—Sérizier, the colonel of the 101st battalion ;
Sérizier, the hero of Issy and Chatillon. The colonel is gone,
and the battalion is scattered.'

The Dominicans ! At that name Kathleen drew closer to
the group, as near as she could to the speaker, gazing at him
with wild wide-open eyes. The Dominicans ! Almost the last
words she had heard from her husband's lips were an
indignant protest against the ill-treatment of these good
monks.

'I would shed my last drop of blood rather than that a
hair of Father Captier's head should be hurt by those devils,'
he had said a few minutes before he left the house.

She went close up to the man who had spoken, and who
was now staring, open-mouthed, at the burning theatre.
She laid her hand upon his arm.

'Is that true?' she asked. 'Has there been any harm
done to the Dominican Fathers of the school of Albert the
Great? My husband was at school there, and he loves them
as if they were his own flesh and blood.'

'Your husband's sons will have to find another school,
citoyenne,' answered the man, with a cynical air. 'The
Dominican School is sacked, and the shaven-polls have been
given their passports for paradise.'

'Murdered !'

'Every one of them. Shot down like pheasants in a
battue, this afternoon, yonder in the Avenue d'Italie,' pointing far away to the south. 'There is nothing left of the
nest or of the magpies, citoyenne.'

She clasped her hands before her face, and reeled against the
parapet of the bridge. Nobody noticed her, or cared for her.
The roof of the theatre was falling in—a shower of burning
fragments was blown across the dark water like a fiery rain.
On the other side of the river the glare, the smoke, the
stench of burning were intensifying with every moment.

'Will there be anything left of Paris but dust and ashes when the sun rises?' asked one of the bystanders.

Kathleen leant against the bridge, motionless, speechless, paralysed by fear. She tried to think. But for some moments thought was impossible; her brain was clouded, benumbed, frozen. Then came reflection. Gaston had said that he would die to save them, fight for them to the death, these good fathers; and they had all been murdered, and Gaston was missing. He who had given her such faithful love had abandoned her to desolation and despair.

Was it likely that he would so abandon her, unless a higher duty claimed him? Was it likely that he would leave her for a space of four days in ignorance of his fate, unless he were a prisoner—or unless he were dead? Paris reeked with blood, every street was the scene of murder, and he was gone from her—gone with the rest of those victims of whom the crowd spoke with such seeming lightness, while it looked on at the burning of the city as at the fireworks which conclude some grand fête.

They were waiting for the conflagration to burst from yonder mighty pile, from painted window, and tower and battlement, from nave and transept, from clerestory and roof: Notre Dame was to be the bouquet.

'Tell me, sir,' said Kathleen, in a hoarse, half-strangled voice, 'was there any one else killed in the Avenue d'Italie —any one besides the Dominicans—any one who was in company with the good fathers?'

'Yes, there were a few understrappers, I believe, servants of the school.'

'No one else?'

'What do I know? The news has passed from mouth to mouth. There is no official bulletin, citoyenne. The Commune keeps these things quiet. It is only hearsay.'

Only hearsay! A ray of hope lit up the blackness of her soul. Only hearsay! And how many wild stories had been told in Paris within the last week, how many horrors had been bruited about which had been but bubbles of foul imagining! The story of the bodies found in the church of Saint-Laurent, for instance. The desecrated corpses exposed at the church-door, the supposed victims of priestly crime; foul fictions invented to stimulate the populace to carnage and spoliation.

'Is it far to the Avenue d'Italie?' she asked.

The bystanders answered carelessly, one saying one thing,

one another, each and all absorbed in the awful rapture of the scene, and caring not at all for individual needs and feelings.

One o'clock struck from the clock-tower of Notre Dame. Kathleen was footsore, faint, her eyes burning with fever, her mouth parched with thirst. She looked down at the river, but the stream seemed to be running with liquid fire, not water. There was no fountain near. She must get on somehow, without the longed-for refreshment of a cup of cold water. There was no use in asking for information here, where the news was only hearsay, where people answered her carelessly. In the Avenue d'Italie, on the scene of this hideous crime, if the thing were true, she must more easily learn the actual facts—who had fallen, how many. There she might learn the worst

She crossed to the left bank of the river, and began her pilgrimage of despair. The distance was long, every step was weariness and pain after her day's wanderings. All the length of the Boulevard St. Michel, along which the ambulance-waggons were passing in dismal procession, crimson with blood. Under their scanty coverings were heaped a confused mass of corpses. The dead were being carried away by waggon-loads. On and on, past a barricade at which the men of the quarter were working, old gray-headed men among them, men who only wanted to die peacefully at home with wife and children, and who, knowing that death was inevitable, stuck heroically to their posts. On and on, till the blaze of the conflagration, the roar of the flames, seemed to be left behind. But not the dull thunder of the cannonade, the sharp crack of pistol-shots. Carnage was audible on every side.

Blood everywhere—the pavement was stained with it ; the doors and door-posts were splashed with it ; the gutters ran with it. Refuse of all kinds littered the road ; butt-ends of muskets, fragments of belts, tails of coats, strips of blouses, caps, cartouch-boxes, shoes ; and here, on the open space in front of a barricade, the soldiers who had eaten their soup had lain calmly down to sleep by the side of the slain, the living mingled with the dead. Kathleen looked at the sleepers shudderingly in the cold clear moonlight. The smoke had drifted away, and that scene of carnage was steeped in silvery light. Impossible to pass that spot with feet undyed in blood, impossible to avoid seeing those dead faces. There, with arms thrown wide apart and face turned to the sky, calm, proud even in death, lies the young lieutenant of artillery whom Kathleen remembered to have seen in the early morning, sitting astride a cannon, thoughtful, with arms folded, and a face prophetic of doom. Yes, it is he and no other. His vest is open, as he flung it apart when the victors called upon him to surrender. His heart is one wide bloody wound. All the gladness and pride of youth have welled out in that purple stream.

No lack of traffic upon the boulevard or in the street, albeit the night is far advanced towards morning. The omnibuses are going again—those useful omnibuses, the luxury of the poor—but their fares are not the living, but the dead. They carry a ghastly load of blood-stained corpses piled at random, thrust in helter-skelter. There are not vehicles enough for this dismal traffic. Railway-waggons, breaks, all are pressed into the funeral service. Men with sleeves turned up collect the dead, the hideous train moving slowly from barricade to barricade.

One man stands looking with horror at his naked arms, steeped up to the shoulders in blood. 'Is there no fountain hereabouts, where I can wash off these stains?' he asks of the crowd. Mighty fountains, rivers of water are needed to purify this Paris, drowned in the blood of her children.

It is deep in the night, but the stillness of night is not here. Men, women, families are grouped in the doorways. No one knows where the conflagration will end, how near the carnage may come; no man knows if he and his dear ones will see the daylight above the roofs and steeples of eastern Paris. Heavily, drearily the waggons go by with their silent burden. This may be called the night-watch of the slain. On the Boulevard d'Italie the insurgents have erected a monster redoubt, a fortification in triple stages, with trenches, loopholes, tunnels, defended at first by five hundred men. The defenders have dwindled to five, but these five will not yield. Their fortress is bombarded, the adjoining houses are in flames; but still the five refuse to surrender, and after a deadly fight, that has lasted thirty-nine hours, they are taken and shot by the Versaillais.

Such conflicts, as bloody as resolute, have been enacted all over Paris in the day that is not yet old. And now the moonlit hours, the calm of night, are given to the gathering up of the dead. Victors and vanquished lie cheek by jowl on the stones of Paris; hecatombs sacrificed to discord and civil war. The red flag flies yet here and there above the carnage, the bloody ensign of a bloody reign.

CHAPTER X.

WIDOWED.

It is morning, dim early morning, dawn pink and pearl-coloured above the housetops, an odour of verdure, of lilacs and acacias in the fresh sweet air ; and Kathleen wanders up and down the Avenue d'Italie, always coming back to that house which has been used as a prison by Citizen Sérizier, Colonel Sérizier, the leader of the 101st battalion. From one and from another, from many informants who all seem to tell their story differently, she has gathered the history of the massacre. She has heard how those harmless Dominican Fathers were hunted down, slaughtered like sheep in the shambles. It is after much questioning that she hears from a woman in one of the houses opposite the prison that there was another victim, one who was neither Dominican nor subordinate of the Dominican school—a young man, handsome, with dark hair and eyes. He would have escaped in the *mêlée*, only he lost time in trying to save Father Captier, the Prior ; and it was only when the Prior had fallen, when the fathers had been shot down all along the street, that this generous youth had turned to fly. And then, like a young antelope, he rushed through the savage crowd. He would have got off even then, perhaps, if it had not been for a Pétroleuse, a veritable she-devil, who gave the view-halloa, and rushed after him with half a dozen ruffians. He fell at the corner of a side street—that new street to the left yonder— the woman thought.

Kathleen listened to the woman's story, questioning her closely at every stage. She was so calm in her white despair, she listened and pondered the details of the tragedy with such a tranquil air, that one could have hardly guessed that each word was a death-blow.

'Do you recognise this young man as any one belonging to you ?' asked the woman compassionately.

She was a sempstress, who cared neither for Peter nor Paul, a decent person who had descended from her attic in the roof to see what this new dawn was bringing to Paris—deliverance or death. She was not one of those furies who had stood at their windows shrieking and applauding during the butchery.

'I believe he was my husband.'

'Heavens, that is sad !'

'Whose fault was it ? Whose work, the massacre ? Can you tell me that ?'

'They say hereabouts that it was Sérizier, Colonel Sérizier. He was at the head of it all. He ordered the Dominicans and the others to be brought here ; he ordered them to be shot ; he was there, in the midst of the massacre, directing his men, encouraging those vile women who were even more savage than the Federals ; his own hand fired upon those helpless priests ; he mocked them with abusive epithets ; he was pitiless, devilish, murder incarnate. You look ready to sink with fatigue,' said the sempstress, moved with pity for Kathleen, whose eyes were fixed and glassy as the eyes of death ; 'come up to my room and rest ; it is a poor place, but you are welcome. And I can give you a cup of coffee and a bit of bread ; it is not so bad as in the siege.'

'Not so bad ? the streets were not drowned in blood then,' said Kathleen. 'No, you are very good, but I am not tired,' with a ghastly smile. 'I will go and look at the corner where he fell. Stay, what did they do with the bodies ?'

'The Versaillais came an hour after and carried them all away.'

'Where—where ?' gasped Kathleen.

But the woman could not tell her. Among so many waggon-loads of dead, who could tell, who cared, whither one particular batch had been taken? Perhaps they had all been carried to that gaping chasm behind the chapel in the Cemetery of Père Lachaise, into which the Federal corpses were flung *en masse* after the battle of Asnières. The sempstress had seen that pit of death, sixty corpses waiting for recognition, a sight to freeze one's blood.

Kathleen left her, and walked wearily to that side street, a narrow shabby street : doors and windows were all closed, most of the houses had an evil aspect. There was no one standing about whom she could question.

A few paces from the corner of the street, at the foot of a lamp-post, she saw the spot where the victim had fallen. A pool of blood had stained the summer dust. It was dry now, but she could see how the corpse had lain in blood and mire. The figure had printed its outline on the ground. There was no other trace of the massacre in this quite street. One victim, and one only, had fallen here.

She knelt beside that awful stain ; she watered it with her passionate tears, the first she had shed throughout her pilgrimage of two and-twenty hours. The church clocks were striking four. Yesterday morning at six she had left the Rue Gît le Cœur. And now she had come to the end of her journey ; she had reached her destination. She knelt alone, unnoticed, with her hands clasped over her face, praying, first for her beloved, for the repose of his soul ; then followed a prayer less pure, less Christian, a passionate appeal to Heaven for revenge upon his murderer, the destroyer of her happiness.

Who was his murderer ? Not the blind mad mob, not even the devilish woman, the Pétroleuse, lashed into crime and murder by the scourges of insurgent tyrants. Sérizier, the man in authority, the wretch who brought those good Dominicans from their peaceful seclusion to the goal and the shambles. It was Sérizier of whom she thought when she prayed for vengeance.

'Let it come, O Lord ; long or late, let Thy thunder come and strike him as he struck them ! Let Thine hour of vengeance be sure and swift ! Lo here, looking up to Thee, I swear never to know rest or respite till I have tracked him to his doom !'

Sérizier, colonel of the 101st battalion. She wanted to know more about him—whither he had vanished after the carnage ; in what cellar or what garret this craven hound had hidden himself.

When she had exhausted her passion in prayer, she calmed herself and began to think.

She was tired to the point of being fain to cast herself down upon the dusty road, and to lie there till sleep or death came to give her rest from the fever of her brain and the dull aching of her bones. But she struggled heroically against this overpowering lassitude, and went back to the boulevard, and hobbled on till she came to a workman's café that opened early for the accommodation of the neighbourhood. Here she entered, and seated herself at a table near the door. The fresh morning air blew in upon her face as she sat there, and she felt as if that alone kept her from fainting. Never in all her life before had she entered such a place alone, or sat alone among such company. Her girlhood and brief married life had been as closely guarded as if she had been a duchess. To sit alone among rough blouses and Versaillais soldiers in their stained uniforms was a new experience.

She ordered some coffee, and the waiter brought her a roll and butter. She had eaten nothing except one piece of bread since she had left home. The coffee and the food revived her, and she was able to look about her, and listen to the eager voices of the blouses and soldiers, as they sat eating and talking, smoking, drinking all at once, as it seemed to her, with their elbows on the table, seen indistinctly in a cloud of tobacco.

'*Hé le père*, two little glasses of cognac, and one of absinthe,' called a blouse.

'*Garcon, une gomme*,' drawled another blouse, with sublime affectation, imitating the expired, or temporarily obliterated race of foplings, the *petits crevés* of the Empire, known afterwards as *gommeux*, elegant consumers of absinthe considerably diluted with gum arabic.

Presently came a name which riveted Kathleen's attention to the next table. The name was Sérizier. They were discussing the delegate of the 13th arrondissement, the commander of the 101st battalion.

'They say that he has decamped, this good Sérizier, the hero of our battles,' said one of the men.

'It was time,' answered a soldier: 'our cavalry were at the end of the street when *cette bête* took to his heels. They have been hunting for him ever since, but the rat has run into some hole where he is not easily found. We shall have him, though. *Nom d'un chien*, such butchers must not be allowed to escape. Those good Dominican Fathers ! No, the *canaille* shall not get off ?'

'He is a man of yesterday, this Sérizier, a creation of the 18th March, is he not ?' asked the other.

'He is a Communard, *crapule* among the Communards. He is a currier by trade, but he got into trouble under the Empire, and was a refugee in Belgium up to the 4th of September. He hates all priests with a diabolical ferocity, and has prided himself upon desecrating the churches by his brutal orgies. He is more tiger than man ; but we shall cut his claws and draw his teeth when we find him.'

'When we find him, yes !' answered the other, lolling over the table, and eating his soup with an air of luxurious repose.

His hands and face were blackened by gunpowder ; his hair was clotted with dust and blood. There had been no leisure yet for the victors to make their toilet.

'You think he has taken the key of the fields?'

'I should say he was across the frontier by this time; or on board one of the American steamers at Havre. He would not let the grass grow under his feet.'

'Not so easy to get out of Paris, my friend. Look at Raoul Rigault. He tried to hide himself yesterday afternoon, but they unearthed him, and set him with his back to the wall—his favourite attitude for other people. And this Sérizier is a marked man. He commanded twelve battalions at Chatillon and at Issy. All the army know him. He will never be able to pass our outposts unrecognised.'

'I hope not,' answered the other. 'They say that some of the communist dogs—the leaders of the sheep—have provided themselves with balloons, and that, as soon as they have burned Paris, they mean to take flight for England or Belgium.'

There was no more said about Sérizier, and Kathleen left, after paying for her refreshment, and walked homeward slowly, feebly, in the bright cool morning. The sun was rising over the heights beyond Paris. It was shining on the faces of the dead, on the dreadful crimson dye which stained the streets, on rags and tatters and fragments of arms strewed thicker than autumn leaves on roadway and pavement.

Some of the street-lamps were still burning—a pale and sickly light in the glow and glory of the morning. The barricades were deserted. This side of Paris was in possession of the regular army, and a comparative quiet reigned— the quiet of death and desolation. But mighty masses of flame and smoke yonder, as of a burning volcano, told that the conflagration still raged with unabated fury—the Rue du Bac, the Rue de Lille, the Public Granaries, the Palace of Justice: enough material there to last for a few good hours yet.

Half-way towards the Rue Gît le Cœur, Kathleen met a melancholy procession. Forty Communards, men and women, prisoners in chains, silent, with bent heads, in the midst of the soldiers who are leading them to the place where they are to be shot. No trial—no formula of any kind. They have been taken red-handed among the ruins they have made, in ditches behind heaps of stones. They have been forced to fight, no doubt. The Commune would take no excuse. Her children must give her their hearts' blood. To refuse was treason; and death to all traitors was the cry of those last days. Rebellion, in her death-agony, was merciless. 'As good one death as another,' said the sheep, as they went to the barricades ; and they worked and drank —they were passing liberal with the strong drinks, these Communard leaders—and they fought with the desperate courage of men who knew that death was certain either way.

And now, meekly as they have obeyed their leaders, they suffer themselves to be led to their doom. Not theirs the brains that hatched rebellion ; not theirs the pockets that were filled by pillage and theft ; not theirs the profligate orgy or the brief spell of power ; but theirs the penalty—death.

It was nine o'clock when Kathleen toiled slowly up the staircase, and knocked with tremulous hand at her sister's door. That last portion of her pilgrimage had been the worst of all. She had crawled along, half asleep, hardly knowing where she was or what she was doing. She had stumbled against the passers-by, and had been accused of drunkenness more than once by an enraged citizen. And now, as Maman Schubert opened the door, she fell into her arms, and sank from that matronly bosom to the floor in a dead faint.

The door of the inner room—Rose's bedroom—was ajar. The good Schubert lifted up Kathleen's lifeless form and laid it on the sofa. She ministered to her with the skilfulness of an experienced nurse, and then ran to close the door of communication, lest Rose should hear too much. Already Rose had inquired several times for her sister. Was Kathleen better ? Would she be well enough to come down to see Rose and the baby ? The mother had an idea that Kathleen would find the little one grown. He seemed to develop so quickly. He was all perfume and bloom, like an opening flower. His breath was sweeter than summer roses.

Durand was lying down on a mattress spread upon the floor of the tiny kitchen. He had taken his turn at the barricade last night, and had received a bullet in the fleshy part of his arm. He was feverish with the pain of his wound, devoured by perpetual thirst.

'You good soul, what would become of us without you ?' he said, as he took a glass of water from Maman Schubert's hand. 'How shall we ever repay you ?'

'My friend, do you think I need any payment ? What has a lonely old woman with a small annuity to do in this world except care for her neighbours ? And Rose and Kathleen are to me as my own daughters. Did I not see them when they first entered Paris, footsore and dusty, but

so gentle and so pretty in their weariness ? Was I not the first
to welcome them to this great city, which is now the city of
death ? Heaven help us ! Lie still, and keep your mind
tranquil, my friend, and as soon as I have given baby his
bath—how he loves the water, the dear innocent !—I will
come and put a fresh dressing on that poor arm.'

Madame Schubert was surgeon, nurse, intermediary between
the sick room and the outer world—everything to the Durand
household in their affliction.

From his bed in the kitchen Philip heard Kathleen's return—her feeble voice presently talking in low murmurs with
Madame Schubert. She was safe ; she had returned. Through
fire, and smoke, and carnage she had passed unharmed. Here,
at least, was a blessed relief—one burden lifted from their
anxious hearts. But he, the husband ? What of him ?

Kathleen told Madame Schubert the story of her pilgrimage ; told how she had knelt upon the bloodstained
ground where her husband's corpse had lain. But the good
Schubert refused to be convinced, would not see any sufficient
evidence of Gaston's death. What did it come to after all,
this story which Kathleen had heard in the Avenue d'Italie ?
A young man, nameless, with dark hair and eyes, had been
killed with the good Dominicans. But why should that young
man be Gaston Mortemar ?

'There are enough young men in France, my faith, with
dark hair and eyes ! *Ça ne manque pas*,' said Madame
Schubert.

' Has my husband come home ?' asked Kathleen.

The good Schubert shrugged her shoulders and shook her
head despondingly.

' Alas, no ! '

' Then he is dead—no matter how or where. He is dead !
Do you think that if he were living he would forsake me ?'
asked Kathleen.

' He may be a prisoner.'

' Would to God it were so ! But I know ; there is something here,' touching her breast, ' something stronger than
myself, that tells me he fell yesterday—on that spot.'

' Kathleen,' called a voice from behind the closed door,
' Kathleen ! '

Rose had heard those murmurs in the next room, and had
recognised Kathleen's voice.

Madame Schubert grasped Kathleen's arm as she was going
to answer that call,

'Don't go to her yet,' she said. 'You will frighten her with your ghastly face and your dust-stained gown. She was very ill yesterday, weak and feverish. She is weak to-day, but the fever is better. She must not be agitated in any way. Go to your room, and wash and change your clothes, and come down presently looking bright and happy.'

'It will be easy,' said Kathleen, with a ghastly smile. 'Yes, I understand.'

'And not a word about Gaston or your wanderings. We told her nothing but lies yesterday—told her that you were in your own bed, ill with a cold. Don't undeceive her. She is so happy, poor soul, nursing her first baby. Yet, even in the midst of her new happiness, she was full of anxiety about you.'

'I will be careful,' said Kathleen. 'I think I am getting used to sorrow. I ought to be able to hide it.'

She obeyed Madame Schubert in every particular, and came back in less than hour, fresh and bright in her clean cotton gown and black silk apron, her lovely hair brushed to silky softness, and coiled in a smooth chignon at the back of her head. She smiled as she kissed Rose. She sat beside the bed and rocked the baby on her knees, and talked to him, and cooed at him, trying to awaken some faint ray of intelligence in the little pink face, which seemed to the mother to be full of soul.

'Do you think he has grown?' asked Rose fondly.

'I think he is wonderfully improved since the day before yesterday,' answered Kathleen.

'Improved!' Rose felt inclined to resent the word. Could there be room for improvement in a being so perfect as that child had been from the very first hour of his life? But Kathleen had vague memories of an unlovely redness and spottiness in the infant's earliest idea of a complexion; and the soft, rosy tints of to-day seemed to her a marked advance in the baby's development.

Rose lay with her face turned towards her sister, her hand in Kathleen's hand, perfectly happy. Happy in the fulness of her love, albeit fort still answered fort with sullen thunder, and cannon and mitrailleuse, chassepot and revolver, still made deadly music in the streets. There was peace here for Rose Durand in the narrow circle of home. She had suffered all anxieties about the outside world to be lulled to rest by Madame Schubert's cheerful assurances. And then, since the birth of the Commune, Paris had grown accustomed to the

sound of bombardment, to the smoke of cannon. Polichinelle
had made his jokes, the merry-go-rounds had revolved, the
barrel-organs and fifes and drums had sounded cheerily in the
Champs Élysées, albeit Versailles was bombarding Paris. The
roar of guns, the noise and havoc of war, had become the
every-day sounds of the city. Rose, lying in her curtained
bed, windows closed and muffled, hardly knew that the guns
to-day sounded louder and nearer.

'Philip will go no more to the barricades,' she told Kathleen. 'He was wounded in the shoulder yesterday—a very
slight wound, praise to Heaven! but enough to prevent his
fighting any more.'

Kathleen heard with a shudder, remembering that file of
prisoners, with fettered limbs and downcast eyes, pale, despairing, submissive. She had heard people say that all who
had carried arms against the Republic would be served thus.
'*Passés par les armes!*' The phrase was familiar enough
now. A short shrift, and your back against a wall, citizen,
your waistcoat open, so! and eight muzzles pointed at your
heart.

'Where is Gaston!' said Rose presently. 'Maman Schubert said he was at the office all yesterday. His newspaper
is to be revived now that Paris is more tranquil, she told me.
Are you glad of that, Kathleen? I hope he will not preach
revolution any more. We have had enough of the
Commune.'

'Yes, enough—more than enough,' said Kathleen, her pale
lips quivering as she turned away her head.

All that day the sisters spent together, Kathleen devoting
herself to Rose and the baby, smiling upon both, speaking
hopeful words; but after dark, when Rose had fallen asleep,
Kathleen stole away from the sick room just as Madame
Schubert re-entered, after having attended to her own home
affairs. Before Madame Schubert had time to ask her a
question, Kathleen was gone. She ran up to her own room,
put on her neat little bonnet and shawl, her thick black veil,
and then back to those terrible streets, to the stifling smoke,
the glare of the conflagration, the tramp of soldiery, the cry
of 'Stand, or I fire!'

The struggle was over in the centre of Paris. The insurgents had retired to Père Lachaise, Ménilmontant, Belleville,
the Buttes Chaumont. The huge storehouses of Villette
filled half the sky with lurid flame, across which flashed the
swift white light of the cannon. The Hôtel de Ville stood

sharply out against the sky of flame and moonlight—a ruin, grand as any wreck of Roman greatness ; airy columns, fairy arches, doorways without rooms, spectral corridors, cornices of delicate tracery ; and, above all, unharmed, in big golden capitals, might still be read the legend, ' Liberty ! Equality ! Fraternity !'

And still the thunder of the cannon peals across the city. Montmartre, from its superior height, rains death and destruction upon Belleville and La Roquette. Belleville and La Roquette reply with mitrailleuse and shell.

'Any news—any news of Colonel Sérizier ?' Kathleen asks of a group of women at a street-corner.

But they do not even know who Sérizier is. They are full of their own troubles, their own fears. One of these weeps for a husband whom she has not seen for four days ; called out against his will—he, the peaceable father of a family—to go and work and fight and die at the barricades.

'Ah, *ma bonne !*' she says to Kathleen, with streaming eyes, 'the Commune was very cruel ; and now they say Monsieur Thiers will be cruel too. Those foolish people have pulled down his house, and that will not help to arrange matters.'

Sérizier ? No ; no one in the streets knew anything about Sérizier.

What was this dark rumour which the loiterers in the streets repeated to each other with awe-stricken faces ? The hostages had been murdered at La Roquette three days ago, slaughtered within the walls of the prison. The Archbishop of Paris, the Curé of the Madeleine, Monsieur Bonjean the President—eighteen victims in all.

Yes, it was true. True also that at five o'clock this afternoon, in the bright May sunshine, another band of hostages—priests, soldiers, civilians—to the number of fifty-two, had been done to death by a savage mob in the Rue Haxo, on the heights of Belleville ; but this new horror had not yet become town talk.

It was one o'clock in the morning when Kathleen went home, worn out by wandering up and down the streets, standing at corners or on the bridges listening to the passers-by, to the people who stood at their doors ; but nowhere could she hear anything which threw new light upon the tragedy in the Avenue d'Italie, or the wretch who had planned that bloody deed.

CHAPTER XI.

KATHLEEN'S AVOCATION

WHIT SUNDAY. May on the threshold of June, the very dawn of summer; but the sun, which hitherto has shone with pitiless searching light upon scenes of death and horror shines no more. Stormy winds beat and bluster against that feeble old house in the Rue Gît le Cœur, with a sound and fury as of thunder : the cannonade of heaven takes up the cannonade of earth, and echoes it with hundred-fold power. Tempestuous rain lashes the windows, like the spray from a seething ocean. Again the cannon of Montmartre thunders against the heights of Belleville and Ménilmontant. Again the insurgents reply with savage fury, blind, reckless, deluging Paris with shells.

And while the pitiless struggle still goes on upon the heights of Belleville, the day of reprisals has already begun for the insurgents. From Mazas they bring a hundred and forty-eight prisoners, hastily huddled into the prison yesterday. In the stormy Sunday morning, Whitsuntide morning, they are marched to the cemetery of Père Lachaise, among the trees and the flowers, and the marble crosses, and urns, and temples : and there, hard by that common grave where the murdered Archbishop and his companions lie in their bloody shrouds, the Federal prisoners are divided into batches of ten, and shot to death. They die bravely, joining hands and crying, 'Long live the Commune!' with their last breath.

In the prison of Little Roquette, at about the same hour two hundred and twenty-seven insurgents meet the same doom ; not quite so boldly, for some of these, said an eye-witness, were snivellers, and begged for mercy.

The final hour has come ; those shells are verily the death rattle of the Commune. Thirty thousand men are said to be concentrated upon this point of Paris, where they have built up giant barricades, almost impenetrable fortresses, communicating with each other by underground passages, a wonder of rough and ready masonry and skill. They are held in this supreme hour by men of desperate courage, men who have sworn not to surrender.

Two o'clock on that stormy Sabbath ; and so far there has been neither rest nor respite. Cannon, mitrailleuse, chassepot, thundering, rattling, roaring, hissing ; but now as the afternoon wears on there come intervals of silence. The cannonade pauses to draw breath. The sounds of battle seem more remote—they die away in the distance. Then silence.

Silence ! Are they all dead ?

This is Sunday, the day when the labourer rests from his toil ; but to-day there has been only one labourer, and his name is Death.

Evening, and for the first time for many weeks and many days no more cannon. O happy silence, silence of peace ! Or should we not rather say silence of death ?

A column of six thousand prisoners who have surrendered at Belleville slowly defile along the boulevard : and this is verily the end. Yes, the cup of desolation has been drained to the dregs. There have been the sword to slay, and the dogs to tear, and the fowls of the heaven and the beasts of the earth to devour and destroy, as in the day of the Prophet ; only the dogs have been human dogs, and the beasts have been human beasts ; and the whirlwind of the Lord has gone forth with fury, a continuing whirlwind, and it has fallen with pain upon the head of the wicked : and on the head of the good and just, and innocent and gentle also.

The sacred month of May, month dedicated to the holy Mother of God, was over—month of May never to be forgotten by the French people, May which has left its indelible mark upon the city of Paris—and now all the gates of the city were opened, and the world came to see the work of destruction. English, Americans, foreigners of all kinds went about looking at the ruins, as at Pompeii or Herculaneum, criticising, examining, somewhat disappointed that the havoc was not more universal.

On the 7th of June came the funeral procession of Monsignor Darboy, the third Archbishop of Paris murdered within a quarter of a century. Under a gray and sunless sky the car with its long train of mourners, soldiers, people, solemnly, silently defiled along the quays, past the still smouldering ruins of palaces and mansions. No roll of drums, no funeral music broke that awful silence; only the rhythmical tread of the soldiers, the hollow rumble of gun-carriages. In the dumbness of a broken-hearted city, a city reeking with blood newly shed, the martyr was carried to his tomb in the great cathedral—last stage of a journey that had known so many dismal halting-places—from prison to prison, and then to the common grave at Père Lachaise, from there to the bed of state in the archiepiscopal palace, and now to the final resting-place among the historic dead.

In the Rue Gît le Cœur life had resumed its wonted way, save for one empty place. Rose was again astir, the careful *menagére*, the attentive wife, nursing her baby, busy with her domestic work, cleaning, cooking, keeping the little apartment as neat and bright as a palace. There were flowers on the window-sill again, a bunch of flowers on the table at which Philip wrote or read, a bouquet of lilies of the valley, pure, spotless, telling no tale of a ruined city, a humiliated and impoverished nation. Within, by the domestic hearth, all was peace. Philip's arm was slowly mending. He was able even to work a little at the famous carved sideboard in his workshop, or to bring one of the panels into his wife's sitting-room, to sit there by the open window, chiselling a group of fruit, bird or fish, and whistling softly to himself as he worked, while Rose sat in her rocking chair crooning to her sleeping babe.

And Kathleen, the widowed, the heart-broken, what was her life in these days of restored peace? She was very quiet. She bore her sorrow with a silent resignation which was more pathetic than loud wailings or passionate tears. But Rose would have liked better to see her weep more. That bloodless face, those fixed and hollow eyes, that slow and heavy step— the step which had once been so light and swift upon the stair—those long intervals of silence and apathy, were not these the indications of a broken heart?

Rose Durand did all in her power to comfort the mourner. She tried to persuade her sister to surrender the apartment on the upper story, and to occupy a little room off Philip's workshop: a mere closet; but Rose could furnish it, and make it a pretty nest for her darling; and then Kathleen would be her child again, always under her watchful care. She would share all their meals, live with them altogether; and the company of the little one, who showed himself full of intelligence, would soothe and amuse her.

'You are very good, dear,' answered Kathleen meekly, when this scheme was pressed upon her; 'you and Philip have been all goodness to me. But I like to live alone just now. I am not fit company for any one. And again, if—if—' with a profound sigh, 'if—he should come back, and find his rooms altered, his books disturbed—it would seem as if I had not really loved him.'

Rose was silent. Till this moment she had supposed that Kathleen was absolutely convinced of her husband's death, that the black gown she wore was the sign of hopeless widowhood; but these words told of a lingering hope, and after this Rose no longer urged her sister to give up the apartment. It was better she should go on hoping until the thin thread of hope wore out, than that she should sink all at once into absolute despair. Better, too, that she should have the daily occupation of arranging her rooms, dusting Gaston's books, opening a volume now and then and looking at a page, as if it held his own words. There were pages of Musset's poetry which seemed to speak to her with her husband's voice, so often had he read the lines to her in their brief married life. She knew all his books, and knew the measure of his love for each.

Every morning she put a little bunch of flowers on his writing-table by the window. And yet in her inmost heart she was convinced that he was dead, and that it was his blood she had seen staining the dusty ground in the street off the Avenue d'Italie. And then when this work of dusting, polishing, and arranging everything was done, work over which she lingered lovingly, she would put on her little black bonnet, with a thick crape veil over her face, and go out and wander about the streets and the quays, and loiter on the bridges, hearing all that could be heard of the public news. People respected that black gown and bonnet, and the thick mourning veil. She was recognised as one of the many mourners who had been left behind after that awful tide of blood and fire had rolled over Paris. Lonely as she was, young, beautiful, no one molested her. She went from place to place, secure in the majesty of her desolation.

She saw the long files of insurgent prisoners led along the streets, fastened together by their elbows, with lowered heads, still fierce and shuddering from the bloody battle, guarded by a *cordon* of soldiers. She saw the exasperated crowd flinging itself savagely upon these victims of their leaders' folly, trying to break through the *cordon* of soldiers, the women more furious than the men, striking at the prisoners with their umbrellas, crying, 'Death to the assassins! To the fire with the incendiaries!'

When some poor panting wretch, exhausted by fatigue,
tottered and fell, and was picked up by the gendarmes and
put in one of the vehicles which followed the convoy, there
was a howl of fury from the mob :

' No, no,' they cried, ' shoot him on the spot ! '

And as the dismal train passed through the villages, on
the quiet country roads, there was the same chorus of insults
and execrations, a torture that knew no cessation till the
prisoners reached the camp at Satory, where they had the
naked earth for their bed, and the sky for their shelter.
Perhaps some among these pilgrims of the chain may have
assisted in that other procession on the 27th of May, when
Emile Gois and his myrmidons drove the priests and the
gendarmes to the place of butchery in the Rue Haxo.

The day of reprisals had come, and the day was bitter.
And the cry of Paris is like the voice of the daughter of
Zion that bewaileth herself, that spreadeth her hands, saying,
' Woe is me now, for my soul is wearied because of murderers!

In all her wanderings, those loiterings under the limes
and the maples, on the boulevard, or on a bench in the
Champs Elysées, where the old air of gaiety began once
more to enliven the scene, Kathleen had as yet heard nothing
of the missing Sérizier. The people whom she questioned
were either densely ignorant—they had never heard of the
man—or they remembered him vaguely as one of those
heroes of the hour, a shoddy Achilles, who had strutted in
a gaudy uniform and played the soldier in a passing show ;
or they were indifferent, shrugged their shoulders, believed
that Sérizier had been killed on one of the barricades at
Belleville yonder, or that he had been shot at Mazas with a
gang of insurgents.

At last, however, one tender June evening, when the
storied windows of Notre Dame flung broken coloured lights,
like scattered jewels, upon the placid bosom of the Seine,
hard by the Morgue, which lay low in the shadow yonder,
like the black hull of some slave-ship, Kathleen, standing by
the low parapet, listening to the deep-toned harmonies of the
distant organ, was startled from her melancholy dreams by
the voices of two men near her who were talking of Sérizier.

They had known him evidently ; he had been one of their
intimates at some period of his career ; but they were not
talking of him with any warmth of friendship. The man
had been too great a brute to conciliate even his own class.

'He got off, sure enough,' said one. 'He was cleverer than Théophile Ferré, or Raoul Rigault, or Mégy, and the rest of them. I met him after dark, on the 25th of May, in the Place Jeanne d'Arc. He was in a fever of fright, poor wretch, shaking from head to foot with agitation and excitement. After all, there is a difference between killing and being killed, and Sérizier thought his turn had come. His boots and trousers were red with the blood of the Dominicans, and he complained of having to wear a uniform that was likely to betray his identity. He was Colonel of the 101st battalion, you may remember, and had been very proud of his uniform—bulldog that he was. Well, he had never done me any good turn that I could remember; but one is glad to hide a hunted beast when the hounds are close upon him; so I told him I had a married sister living in the Rue Château des Rentiers, and that I could get him shelter in her lodging, which was on the ground-floor, at the back, looking into a walled yard—a safe kennel for any dog to hide in. He jumped at the offer, and I took him to my sister's place, gave him a supper, and a bit of carpet to lie upon, and a blouse and a pair of linen trousers in exchange for his fine feathers, and lent him a razor to cut off his military moustache; and at break of day he left us, clean-shaved and dressed like a workman.'

'And you conclude that he got out of Paris that morning?' asked the other man.

'He was a fool if he did not, having a fair chance.'

'The question is whether he had a chance. That bulldog muzzle of his would not be easily forgotten, and the Government was hard on his track on account of the slaughter of the Dominicans, which really was a little too much; even we of the International thought he had gone too far. I should think it would be easier for him to hide in Paris than to leave Paris just then.'

'Perhaps; but there has been plenty of time since for him to get clear off. I dare say he is living by his craft as a currier in one of the big provincial towns. He would have to live by his trade; for I know he carried no money with him when he made off that morning.'

'A currier! Here was something gained, at least,' Kathleen thought. Until this moment she had not known the original avocation of the warrior Sérizier, commandant of the famous 101st, the hero of Issy and Chatillon. A currier! Here was a falling off indeed for the Ajax of the gutter.

One of the big provincial towns ! Alas, this was but a vague clue. Rouen, Havre, Lyons, Tours, Rennes—the names of a dozen great cities came into Kathleen's mind as she went slowly homeward, downcast and disheartened. He lived ; that was something for her to know. He lived to expiate his crime, to suffer as she suffered, to render blood for blood. Her life, her brain, her heart should be devoted to the task of finding him ; her hand should point him out to the law he had outraged.

All that night—the soft summer night, full of the murmuring of leaves—even here in desolated Paris, where the ruined houses stood up blank and black, with shattered windows, through which the moonlight shone and the June winds blew ; a handful of dust or a fragment of crumbling mortar falling every now and then as the zephyrs touched the broken walls—all that night Kathleen lay broad awake, staring at the casement opposite her bed ; and when day dawned—the sweet summer dawn that came so soon—she sprang up, and began to wash and dress. Her plan was formed.

One of those two men had said there was safer hiding for such as Sérizier in Paris than outside Paris ; the other had said that he had no money upon him at the time of his supposed flight. Without money how could he have taken a long journey ; unless he had walked, like the two sisters ? But the colonel of the 101st—the man who had wallowed in feasting and drunkenness, who had held his impious orgies in the violated churches of Paris—was doubtless too luxurious a person to tramp for weary leagues along the white dusty roads, under the pitiless sun. No, he would stay in Paris. He would think himself safe in his workman's blouse, among workmen, most of them members of the International Society, that fatal association which had sown the seeds of anarchy all over Europe. Amongst these men the assassin would be safe ; they would not betray a brother, even were he known as the murderer of the helpless.

She was in the streets before any of the shops were opened, before workaday Paris—no sluggard, whatever her vices—was beginning to stir. This was sheer restlessness, for she could do nothing without the help of her fellow-men. At eleven o'clock she was in a small office in the Marais—an office to which she had gone with Rose years ago, soon after their first coming to Paris, to inquire for work. It was a registry for servants, for clerks in a small way, for shopmen and workers of all kind. Here she asked how many curriers' workshops there were in Paris. She thought there might be several, ten perhaps, or even twenty.

The agent gave her a trade-directory, opened it for her at a page headed 'Curriers.' There were two hundred and thirty-two master curriers in Paris—two hundred and thirty-two workshops at any one of which the man Sérizier might be plying his trade.

Hardly strange, taking this fact into consideration, that the law had hitherto failed to touch this offender; more especially as the government, though ready to administer stern justice upon such of the Communist assassins who came in its way, did not give itself very much trouble in hunting down those who had made clean off.

And then, again, the harmless Dominicans were solitary men. There was no wife or child, no friend or sweetheart, to avenge *them*.

'It will be longer than I thought,' Kathleen said to herself, as she stood at a desk in the shadow at the back of the little office, copying that long list of names and addresses.

Two hundred and thirty-two workshops! There were names of streets which she had never heard of—districts, suburbs, of whose very existence she was ignorant. The work of copying those addresses alone occupied her for nearly two hours; she was so careful to write every address correctly, to be sure of every name.

When her task was done, she gave the agent a franc for the use of book, ink, and paper, and asked him where she could buy a good map of Paris. He directed her to a shop in the next street, where she got what she wanted; and this done, she went home.

Rose was singing over her baby, singing in the sunlit window, bright with flowers. Philip had fitted the windows with flower-boxes of his own designing—Swiss, rustic, what you will, constructed out of odd pieces of rough oak, the refuse of his cabinet work. Rose was the gardener, who bought and planted the flowers, and tended these humble gardens day by day ; and never had bloomed finer carnations than Rose's Souvenir de Malmaison yonder, or lovelier roses than her Maréchal Niel.

Durand was at work in his carpenter's shop hard by, with a sheaf of chisels, carving a bird, whose breast feathers seemed ruffled with the summer wind, so full of life was the chiselling. What a happy home it looked in the July afternoon ! The tide of blood and fire had rolled by, and left this little household unscathed, untouched. Nay, in the midst of death and doom the babe had been born ; and the trinity of domestic love had been completed.

Kathleen sank down into a chair near her sister's, sighing faintly in very weariness.

'My love, how tired you look !' said Rose tenderly. 'Have you been far ?'

'No : only to the Marais.'

Rose had of late abstained from all close questioning of her sister. She knew that Kathleen wandered about the streets aimlessly, wearied herself with long walks that seemed utterly without end or motive. But this idle wandering might be one way of living down a great grief. It was well perhaps to let the mourner take her own way. Nothing so oppressive as obtrusive sympathy. Rose sympathised and said very little.

At his wife's instigation Durand watched the girl's lonely walks on two or three occasions—saw that she suffered no harm, went into no vile quarters, provoked no insult ; and after being assured of this, Rose was content to let her follow her own devices.

'The angel of consolation may be leading her,' she said ; 'saints and angels know what is best for her.'

And in her high-strung faith as a Papist, Rose Durand believed that her sister's pure spirit here on earth might be in communication with the souls of that mighty company, which had gone before, that great cloud of witnesses hovering round us, invisible, impalpable—the spirits of the faithful departed.

Kathleen sat silent, those dreamy eyes of hers gazing across the flowers to the blue cloudless sky. The dark-violet eyes seemed larger and more lustrous than of old now that her face was pinched and thin ; but oh, so unspeakably sad !

'Why were you not at home at dinner-time, dear ? Have you had anything to eat since the morning ?'

'I think not,' Kathleen answered absently.

'And you went out so early ! I was at your door before six, and found you were gone. You must be faint for want of food.'

'I never feel hungry. I am a little tired, that's all.'

The boy had dropped off to sleep by this time. Rose laid him softly in his cradle, and then busied herself preparing a meal for her sister.

She made some coffee in a little brown pot, which

needed only a handful of burning charcoal to heat it. She brought out some Lyons sausage, a plate of salad, a hunch of crisp light bread, a roll of butter in a little covered dish half-full of ice. Everything in Rose's domestic arrangements was fresh and clean and neat. The cloth she spread on the table was spotless damask, washed and ironed by her own hands.

'Come, pet,' she said, and coaxed her sister to the table, taking off her bonnet, smoothing the soft golden hair, kissing the pale brow, so full of gloomy thought.

Kathleen took a little coffee, but ate nothing. She sat with her eyes fixed on vacancy, scarcely conscious of the meal that had been spread for her, quite unconscious of Rose's face watching her.

'My dearest, if you don't eat—if you go wandering about and fasting for long hours—you will be fit for nothing; you will drop down in the streets; you will be carried off to a hospital.'

Kathleen looked up at her with a startled expression.

'Yes, yes; you are right,' she said hurriedly, and with a sudden agitation in tone and manner. 'If I become too weak, ready to faint at every turn, I shall be useless—I can do nothing; and I have so much to do. Yes, dear, I will take some of this nice bread and butter. I want to be strong. I am a reed—a poor, feeble reed; and I ought to be made of iron.'

'Only be reasonably careful of yourself, dear, and you will soon be strong again. Those long wanderings and long fastings must kill you if you go on with them. You ought to be careful of yourself, Kathleen,' added Rose, with tears in her eyes—for there were times when she felt as if it were but a question of weeks and days how long she might keep this idolised sister—'you ought to be careful, for my sake and Philip's. We are both so fond of you.'

'Yes,' Kathleen answered, in a low voice, 'and for *his* sake.'

She forced herself to eat, and did tolerable justice to the white sweet bread and the fresh salad. Her meals in her own apartment were less luxurious. A slice of dry bread, eaten standing, a handful of cherries and a crust, a cup of milk. She had hoarded her little stock of money ever since Gaston's disappearance. She held it ready for any expenditure that might help her in her scheme of vengeance.

'I want to be strong,' she said quietly, when she had finished her meal. 'I have got some employment—a—a kind of place to which I shall have to go very early every morning.'

'Indeed!' exclaimed Rose, sitting at work by the window, moving the cradle gently with her foot. 'Why did you do that, dear!'

'I hardly know,' answered Kathleen, with her eyes on the ground. 'I thought it would be better for me to be employed.'

'But I don't think you are strong enough for employment of any kind just yet, dear,' said Rose anxiously.

The idea seemed to her fraught with peril, with madness even.

'Oh, but I shall get stronger now that I have a motive, a settled purpose in life, a task to perform. You will see that I shall do so, Rose. Have no fear.'

Her eyes brightened and flashed as she spoke—a hectic fatal light, Rose thought.

'I hope, whatever place you have taken, that the work is very easy,' said the elder sister, after a pause.

'Oh, yes; it is easy enough—very easy; in the open air mostly. You will see that my health will improve every day.'

'I shall be full of thankfulness if I see that; and if the employment adds to your happiness.'

'It will!' cried Kathleen eagerly. 'It will make me very happy, if I succeed.'

'Dearest, I never like to question you about yourself,' said Rose, in a pleading tone, 'for I know there are heart-wounds which should never be touched. But I should be so glad if you would tell me frankly, fully, what you are going to do?'

'I cannot, dear.'

'Cannot! Oh, Kathleen, is not that hard between such sisters as you and me?'

'All my life has been hard since the 21st of May.'

'And I am to be told nothing?'

'Nothing more than I have told you already. I have taken upon myself an avocation which will oblige me to go out very early every morning: to be out sometimes at dusk. I want you to understand this, and not to be uneasy when I am away from home.'

'I cannot help being uneasy. I am anxious about you every hour of the day. Why cannot you stay at home, Kathleen, and let me take care of you? I could get you work that you could do in your own room; sheltered, safe, protected from the pollution of the streets, from the hearing of foul language, from brushing shoulders with disreputable people,'

'I hear nothing; I feel no degradation. I think of nothing, am conscious of nothing, but my own business.'

'Is this business—respectable—worthy of a good Catholic?'

'Yes it is respectable. There is a warrant for it in the Scriptures.'

Rose looked at her with acutest anxiety. That pale fixed face, the strange brightness of the eyes, suggested an exaltation of spirit, a state of mind which touched the confines of madness. And yet the girl's voice was soft and gentle, the girl's movements were quiet and deliberate. There was no wildness of gesture, no sign of actual aberration. Kathleen was terribly in earnest, that was all.

From that hour the girl's health seemed to improve : both mentally and physically there was a change for the better. Her eye had a steadier light ; there seemed less of exaltation, of feverish excitement. Her whole being seemed braced and strengthened, as if by some heroic purpose. Yet there were times when the light in those steadfast eyes, the marble lines of the firmly set lips, were almost awful.

'What a woman that is, that sister-in-law of yours!' said Durand's artist-friend, the graybeard who had been one of the witnesses at the double wedding. 'That face would be magnificent for Jael or Judith, for Charlotte Corday or Salammbô. That girl is capable of anything strange or heroic or deadly. She has the tenacity of a Redskin.'

Durand smiled a sad incredulous smile.

'Poor child, how little you know her!' he answered. 'You clever men are so easily led away by a fancy. Kathleen is one of the gentlest souls I know. She adored her husband, and her grief at his death has turned her a little here,' pointing to his forehead. 'But she is incapable of any violent act.'

'She is capable of a great crime in a great cause, as Charlotte Corday was ; the gentlest of souls, she, till she took the knife in her hand to slay him whom she deemed the scourge of her country. I am not led away by fancies, Durand. Faces are open pages to the eye of a painter. I can read that one, and know what it means.'

Philip took this for the illusion of an habitual dreamer, and attached no weight to the opinion. Kathleen had given them no cause for uneasiness since she commenced her 'avocation.' Her life passed with an almost mechanical regularity. She left the house every morning before seven— sometimes even before six. She had been observed to go out as early as five. She came home again at any hour between nine and eleven, breakfasted alone in her own sitting-room, did her housework, her little bit of marketing, and then slept or rested for an hour or two. Then, latish in the afternoon, she went out again, to return after dark.

This was her manner of life, as seen by her sister and her sister's husband. They puzzled themselves exceedingly as to the nature of that employment which obliged her to keep such curious hours. They talked, and wondered, and speculated ; but they did not venture to question her. She had entreated Rose to forbear : and Rose, who so fondly loved her, was content to remain in ignorance, seeing that the mourner seemed more tranquil, more resigned than before she began this unknown labour.

Yet they could not refrain from speculations and wonderings between themselves, the husband and wife, for whom life was free from all care save this one anxiety about the widowed girl.

Was her occupation that of a governess ? Had she found two sets of pupils in some humble circle, where superior accomplishments were not demanded in a teacher ? Did she go to one family in the morning, to another in the evening ? This seemed a natural and likely explanation. But if it were so, why had she made a mystery of so simple a matter ?

They could only wait and watch. They were too high-minded to follow or to play the spy upon her. But they watched her face, her bearing, when she was with them— which was but rarely now—and they waited for the revelation of her secret.

She would not make her home with them. That was Rose Durand's worst grief. If she could have had that beloved mourner beside her hearth every day ; if she could have seen her bending over the little one's cradle, beguiled by the sweetness of his dawning intelligence ; if she had but been allowed to soothe and console her sister, Rose would have been quite happy. She would have trusted to her own loving arts, and to the great healer, Time, and she would have looked forward to a day when Kathleen's wounds would be healed.

But Kathleen hugged her loneliness as if it were the one precious thing left to her. She would not be tempted from her solitude in the two quiet rooms upstairs. ' I am tired when I come home from my work,' she said one day, when Rose upraided her with unkindness in refusing to spend her leisure hours in the Durand *ménage*. 'It would be no rest to me to be with you and baby, dear as he is. I want to be quite alone with my dreams of the past.'

'They are not good for you, Kathleen, those dreams of the past.'

'Oh, yes, they are. They are my greatest comfort. Sometimes, sitting here in the afternoon sunlight, with a volume of Hugo or Musset in my lap, I almost believe that Gaston is sitting in that chair where you are now, by my side. I dare not lift my eyes to look up at him.'

'Why not ?'

'Because I should know then that he was not there, and the spell would be broken. You don't know how real daydreams are to me.'

'Too real, Kathleen; such dreams as these lead to madness.'

'Let me be mad, then. I would rather be mad and see him there, than sane and not see him. I would welcome madness to-morrow if I could believe that he were still alive— if there need be no lucid interval in which I should remember that he is dead.'

'Kathleen, you frighten me ! '

'Forgive me, dearest,' the girl answered, gently. 'There is no cause for fear. You do not know how steady my brain has been, how regularly my heart has beaten, ever since I have had—employment—business to do—a purpose in life. Before, I felt as if I were wandering in a desert, under a midnight sky. Comets were blazing in that sky—shooting stars darting their light, now this way, now that ; but there was no star to guide my steps—there was no road across the waste. Now I feel as if I were travelling on a straight level road, with my guiding-star shining steadily before me : there is such a difference.'

'You look so white this afternoon, darling. Have you worked harder than usual to-day ?'

'Yes, it was harder to-day—very, very far ! ' Kathleen answered, with an absent air.

'You had further to go to your employment ?' faltered Rose, looking at her wonderingly. 'Is it not always in the same place ?'

'Not always.'

'That is very strange.'

'Life is strange,' answered Kathleen, 'almost as strange as death. Oh, Rose, my best of sisters, don't look so troubled

about me. Believe me that all is going well with me. I am
doing no harm. I am doing my duty. And all will come
right in the end.'

This was spoken with a fervour which in some measure
reassured Madame Durand. She had never suspected evil of
her sister. She knew that pure nature too well for doubt to
be possible upon this score. Her chief fear, her ever-present
dread, was for the soundness of the girl's reason, for the
capacity of her mind to stand against the strain of a great
sorrow.

Kathleen would not go to her sister's rooms; but Rose went
to the widow's lonely home two or three times in every day ;
she would not be put off by Kathleen's desire for solitude.
She went to her the last thing every night, and knelt and
prayed with her; but Kathleen's lips were dumb. That
spirit which had once been fervent in prayer was now voice-
less. The widow knelt beside her sister with bowed head :
but there were some of Rose's prayers to which she would
not even say Amen.

' Why do you not join in the Paternoster, Kathleen ? ' Rose
asked tenderly.

' Because I cannot join with all my heart when you pray,
" Forgive us our debts as we forgive our debtors." If I said
that with my lips my heart would be the heart of a liar.
There are some debts that cannot be forgiven, some wrongs
that must be avenged.'

' Vengeance belongs to God,' answered Rose quietly. ' And
with Him it is not vengeance, but justice.'

' That is all I want,' said Kathleen. ' Justice, justice,
justice ! '

And then she lifted up her face, which had been bowed
upon her clasped hands until now, and prayed aloud :

' O God, Thou art my help and deliverer ! O Lord, make
no tarrying ! The wicked walk on every side when the vilest
men are exalted. As the fire burneth the wood, and as the
flame setteth the mountains on fire, so persecute them with
Thy tempest, and make them afraid with Thy storm.'

CHAPTER XII.

FOUND

THE days and weeks wore slowly on; July came and passed, and it was mid-August. Paris was at its hottest. It might have been a city in the tropics. Thick white mists rose from the boulevards and clouded the evening air. The stones in the courtyards of hotels and great houses were baked in the sunshine. The very sound of water splashing upon the hot streets was rapture. The atmosphere was heavy with heat; and it seemed as if the low thunder-charged sky were a cast-iron dome which roofed in the city and suburbs.

That city, once called beautiful, still wore the aspect of devastation. The ruined houses still gave forth an odour of smoke and burning. The fierce meridian sun drew out the stench of charred wood. On every side were the signs and tokens of destruction. On every side one heard of loss, and sorrow, and death.

The herd of tourists went tramping through the city, staring, gaping, expatiating on the spectacle—disappointed somewhat that things were no worse. They had expected to find Babylon a heap; and here were her palaces and churches still standing, her spires and pinnacles still pointing heavenward, her domes glittering against the hot blue sky. The tourists were disillusionised, and felt they were getting very little for their money.

The mightier of the ruins remained as anarchy had left them; but here and there the work of reparation had begun. Trade was reviving. The markets had resumed their normal aspect, and food was to be had at the old prices. The theatres were beginning to reopen their doors. Restaurants and cafés had smartened themselves up to accommodate a floating population of travellers, taking this desolated Babylon on their way to fairer scenes. Again the clinking of teaspoons and the clash of glasses were heard on the boulevard. The *petits crevés* and the *cocodettes* had emerged from retirement, or had come back from exile. Alcibiades and Aspasia had returned to look at the ruins, and had hurried off again to the mountains or the sea. Paris was Paris again; but a sorely impoverished, somewhat humiliated Paris.

Kathleen's life pursued its beaten round all this time. The oppressive heat of those August days did not deter her from her labour. Every morning before the shops were opened she was in the streets, neatly clad in her black gown and close black bonnet, a little market-basket on her arm, as of one who went upon a housewife's errand. In the dim early morning she walked to her destination—one of those two hundred and thirty-two workshops which she had written down in her list. Some of these were in the remotest corners of Paris, and many of her morning walks were long and weary ; but she was careful to allow herself ample time for these long distances. She always studied her map overnight, and learned the names of the streets by which she had to go. She was thoroughly systematic in her work ; and she had by this time acquired a wonderful expertness in finding her way, a wonderful knowledge of the great wide-spreading town. It seemed to her as if there were not a corner of Paris, not a nook or an alley, which she had not explored.

Sometimes her destination was some foul-smelling lane at Belleville, some dingy street near Montmartre. She went as far as Vincennes on one side, beyond Passy on the other. But whatever the distance, she went to her work with the same quiet patience, the same tranquil aspect. Nobody ever remarked her as an eccentric-looking person ; no one ever saw wildness or exaltation in her manner. She walked quietly onward, at a moderate business-like pace, her little basket over her arm ; her pale earnest face shaded by the neat little crape veil, tied closely round the small black straw bonnet ; and she inspired no one's wonder or curiosity. A clerk's wife, catering for her little household ; a sempstress going to her work. She might be either.

When she reached her destination, and stood in front of the curriers' workshop, her task became more difficult. She watched for the going and coming of the workmen at their breakfast-hour, between nine and ten o'clock. She had to observe without being observed. She hovered near the door of the restaurant where they took their *soupe au fromage*. She had to loiter in the street or the lane, without appearing to be a loiterer. This exacted all her powers as an actress; but, as every intelligent woman is instinctively an actress, she contrived to perform this part of her task so skilfully as to escape, for the most part, unquestioned and unremarked.

If there were shops in the street all her little purchases for that humble *ménage*, which was not much better than genteel starvation, were made upon the spot. This gave her the opportunity of wasting time, and of making inquiries. It was so easy while buying a pear or a handful of plums at the little fruit-shop, or a roll at the baker's, to ask a few questions, in mere idle curiosity as it seemed, about the currier's on the other side of the way. Was it a small or a large trade for instance? How many workmen were employed—and what kind of men? Then if the shopkeeper were inclined to gossip, and were friendly, she could watch the men go to their work from the threshold of his shop, and hear his remarks upon them, and be sure that she saw the full complement employed there.

Now and again it happened that a workman was ill or drunk, or idle, and did not go to his work; and then, after ascertaining this fact, she had to come back to the same spot again, once, twice, thrice even, to make sure of that one errant workman. For the man she wanted was one man among all the curriers of Paris, and to let one escape her might be to lose him.

She hunted her prey with the tenacity of a Red Indian.

The work was very slow work. August was nearly over, and she had not completed the third part of her list. The curriers' shops were scattered. It was rarely that she could do more than two in a day—one in the morning, when the men went to their work; one in the evening, when they left work. She was getting to be curiously familiar with the curriers of Paris, their ways and their manners; the restaurants where they dined or supped late in the evening, at long narrow tables in low dingy rooms, by the light of tallow candles, and amid overpowering odours of cognac and cheese soup; the wine-shops where they swilled gallons of 'little blue,' or stupefied themselves with cheap cognac.

She learned a great deal; but in all this time there had been no sign of Sérizier, no clue to the whereabouts of that one workman.

Now and then she ventured to accost one of these blue blouses, who answered civilly or brutally, as Fate willed. But, for the most part, they were civil in their rough way. She told her little pathetic story of a brother, a currier by trade, of whom she had lost all trace since the Commune. His chief friend was a man—also a currier—called Sérizier: and she thought it likely that, wherever Sérizier were working, her brother would be working too.

Did monsieur happen by chance to know anything about

a currier called Sérizier ? No, nobody knew of such a man. Some to whom she spoke remembered the name and the man in the day of his splendour—with a cocked hat, and a red scarf round his waist. There had been a passion for red scarves among the Communards. Perhaps it was the colour that charmed them, the hue of that blood which was to them as an atmosphere.

Those who knew all about Sérizier's past career could give her no enlightenment about his present whereabouts. She always made her inquiries judiciously, indirectly, putting forward that mythical brother as the motive of her questionings. She did not want to be known as a woman who had inquired for Sérizier, lest the hunted should get wind of the hunter. And so she came to September, and in all the blue blouses, the heavy figures, and stooping shoulders, the toil-stained hands, the close-cropped bullet heads, she had seen no sign of Sérizier. How should she know him when she saw him ?

Easily enough. First, she had his photograph, which she had discovered, after a diligent search, in a shop on the Boulevard St. Michel, among other heroes of the Commune. Secondly, she had seen him once in the flesh, and his face had impressed itself upon her memory in a flash, as if it had been photographed upon her brain. It was not a common face ; it was original in its sinister ugliness, and she could recall every line in that bulldog visage.

She had seen him soon after the skirmish at Issy, when his laurels were yet green, and the street-arabs cheered him as he passed at the head of his regiment, in gaudy uniform, red scarf, waving plumes, clanking sword, on a horse which he could not ride, boastful, triumphant. It was in the spring evening, the clear cool light of declining day, when she stood on the quay, hanging on her husband's arm, and watching the soldiers go by.

Gaston told her all about Sérizier. A brute, but a brave brute, he said, and good at training his soldiers—a man who was likely to come well to the fore, if the Commune could hold its own.

And so, with the evening sunlight on his face, Sérizier rode slowly by, she watching him, open-eyed with wonder that such a brute face as this should belong to one of the heroes of the people.

The face was as vividly before her eyes to-day as it had been that April evening. She looked at the photograph every

night before she went to her rest. Let him disguise himself
as he might, let him die his skin like a blackamoor's, or hide
cheeks and mouth and chin behind a forest of beard and
whisker, he could never hide himself from her. His face
was never absent from her mind.

So she went on with her work doggedly, hopefully, albeit
there were times of fear—times when she recalled how little
foundation there was for any certainty that Sérizier was in
Paris, or even that he lived. The man for whose going in
or coming out she watched morning and evening might be
far away in the New World, rioting and revelling upon the
spoils of revolution, conveyed to him yonder by some faithful
friend; or his corpse might have been huddled into one of
those common graves which had yawned to receive hecatombs of nameless dead.

The Durands had both been curious as to the fate of Suzon
Michel. It was known in the Rue Gît le Cœur that she had
been active amidst the atrocities of the Commune, a shining
light in that fiery atmosphere. She was known to have
carried the chassepot and the petroleum can, to have been
busy amidst scenes of riot and death. There were some who
declared that she was the Pétroleuse who had ridden, dressed
as a vivandière, at the head of that hideous procession to the
Rue Haxo, when the priests and the gendarmes were led to
the slaughter, less happy in their doom than the Archbishop
and his companions, who were massacred within the walls of
La Roquette. Certain it is that she had been seen more
than once in a vivandière's costume, and that she was known
to be one of the fiercest of that hellish crew.

Some said that she had been shot down on the last of the
barricades, yonder at Belleville ; others declared that they
had seen her in a gang of prisoners bound for Satory. No
one regretted her ; but there was a morbid curiosity in the
Rue Gît le Cœur, and two or three adjoining streets, as to her
fate. Details of her last hours, seasoned with plenty of
blood, would have been welcome.

The *crémerie* had been closed from the first day of the barricades, and had never reopened. A board in front of the
shop announced that it was *à louer presentement*. Either
la Michel was verily gone to give an account of her sins in
the land of shadows, or she was keeping out of the way, lest
she should be called upon to answer for her misdeeds before
an earthly tribunal. This was what was said of her in the

Rue Gît le Cœur. Kathleen knew the popular mind upon this subject, and she heard Durand and Rose discuss the question on one of those rare occasions when she consented to join them at the neat little supper table. It was almost a festival for Rose when she could induce her sister to spend the evening with her.

'I always hated that woman,' said Rose, speaking of Suzon Michel ; 'a bold bad woman, capable of any crime.'

'A creature of strong passions, no doubt,' answered Durand, 'terribly capable of evil. But I do not know that she was quite incapable of good. These women who feel so strongly are as fitful as a summer thunder-storm ; they will adore a man one day and murder him the next. But they have the power to love as well as to hate ; they have strength for self-sacrifice as well as for crime.'

'I do not value their love any higher than their hate,' said Rose, who had never forgotten her early impressions about Suzon, never ceased to be jealous and suspicious of the woman who had dared to love Kathleen's lover ; 'their hearts and minds are all evil, their love is a snare. If she is dead, well —God give me charity—let her rest in her grave ; if she is living, God grant that she and I may never meet.'

It was only a few days after the evening upon which this conversation occurred that Kathleen had startling evidence of Suzon Michel's existence in Paris, at the very time when people believed her to be either dead or in exile.

Those first days of September in '71 were as sultry and thunderous as the last days of August. Indeed, it seemed as if the summer grew hotter as it waned. The sun shone with tropical splendour all day, and at eventide the atmosphere was thick with heat.

It was between eight and nine, after her evening watch in a street near the Barrière d'Enfer was over, that Kathleen went to a spot which she had visited in many a twilight hour, since she first gazed upon it in the dim early morning on the 25th of May.

This was the narrow side street in which she had seen the bloody traces of her husband's death, at the foot of the lamp-post. That dreadful spot was to her as his grave, and her coming hither had all the solemnity of a pilgrimage to a grave. The street was dull and solitary—a street of shabby houses, shabbily occupied by the working classes. It was a new street which had never attained prosperity, and three or four of the houses were empty, staring at the sky with curtainless windows, and boards announcing that they were to let. Here and there appeared a shop, but a shop which looked as if customers were the exception rather than the rule.

On this September evening the street was empty, save for a couple of women standing talking at a street-door, a little way from the lamp-post by which Gaston fell. The house facing this fatal spot was empty, had been empty ever since Kathleen had known the street. The windows were clouded with dust ; the board which invited an occupant had fallen on one side, and hung disconsolate. The proprietor had, doubtless, abandoned all hope of finding a tenant until the evil days had passed, and a new birth of prosperity had come about for this fair land of France. It was a dreary-looking house in a dreary street ; a new house which had grown old and shabby without ever having been occupied.

Kathleen walked slowly up and down the street two or three times, coming back to the fatal spot, and standing beside it for a few minutes with bent head and clasped hands, and lips moving dumbly in prayer for the beloved dead. On the last time she saw a woman coming towards the same spot—coming as if to meet her, a woman who looked to her like a ghost. Yes, like one dead, who had come back to life purified and chastened by her pilgrimage through the valley of the shadow of death.

It was Suzon Michel, but not the Suzon of old. The fire in the large black eyes was quenched ; the face had lost its brazen boldness; the rich carnation of sensual, vigorous beauty had faded from the cheek. The pale, grave face, with serious mournful eyes, looked at Kathleen, and, recognising her instantly, blanched to the ashy whiteness of a corpse.

The women looked at each other in silence, and then each passed slowly upon her way. They met and parted without a word.

Two minutes afterwards, before she reached the corner of the street, Kathleen turned suddenly, and looked back, wanting to speak to Suzon Michel, to question her, she hardly knew wherefore or to what end. She thought of Suzon with horror and detestation ; and yet they two had loved the same man : Suzon might know more of the details of Gaston's death than she, his wife, had been able to discover. She might know into what common grave his corpse had been flung, beneath what clay his bones were mouldering.

She turned and the street was empty. There was not a

sign of Suzon in the distance. Had she run ever so fast she could not have reached the end of the street. It was clear, then, that she had gone into one of the houses.

But which house? Kathleen loitered in the street for some time, contemplating those dreary-looking houses, trying to divine which of them had swallowed up Suzon Michel. Presently a woman came and stood at her door on the opposite side of the street. Kathleen went over to her and questioned her, describing Madame Michel, and asking if she knew of such a person.

The woman was only a lodger on the fourth story, and had not long lived there. She worked in a mattress manufactory a little way off, was out all day, and knew nothing of her neighbours.

There was no one else in the way to answer an inquiry. And, after all, what good could come of any meeting between Kathleen and Suzon?

'She hates me, and I do not love her,' thought Kathleen. 'But she is strangely altered. I thought Rose was right when she called her a creature altogether evil, a soul given over to wickedness. Yet to-night her face had a softer look; the unholy fire seemed to have gone out of it, as if the face and the soul had been alike bleached and chastened by suffering.'

The days and weeks wore on, and the mornings and evenings grew brisk and cold. That curtain of sultry heat was lifted; the dome of white-hot iron was taken off the city, which no longer seemed like a cauldron seething and bubbling over subterranean fires. The white vapours of summer floated away from the streets and quays, from river and woods and gardens. It was October, and the leaves were falling from the poor remnants of trees in the mutilated Bois, that lovely wood which had been hewn down and converted into an *abattis*. Autumn had come, and Kathleen's work was still uncompleted, still went on; the worker patient, secret, dogged, never for one moment abandoning her purpose, never losing faith. Not till she had seen every journeyman currier in Paris would she falter or waver in her work. Then it would be time to say, 'I have deceived myself; Sérizier has left Paris;' and then it would be time to think of following and hunting him down in the place of his exile, be it far or near, in the Old World or the New. Sea or land should be as nothing to her in that search—distance and time as nothing. She felt as if she were the spirit of vengeance, a disembodied soul, free from those fetters which make humanity feeble.

Day after day she went to her task—monotonous, dreary, full of weariness for mind and body ; and yet she knew not weariness. That iron purpose within her buoyed her up and sustained her. The spirit conquered the flesh.

There were days when she felt ill, very ill—sick to death almost ; but she flung her illness aside, as if it had been a garment that embarrassed her movements, and went out to her work. Her white face in those days evoked the pity of strangers.

'A poor creature that ought to be in the hospital rather than in the streets,' thought the passers-by. 'Not long for this world,' said one. 'There is death in that face,' said another.

Other days there were when all her limbs seemed one great aching pain ; yet she crawled down the steep old staircase and into the dim morning streets ; and, like an old horse which begins his day stiffly and feebly, and shuffles himself into a trot under the goad of the whip, she gathered up her strength for the journey, and quickened her pace as she neared her goal.

Not one day did she miss in all those toilsome weeks. Happily there were the Sundays, blessed intervals of respite and rest, which gave her new strength for the coming six days.

On these quiet Sabbaths she rested all day long, lying on her bed like a log, hardly moving hand or foot, reading a little now and then, but, for the most part, resting—only resting—in a state of apathy, which was little more than semi-consciousness.

Again and again the Durands urged her to go out with them on the Sunday, to get fresh air, change, a little innocent gaiety, a few hours of forgetfulness in some pretty rustic spot. They offered to take her to Asnières, to Bougival, to Marly le Roi.

In vain.

'I have a good deal of walking every day,' she said. 'I like to rest—only to rest—on Sundays.'

She did not tell them that the agony of weariness was sometimes so acute towards the close of the week that nothing but this long day of total inertia could have enabled her to resume the round of toil.

'But you never go to mass now, Kathleen,' said Rose, with gentle reproachfulness. 'You used to go regularly to the dear old church yonder,' with a little motion of her head towards Notre Dame.

'Used—yes. But he was alive then, and I went to pray for him. Now—no, I could not kneel and pray in a church. Not yet, not yet. There is a cloud of blood that swims before my eyes when I try to look up to heaven.'

October was passing. It was the middle of the month—the 16th—and still no sign of Sérizier. Her day's work was over, and Kathleen was walking slowly, with downcast eyes and drooping head, along the Rue de Galande, in the dusk of evening. She had been watching for more than an hour in front of an obscure workshop at the end of the street. There was a Belgian name over the door. She had seen two men leave the house, one a workman, the other a man of somewhat superior appearance, who looked like the master. The workshop was small, poor-looking ; and, according to her knowledge of the trade, these two men would be in all likelihood the complete staff. But she made up her mind to go back next morning to watch the men going to their work, and to make inquiries as to the number employed. She never struck a workshop off her list until she had made herself mistress of her facts.

Suddenly, in the autumnal dusk, she looked up, startled by the rattling of an empty truck over the rough stones of the roadway. She looked up, and found herself face to face with a man in a ragged blouse, wheeling a truck.

The man was Sérizier.

She had not one moment of doubt ; not a passing shadow of hesitation clouded the clearness of her mind. This was Sérizier.

She had seen him last in the pomp of his warlike accoutrements, plumed hat, clanking sword, and sabretasch, red scarf, breast bedizened with gold embroidery, chin and lip shrouded by a heavy military moustache, erect, audacious, arrogant, lording it over an admiring crowd.

To-day the man was clean-shaved ; he seemed to have grown smaller, as if bent double with a load of ignominy, shrunk into his sordid inner self, lessened morally and physically by the loss of plumes and gold lace, and the insolence of successful audacity.

But Kathleen was not the less sure of his identity. Those restless shifty eyes, more unquiet than ever now that the man had fallen to the level of hunted criminals—those evil-looking eyes were not to be forgotten. It was he.

Cold and trembling, Kathleen tottered, and reeled against the wall. For a few moments her eyes were dim, and her brain was clouded, the passionate beating of her heart was almost unbearable; then, collecting her senses with a supreme effort, she turned and followed her prey, keeping at a respectful distance, and in the shadow of the houses. She saw him wheel his truck into a little yard belonging to the currier's workshop—watched him come out again and go into a wine-shop on the other side of the street, where he sat drinking and talking with another blue blouse. Kathleen stood outside in the dusk—as she had stood outside many such a window in the course of her evening watches—and studied the man's face by the light of the flaring candle, which stood in front of him, as he hobnobbed with his friend.

Yes, her patience was rewarded. She had found him—the assassin of the defenceless. The man to whom tears and blood had been as strong wine, for whom power had meant the power to slay and to burn. This bulldog-visaged workman, crooning over his pipe, talking with bent brow and angry eyes, this was the murderer of the Dominicans and of Gaston Mortemar.

She went straight to the office of the Commissary of Police of the Quartier de la Gare; but by this time it was ten o'clock, and too late for her to be admitted to an interview with any of the officials. She was told to return in the morning, when she could see the chief officer. She was there again when the office opened, saw Monsieur Grillières, and told him her story.

The intelligence was welcome, for Monsieur Grillières, misled by erroneous information, had already made more than thirty useless investigations in search of Sérizier. Monsieur Grillières started instantly, accompanied by two inspectors; but on arriving at the Rue Galande he was told that the Belgian currier had left the night before. He and his workmen had removed the stock-in-trade—some of the things had gone away in a van, some in a truck. The last truckload had been wheeled away at midnight.

Where had he gone?

Nobody knew exactly; everybody had some suggestion to offer; the ultimate result of which statements and counter-statements, assertions and contradictions, was that the Belgian currier had been heard to say that he was going to establish himself in the neighbourhood of the markets.

Thither Monsieur Grillières started in hot haste, and

searched every shop occupied by a currier, leather-seller, or morocco manufacturer ; but to no purpose. He found no one resembling Sérizier among the hard-handed sons of labour smelling of leather. He began to despair, when towards five o'clock in the afternoon, crossing a street which abutted on the corn-market, he saw a van standing near a door—a van full of bundles of leather, dressed skins, and currier's implements. A man was unloading the van, and carrying the contents into the house near which the vehicle waited. Grillières went into a shop where he saw a man who looked like the proprietor.

'You are a currier ?' said the magistrate.

'Yes, monsieur.'

'I am a police magistrate, and I must beg you to answer my questions.'

'Willingly, monsieur.'

'How long have you lived in this part of the town ?'

'Since last night.'

'Where were you before ?'

'Rue Galande.'

'How many workmen do you employ ?'

'Two : the man who is unloading the van, and who has been with me fourteen years ; the other who has been working for me only a fortnight, and who is now in my workshop on the third floor of this house.'

'What is his name ?'

'Chaligny.'

'His name is not Chaligny,' answered Monsieur Grillières. 'He is Sérizier, and I am here to arrest him.'

Grillières went upstairs, followed by his two men. On the third floor there was a door half-open, and in the room within they saw a man sharpening his knives. The man looked up, and, seeing a stranger, was seized with an instant suspicion, and stretched out his hand to snatch up a shaving-knife, the first instrument of defence or attack which offered itself. But Grillières threw himself upon him. 'You are my prisoner,' he said.

'Why do you arrest me ?' cried the man. 'My name is Chaligny.'

Duprat, one of the police-officers, had been immured as a hostage at the prison of La Santé during Sérizier's reign of terror. He recognised the *ci-devant* colonel at a glance.

'You are Sérizier,' he said ; 'I remember you perfectly.'

'Yes,' answered the other doggedly, 'I am Sérizier. The

game is up, and I know what I have to expect. But if I had seen you fellows ou the staircase just now, you should uot have lived to take me.'

He made no resistance, and was taken to the police-office, where he himself dictated his deposition. Thence he was transferred to the Prefecture. Thence again, after the usual formalities, he was sent to the Depôt.

'My affairs are settled,' he said to his custodians. 'I have done enough to get my head washed in a leaden bath; but it's all the same to me. I regret nothing; I only did my duty.'

Colonel Sérizier was right in his prophecy. His doom was to be the leaden bath; but the law's delays are tedious, and the murderer arrested in October was not to be despatched until the following February.

CHAPTER XIII.

ATONEMENT

KATHLEEN'S mission was accomplished. There was no more for her to do. She went back to the Rue Gît le Cœur, broken in spirit and in body. She lay on her bed, and it seemed to her that her life now was one long Sunday, a time of apathy and dumb dull rest—joyless, hopeless. There was nothing more for her to do in this life. She had given the victim over to his executioners. She was told that the end was certain. There could be no pardon, no commutation of the law's last penalty for such a wretch as Sérizier. France would rise up with one loud cry of vengeance were there any puling for mercy here.

The slow days wore on—dull gray days ; storms of wind, driving showers, anon the fogs of November floating up from the neighbouring river—and still Kathleen lay on the bed or the sofa, helpless, prostrate, as some wild flower that has been torn from its stem and flung aside to wither. Rose had brought a doctor to see her ; but he did not even profess the ability to cure.

'There is nothing organically wrong,' he said. 'Your sister must have had a very fine constitution to survive what she has gone through. It is a case of extreme weakness, loss of appetite, sleeplessness—things that tell without actual disease. If you could get her away into the country, fresh air and change of scene might do something ; but she is too weak to be moved.'

'We will take her away directly she is strong enough to go,' said Rose.

The doctor thought that time would never come ; but he held his peace, took his fee, and departed.

Rose and Philip watched the fading life in that quiet room on the upper story as devotedly as if the thread of their own lives had been intertwined with it. But their tenderness, their little plots and expedients, were all useless. They could not lure Kathleen from her solitude, or beguile her into forgetfulness of her grief.

'While I was watching for that man I forgot everything, except the task in hand,' she said ; 'I lived and breathed only for that. My brain was burnt up with one fiery thought; and in those days I hardly grieved for Gaston—I hardly knew how much I had lost. But now I think of him, and brood upon his memory all day long.'

'But if this goes on you will go mad or die,' said Philip, standing beside her sofa, looking down at her with honest earnest eyes, full of affection ; 'and that will break Rose's heart. Remember how she has reared you and cared for you! To her you are more than a common sister. She has been to you as a mother; and you owe her a daughter's love and duty.'

'Let her ask me anything, except to live,' answered Kathleen. 'I *cannot* live without him. O, she must let me go—in charity she will let me go—where I shall be at rest for ever, as he is. She has you and the little one. She can spare this broken life.'

'But she cannot spare you—nor I, nor the little one ; and it is your duty to live for our sakes. Your natural grief we would respect, Kathleen ; but this inordinate sorrow, this obstinate despair——'

'Had he died a natural death, I would mourn for him as other widows mourn for their husbands ; I would bow to the will of God. But he was murdered.'

'And you have brought his murderer to justice. Is not that enough, Kathleen ?'

' I wonder whether I shall live to hear his sentence, to know that he has suffered a murderer's doom ?' she murmured ; and then she turned her face to the wall, and would talk no more that day.

Rose and her husband began to despair. It seemed to them that Kathleen's vital power was ebbing day by day, gradually, imperceptibly. The loss of strength was only indicated by the facts of her daily life. Last week she had risen early every morning, and had swept and dusted her rooms, with only a little help from Rose, who was ever on the watch to aid and comfort her. This week she could only crawl about a little, dusting Gaston's books with tremulous hands, arranging and rearranging his desk or his bookshelves, with a fluttered nervous air. A few days ago she had lain on her bed or her sofa, as if in mere apathy. Now the time had come when she lay there from sheer weakness, broken down, fading before their very eyes.

They had gradually schooled themselves to bow to the rod.

They began to talk to each other about her as of one fore-doomed, unspeakably precious, inasmuch as she was to be with them but a few weeks—perchance but a few days. They talked sorrowfully, yet with resignation, of a future in which she was to have no part, save as a sweet sad memory.

'How fond she would have been of you, my angel!' said Rose, prattling mothers' tender prattle to the baby on her knees, 'if she could but have lived to see you grow up!'

One day, when the invalid up-stairs had sunk so low that it seemed as if she could hardly last to the end of the week; Philip Durand came past the little *crémerie*, which had once been Suzon Michel's, on his way home. It was between four and five, and already dusk, and he was startled to see the door of the shop open and a light within.

While he stared, wondering whether a tenant had been found for the deserted house now that trade was looking up a little, Suzon herself emerged from the darkness within, followed by a man who blew out a candle, and came into the street, carrying a bunch of keys. The man was the landlord, who had been making an inspection of the premises with his old tenant.

'Come, Madame Michel,' he said, as he locked the door on the outside, 'you cannot do better than take down the shutters to-morrow morning ; no one will do so well as you in that shop, and now that business is brisk everywhere, you may make a better trade than ever. I shall not raise your rent——'

'Oh, but monsieur is so generous !' cried Suzon ironically; 'everybody knows that rents are going up in Paris.'

'Well, I say it shall be the old rent.'

'I'll think it over,' replied Suzon ; 'but it will be at least a week before I can decide. Certain it is that 1 must do something : one cannot live upon one's savings for ever.'

'It was a suicide to shut up such a shop as that, except for just the week of the barricades,' said the proprietor. 'But you are not half the woman you were, Madame Michel ; the air of your present abode cannot agree with you.'

He wished her good evening and trotted away, fingering his bunch of keys. Two minutes afterwards she met Philip Durand face to face.

Yes, she was changed. The woman of the people, the amazon, the pétroleuse, was curiously subdued and softened. Some chastening influence had subjugated her vehement nature, and altered the expression of her countenance to a degree that was almost a transformation.

'Monsieur Durand!' she exclaimed, with a startled look; and then she said quietly, 'I am a stranger in this neighbourhood now. It is like coming back to an old half-forgotten existence. How is your wife?'

'She is tolerably well.'

'And her sister—Madame Mortemar?'

'She is—dying.'

'Dying! That is a strong phrase.'

'It is the truth. We have done all that care and love could do, but she is slipping away from us. I have no hope that she will last to the end of the month.'

'What is her malady?'

'A broken heart.'

'Ah, that is more common than doctors believe! Has she never got over the loss of her husband?'

Suzon had turned to accompany Philip, and they were walking side by side towards the Rue Gît le Cœur.

'Never.'

'I suppose, though, she is glad that Sérizier was taken the other day?'

'She was glad; it was her own work. She only lived to bring the murderer to justice, and that being accomplished, it seemed as if the mainspring of her life were broken.'

'*She* brought him to justice!' cried Suzon. 'What do you mean?'

'Simply what I say; Sérizier's arrest was brought about solely by my sister-in-law; she watched and waited for him, day by day, for three months. It was she, and she only, who brought him to his doom.'

'I read in the papers that it was a woman, but I thought it was a jealous woman—some discarded mistress, perhaps. And you say that it was she—that lily-faced girl—*she* who tracked the murderer to his hole?'

'She, and no other.'

'And she is dying?'

'Yes, she is dying. The task weakened the sources of life; body and mind were alike exhausted by the long patient effort—unshared, unknown by those who loved her—and now a broken heart has done the rest.'

'She shall not die!' cried Suzon, with a voice so loud that it startled the passers-by, who turned and stared at her; 'no,' she went on hurriedly, breathlessly, 'if there is a God

in heaven she shall not die.   If there is no God, well, then,
this earth is a shambles, and the innocent have no friend.
She shall not die !'

'What can you do to save her ?'

'Give her something to live for, give her so strong a reason
why she should live that the tide of life will flow back to her
veins, the weary heart will beat strong with hope and love.'

'You are mad !'

'No, I am not mad.   Go and get a fly.   Can she be moved,
do you think ?   Could she bear to be driven a little way?'

'God knows.   She is as weak as an infant !'

'Oh, only go and get the carriage.   We will manage it, we
will carry her.   Go ; I have but to whisper in her ear, and
she will have the strength of a lioness.   Bring the carriage
to the door yonder ; I will run on and see your wife.'

Durand thought the woman must be mad ; but her earnestness, her energy were electrical, and he obeyed her.   In a case
so desperate any gleam of hope was welcome.   There was some
secret to be told, some revelation coming.   He scarce asked
himself what, but hurried off to engage the first prowling fly
he could find.

Suzon ran upstairs to the third floor.   She listened at the
door of Kathleen's sitting-room.   There was a faint murmur
of voices within.   She entered without knocking.

Kathleen was lying on the sofa near the fireplace, her
wasted cheek white as the pillow on which it rested.   Rose
sat by her, bending over her, talking to her in low murmurs.
The room was dimly lighted by a lamp on the mantelpiece.

Suzon went across the room and knelt by the invalid's side.

'It is I, Suzon Michel,' she said, 'the woman who once
hated you, but who has since learnt to pity, and who now
honours you.   Is it true that you tracked that wild beast
to his lair ? that when all the police in Paris had failed to
find him, you hunted that tiger down ?'

'Yes, I found Sérizier.   They say he will be shot.'

'*Sacré nom*, yes, he shall be shot.   The women of the Place
d'Italie—the people who lived in fear and dread of him, to
whom his name was a terror—they will not let him escape,
now the law has got him.   Madame Mortemar, will you
come with me ?   I want to take you to my home, yonder,
close to the spot where your husband fell.'

Kathleen started up into a sitting position.   It was like a
sudden awakening to life, as if some magic wand had been
waved over her, magnetising the feeble clay.

'What!' she cried, 'you live there? I thought it must be so, that night. Yes, yes, take me to the spot where he fell. Let me see it once more—once before I die. To me it is as sacred as a grave. I cannot go to his grave,' she added despairingly.

'Dear love, you are too weak to stir,' pleaded Rose tenderly with her arms about her sister's wasted form.

'She is not too weak to come with me. She should come if she were in her grave-clothes. You can come with us—you can help me to carry her down-stairs. Your husband will have a fly ready. Yes!' cried Suzon, running to the window, 'it is there, at the door below. Bring some brandy in a bottle—wet her lips with a little first. A warm shawl, so,' wrapping it round Kathleen's wasted form as if she had been a child. 'You are not afraid to come, are you, my little one? I have good news for you at the end of the journey.'

Her impetuosity evolved a corresponding energy in Kathleen, who was tremulous with excitement. Rose understood that there was new life at the end of this sudden journey. Yes, there was a revelation at hand, about Gaston. She kept herself calm and steady while those two others were on fire with excitement. Between them she and Suzon Michel carried Kathleen down-stairs to the fly, the three women got inside, Kathleen wrapped up in thick shawls. Philip got on the box beside the driver; in a crack or so of his whip they were rattling into the Boulevard St. Michel.

It was a longish drive to the Place d'Italie; but urged by Suzon, the man got over the distance very quickly. The dull side-street looked unspeakably dreary in the wintry gloom, the lamps burning dimly, the windows showing little light —signs of failure and poverty on every side.

The fly stopped before that empty house which Kathleen had noticed in the summer gloaming. The board was still hanging above the door, the windows were all blank and dark; but Suzon opened the door with her key, while Durand lifted Kathleen out of the vehicle.

'Carry her upstairs, following me,' said Suzon; 'but she and I must go into the room alone. You others must stay outside.'

'It is not a trap, is it?' asked Rose, frightened. 'You mean her no harm?'

'I mean her all the good in the world, and she knows it,' answered Suzon, holding Kathleen's hand, which feebly pressed hers in response to these words.

They stopped at the door of the back room on the first floor, Suzon first; then Philip, with Kathleen carried on his shoulder; Rose in the rear, but pressing close against them, lest there should be danger ahead.

Kathleen slipped from Durand's arms, and clung to Suzon Michel, as the latter opened the door. The two women went into the room together, and Rose and her husband were left outside.

There was one instant's silence, and then a wild shriek, a shriek that might be terror, grief, or joy. One could not tell what it meant, outside the door.

Rose was in an agony. She would have dashed into the room, but Philip held her back.

'Let them be for a few moments,' he said. 'Mortemar is alive. The mystery can be only that—alive, and shut up in this house, under watch and ward of that woman.'

Two minutes after, the door was opened by Suzon, and the Durands went in. The room was comfortable enough within, desolate as the house looked outside. The furniture was humble, but neat and decent. There was a fire burning in the grate, a lamp on the table.

In an easy-chair in front of the fire sat a man with his leg in splints from the hip downwards. He was pale to ghastliness, and had the look of one who had but begun the slow progress of recovery from a sickness nigh unto death. His hair and beard were long, his hands thin to transparency.

Yes, it was Gaston Mortemar, and his wife was kneeling at his feet, kissing the wasted hands, murmuring sweetest words, nestling her head in his bosom, ineffably happy.

'I give you back your dead,' said Suzon solemnly. 'He was left for dead when I picked him up and brought him in here, shot through shoulder and hip and leg with half a dozen bullets. The surgeon I brought to him said it was a hopeless case; but for the sake of surgery, as an amateur, he would try to cure him. For two months he lay in instant danger. For seven weeks he was mad with brain-fever— fever that came from the pain of his wounds. I have nursed him through all. The surgeon will tell you if I have been a faithful nurse. And now I give him back to you, not healed, but on the fair road to recovery; although he will be lame all his life, poor soul; but that does not count in a writer, does it? He will be all the greater with his pen if he has less temptation to roam.'

'Bless you! May God bless and reward you for your devotion!' cried Kathleen.

'Bah! There is no question of blessing or reward. I have been a wicked woman. I kept him like a bird in a cage, and I let you think him dead, and I told him you had perished on the last day of the barricades, and I let him mourn for you. He was helpless, in my power, and I lied to him and cheated him. But I snatched him from the jaws of death; the surgeon who has attended him will tell you that. I dragged him into this empty house, dragged him away just as the last batch of Sérizier's bloodhounds were turning the corner of the street, whooping for more blood ; and I kept him here, closely guarded, hidden from all the world, except the surgeon, who believed that he was my brother. Monsieur Mortemar could tell no tales, poor fellow ; for it is only within the last three weeks that he has been in his right wits.'

Gaston's head was leaning forward against Kathleen's, the husband's haggard brow against the wife's wasted cheek. Both faces were the image of death, and yet radiant with a new-born life—the sublime light of happy love.

'She told me you were dead, Kathleen,' he murmured.

'Forgive her, dear. She saved you, and I have avenged you. O my love! my love! God is good. He has given you back to me, out of the grave.'

'How did you manage to occupy this house, and to keep your existence here a secret?' asked Durand of Madame Michel.

'There was no difficulty. I was not without means. I went to the landlord, and offered him half the rent of the house for the use of two or three rooms at the back. The house had been unlet a year and a half—the street is a failure—so he was glad to accept my offer, and the board was left up over the door to avert suspicion. The people who saw me go in and out took me for a caretaker ; nobody asked any questions. I had a truck-load of furniture brought here after dark from my rooms at the *crémerie*, and I made things as comfortable as I could for my patient. If he had any knowledge of those dark days he would know that I nursed him faithfully. For six weeks I scarcely knew what it was to sleep for an hour at a stretch. I had a mattress at the foot of his bed, and I lay down now and then like a dog, and slept a dog's sleep, with my ear on the alert for the first groan of pain.'

'God bless you!' cried Kathleen, taking her hand and kissing it.

' You are a strange woman,' said Durand ; ' but let no one
say that you are wholly bad.'

' I was a devil in those days of the barricades. I was mad
like the rest of them, maddened with the thought of all the
wrongs that we *canaille* have suffered from the beginning of
the world. Yes, from the days when Herod put John the
Baptist in prison, and cut off his head, to keep faith with a
princess who danced. I was drunk with blood, like the rest
of them. But in six weeks of watchfulness and watching
one has time to think ; and, in the silence of the night, sometimes I used to wonder whether it was good for a woman to
be an *esprit fort*, whether it was not better to be cheated,
even, and to believe in Some One up yonder, who can set the
riddle of this world right when He chooses—some hand
turning the great wheel of destiny yonder behind the clouds.
No, Monsieur Durand, I am not all evil.'

It was not till the end of the year that Gaston was well
enough to be removed to the Rue Gît le Cœur, and, in the
meantime, he and his wife occupied the rooms in the empty
house near the Place d'Italie, with that good-natured busybody, Madame Schubert—generally known as *c't bonne
Schubert*—to take care of them. Suzon Michel went straight
from the house where those two whom she had held apart
were lost in the bliss of an unhoped-for union, and gave
herself up to the police. The account against her name was
heavy, and payment in full was exacted. She was despatched
with a gang of Communards on board a rotten old ship bound
for Cayenne, and in the unutterable miseries of that dreadful
voyage she was like an angel of mercy to her fellow-sinners.
And at the convict settlement the pétroleuse, the amazon,
became the nurse and ministering angel of the fever-stricken
wretches in the prison hospital, a source of comfort and of
hope to many a dying captive, till the deadly climate did its
work, and the pestilence struck her down as it had stricken
others—a woman young in years, but old in strange and sad
experience ; a sinner, but not without hope of pardon.

The dark days of November and December were blissful
days for Kathleen. Health and strength returned to her as
if by magic ; and in a week after her restoration to happiness
she was able to help in waiting upon her husband. Another
week and she would hardly allow Madame Schubert to do
anything for him. In the third week she was walking to and
fro the printing office of Gaston's old journal, which had been

resuscitated under a new name, as *The Friend of Freedom*,
and the proprietor of which was enraptured to receive ' copy '
from the brilliant pen of his old contributor, given up as lost
to literature for ever.

Yes, those were happy days. That poor shattered leg of
Gaston's had shrunk and shortened, and he would go limping
along the road of life to the end of his journey ; but his mind
was clear and vigorous as ever, and his heart was content.
During the enforced quiet of those December days he made
a vigorous beginning upon that scheme of a novel which he
had mentioned to Kathleen on their wedding-day. But
he did not keep his work secret from his wife, as he had
threatened. He garnered up no surprises, being in too much
need of her sympathy to sustain his belief in himself.

He read the day's portion aloud to Kathleen at night, the
last thing, when that good old Schubert, who insisted upon
coming every day with her market-basket, smelling of *les
Halles Centrales*, to cook and attend upon them—when
Maman Schubert had taken her modest little nip of *eau de
vie*, put her arm through the handle of her empty basket,
and wished them good-night for the sixth or seventh time.
Then Kathleen perched herself upon the arm of her husband's
chair and nestled her head upon his shoulder while he read
his manuscript. It was a love-story, full of passion and fire,
and Kathleen felt that it must make a mad, a furious success.
Nor was she far out in her reckoning. When a man, whose
pen has grown bold and brilliant in the work of a literary
journeyman, whose memory has garnered the experience of a
youth and manhood spent in the very whirlpool of metropolitan life, and who has read and dreamed and thought super-
abundantly in his leisure hours and his wanderings to and
fro—when such a man girds up his loins and says, ' Enough
of the hard facts of life—now I will give myself full play in
the garden of fancy,' the chances are that he will write a
novel that shall be famous.

Sérizier was condemned to death on the 17th of February,
1872, by the sixth council of war. He appealed against this
sentence, setting forth the service which he had done to
General Chanzy, on the 19th of March '71, in defending him
against the revolutionary mob. It was rumoured in the
neighbourhood of the Place d'Italie that Sérizier would not
be executed ; whereupon an unprecedented agitation arose
among the people. The inhabitants of the neighbourhood,

remembering the agony of terror under which they had lived on account of this man, signed a petition demanding that no commutation of the extreme sentence should be accorded to the late chief of the 13th Legion, and entreating that, as an example and a just expiation, he should be executed in front of the prison over which he had ruled, and on the very spot where he had presided over the massacre of the Dominicans.

This strange request could not be granted ; but Sérizier's crimes were of too black a dye to admit of mercy. He and his lieutenant Bobèche were shot on the plain of Satory.

Gaston Mortemar's novel was published in the following autumn, and obtained a more brilliant success than any book that had appeared since Madame Bovary. There was a fire and a freshness in the style which made the appearance of the story a sensation, an event ; and Gaston saw himself released for ever from the treadmill routine of a third-rate newspaper, a man with place and name in the ranks of literature, free to write what he liked, and secure of publisher and public. And as the years wore on—years of peace and prosperity—those two households of the Durands and the Mortemars were undarkened by so much as a passing cloud. Industry, honour, and domestic love ruled in each *ménage*, and there was no break in the union between the sisters ; albeit, Durand and Rose remained constant to their town quarters in the Rue Gît le Cœur, while Gaston and his wife transferred their household gods to a dainty little villa at Passy, where the husband could write in his garden among the birds and flowers, while his young wife guided the footsteps of her yearling baby up and down the little grassplot.

The carved-oak sideboard was bought by Sir Richard Wallace, and Durand's fame as a craftsman and artist was safely established from that hour : and so, where there had been cloud there was sunshine, where there had been storm there was perfect and holy calm.

DROSS; OR, THE ROOT OF EVIL

DRAMATIS PERSONÆ.

TREMAINE DARRACOTT.	LADY SKIMPER.
THOMAS CHUGG.	LEONORA SKIMPER.
RICHARD AVERY.	SYLVIA SCOBELL.
NICHOLAS PUSSLEY, *groom.*	MARY CHUGG.
BATES, *grocer*	MRS. HAMMICK.
CAPTAIN VANDEAN.	

ACT I.

SCENE.—*A farmhouse interior. Summer landscape seen through open lattices. Village in the distance. Furniture good and substantial, but very old-fashioned ; bureau, eight-day clock, &c., &c.*

> MRS. HAMMICK *seated shelling peas,* MARY *standing by her chair ;* RICHARD, *with his hat in his hand, near the door.*

MRS. HAMMICK. I do wish you would go out or come in, Dick. It's so uncomfortable to have you hovering there, as if you wanted to go, and didn't know how to carry out your intention.

RICHARD. That's just what I almost always feel in this house, Mrs. Hammick—not the wanting to go, but the not being able to do it. And to-day I'm rather more unsettled than usual. I suppose it's in consequence of the old Squire's funeral. That is an event, you know, Mrs. Hammick ; we don't bury an old Squire every day.

MRS. HAMMICK. Ah, well, he was quite one of the old school, wasn't he ?

Mary. If he were still alive, I should say he was a nasty old man ; but, I suppose, now he's dead we are all to make believe that we always thought him nice.

Richard. I wouldn't say anything against him for the world, as he is dead ; but he certainly was the meanest old hound——

Mary. Richard !

Richard. The falsest old hypocrite, and the most tyrannical old skinflint——

Mrs. Hammick. Richard !

Richard. See how he treated Tremaine Darracott, his own grandson.

Mary. Ah, that was a cruel act—to turn his grandson out of doors, because he had fallen in love with a penniless girl, and that girl one of the sweetest young ladies that ever lived.

Mrs. Hammick. Yes, and the orphan daughter of one of the Squire's dearest friends. I used to think the Squire was very much attached to Miss Sylvia Scobell, in his way.

Richard. Yes, his way of being fond of a person is rather like anybody else's way of detesting them. However, I suppose Mr. Tremaine will be able to do what he likes now, and that the first thing he will do will be to marry Miss Scobell—that is to say, as soon as he decently can after his grandfather's death.

Mary. But what if the Squire should have altered his will, and left his fortune to a hospital, as he often threatened? I know people who have heard him.

Mrs. Hammick. Nonsense, Mary. The old Squire would never leave his money to a charity, it would vex him to think of having done so much good. Besides, Mr. Tremaine Darracott is the only son of his only son—his natural heir.

Richard. There's not an acre of Darracott Manor entailed. The Squire could dispose of his estate as freely as if it was one of his old hunting coats——

Mary. He usen't to like giving them away, Dick. I'm sure he wore them till they were too shabby for anything but a scarecrow.

Richard. He was a close-fisted, obstinate old man, Mary. I shouldn't be a bit astonished if Tremaine Darracott were left a pauper.

Mary. Then all I hope is that he'll marry Sylvia Scobell next week, and that they'll live happy ever afterwards.

RICHARD. Without a penny between them, Mary? They can't live upon love.

MARY. Oh, yes, they can, if it is *true* love. Providence always takes care of true lovers, just as the dear little robins took care of the children in the wood.

RICHARD. Gave them decent burial after they were starved to death. That's about as much as Providence, in the shape of wealthy relations, generally does for a foolish young man and woman who marry for love. But here comes Mr. Chugg; and now, I suppose, we shall hear all about the Squire's will.

[CHUGG *heard singing outside.*

"I'll sell you for a crown, my boy,
And that won't be too dear;
For 'tis my delight on a shiny night,
In the season of the year."

[*Stops himself suddenly as he enters, dressed
in deep mourning.*

CHUGG (*handing his hat to* MARY). Take the band off Polly, my pet. And you, Dick, give us a hand with this double-milled doeskin imposture. (*Pulls off his coat.*) Away with melancholy! I feel like a gigantic Spanish fowl trussed ready for roasting, with all his feathers on him. Ah! now I begin to breathe again. (*Takes off his hat.*) Bring me my liveliest waistcoat, Mary, the brightest bit of colour you can find in my wardrobe, lassie, and the cheerfullest thing you can lay your hand on in the way of a necktie. (*Exit* MARY.) I do believe I never had such a sickener in my life as when I stood in that churchyard among a lot of other hypocrites, all of us pulling the longest faces we could, and not one of us honestly sorry in his heart. Why, the very parson never had a good word for the Squire while he was alive; and Mr. Carlyon, the J.P., who kept his face smothered in a pocket-handkerchief, as if he was convulsed with grief, hated the old man like poison. And there was poor Tremaine Darracott, who had been kicked out of doors by that old tyrant, standing beside his grave as chief mourner, with a pale, steady look upon his handsome face, but not making believe half so much as the others.

MARY. How about the will, father? What has the Squire done with his money? We're all dying to know that.

CHUGG. Then I'm sorry to say I can't bring you to life, for

I don't know anything about it. 'Come along with us and hear the will read, Chugg,' says Mr. Brooke, the lawyer; but I wasn't going into that gloomy old manor-house again, just for a chance of a glass or two of the Squire's '47 port.

MRS. HAMMICK. There may be a legacy for you, Tom. The Squire and you were always friendly.

CHUGG. Well, I was about the most improving tenant he had, and I was able to be useful to him in a good many ways. That's just what Brooke said—'There may be a legacy for you, Chugg; who knows?' and by the significant way Lawyer Brooke spoke, I should rather think I do stand in for a trifle. But I'm no legacy-hunter. If the old man should have left me fifty guineas or so, why, I'll divide it between you and Mary, Betsy my dear, and you shall buy a new gown apiece.

MARY. Oh, father, you don't suppose our gowns cost five-and-twenty guineas?

CHUGG. Of course not, my dear; but that's my delicate way of putting it. You may want other things—cuffs and collars, sashes and neckties; young women are always wanting some kind of finery.

MARY. You are a dear, generous old dad!

CHUGG. Well, my love, I hope I shall never be mean. I am not a rich man. It's about just as much as I can do to keep things going comfortably, so that everybody in the neighbourhood should be able to say, 'If you want to see a farm, look at Chugg's farm; that *is* farming. When I grow corn I like it to be corn, not half thistles and hogweed. When I breed sheep I like 'em to be sheep. And as for the house I live in, why, I like it to be home—home for me, and open house for my friends: a house in which a man can feel sure of a hearty welcome, a good cut out of a joint, and a tankard of home-brewed beer—no pretence, no finery, but solid English comfort. That's my motto. (*Putting on waistcoat and tie which* MARY *has fetched from adjacent room*) Here goes for the coloured waistcoat, and away with melancholy. That's another of my mottoes.

MRS. HAMMICK. Well, Mr. Chugg——

CHUGG. Who are you talking to? Where's Mr. Chugg? There's no such person here, that I'm aware of, for you. Why can't you be friendly, and say Tom?

MRS. HAMMICK. I always feel as if I were taking a liberty.

CHUGG. Well, that's rank nonsense. Don't I call you Betsy? Wasn't your poor husband my second cousin, and ain't you my own flesh and blood, in a manner of speaking?

Mrs. Hammick. Oh, Mr. Chugg! Tom, it's only your goodness which tries to make out a tie between us, as an excuse for giving me a home, and so that I mayn't feel as if I were eating the bread of charity.

Chugg. Bread of charity, indeed! Why, you're the most useful person in the house. In fact, the house couldn't go on without you, could it, Mary?

Mary. No, indeed, father. My poor giddy head would never be equal to all the care and thought that are needed to keep everything as you like it kept—the dairy, and the poultry-yard, and the brewing, and the cider-making, and the cheese. There isn't room enough in my mind for half of it.

Chugg. I don't believe there is, Mary, especially as a very large portion of your mind is let off to Mr. Richard Avery. Don't blush, Dick, we all know all about it; and it shan't be my fault if that little story of yours doesn't end happily.

Richard. You are so thoroughly good-natured, Mr. Chugg.

Chugg. Well, I don't come of a bad-natured lot, anyhow. There's very little ill-nature in my family history. The Chuggs were never grand—never troubled themselves about coats-of-arms, or quarterings, or crests, or such-like foolery; although, mind you, the old Squire and I came of the same stock, for my great-grandmother was a Darracott.

Mrs. Hammick. Ah, to be sure! You're a kind of cousin of the Squire's. I've heard people say so.

Mary. Goodness gracious, father, suppose he has left his estate to you—as his only surviving relation, except Mr. Tremaine!

Chugg. No fear, Mary. The Chuggs were never what you can call a lucky lot. No dropping into fortunes promiscuously; no finding a tin mine in a meadow; no unexpected legacies for them. The Chuggs began poor, and they've gone on poor; but who cares? We've never been in debt, or out at elbows, any of us; and we've always had a crust of bread and cheese to share with a friend. Jolly Chugg, folks call me; and I don't envy any man living his riches. If I was a rich man—well, I believe I should do a power of good in the world, for my greatest delight would be in spending my money freely and making other people happy.

Mary. I'm sure it would, father.

Mrs. Hammick. I know how generous you've been with moderate means, Tom.

Chugg. Well, I hope, if Providence ever was to make me

a rich man—but of course it won't—I should be like the
gentleman in the song, who meant to make everybody happy,
provided he could first lay his hand upon the four-leaved
shamrock—

"And hearts that had been long estranged, and friends that
    had grown cold,
Should meet again, like parted streams, and mingle as of old.
Oh! thus I'd play the enchanter's part, thus scatter bliss
    around,
And not a tear or aching heart should in the world be
    found!"

          [*As he sings the last line he knocks up against*
          TREMAINE, *who enters while he is singing.*

CHUGG. I beg your pardon, Mr. Tremaine. Nothing should
have tempted me to burst into a secular song on such a—a—
melancholy occasion, if I'd known you were near.

TREMAINE. Don't apologise, my dear Chugg. I am very
glad to know there is some one cheerful in this world; for my
own outlook at this moment is so black that——

CHUGG. Yes, no doubt you will be expected to wear black
for some time—for a grandfather—and it is *not* a cheerful
colour. In double-milled Saxony or doeskin it is certainly
the reverse of lively, especially in hot weather, and with the
lanes so given over to dust—I say given over to dust, and not
a water-cart in the parish.

TREMAINE. It is not the idea of a mourning suit that
troubles me, Chugg. In fact, my troubles are much more
likely to take the form of no clothes at all—when these are
worn out.

CHUGG. Why, you don't mean to say that the Squire
has——

TREMAINE. Disinherited me. Yes, he has, Chugg. When
he turned me out of his house six months ago, for no other
reason than that I was true to the girl I loved, and with the
change of a five-pound note between me and starvation, he
told me he meant to cut me off with a shilling. He has
carried out his intention most completely—except that he
has forgotten the shilling.

CHUGG. You'll dispute the will, of course. I'll help you.
I'll back you up. I'll lend you my last shilling to fee the
lawyers, and I'll swear the Squire was a lunatic—*non compos
mentis*—when he made this most unnatural and iniquitous

will ; for that it is a most unnatural and iniquitous will I do declare before all men—and——

MARY. And so it is, Mr. Tremaine.

TREMAINE. You're a good fellow, Chugg, an excellent fellow—you've always been kind to me. Perhaps you'll modify your views when you know all. Circumstances alter cases, you see, Chugg. That's an old saying, and there's wisdom in it. I have come here to ask you to do me a kindness. You and my father were boys together.

CHUGG. I should think we were, indeed ! Boys together! Why, in the hunting field we were like brothers. No place like that for finding your level. Every man is equal across a stiff bullfinch ; and your father and I have taken many a rasper neck and neck. My father bred the first hunter your father ever rode to hounds, and I broke him. Wasn't he a devil to go ? But, I say, Mr. Tremaine, you don't mean to let this will of your grandfather's stand, do you ?

TREMAINE. Well, I don't know, Chugg. I am going to London by the evening mail.

CHUGG. And you want a few pounds to start you in life ? I understand. You shall have it, Mr. Tremaine. I've got a little sum put away in a stocking for one of those new-fangled reaping-machines. Now, I don't much care for these iron contrivances, which cost a power of money to buy, and which throw flesh and blood out of work ; so you're welcome to the hundred I've put by, and Jack and Bob and Bill and Joe shall reap my corn, as they used to do in my old father's time.

TREMAINE. My dear Chugg, you are the most generous of men ; but I've not come here to sponge upon you—at least, not in that way. I'm off to London to fight the battle of life I've been called to the Bar, you know ; and I suppose if I sit in my chambers and read law, and wait for the turn of the tide, briefs will begin to drop in—some day. The favour I have to ask is this : Miss Scobell is now without a home ; if we were to marry at once, matrimony would mean starvation. We must wait for better days. But what is to become of her in the meantime ? She is not the kind of girl to go into the world and get her own living. I know Miss Chugg and she are great friends. Now, if you and your daughter would——

CHUGG. Make her happy here until you can afford to marry ? Why, of course we will. Let her consider Hazle Farm her home from this hour. She shall have the spare bedroom with the bow window facing south and looking over Mary's flower-garden. She shall have larks and blackbirds in fanciful cages to hang in her window, and sing to her when she feels melancholy. I say, Mrs. Hammick, suppose you run across the fields to the Manor and fetch Miss Scobell. She'll be glad to get away from that melancholy old house. And I daresay she'd like to have a chat with Mr. Tremaine here before he starts. Go as fast as you can, like a good soul. It's only ten minutes' walk. (*Exit* MRS. HAMMICK.) We'll make her comfortable, won't we, Mary ?

MARY. Yes, father ; she shall be my adopted sister, if she will.

TREMAINE (*clasping their hands*). Chugg, you are a good man. I felt that I might depend upon you. My dear Mary, I am more grateful than words can say. And now that I've tried your metal it's time I should tell you what the Squire has done with his estate. There are men in my position who would hate you, Chugg.

CHUGG. You hate me, Mr. Tremaine ! Why, I never injured you by so much as an unkind thought.

TREMAINE. I am sure of that, and you have done me many a kindness. When my grandfather turned me out of doors you offered me free quarters here, and you lent me money to carry on with in the Temple. I am not likely to forget that you were my best friend when I most wanted one. But you have been made the instrument of my grandfather's revenge upon his only son's only son.

CHUGG (*puzzled*). As how, Mr. Tremaine !

TREMAINE. He has left the whole of his fortune, real and personal, to you, with a request that you will, as speedily as may be practicable, assume the name and arms of Darracott.

MARY. Oh, Mr. Tremaine, what a wicked, unjust act !

CHUGG (*absorbed in himself*). Squire Darracott —Chugg Darracott. Yes, Squire Chugg Darracott. That sounds uncommonly well. And every rood of his land is mine ! It is land on which I was born and reared. His woods and commons, the meadows and corn-fields, that we Chuggs, father and son, have farmed for fifty years, and on which he wouldn't let me shoot a rabbit, all mine ! The old Manor House, pictures, plate, armour ; the orchards I used to rob when I was a boy ; the gardens which I fancied were the exact copies of the Garden of Eden—mine, all mine ! (*Walks slowly across the stage, and comes face to face with* TREMAINE).

TREMAINE. Well, Chugg, do you still maintain that my grandfather's will is unnatural and iniquitous?

CHUGG. My dear Tremaine, as you most shrewdly observed just now, circumstances alter cases. Had your grandfather bequeathed his wealth to a hospital or an almshouse, had he impoverished you, his own flesh and blood, in order to fatten the widow and orphan of the indifferent stranger, I should have held to my opinion that the will was an unnatural will, an iniquitous will, a will to be held up to universal contumely and reprobation. But when this fine old country gentleman shows his respect for the claims of consanguinity, even in a somewhat distant relative ; when he testifies that the blood of the Darracotts, filtered through three generations of Chuggs, is still to his mind the true Darracott blood ; when he passes over the Darracotts of the present to recognise the Darracotts of the past, I say that he gives evidence of those good old true-blue Church and State principles which every true-born Englishman must honour.

TREMAINE. Good-bye, Mr. Chugg——

CHUGG. Darracott, sir, Darracott. From this instant I assume the name of my maternal great-grandmother.

TREMAINE. Good-bye, Mr. Darracott. You'll be kind to Sylvia, won't you ? I suppose you'll be taking possession of the Manor House in a day or two ?

CHUGG. I shall sleep there to-night. Nobody shall say that I shirk my responsibilities. The old Squire looked to me to maintain the honour of the Darracotts, and he shall find me equal to the occasion. He was a shrewd old man, and no doubt he had taken my measure before he made that will.

TREMAINE. You'll not forget Sylvia ?

CHUGG. Certainly not, my dear fellow. (*Re-enter* MRS. HAMMICK *with* SYLVIA). Ah, here she comes. My dear Miss Scobell, Tremaine has told me everything. Hard for him— hard for you. But you have youth, health, hope, kind friends left. Money is not everything. So long as I live you shall have a home at the Manor.

SYLVIA. Ah, Mr. Chugg, such an obligation—what claim have I ?

CHUGG. Don't mention obligation. We shall be able to make you useful, I've no doubt. Mary likes you, and Mary shall find a groove for you—a groove, you know. (*Looking at* MARY, *who sits at the table with her face hidden in her hands,* RICHARD *standing by her.*) Why, Mary ! I declare the girl is crying ! What's the matter now, child ?

MARY. Oh, father, it seems so strange, so wrong, that you should profit by Mr. Tremaine Darracott's loss.

CHUGG. My dear child, no man can profit except by somebody else's loss. It is the inevitable law of property, which is always changing hands, somehow or other. As for Mr. Tremaine—why, at *his* age a fortune would be a millstone round his neck. He doesn't see it in that light just at present, perhaps, but he will when he is Lord Chancellor.

TREMAINE. At any rate, Mr. Chugg—Darracott, I can admire the philosophy of my friends.

[Chugg goes up the stage, leaving Tremaine and Sylvia together.

TREMAINE. Sylvia, my best and bravest of girls! You were never afraid to stand between me and my grandfather's anger when I was a boy. I don't think you'll be afraid to stand by my side in poverty now that I am a man.

SYLVIA. Afraid? no, Tremaine. But how can I ever forgive myself for having brought that poverty upon you? If you had never loved me——

TREMAINE. Don't talk about impossibilities, Sylvia. Who could know you and not love you? Besides, if he hadn't thrown me off on your account, the old squire would have found some other reason for quarrelling with me. He had the genuine disinheriting disposition.

SYLVIA. If I could only help you in any way, Tremaine! I wish the people who educate girls would teach them to do one thing well instead of a good many things badly ; for then a woman would not be a useless creature in the time of calamity.

TREMAINE. Your love will help me to be patient, and steadfast, and brave, and honest, Sylvia. That is enough.

[They go up the stage.

MARY. Father, aren't you going to offer Mr. Tremaine some compensation for that wicked will? Won't you make some division of the property, giving him at least half?

CHUGG. I blight that young man's prospects, cripple his ambition? No, Mary! Who ever heard of a wealthy young man working his way to the front? They never do it, my dear. There's no incentive for them. Poverty is the true school for greatness. Go and pack your trunks, Mary.

MARY. Oh, father, do you really mean that we are to leave Hazle Farm—the dear old house in which I was born, where my dear mother lived and died!

CHUGG. My dear, we must not shirk our responsibilities. Property has its duties as well as its rights. That is an observation which you may have heard before.

MARY. I'm sure I shall never be so happy in any other house.

CHUGG. Mary, you are sadly deficient in self-respect—you have no proper idea of your own value, I'm afraid. The blood of the Darracotts suffered a good deal by adulteration before it came to you. Now, then, Mrs. Hammick, stir your stumps, and let us have dinner. Tremaine, you'll dine with us, of course. I can't give you such a bottle of port as I shall be able to crack with you by-and by at the Manor but as far as home-brewed goes you'll have no cause for complaint.

TREMAINE. I shall be delighted.

RICHARD. Good day to you, Mr. Chugg. Good-bye, Mary. (*Aside to* MARY) I'm afraid I shan't be quite so welcome at the Manor as I have been at the Farm.

MARY. Oh, yes, you will. Father, Dick thinks you are going to forget old friends now you are rich.

CHUGG. Forget! No, Richard. The Darracotts are staunch—staunch, sir. I shall not forget you. No, Richard, I shall find a groove for you, as well as for Sylvia Scobell. You are an intelligent young man, and I can turn your intelligence to account. You shall have the management of this farm, and you shall help to look after my affairs at the Manor—examine the tradesmen's accounts, see that I don't get cheated. It will be a position of trust, and I shall be able to give you a very comfortable salary—say fifty pounds a year, with the run of your teeth at the Manor House.

MARY (*aside to* CHUGG). Fifty pounds a year! Why, father, a little while ago you were going to give me five-and-twenty pounds to buy a gown.

CHUGG. That was when I was a poor man, my dear. The poor are always improvident.

RICHARD. Gentlemanly drudgery at fifty pounds a year. It isn't a brilliant prospect for a young man with his future to make ; but to be near Mary is worth a sacrifice. (*Aside*.)

CHUGG (*to* MARY.) Now I hope you're happy.

MRS. HAMMICK. And now that such a change has taken place in your circumstances, Tom—Mr. Chugg——

CHUGG. I beg your pardon, Darracott.

MRS. HAMMICK. He doesn't tell me to call him Tom now. (*Aside*.) I had better look out for another home.

CHUGG. No, Mrs. Hammick. You shall have a corner at the Manor House. We'll find a groove for you, madam. Come, bustle, bustle, let's have dinner soon, and be sure it's a good one. It's our last day in this shabby old hole, remember. You might send to the village for a dozen of champagne, if there is such a thing as a dozen of champagne in the village (*giving money*). Stay, what a fool I am· Send across to the Manor, to my cellar, for a dozen or so. Where's the key? Here's a pretty thing, for a man not to be able to put his hand on the keys of his own wine-cellar. Come, I say, bustle, bustle, you seem all struck slow and stupid. (*Aside crossing in front of the stage, while they all watch him in astonishment and anxiety.*)

Chugg Darracott! It's all like a dream! Property—responsibility—the land—the Manor House—all mine! (*Clutching at his throat*) There's a kind of choking here as if I were· going to have a fit. (*Snatching off his necktie*). Upon my soul, I don't know yet whether I'm glad or sorry. (*He sinks into a chair in the centre of the stage, and they all cluster round him, alarmed at his appearance*)

END OF ACT I.

ACT II.

Scene, Winter Evening.—*Hall at the Manor House, used as a living-room, opening at the back into gardens. Door on one side leading to drawing-room, on the other to* Chugg's *private sitting-room. Easy-chairs; occasional tables in foreground.*

Mrs. Hammick *seated at afternoon tea-table in front of a wide early-English fire-place.* Richard Avery *seated at writing table on opposite side of stage, dismissing* Bates, *grocer.*

Richard (*handing cheque to* Bates). There is your account, Mr. Bates.

Bates. Ten per cent. discount, sir? That brings down my profits to next to nothing. I'm almost out of pocket by such an account, sir. The old Squire was close, but he never asked for ten per cent. discount on a quarterly account.

Richard. Mr. Chugg Darracott is a man of business, the old Squire wasn't. Besides, the present consumption is about six times what it was in the old Squire's time. However, if you're dissatisfied we'll close the account. We can deal with the Co-operative Stores.

Bates. No, sir, no. I would rather supply you at a loss. I'd rather give you my goods, sir, than knuckle under to them

Co-operatives. But Mr. Chugg Darracott does cut things a little too fine. Good night, sir. [*Exit* BATES.

RICHARD. Good night to you. Upon my soul, Mrs. Hammick, I feel ashamed of myself when I have to grind down those poor fellows like that. I've no doubt they all cheat and over-charge, more or less. But for a man in Mr. Darracott's position, and with his large means, to grind and screw as he does! It's dreadful.

MRS. HAMMICK. Ah, and if you only knew what a noble-hearted fellow he was before he came into this fortune—how frank, how confiding!

RICHARD. Now he suspects everybody—thinks we are all in league to cheat him.

MRS. HAMMICK. And although he doesn't care how much he expends upon splendour or display, he grudges five shillings given away in charity.

RICHARD. Unless it is for one of those local charities in which his name appears at the top of the list as the largest donor.

Enter SYLVIA.

SYLVIA. I shall be so glad of a cup of your excellent tea, Mrs. Hammick. Still at your accounts, Mr. Avery? I've had such a skirmish with the head-gardener in order to get enough hot-house flowers for the dinner-table and drawing-room. He's such a very grand man, compared with old Peter, who was head-gardener in the Squire's time, that I'm afraid to speak to him. And Mr. Chugg Darracott was quite angry with me yesterday, because there were not enough flowers on the table, and I believe he expects some very stylish people this evening. Staying company, as the butler calls them.

MRS. HAMMICK. Yes; I have been told to prepare three of the best bedrooms, and that the dinner is to be something superlative; but Mr. Darracott did not honour me so far as to confide the names of his guests.

Enter MARY, *overhearing last speech.*

MARY. Don't you be grumpy, auntie dear. I'll tell you all about our fine visitors. They are some people whose acquaint-ance father made the day before yesterday in the hunting-field. There are two ladies; Lady Skimper—the widow of a City knight, I believe, but altogether a very superfine person—and her daughter, Leonora Skimper, who is supposed to be a very nice acquaintance for me; and then there is

Captain Vandean, of the 19th Lancers, a tremendous individual.

RICHARD. Also supposed to be a very nice acquaintance for you.

MARY. Don't be disagreeable, Richard. They are all coming in time for dinner; and they are to stay till after Christmas, or as much longer as they like. I think Lady Skimper would like to stay here all her life; but I hope my father will be too wise——

RICHARD. To fall into that trap. I don't know, Mary. A man who has great confidence in his own wisdom is generally an easy victim under such circumstances. Do you like these people?

MARY. No, Richard; I only like old friends. (*Putting her arm round* SYLVIA.) How grave you look, darling! Was there no letter from *him* this afternoon?

SYLVIA. Yes, dear, there was a letter, and he wrote in very good spirits. He even talks of running down to see me before Christmas is over. But I have been a little troubled about the table decorations. Your father was not quite satisfied yesterday, and I am so anxious to please him—I am under such heavy obligations——

MARY. Sylvia, if you have any sense of obligation we must be treating you badly. There must be something wrong, somewhere. Obligation, indeed! Why, all the obligation is on our side; for what would my father and I have done in this fine old house, and at the head of a large establishment, if you had not been here to tell us all the ways of the landed gentry—how to write a note of invitation, and how to answer one; how to order a dinner, and how to decorate a table?

SYLVIA. You learnt everything so quickly, Mary; it was a pleasure to teach you. But Mr. Darracott—I don't want to be ungrateful—but I can't help saying that Mr. Darracott has ways of his own.

MARY. Decidedly his own. My father is a dear, good man, but he is obstinate. I dare say, many dear, good men are obstinate. Now, I begged him not to invite these people who are coming to-day, but he would do it. He thinks they are high-bred, aristocratic, everything that is delightful. I think them flashy, vulgar adventurers. But it was no use talking. Father always will have his own way.

Enter CHUGG.

CHUGG. His own way, indeed! I should think he ought to have his own way. What's the use of a man being Lord

of the Manor, if he is to be domineered over by his daughter?
You hear that, Mary—no domineering. I hope you are
going to make the drawing-room a bower of roses this
evening, Sylvia, and the dinner-table something to dream of.
That's your groove, you know—the elegances of life. You
are to look after the elegances; push about the chairs in a
degagé way, as if people had been sitting on 'em ; scatter about
the books and magazines as if people had been reading them ;
arrange the old china in an artistic way—ascetic, you know,
ascetic—one must be ascetic nowadays.

MARY (*gently*). Æsthetic, papa.

CHUGG. Mary, no domineering. Now, Mrs. Hammick,
your department is the substantialities, and that's still more
important. We can't get on without the substantialities.
Where's your menoo ?

MRS. HAMMICK. I beg your pardon, Mr. Darracott.

CHUGG. Your menoo—menoo—m-e-n-double-o.

MARY. Father means the bill of fare.

CHUGG. No domineering, Mary. When your father means
English, he speaks English. When he means French, he
speaks French. Where's your *menoo* ? (MRS. HAMMICK
hands bill of fare.) *Potage à la bonne femme, Saumon à la
Pompadour*—Pompadour's French for lobster sauce, I suppose
—*Cotelettes aux truffes, Petites timbales de gibier, Dinde aux
huitres, Selle de mouton, Gelée à la Marischino, Charlotte
Plombieres, Fondu de Parmesan.* Ha ! humph ! a tidy little
dinner—nothing original, no inventive power, but I suppose
it's about the best Mounseer Bainmarie can produce. The
man is not a genius ; he can cook, but he doesn't soar. Snow
again ; no chance of a run on Boxing-day. Rather hard to
have a stud of hunters eating their heads off in one's stable.

RICHARD. Harder for the man who can't afford to keep a
horse at all.

CHUGG. Ah, that's your confounded radical way of looking
at things. Have you settled all those accounts ?

RICHARD. Very nearly. Bates called for his cheque just
now. He was rather cut up about the ten per cent. discount.

CHUGG. He'll be cut up a good deal smaller if he doesn't
take care what he's about. I've half a mind to transfer my
custom to one of the Co-operative Stores. I had a catalogue
by post this morning. What does Bates charge us for the
best Patna rice ?

RICHARD. Fourpence a pound.

CHUGG. I thought so. Bates is a swindler ! a bird of prey !

I can get Patna at the Stores for threepence-three farthings.

MARY. Oh, father, what can a farthing matter?

CHUGG. What can a farthing matter? Everything! Colossal fortunes are made by economy in farthings. The millions of the future are created from the farthings of the present. How are you to keep your sovereigns if you let them leak away in unconsidered farthings? You'll tell Bates that in future he must supply Patna at threepence-three farthings.

RICHARD. Yes, sir.

CHUGG. And I have an idea that his sugars contrast un-favourably with the Co-operative Stores. Let him look to his sugars. And now to a more agreeable subject. We have to arrange our Christmas festivities. Christmas in the olden times, as depicted in the Christmas number of the *Illustrated London News*—the old English gentleman's Christmas, with carol-singers, bell-ringers, mummers, the whole business. Have you been making your preparations, Richard?

RICHARD. Yes, sir. Everything is arranged. The carol-singers will be in front of the hall-door at nine o'clock this evening. The mummers reserve their sports for to-morrow afternoon. I have been making a list of the poor in the three parishes in which your property lies, thinking that you would wish to make a distribution of coals, blankets, and beef, and perhaps a little money, at this season.

CHUGG. Beef, coals, blankets, money! Did the old Squire make any such distribution?

RICHARD. You know what he was. Christmas was to him like any other time. He took no notice whatever of the festival.

CHUGG. Then I will not be so disloyal to my benefactor as to set myself up in opposition to him by ill-advised benevolence. I will not have it upon my conscience that I have pauperised my neighbourhood.

MARY. But, dear father, it is surely right for the rich to help the poor, especially in such a hard winter.

CHUGG. Mary, I will have no domineering. Richard, my good fellow, I should like you to stick to those accounts until you dress for dinner (RICHARD *goes off to study*). Mrs. Hammick, I wish you'd give an eye to the rooms that have been prepared for Lady Skimper and her daughter.

MRS. HAMMICK. Yes, sir. There are only a few finishing touches wanted. [*Exit.*

SYLVIA. And I must see what can be done with that terrible Mr. MacCandlish.

[*Wraps a shawl round her, and exit to garden.*

CHUGG. And now, Mary, that we are alone together, I want to talk to you--seriously. What do you mean by your unjustifiable condescension to my steward, Richard Avery?

MARY. Unjustifiable condescension to Richard—to your old friend's son—to the man whom I, and everybody else, have always looked upon as my future husband! Surely, father, you can't forget? If we have never been formally engaged, still it has always been understood that Richard and I would be married some day, and with your complete approval.

CHUGG. With *my* approval! *I* approve of the heiress of all the Darracotts throwing herself away upon a small farmer's son! Why, the girl must be mad. While you were Miss Chugg of Hazle Farm, it was all very well for you to play at sweethearting with my old friend Avery's only son, who will come into a tidy little freehold of a hundred and fifty acres, there or thereabouts, when his father's under the sod. But Miss Darracott must look higher; Miss Darracott must aspire. That's an involuntary burst into poetry, which I was not prepared for.

MARY. Whether my name is Chugg or Darracott, father, my heart is made of exactly the same stuff; and as long as it beats it will always belong to Richard Avery.

CHUGG. How she ups and talks to me! Have a care, child. Take care that I do not disinherit you. I could do it, in more ways than one. I am not an old man, Mary. The bloom of youth has not yet faded from these locks. I might marry again.

MARY. Nothing would please me better, father, if you were to marry wisely, choosing one who loves you and would make your declining years happy.

CHUGG. You may be sure of one thing, that if ever I should enter into matrimonial bondage, I shall marry as beseems a Darracott. I shall not degrade that ancient name by a low alliance. I shall choose a lady whose rank and fashion will be an ornament to my table, an embellishment to my home.

MARY. You'd better have true love than all the rank and fashion in the world, father.

CHUGG. Mary, I will not be domineered over. With regard

to Richard Avery, you will be kind enough in future to
consider him as my house-steward, and in no other light.
Captain Vandean is a gentleman of old family, and, as I
hear, of good means. His father is an honourable, his grandfather was a nobleman.

MARY. If his father were a duke it would be all the same
to me. Let us understand each other, father. Richard and
I loved each other when we were boy and girl together in
the old happy days at the farm, and you smiled upon our
love. What would you think of me, what could I think of
myself if my feelings could change now because of the change
in our fortunes ? If we were ten times richer than we are I
would never marry any one but the man I loved when we
were poor?   [*Exit.*

CHUGG. How that girl has deteriorated since she became a
Darracott ! Faults which in a Chugg were hardly noticeable,
stand out in fiery characters upon the front of a Darracott.
Let me see, what have I to do next ? (*Looks at his watch.*)
Lady Skimper and her daughter are to arrive about seven ;
they will drive over from the hotel at Dawlish, where they
have been staying. Deuced fine woman, Lady Skimper—
took her fences admirably, though I didn't think much of
her cattle. Such a woman would be an ornament to any
gentleman's table. What bosh Mary talks about true love !
There was a time when—when I had a sort of sneaking
kindness for Betsy Hammick, and when I fancy Betsy Hammick had a sort of sneaking kindness for me. But that
would never do now. She's a good-looking woman, a nicely
rounded figure, no angles, a fine fresh complexion ; but she's
vulgar, decidedly vulgar—a thoroughbred plebeian. No,
Thomas Chugg Darracott, property has its duties as well as
its rights.

Enter FOOTMAN.

FOOTMAN. If you please, sir, Pugsley would be glad to
speak to you.

CHUGG. What does he want ? Tell him I've no orders for
him.

FOOTMAN. He knows that, sir ; but he would like to speak
with you on a little matter of business.

CHUGG. Business, indeed ! One would suppose I owed the
fellow money. Let him come in. (*Exit* FOOTMAN.) I don't
know how it is, but I've a most uncomfortable feeling about
that old stud-groom of the Squire's. He's the only one of

the old servants I kept. I made a clean sweep of all the rest—no domestic tyranny from old retainers for me ; but there was a look in this one's eye which stopped me, somehow, when I was going to dismiss him. He's not a bad servant, knows a lot about horses ; but he has no figure for a hunting-groom, and he's got a masterful way that I don't half like. There are looks and tones of that man's which make me feel as if I had cold water down my back. But I'm not going to be domineered over by a servant.

Enter PUGSLEY.

Well, Pugsley, what's the row ?

PUGSLEY. The row is, that Mr. Avery have been tampering with my accounts, and I don't mean to stand it.

CHUGG. Your accounts ?

PUGSLEY. Yes, my accounts—my corn merchant, and my saddler, and my carriage-builder. Mr. Avery have been taking ten per cent. off the stable accounts : and how do you suppose the tradesmen are to give me my commission if they are to be swindled out of ten per cent. discount by you ?

CHUGG. Pugsley, this is not over-respectful.

PUGSLEY. It is not meant to be respectful. Quite the contrairy. Ain't you ashamed of yourself, for trying to intercept your own servant's legitimate profits ? Don't you think poorly of yerself, now, for taking the bread out of an old servant's mouth ? Aren't you ready to blush for your meanness ?

CHUGG. Pugsley, when I took you into my service——

PUGSLEY. You didn't take me into your service. I was here before you was. You're a parwenny compared with me.

CHUGG. Pugsley, as I remarked before, your language is the reverse of respectful. I was about to observe that when you became my servant there was no question of your receiv-ing commissions from the tradespeople. If such a question had been mooted I should have said no—emphatically no.

PUGSLEY. Then I wouldn't have stayed.

CHUGG. In that case, my good fellow, I should have been compelled to dispense with your services. (*Aside*) I feel the cold-watery sensation creeping over me ; but it won't do to quail before a hireling. (*Aloud*) I must repeat, Pugsley, that you don't appear to know your place.

PUGSLEY. Me not know my place ! Perhaps it's you don't

know your place, Mr. Chugg Darracott, or Mr. Darracott
Chugg, or Mr. Chugg without the Darracott. Me not know
my place ! I've been on these premises, man and boy, over
thirty year, and I ought to know my place by this time. I
know every inch of this house, and all that belongs to it. I
know a precious deal more than you know, Mr. New-comer ;
and you'd better be careful.

CHUGG (*aside*). This is dreadful ! The man must know
something—some horrible secret, the very thought of which
turns my blood to ice. He would never dare to be so insolent unless he had some kind of power. Perhaps he is a son
of the old Squire's by a secret marriage—the rightful heir.
He isn't like the Squire ; but that's neither here nor there.
He may take after his mother. I must conciliate him at any
price. (*Aloud*) Well, Pugsley, we'll say no more about the
ten per cent. discount. You can tell the tradespeople that
will be made all right. It wasn't I who cut down their
accounts ; but I have a steward, Pugsley, and he has his own
view of these little matters. For my own part I like things
done in a large-hearted, liberal manner. And as for your little
commission —why, you're a valuable servant, and you deserve
it. Go along, Pugsley, and make your mind easy. I am not
the kind of man to stint a faithful old servant.

PUGSLEY. You'd better not try it on with me. [*Exit.*

CHUGG. He doesn't even pretend to be grateful. There
must be some secret. I begin to think he really is the rightful heir. But in that case why doesn't he declare himself,
and claim his own ? Perhaps there is some difficulty about
his mother's marriage certificate. He may be waiting for
documentary evidence. This is terrible ! I am to live with
this danger constantly threatening me—a sword of what's-
his-name suspended above my head by a single hair.

Enter BUTLER *announcing*

LADY SKIMPER, MISS SKIMPER, *and* CAPTAIN VANDEAN.

SYLVIA *and* MARY *re-enter at the same time.*

CHUGG. My dear Lady Skimper, charmed, too charmed at
this delightful visit. My daughter you already know ; my
daughter's friend, Miss Scobell—Lady Skimper, Captain
Vandean.

LADY SKIMPER. What a delicious old house ! I was prepared for something unique, but this is really——

VANDEAN. Yes, this is really——

Miss Skimper. Quite too distinctly precious. Mother, do observe the panelling.

Lady Skimper. And the chimneypiece, so truly Jacobean——

Sylvia (*aside to* Mary). How much more impressed she is by the furniture than by us!

Lady Skimper. Mr. Darracott, I congratulate you upon being the owner of such a noble old house.

Chugg. Yes, it has been in my family for a good many generations. It was built by a Darracott in the reign of Henry the Seventh.

Lady Skimper. How you must love it! You were born beneath this fine old roof-tree, of course?

Chugg. No, I was not actually born in this house, not actually—in point of fact, I happened to be born elsewhere.

Lady Skimper. I understand. Your parents were travelling at the time of your birth. Have you travelled much, Mr. Darracott?

Chugg. Yes, I've been a goodish bit of a rover in my time. I've been to Torquay, and to Ilfracombe, and to Weston-super-Mare, and I *have* been to London ; but that was rather a long time ago,

Lady Skimper. I think I begin to read your character, You are the real, true-blue, fine old English gentleman, fond of hunting, shooting, sport of all kinds—a character one too rarely meets in these days of tinsel and shoddy. And how splendidly you ride ! It is a delight to follow any one with such a seat, and such hands.

Vandean. And such a horse! Very fine animal that second horse of yours the other day.

Chugg. Yes. I rather pride myself upon my hunters. I have ridden to hounds ever since I was seven years old. My daughter has ridden to hounds ever since she was seven years old.

Vandean. And most magnificently she rides in consequence. Nothing like early training. (*To* Mary) I suppose you adore hunting, Miss Darracott,

Mary. I like a good run when my father and I are out together, but there are many things I like just as well.

Vandean (*aside*). I see. No gush, not enthusiastic. Common sense is the line here. Pretty, and as things stand at present, the natural inheritor of this place and all the father's money. But the father is young enough to marry ; and Lady Skimper means to have him.

LADY SKIMPER. And now, dear Mr. Darracott, before we dress for dinner, I should so like you to show me this lovely old house. I am pining to see the picture-gallery—of course you have a picture-gallery. And you must tell me all about the ghost—of course you have a ghost. Come, Leonora, I hope you are making friends with Miss Darracott.

LEONORA. Yes, mother. We are going to be no end of chums. I have just been telling Miss Darracott that she must try my dressmaker, and that her sleeves have been out for the last six months.

CHUGG (*severely*). What do you mean, Mary, by going about the house with your sleeves out? Haven't you your own lady's-maid to mend your clothes for you?

LEONORA. I only meant that your daughter's sleeves are out of fashion, Mr. Darracott. You middle-aged gentlemen are so awfully practical.

CHUGG (*aside*). Pert minx! calls me middle-aged to my teeth.

LEONORA. Mayn't I come with you, mother, and be introduced to the ghost? Come, Mary. Please let me call you Mary; Miss Darracott is so awfully formal.

MARY. I'd much rather be called Mary.

LEONORA. Of course you would. Call me Nora, please. That's what all my spoons call me.

[*Exeunt* CHUGG, LADY SKIMPER, LEONORA, *and* MARY.

SYLVIA *moves about, arranging flowers.* VANDEAN *lounges in doorway, lighting cigarette.*

SYLVIA. His letter says *very* soon. I wonder whether that means immediately. Poor, dear Tremaine! Last Christmas Eve we were so happy together, hanging up holly in the old church, and sitting telling each other ghost stories in the evening, while the Squire enjoyed his after-dinner nap. There were no visitors; there was no feasting. It was what most people would call a very dreary Christmas. But oh, how happy we were! Love makes all the difference.

VANDEAN (*aside, watching her*). Very nice little girl. Poor dependent, evidently, from the way in which our friend introduced her. (*Aloud*) How very sweetly you are arranging those flowers! Quite artistic, upon my word.

SYLVIA. Do you know that people don't generally smoke in this room?

VANDEAN. Don't they? I thought, from the look of the

place, that it was liberty hall. Guns, whips, fishing-rods, rackets ; why not tobacco ?

SYLVIA. Perhaps, partly because this room is used by the ladies of the family, and partly because Mr. Darracott detests tobacco.

VANDEAN. Say you dislike it, and I throw my cigarette away that instant ; but if you'll join me (*offering cigar-case*), I'll go on and defy Darracott.

SYLVIA. No, thank you. I neither like cigarettes, nor people who smoke, unpermitted, in a room occupied by ladies.

VANDEAN. Don't be severe ; it doesn't suit your cast of features. A pretty girl should never frown. When she does, she unconsciously invites the approach of wrinkles. Why weren't you out with the hounds the day before yesterday ?

SYLVIA. Because I have no horse, and never hunt.

VANDEAN. Ah, but you ride, splendidly ! I am sure of that. You have just the figure for a habit ; you have really.

> [SYLVIA *tries to cross towards drawing-room.* VANDEAN *intercepts her.*

VANDEAN. Why are you running away ? Can't you be sociable ? I want you to tell me all you can about Mr. Chugg Darracott and his daughter. I have been dragged here by Lady Skimper, and, of course, care nothing for the people, so you can say what you like. I can't quite make the gentleman out. He has all the bad style of a *parvenu*, and yet Darracott is a good old name.

SYLVIA. I had rather you obtained your information from somebody else. Mr. Darracott is my benefactor.

VANDEAN. Your benefactor ; yes, and he lets every one see that you are here in a subordinate position. I knew at a glance that you were thoroughbred, and that he isn't. The daughter's a nice girl —uncommonly nice ; and will have plenty of money, I suppose——

SYLVIA. You had better go and ask her.

VANDEAN. No, I shan't. I'd rather ask you. Why are you so unfriendly ? You can see how much I admire you. Why are you making for that door ? I suspect there's a bit of misletoe over it, and you mean a fellow to steal a kiss, don't you, now ? (*Trying to kiss her.*)

> [TREMAINE *enters at* c. *door, with rug and travelling-bag, comes down stage, takes hold of* CAPTAIN VANDEAN'S *collar, and pushes him aside.*

Sylvia. Tremaine!   What a delightful surprise!

Tremaine. Yes, I held my first brief last week, so I thought I'd take advantage of the Christmas excursion trains and come and tell you all about it. I hope I didn't startle you.

Sylvia. Just a little, but it was a very pleasant surprise.

Vandean. You startled me, sir, in a manner which I consider particularly unpleasant, and for which I must request an apology.

Tremaine. You had better apologise to this lady, to whom you were making yourself exceedingly offensive.

Vandean. I was merely expressing my admiration for the lady, sir.   I don't think that is an offence for which a man ought to be collared by an unknown individual.

Tremaine. My name is Darracott—Tremaine Darracott.

Vandean. Son of the present proprietor ?

Tremaine. Grandson of the late Squire—no relation, or only a very distant one, to the present Mr. Darracott—and this lady's affianced husband.   The next time you wish to express your admiration for a lady, sir, you had better take the trouble to ascertain beforehand that your compliments will be welcome.

Vandean. Oh, hang it!   Every woman likes to be told she's handsome ; (*aside*) even if she is engaged to a cad who travels by an excursion train.

Re-enter Chugg, Lady Skimper, Leonora, *and* Mary.

Lady Skimper. The more I see of this delicious old place, the more I adore it.   So historical, so mediæval, so thoroughly sweet.

Chugg. Well, I flatter myself that in the matter of drainage my house leaves nothing to be desired.   No sewage gas, no ugly smells.

Lady Skimper. Oh, but I meant sweet in its æsthetic sense.

Chugg. Tremaine!   How d'ye do ?   This is a surprise. I thought you were sticking to your work in your Temple chambers.

Tremaine. "All work and no play "—you know the adage. Besides, I rather distinguished myself last week defending a West-end dairyman who was sued by the proprietor of a monster hotel for supplying adulterated milk.   I brought the adulteration home to the hotel servants, and brought off my dairyman with flying colours.   So I thought I'd run down and spend Christmas in the old home.   I may have a room somewhere, mayn't I, Chugg—I beg pardon, Darracott ?

CHUGG. Yes, no doubt we can find you a shakedown some-where.

TREMAINE. My own old room, perhaps.

CHUGG. Why, no; your room has been appropriated to Miss Skimper. Lady Skimper, allow me to present to you my young friend and kinsman, Mr. Tremaine Darracott, a scion of the old stock. Mr. Darracott—Lady Skimper, Miss Skimper. (*Gong sounds in vestibule.*) Ah! there goes the gong. Cheerful sound, isn't it!

VANDEAN. Delightful, after a cross-country drive.

CHUGG. That's the warning gong. I hope you'll make a very quick toilet this evening, ladies. You can reserve your last new gowns for Christmas Day. My poor old mother always sported a new gown on Christmas day, and a new bonnet on Easter Sunday. It was part of her religion. You girls can show Lady Skimper her rooms.

VANDEAN (*aside as he goes out*). Talks of his poor old mother's gowns and bonnets. What a howling cad!

[Exeunt LADY SKIMPER, LEONORA, MARY, SYLVIA,
and CHUGG and VANDEAN.

CHUGG. Oh, here's Mrs. Hammick.

Enter MRS. HAMMICK.

CHUGG. Just see about a room for Tremaine somewhere, will you, Mrs. Hammick? He'll be with us till Boxing Day.

TREMAINE (*aside*). A room somewhere! Rather an off-hand way of putting it. I'm afraid my grandfather's fortune has not improved my old friend Chugg. Sylvia does not look happy.

MRS. HAMMICK. Mr. Tremaine! This is indeed an un-expected pleasure (*shaking hands with him*).

TREMAINE. Thank you, Mrs. Hammick. That sounds like welcome.

MRS. HAMMICK. I'll go and get you a nice room ready.

[Exit.

TREMAINE. Well, Mr. Darracott, I suppose by this time the novelty of your position has quite worn off, and that you've settled down into the country squire.

CHUGG. I hope, Tremaine, that the duties of that position do not sit ill upon me. I have done my best to uphold the dignity of the order. The style of housekeeping at the

Manor House has undergone considerable expansion since I have been master here. I have a French cook, a pair of match footmen, a fine stud of hunters, and if I could find a woman fitted to take the lead in such an establishment—a lady, sir, whom I could proudly place at the head of my table——

TREMAINE. You have some thoughts of matrimony.

CHUGG. I was forty-five on my last birthday, Tremaine. I hope that age does not forbid a man ruminating upon a wedding-ring.

TREMAINE. My dear sir, it is the prime of life. And if you are happy in your choice, you could hardly do a wiser thing than marry. Do you know, I used once to think you were rather sweet upon Mrs. Hammick.

CHUGG. Tremaine, you astonish me. Mrs. Hammick is my housekeeper. I pay her a salary, or to put it with broad vulgarity, wages—wages, sir, wages.

TREMAINE. Ah, you didn't pay her anything, except kind attentions, in the days I am talking of. She was not your paid servant, but your honoured friend. I wonder she can lower herself to take payment for her services.

CHUGG. I insisted upon it. I would have her here on that footing and no other. My housekeeper—a lady housekeeper, as they call it in the advertisements. That was the groove I made for Mrs. Hammick.

TREMAINE. I'm sorry I was mistaken. She's an admirable woman—good-looking too—buxom. I should have thought she possessed every quality which a sensible man of five-and-forty would desire in his wife.

CHUGG. Except blood, sir, blood! Old family, ancient lineage, a place in the sacred pages of Burke. The wife of a Darracott must be born in the purple. Fine woman Lady Skimper. I don't know whether you noticed her.

TREMAINE. Rather a showy outline, but badly filled in.

CHUGG. Good points, Tremaine ; a trifle weedy, perhaps—but uncommonly good points.

TREMAINE. Who is she ?

CHUGG. A widow.

TREMAINE. That is obvious.

CHUGG. How so ?

TREMAINE. She has the adventurous eye, the brazen front, the hardened manner of a woman accustomed to fight her own battles, to bully landlords, and quarrel with livery stable keepers, and cheat at whist, and pounce upon the wings of the chickens at table d'hôte. She has the keen outlook of the woman who has been occupied for the last ten years or so in trying to catch a second husband. How long has she been a widow ?

CHUGG. I haven't asked her.

TREMAINE. And who and what was her husband ?

CHUGG. Sir Paul Skimper.

TREMAINE. Baronet ?

CHUGG. Knight.

TREMAINE. I thought so. The flimsiest rag of gentility which can do duty as a title. I remember there was a Bristol brewer called Skimper, who was knighted when the Queen opened a local hospital.

CHUGG. Tremaine ! I consider Lady Skimper a woman of the highest ton, and I do not seek to pry into her husband's antecedents. If he perchance belonged to the trading classes, some of the bluest blood in the country flows in her veins. She told me as much the day before yesterday in a quiet corner to leeward of Simmons's windmill : and I can see it in her countenance.   There is race in every feature.

TREMAINE. Well, I'm not going to quarrel with an old friend about Lady Skimper. And if your matrimonial ideas do tend that way, I can only wish you happiness. I wish my own marriage could be as easily managed. I fancy Sylvia is not looking particularly well ; she has rather an anxious, worried look.

CHUGG. I can't see what she has to worry her. She has a good dinner every day, a good gown to wear, and a carriage to ride in—now and then. Anything over and above that is mere fancy.

TREMAINE. Perhaps ; but fancies go a good way with a girl of nineteen.   However, I hope, before another year is over, I may be able to relieve you of the burden of Sylvia's maintenance.

CHUGG. Don't give yourself any uneasiness about that. The girl is useful. She has a good deal of taste, and is very handy in various small ways. How do you like my improvements ? I've smartened up the old place a bit, you see ?

TREMAINE. You've made it absolutely gorgeous ; but I hear you've dismissed all the servants, except Pugsley.   I wonder you made an exception in his favour.

CHUGG. Well, you see, Tremaine, I don't particularly like the man, but I'm passionately fond of horses, and Pugsley is a first-rate fellow for horses.

TREMAINE. I'm not so sure of that. If I were passionately fond of a horse I should never trust him to Pugsley. The fellow may be a good groom, but he's a bad man. Do you know that I once thrashed him to within an inch of his life for ill-using an old mare that used to carry me to hounds?

CHUGG. Did you, really? I honour you for the act, and for the feeling that prompted the act. But how did Pugsley take it? He seems to be scarcely the kind of man one could horsewhip with impunity.

TREMAINE. Oh, a bully is always a coward. He blustered a good deal; swore he would tell my grandfather, and didn't; swore he would pay me out somehow, and didn't pay me out anyhow. You know the kind of thing. But I don't think he ever handled Grey Molly roughly after that—at any rate, not while I was on the premises.

CHUGG. Then you think that he's afraid of you?

TREMAINE. I do.

CHUGG. My dear Tremaine, I really am very delighted to have you here, at this festive season too; it makes Christmas more Christmasy. You must try and stay a little longer than we originally proposed. Why confine yourself to Boxing Day? Why not make it New Year's Day, or even Twelfth Night?

TREMAINE. My dear Chugg, you may be sure I shall be in no hurry to leave the house that holds Sylvia.

CHUGG. Of course not. By the way, talking of Pugsley, there is a something odd about the man—a peculiar strangeness, a strange peculiarity. Do you know anything about his origin? He is not—not—a poor relation of the old Squire's, is he? (*Aside*) I don't like to put the question plainer.

TREMAINE. Pugsley—that low-bred, illiterate ruffian—a relation of the Darracotts! How can you suggest such a thing?

CHUGG. It's too absurd, isn't it? But the fellow take so much upon himself, he conducts himself with an amount of—cheek, which only some kind of unacknowledged family connection could justify——

TREMAINE. He has grown insolent on the strength of being the only one of all the old servants retained by you. He fancies you can't do without him. The man is a rogue as well as a bully. Sack him, my dear fellow, sack him!

CHUGG. Yes, I'll sack him. (*Aside*). If I could only screw my courage to the sacking-point! (*The gong sounds again. Re-enter Omnes*). There goes the gong. My dear Lady Skimper, may I offer you my arm ? Captain Vandean, you will bring my daughter. Richard, take care of Miss Skimper. Tremaine will bring up the rear with Miss Scobell and Mrs. Hammick.

MARY. I would rather not go into dinner, father, if Lady Skimper will be good enough to excuse me. I was out in the wind after luncheon, and it gave me a headache.

RICHARD. And I dined early, sir. So, if Captain Vandean will take Miss Skimper, the table will be better balanced.

LEONORA. Oh, I daresay he won't mind. Come along, Charlie.

CHUGG (*aside*). Damn the table. That only daughter and heiress of mine means mischief.

LADY SKIMPER (*as they go up stage*). Now, remember you are to tell me all about the family ghost. I am sure there is no skeleton in this happy household, but there ought to be a family ghost.

[*Exeunt all except* RICHARD *and* MARY. MARY *seats herself by the fire and takes up some fancy-work.*

RICHARD. Is your head very bad, Mary ? Do you think it would make you worse if I were to sit here and talk to you for a little bit ? (*Seating himself on a stool at her feet in the firelight.*)

MARY. Well, no, Richard, I think I might endure it. Some voices are very trying when one has a headache ; but yours—I don't want to flatter you, Dick—but yours is a sympathetic voice.

RICHARD. She called me Dick ! Mary, do you know it is nearly six months since you called me Dick ? I don't think you have done it once since you became a great heiress.

MARY. You don't suppose that makes a difference ?

RICHARD. I know that something has made a difference. There has been a gulf between us ever since your father became Squire Darracott.

MARY. If there has been a gulf, Richard, it has not been of my making. If other people choose to be stand-offish, and to keep an old friend at arm's length——

RICHARD. Mary, do you really mean that you are unchanged—that if I, Dick Avery, only a well-to-do farmer's son, with no better prospect in life than to succeed to my father's farm ; if I were to ask you to keep an old promise made years ago when we were little more than children ; if

I were to ask you to be my wife, Mary, what would you say?

MARY. I should say that you have taken a very long time about it.

RICHARD. Oh! my darling! (*Checking himself.*) And you would not think meanly of me? You would not think that the change in your fortune can make you one whit dearer to me than you were in those old days?

MARY. Oh! Dick, I think you and I know each other too well for that. What is the good of our having played together as children if we can't understand each other as man and woman?

RICHARD. God bless you, my darling. You have made me the happiest man in the three kingdoms. But, oh! Mary, how do you think your father will take our engagement?

MARY. Like a dose of medicine : that's to say, I'm afraid he'll make a few wry faces. But whatever poor dear father may do or say under the influence of Mammon—he is a devil, isn't he, Dick, that horrid Mammon?—I know his heart is in the right place, and that it is a warm, true heart if one only appeals to it properly; so I'm not afraid of speaking my mind to him.

RICHARD. You are the dearest, prettiest, pluckiest of girls. (*Voices of carol singers sounding in the distance.*) Mary, do you remember our last Christmas Eve at Hazle Farm?

MARY. When we all sat round the parlour table playing speculation, with Barcelona nuts for counters; and when we all went out to the kitchen to stir the pudding : and when you beat the eggs for the flip; and when father was so—so *very* cheerful after drinking it? Of course I do.

RICHARD. It was all very vulgar, wasn't it?

MARY. Awfully vulgar.

RICHARD. Which Christmas Eve did you like best?

MARY. Last year's.

RICHARD. So did I, Mary, ever so much; for I was able to steal a kiss in the dark passage as we came back from stirring the pudding; and I don't see any chance of such luck to-night.

MARY (*coyly*). Ah! but to-night we are engaged, Dick, and you need not steal kisses. You can take one.

He kisses her. Enter VANDEAN *and* LEONORA.

VANDEAN. Pray don't apologise. You made such a pretty group in front of that Jacobean mantelpiece, under the mistletoe. Just the kind of thing for the "Illustrated" or the "Graphic;" old as the hills; been done over and over again for the last forty years, but its a kind of thing that always fetches the British public.

MARY. Did you find the dining room unpleasantly warm, Miss Skimper?

LEONORA (*seated, fanning herself languidly*). No, Miss Darracott; the dining room was comfortable enough, and the dinner was excellent—I pride myself upon being a judge of a good dinner; but your poor dear father and my poor old mother became so intolerably prosy that I was obliged to come away. You see there was no one to give the signal for departure, and though I scowled at my parent with all my capacity for scowling, I could not make her budge. If your table wasn't so wide I should have kicked her favourite corn. She would have felt *that*.

VANDEAN (*gazing at her admiringly*). Nice girl! *Quel chic.*

LEONORA. Miss—— What's her name, your little friend in the black frock?

MARY. Scobell.

LEONORA. Miss Scoburne sat on like a martyr; but as she and young Mr. Darracott were spooning each other all dinner time, I suppose she didn't find the thing as tedious as I did.

VANDEAN. Rather rough on me. Wasn't I sitting next you all the time?

LEONORA. With your nose in your plate. You didn't begin to be attentive till after the Parmesan ramequins, and even then you divided your attentions between me and Mr. Darracott's Lafitte.

VANDEAN. Clever girl. *Quel zing!*

LEONORA. Nice young fellow, that Tremaine Darracott. Rather a pity his grandfather left him out in the cold. If the old Squire had given him a thousand a year or so, he would not have been such a desperately bad match. (*To* MARY) I suppose those two poor creatures mean to marry and starve?

MARY. I know they mean to marry, and I hope Providence will take care of the rest.

LEONORA (*sighing*). Providence has enough to do with all the imprudent lovers who begin life without any other banker.

VANDEAN (*aside*). Splendid girl. *Quel v'lan!* (*Aloud, looking out into garden*). What a bright moon. I say, Nora, what do you think of a stroll to that lake yonder?

LEONORA. And a cigarette. Delightful ! *Skips across to him. He picks up a wrap from a chair and puts it on her.*

VANDEAN. Smokes like a life-guardsman. *Quel chien ! Exeunt* VANDEAN *and* LEONORA *through porch to garden.* MARY *and* RICHARD *retire to billiard room. Enter* SYLVIA *and* TREMAINE *from dining-room.*

TREMAINE (*aside to* SYLVIA). In spite of your assurances to the contrary, I know you are not happy here.

SYLVIA. Then I must be very ungrateful, for Mary is all goodness to me.

TREMAINE. But how about Mary's father ?

SYLVIA. Mr. Darracott is not unkind, but he is sometimes a little overbearing, just a little spoiled by good fortune.

TREMAINE. So I fancied from his manner. Squire Darracott is not half so good a fellow as Tom Chugg—jolly Chugg, as people used to call him. But never mind, Sylvia, I am beginning to see my way to a modest little income, just big enough for love in a cottage. I have held my first brief not unsuccessfully, and I have earned a few pounds by literature. You don't know what a delight it is to me to work hard for your sake.

SYLVIA. How good and brave you are, and how few young men would have borne such a reverse of fortune as bravely !

TREMAINE. I am pretty much of Horace's opinion, that a man's mind should be prepared for change of fortune—that in prosperity he should fear the approach of evil, and in misfortune expect a change for the better. The very day that I feel myself secure of three hundred a year, I shall write to our old Vicar to put up the banns. Don't you think we might live on three hundred ?

SYLVIA. Don't you think we might manage with two hundred and fifty ?

TREMAINE. My dearest girl, how happy you make me ! That means you will marry me early in the new year. Oh, Sylvia, you don't know how hard a man can work when he is over head and ears in love, and has one dear face always smiling before him, leading him onward over the stony ways of life. And you are not afraid of living in a small house, Sylvia—a house at forty pounds a year, for instance ? You have no idea how small a house London landlords have the conscience to give for forty pounds a year.

SYLVIA. However small it is, Tremaine, it will be big enough for you and me to be happy in it.

TREMAINE. To be sure it will ; and we can change it for a

bigger house by-and-by, when I have made my mark in my profession, and when—there are more of us.

[Carol singers appear before the porch, and sing a carol.

Re-enter CHUGG, LADY SKIMPER, *and* MRS. HAMMICK *from dining room.* CHUGG *seats himself on centre ottoman, between* LADY SKIMPER *and* MRS. HAMMICK. SYLVIA *and* TREMAINE *are seated on one side of stage.* RICHARD *and* MARY *on the other.*

LADY SKIMPER (*at the close of the carol*). Very sweet, really. So suggestive of the good old times.

MARY. The good old times must have been slightly out of tune if they were like that.

CHUGG. It's rather jolly, ain't it ? My idea, you know.

LADY SKIMPER. An idea that does you credit. So truly Shakespearian.

CHUGG. How do you like it, Mrs. Hammick ?

MRS. H. I think it would have been better if Stubbs, the cobbler, had kept time, and if Crow, the saddler, hadn't such a cold in his head. *[Loud laughter outside.*

CHUGG. Richard, will you be good enough to go and see what they are doing in the servants' hall ? There is an exuberance of mirth which indicates recklessness with the beer-barrel.

RICHARD (*to* MARY). You see, I'm not even allowed five minutes' quiet talk with you.

CHUGG. Mrs. Hammick, I hope there is some limit in the matter of beer. I should be very sorry to encourage drunkenness in my household. I should regret extremely that liberality should degenerate into licence.

MRS. HAMMICK. That is rather the butler's department than mine. He would object if I were to interfere.

CHUGG. Nonsense, Mrs. Hammick. Butler, forsooth ! Am I to be domineered over by a butler ? General economy is your department, Mrs. Hammick. Everything that can save my purse is your department. Do you want to see me end my days in a workhouse ? Judging by the present rate of expenditure, I should say that the Union must be my ultimate destination. Beer, Lady Skimper, the profligate use of beer is the curse of this country. The influence of beer is under mining the British Constitution, morally and physically. (*Aside*) Good gracious ! I forgot that her husband was a brewer.

LADY SKIMPER. Come, now, Mr. Darracott, I am sure that a man of your large mind must rejoice in the happiness of others.

(*Laughter outside*). I think those sounds of merriment, though somewhat boisterous, are truly delightful. They suggest so much.

CHUGG. They suggest that a pack of lazy, over-fed ruffians are getting tipsy at my expense, (*Aside*) I begin to think that Lady Skimper is a fool. (*Aloud*) Mrs. Hammick, you'd better go and see what those servants are up to, and bring me the key of the beer-cellar.

TREMAINE. Isn't it rather hard to put a damper on their festivities at such a season ?

CHUGG. Sir, their festivities are damp enough already. If Christmas in the olden time means nothing but beer, I shall take care that in future my Christmases are distinctly modern. Pray pardon me, Lady Skimper, for intruding these sordid details upon your elegant mind ; but a man must be master in his own house ; he must not be domineered over by butlers, nor by lady housekeepers (*looking at* MRS. HAMMICK), who are too fine to attend to their own special groove.

MRS. HAMMICK. I am going, Mr. Darracott. I hope I know my place. [*Exit indignantly.*

CHUGG. I hope you do, madam. I am not going to be trampled upon.

LADY SKIMPER. Old servants are always tyrants. Your Mrs. Hammick seems a very worthy person ; but I think you allow her too many liberties. I never have believed in the lady-help system.

Enter VANDEAN *and* LEONORA *from garden.*

What have you been doing out of doors at such a time of night, Nora ?

LEONORA. Oh, mother, the moon is positively too entrancing. Captain Vandean and I have been as far as the lake to see if the ice would bear.

TREMAINE. And will it ?

LEONORA. Well, it was just thick enough to bear us. We had a most delicious waltz by moonlight. The ice was very shaky. We might have tumbled through at any moment and been drowned together—so deliciously exciting. We shall be able to skate to-morrow.

TREMAINE. Ladies, what do you say to a game at pool? My grandfather's billiard-table is one of the best in Devonshire.

CHUGG. What do you mean by talking about your *grandfather's* billiard-table? What do you suppose *he* can want with a billiard-table in his present condition?

LEONORA. I should like it of all things. Mother, you must come and join us.

LADY SKIMPER. You play pool, of course, Mr. Darracott ?

CHUGG. Occasionally. It's not a bad game for ladies, but there's no real play in it. (*Aside*) I never rose above bagatelle at the George and Dragon till I came into my fortune.

LADY SKIMPER. Then give me your arm to the billiard-room.

Re-enter RICHARD.

CHUGG. Did you ascertain the cause of their hilarity ?

RICHARD. The cause of their hilarity is undoubtedly beer, aided by various drinks of a stronger nature. They have invited the carol-singers to supper, and I am sorry to say there are one or two cases of decided intoxication. Your stud-groom, Pugsley, is the worst of them.

TREMAINE. I really should sack that man if I were you, Darracott. He is a drunken scoundrel, and a disgrace to your establishment.

CHUGG. I will not be dictated to. If I choose to fill my house with drunken scoundrels, that is nobody's business but my own. Come along, Lady Skimper.

> [*Exeunt* CHUGG *and* LADY SKIMPER, *followed by* SYLVIA, LEONORA, TREMAINE *and* VANDEAN. *As* MARY *is following*, RICHARD *stops her and kisses her.*

RICHARD. This is almost as good as the dark passage at Hazle Farm.

MARY. Ah, Dick, how I wish we were back there! I can't help thinking that there are none of us so happy at the Manor as we were at the Farm.

RICHARD. At least, I know of one who isn't.

> [*Exit with* MARY.

Enter MRS. HAMMICK.

MRS. HAMMICK. I've obeyed orders and secured the key of the beer-cellar ; but it was a most unpleasant thing to do. Digges, the butler, was horribly rude ; and that odious Pugsley was most abusive, and even violent in his language. The carol-singers all sat staring with their mouths wide open, and one of them, Joey Stubbs, the cobbler, said that things were better in the old Squire's time, when there was no make believe liberality. I can't think what has come to Tom

Chugg; for Tom Chugg I shall always call him in my own mind, in spite of all their Darracotts. He used to be so kind-hearted and so liberal, delighting in seeing other people happy; and now he seems to grudge every sixpence he spends. What can an extra cask of ale matter to a man who has thousands a year? after talking of a fine old English gentleman's Christmas, too. And he has so changed to me that I can hardly believe he is the same man who used to be so kind and friendly, and who used to treat me like a sister; except that he was ever so much kinder than the common run of brothers are to their sisters.

Re-enter CHUGG.

CHUGG. I call that a humbugging game. I wasn't going to stay to be laughed at by a parcel of young people, and to lose my lives and my sixpences for the amusement of pert minxes. I repeat, pert minxes. Why, I miscued, got fluked, and then Tremaine had the impertinence to say I had played on the wrong ball, and asked if I'd star. As for Lady Skimper, I'm afraid she is a gambler. I saw a fire in her eye which denoted the gamester. (*Seeing* MRS. HAMMICK.) Ah, here's my lady housekeeper, with her handkerchief to her eyes. What's the matter, Mrs. Hammick? You ve been crying.

MRS. HAMMICK. No, I have not, Mr. Darracott. There is the key of your beer-cellar (*offering him an enormous key*).

CHUGG. Thank you. You don't expect me to put it in my waistcoat-pocket, do you? You don't consider that a nice little appendage for a man's watch-chain?

MRS. HAMMICK. You told me to fetch that key, Mr. Darracott.

CHUGG. I did, Mrs. Hammick; because I did not wish my ancestral halls to become the scene of unseemly rioting. I heard the revel degenerating into an orgy, and I knew that beer was at the bottom of it. Now you have secured the key you'd better keep it; and I should wish you in future to give out the beer daily, for dinner and supper.

MRS. HAMMICK. I shall obey you, Mr. Darracott. But you will place me in an unpleasant position.

CHUGG. Why, you used to give out the beer at Hazle Farm. I've seen you do it, many a time.

MRS. HAMMICK. Yes, Mr. Darracott, I know that in those happy days I used to give out the beer; but I must venture to remind you that a style of housekeeping which was suitable to the Farm would be considered unworthy of the Manor.

CHUGG. I understand. I am to be fleeced by everybody. Brewers are to batten on me, butchers are to devour my substance, grocers are to overcharge me, my servants are to wallow in expensive luxuries. I am to contribute to every charity in the kingdom, to be the mainstay of horticultural societies, the chief support of every fancy fair, the backbone of the hunt. Every pauper in the parish is to come to me for food and raiment ; every village brat is to be educated at my expense ; because, forsooth, I am the richest man in the neighbourhood. At this rate I should very soon be the poorest. What is the woman whimpering for?

MRS. HAMMICK. I—I can't help it, Mr. Darracott. You are so changed, everything is so changed. When I remember the happy days at Hazle Farm!

CHUGG. They were not happy days! How dare you say that they were happy days? How dare you insult me by suggesting that I was happier when I was Tom Chugg than I am now?

MRS. HAMMICK. I don't know about *your* feelings, I can't presume to enter into them ; but I know that in those days you used to make those around you happy, while now——

CHUGG. I don't? You have the cool impertinence to tell me that I am not a source of happiness to my family and dependents. I provide them with every luxury, I feed them on the produce of a French cook, I clothe them in silk attire : and you have the base ingratitude to tell me, with that gown on your back, that I don't make you happy. Woman, you are a viper !

MRS. HAMMICK. Mr. Darracott !

CHUGG. I repeat it : you are a viper ! You turn and sting the hand that has warmed and fed you.

MRS. HAMMICK. Very well, Mr. Darracott. After this there is only one course open to me. You have been very good to me in the past, and I hope I shall never forget all I owe you; but after what you have just said, I could not stay another hour under your roof. There is the key of the beer cellar.

CHUGG. D——n the key of the beer-cellar. I will not be pestered by that key.

MRS. HAMMICK. I beg your pardon, Mr. Darracott. (*Laying key on table.*) I forgot your objection to it. Good-night, sir, and good-bye.

CHUGG (*running after her, as she is going out.*) I will not be abandoned in this ruthless manner. I will not be called, sir. Mrs. Hammick, what do you mean by this conduct?

(*Exit* MRS. HAMMICK) Mrs. H——, Mrs. Hammick—Betsy !
She didn't hear me call her Betsy.   She must have melted at
that old familiar name.   I hate to see a woman cry.   I hate
it most of all when I think I've made her cry. But they can all
turn on the waterworks. (*Rings bell.*) Here, John, William !
Where is that pair of powdered blockheads of mine ? Bring
some brandy and soda.   The liqueur stand, sirrah, d'ye hear ?
Do you want to keep all the drinking to yourselves in the
servants' hall ?

> [*Footmen bring spirit stand, glasses, syphons, &c.,
> and arrange them on table at side of stage.* CHUGG
> *helps himself freely.*

Re-enter LADY SKIMPER, MARY, LEANORA, SYLVIA, RICHARD,
TREMAINE, *and* CAPTAIN VANDEAN.

MARY. Father, we are going to have a waltz in the drawing-room.   You don't mind, do you ?   Sylvia and I can take
it in turns to play.   Come, Richard, Tremaine, Captain Vandean, you must all help to move the furniture while the
servants are having their fun in the servants' hall.

VANDEAN. Oh, but upon my soul, you know—Poole doesn't
make a dress coat to stand that kind of navigator's work.   I
should have my sleeves out of the shoulder if I lifted a table.
Can't those flunkies do it ?

RICHARD.   My coat was made by a country tailor.   (*Aside
to* MARY).   I'd move an upholsterer's van for the sake of a
waltz with you.

MARY. Tremaine, will you bring one of the lamps ? and you
another, please, Captain Vandean. Don't spill the oil. Come,
Mrs. Hammick, dear, you must be everybody's chaperon.

> [TREMAINE *and* VANDEAN *each take a lamp, leaving
> only the shaded lamp on a table near front of
> stage.   The background is lighted by the red glow
> of the wood fire.   They all exeunt to the drawing-
> room, except* LADY SKIMPER, *who seats herself on
> the central ottoman, and uses her fan with an
> exhausted air.*

LADY SKIMPER. Giddy, thoughtless creatures ! flitting like
the butterfly from flower to flower—from one pleasure to
another.   Why did you desert us so soon, Mr. Darracott ?

CHUGG. Lady Skimper, I felt that my position was rapidly
becoming ignominious, and I have too proud a spirit to

brook ignominy. If I'm not winning at a game, I cut it. I hope fortune favoured you.

LADY SKIMPER. The fickle goddess was not unkind; I won a pool or two: but I only went on with the game to please those young people. Conversation with a congenial spirit would have been much more interesting to me. I want you to tell me all about this delicious old house, and above all, about the ghost. This old hall, in the red light of that log fire, is the very room in which to talk about ghosts. This dear old house is just the kind of place to be haunted.

CHUGG. Would you like it any better if it were?

LADY SKIMPER. Indeed, I should. I adore ghosts.

CHUGG. Did you ever see one?

LADY SKIMPER. Never. It is the one regret of my existence that I have never been so fortunate.

CHUGG. And if you were to see a ghost you wouldn't run away, as most people do?

LADY SKIMPER. Run away! No, I would interrogate that messenger from the spirit world. I would entreat that dweller in the shadow-land to let me hear his thrilling voice. But I am sure, from your questions, that there is a ghost. The old Squire walks.

CHUGG (*puzzled*). He walks?

LADY SKIMPER. Yes, He has been seen at midnight in a dark corridor, like Hamlet's father, in his habit as he lived. What did he usually wear, by the bye?

CHUGG. Hamlet's father?

LADY SKIMPER. No, the old Squire.

CHUGG. Oh, I'm sorry to say he was a desperate old sloven. He was very fond of hunting, and he liked his hunting clothes better than any other. I used to think he slept in them. His favourite costume was an old red coat, buckskin breeches, and mahogany tops.

LADY SKIMPER. Eccentric old darling! And he has been seen in that picturesque attire?

CHUGG. He was seldom seen out of it during the hunting season.

LADY SKIMPER. But I mean since his death. He has walked! The servants have seen him, after dark?

CHUGG. Not that I know of. (*Aside*) How she harps upon the supernatural! (*Aloud*) My dear Lady Skimper, let us leave this theme for a more congenial topic. I'm glad you like my house; but, Lady Skimper, the most perfect establishment is wanting in its proudest ornament when it lacks

the charming presence of woman—lovely woman. (*Aside*)
I'm not so eloquent as a lover ought to be. Perhaps a
thimbleful of Hennessy might inspire me (*helps himself again
to brandy*).

LADY SKIMPER. That charm is not deficient in this fine old
mansion. You have your daughter.

CHUGG. My daughter is a mere chit, and she would abandon
me to-morrow for a husband. May I offer you a thimbleful of Hennessy, Lady Skimper?

LADY SKIMPER. Hennessy?

CHUGG. Cognac.

LADY SKIMPER. Mr. Darracott, do you suppose that
brandy is ever tasted by women in society?

CHUGG. Not in society perhaps—but I've heard they sometimes take a little on the quiet. You won't? Innocent as
my daughter appears, Lady Skimper, she has a husband in
her eye already.

LADY SKIMPER. And you have your estimable housekeeper.

CHUGG. Estimable undoubtedly—in her place. But that
which this ancestral mansion requires is an aristocratic mistress, a patrician mind, a woman who could take the lead in
county society, and who could assist her husband to climb to
the highest rung of the social ladder. I feel that it is in
me to climb, but I want a helping hand—I want a fellow-
climber. Lady Skimper, will you be that fellow-climber?

LADY SKIMPER. Mr. Darracott, is this a declaration?

CHUGG. It is.

LADY SKIMPER. Mr. Darracott, you have moved me more
deeply than words can describe. There is a fervour in your
language, rare among the hollow-hearted throng. But—I
am no longer in the bloom of youth—I have ties, responsibilities. I married in the nursery, and the consequence of
that girlish folly is that at—(*calculates and counts on her fingers*)
—at five-and-thirty I find myself confronted with a grown-
up daughter. If—if I were to be tempted to marry again,
my daughter must share my new home.

CHUGG. She shall.

LADY SKIMPER. And for her sake, in order to make her future
prosperity secure, I could not marry without a settlement.

CHUGG. You should have a settlement, a liberal one! Every
penny of your own fortune should be settled on yourself. I
wouldn't sponge upon a wife's means for worlds.

LADY SKIMPER. You are all generosity. But I alluded to
the income, the six or seven hundred a year of pin-money,

which a man of your position would naturally settle on a wife.   But that is a question for our family lawyers ; let us not enter upon such sordid details.

Chugg. (*Aside*) Six or seven hundred a year ! She puts herself at a tidy figure.   Then, dearest, I may dare to hope that I am not indifferent to you ?

Lady Skimper (*girlishly*). Mr. Darracott, it is like a dream. I can hardly believe that it can all be real, after so short an acquaintance.

Chugg. Call it not by so cold a name ; call it friendship— call it love.   Sweet one, say thou wilt be mine.

> [*Waltz tune sounds now and again from drawing-room.*

Lady Skimper. You know so little of me.

Chugg. I know that you are the finest woman I ever met ; that you will grace my dinner-table and ornament my home ; that, with you by my side, I can boldly enter the proudest society in my native county.   You shall retain your title— "Mr. Darracott and Lady Skimper." How do you think that sounds as an announcement ?

Lady Skimper. Poor Sir Paul !

Chugg.   Brood not upon the past, beloved one.   The future smiles before thee.   See (*extending his arm in a romantic attitude, and pointing towards back of stage*), behold, how fair a prospect awaits thee !

> [Pugsley *appears at back of stage in an old hunting-coat, hat on one side, buckskins and tops, whip in hand.   The clock strikes twelve.   Pianissimo waltz music from adjoining room.*

Lady Skimper. The old Squire's ghost !   (*Rushes out shrieking.*)

Chugg (*frightened, recoiling from figure and slowly backing towards door*).   I never have believed in ghosts, but this looks like one.

Pugsley (*coming forward, tipsy*). Stop, Tom Chugg—stop, I say ! It's no ghost, but flesh and blood. And flesh and blood that wants to have a word of a sort with you.

Chugg. Fellow, avaunt ! What do you mean by frightening an aristocratic female out of her wits ? How dare you dress yourself up in that ridiculous costume ?

Pugsley. Why shouldn't I ? The togs are my own property. The old Squire always used to give me his cast-off clothes.   Haven't I a right to wear 'em, Tom Chugg ?

CHUGG. How dare you call me Tom Chugg?

PUGSLEY. Why shouldn't I? Will you be kind enough to explain why I shouldn't?

CHUGG. For two very good reasons—first and foremost, because my name is not Chugg; and secondly because I'm your master.

PUGSLEY (*snapping his fingers in* CHUGG's *face*). That for your reasons! Your name *is* Chugg, and you are not my master. I dismiss myself from your service. I give myself a month's warning, and I claim a month's wages, and a month's keep. Hand over.

CHUGG (*aside*). He must be the rightful heir. Nobody else could dare to be so insolent. What shall I do? Shall I defy or conciliate him? I'll defy him first, and conciliate him afterwards. (*Aloud*) Fellow, I refuse to pay wages which you have not earned, and I dismiss you on the spot for drunkenness. You are intoxicated, sir! Leave my house!

PUGSLEY. Your house? I like that! Your house? It's as much my house as it is yours. I've as much right to be here as you have, and I mean to stay here. I repudiate your st i on as my master. I scorn your wages.

CHUGG (*aside*). Defiance won't answer. I must try conciliation. (*Aloud*) Pugsley, my good fellow, you have been drinking! Don't be angry. I do not make the remark offensively. At this festive season it is rather meritorious in a man to be drunk. It bespeaks the open heart, the genial nature, the social soul. But you are not in a state to take a calm view of our relative positions. Grant that you are the victim of a youthful error on the part of our deceased friend. Grant that, as a man of honour, the old Squire ought to have married your mother. But he didn't, you see, my poor friend. He did not.

PUGSLEY. What are you talking about? Drunk, indeed! Why, it's you that are drunk—roaring drunk. (*Taking out paper and flourishing it over his head*) Look at this.

CHUGG (*aghast*). Your mother's marriage certificate!

PUGSLEY. My mother be blowed. I never had a mother—at least, not to know of. Do you see this document?

CHUGG (*aside*). He denies his claim, and I may snap my fingers at him.

PUGSLEY. Tom Chugg, do you see this paper?

CHUGG. Get out of my house, fellow! I discharge you.

PUGSLEY. Do you mean that?

CHUGG. Most distinctly.

Pugsley. Then good-night, Tom Chugg. To-morrow Tremaine Darracott will be in possession of the old Squire's last will and testament—a will made six months after that under which you inherit—and on the following day you'll get notice of ejectment.

Chugg. What do you mean?

Pugsley. Exactly what I say. A fortnight before the old Squire died he began to relent towards his grandson, young Tremaine. He called me into his room one evening. I was his oldest servant, rode his second horse out hunting, and he was more familiar with me than with any of 'em. "Jim," he says, "I don't feel comfortable in my mind about my grandson. I'm going to make a fresh will. Lawyer Brooke is up in London, but I know pretty near as much law as he does, and I know how to make a will. You and Dolly Stokes, the dairymaid, can witness it for me, and don't you say nothing to nobody." Well, he wrote out his will, sure enough, on this sheet of foolscap, leaving everything to his grandson, Tremaine Darracott; and me and Dolly wrote our names at the bottom as witnesses, each in the presence of the other, all reg'lar. And then he put the paper away in a drawer of his old mahogany bureau. I see where he put it, and when he was seized with a fit a week afterwards I got hold of his keys and took out that paper. Mr. Tremaine broke his hunting-whip over me a year ago, and I meant to make that broken whip cost him the old Squire's fortune. Nobody knows of the will, except me and Dolly. Dolly went to America with her father while the old Squire was lying ill; so *she* is out of it.

Chugg. James Pugsley, give me that paper. You must be perfectly aware that at the time the old Squire penned that document he was a raving lunatic.

Pugsley. No, he warn't. He was what the lawyers call of sound disposing mind. He was as right as a trivet. As for this sheet of foolscap, it's either an instrument of retribution to bring down ruin upon your head, or it's a bit of waste paper for you to light your cigar with. If you want it for waste paper you can have it; but the price of the article is ten thousand pounds. (*Folds up paper, puts it in his breast-pocket, buttons coat, and stalks out.*)

Re-enter Omnes, except Lady Skimper.

Mary. Father, we all want you to join in "Sir Roger de Coverley."

Chugg. No, my love, no. I don't feel in a dancing humour.

MARY (*looking at him*). Why, father, how pale you are ! You look as if you'd seen a ghost.

CHUGG. That's it, my dear. It was a kind of a ghost. But no matter ! Sir Roger de Coverley, did you say ? Yes, by all means. Where's Lady Skimper ? If she won't be my partner, perhaps you will, Miss Skimper. Youth and beauty, mirth and jollity. Come along, come along. (CHUGG *dances off with hysterical mirth, followed by the others, to the air of Sir Roger de Coverley.*

END OF ACT II.

ACT III.

MORNING.—SCENE *same as in* ACT II.—MARY *is seated at needlework beside the fire,* RICHARD *standing near.*

RICHARD. Your father does not seem particularly cheerful, Mary, in spite of his matrimonial engagement. Do you think he begins to repent already ?

MARY. I don't know. There is something wrong, evidently. Poor papa has changed very much since Christmas Eve. If I were to tell you a secret, Dick, do you think you could keep it ?

RICHARD. I am not a woman, so perhaps I could manage— with a struggle.

MARY. Don't be absurd, sir. Men are even fonder of hearing themselves talk than women are, and it is people's love of talking which makes it difficult to keep a secret. However, I suppose when you and I are married I shall be bound to tell you everything.

RICHARD. Of course you will, so you'd better begin at once, and get your hand in. What is this tremendous secret ?

MARY (*mysteriously*). The old Squire walks.

RICHARD. What ?

MARY. At midnight on Christmas Eve he appeared to papa and Lady Skimper. They were sitting on that ottoman, when exactly as the clock struck twelve they looked up and saw the old Squire standing facing them in the firelight —in his hunting clothes—just as he looked when he was alive.

RICHARD. My dear Mary, who put this absurd nonsense into your head ?

MARY. It was Lady Skimper herself who told me. I am not sure that it is nonsense. You know how frightened poor father seemed when we all came in here to ask him to dance.

I remember telling him that he looked as if he had seen a ghost. I little thought that he had.

RICHARD You surely don't believe this absurd story ?

MARY. There must be something in it. Lady Skimper was frightened out of her wits. She described the old Squire's appearance exactly as I remember him. If it had been only fancy on her part, how could she, a stranger here, know what old Mr. Darracott was like ?

RICHARD. Has your father said anything about this apparition ?

MARY. Not a word. But any one can see that he has something on his mind. He is sometimes boisterously cheerful, at other times sunk in gloom. It makes me unhappy to see him.

RICHARD. I dare say this is the pleasing device of some practical joker. If I can find out who the gentleman is, I'll —I'll give him a sickener of all such jokes.

Enter LADY SKIMPER.

LADY SKIMPER. Good morning, Mary ; good morning, Mr. Avery. Snow again—no hunting ; and no chance of visitors with the roads in their present state. I really begin to realise in some degree what Noah and his amiable family must have felt during the Deluge. Ah, Mary, what a happiness to be staying with congenial spirits at such a time ! What has become of my Nora ?

MARY. Nora, Sylvia, Tremaine, and Captain Vandean are all on the lake.

LADY SKIMPER. Skimming, swallow-like, across the ice. And your dear father ?

MARY. He is about the grounds—or the stables, I believe.

LADY SKIMPER. Active creature ! Mr. Tremaine is to leave us to-day, is he not ?

RICHARD. Yes. He talked of going this morning, but he allowed himself to be persuaded to join the skaters and defer his departure till the evening mail.

LADY SKIMPER. No newspapers yet, I suppose ?

MARY. No. The post is due at one o'clock ; but I suppose in this weather we must think ourselves lucky if we get our letters and papers at afternoon tea.

LADY SKIMPER (*seated at small table, yawns, takes up evening paper*). It is really dreadful to find oneself reduced to reading yesterday's news over again.

MARY. Do you never read books?

LADY SKIMPER. No, my love. I never waste my intellect upon bygone interests. A woman who wishes to please in the best society should be posted in the facts of the present, should have original ideas about the future, and should leave history and belles-lettres to bookworms and blue-stockings.

MARY. I detest newspapers.

LADY SKIMPER. You are young, my dear, very young.

Enter CHUGG *from garden. He has an absent, abstracted air. He tries to be cheerful, but is evidently full of anxiety.*

CHUGG. Good morning, Penelope. Why is my sun so slow to appear above the wintry horizon? The breakfast-table was desolate without your smile, beloved one.

LADY SKIMPER. I had a slight headache, and these frosty mornings are so uninviting.

CHUGG (*reproachfully*). Uninviting! When thy Thomas pined for thy coming—languished for the sunlight of thy smile. (*To* MARY) I saw Tremaine on the ice just now. I thought he was going by the eleven o'clock express.

MARY. He was, but we all persuaded him to stay.

CHUGG. You did, did you? That was kind.

MARY. I am sure it must be such a pleasure to you to have him here—to see him thoroughly happy in his old home.

CHUGG. Oh, yes, I like to see him make himself at home— almost as if the Manor House belonged to him—as if he were the real owner and as if I were an interloper.

MARY. But, dear father, he doesn't presume in the least.

CHUGG. Doesn't presume—no—no—he doesn't presume as yet. He has not yet begun to presume; but it will come— I shall be trampled upon by-and-by.

MARY. Dear father, you are so needlessly sensitive.

LADY SKIMPER. I can thoroughly sympathise with your father, Mary; and I wonder you are so obtuse as not to understand him better. It must be extremely unpleasant to him to have that young man on the premises—a young man who, no doubt, in his inmost heart, considers himself the rightful heir, and fancies that your father is enjoying wealth which ought to belong to him. Good gracious, Tom, what a convulsive start! Is it lumbago?

CHUGG. No, no—sciatica. The sciatica nerve, which runs from the hip to the heel, a nerve as thick as your wrist, and when that gets a wrench you—well, you remember it.

LADY SKIMPER. I know I shall feel all the more comfortable when Mr. Tremaine has left us. And if I were you, Tom, I should get rid of Miss Scobell. No doubt she's a snake in the grass—a domestic spy, always on the watch for something.

MARY (*indignantly*). I wonder you can talk so, Lady Skimper. Sylvia Scobell is as good as gold and as true as steel ; and even if she were the kind of person you speak of, what have we to fear from a domestic spy ? One would think my father's life were not all fair and above-board.

LADY SKIMPER. I meant nothing of the kind, my dear. But I maintain that it cannot be pleasant to your father to know that his every action is noted and his every word weighed by a young lady who no doubt considers her lover the victim of an unjust will. (CHUGG *starts as before.*) That convulsive movement again, Tom !

CHUGG. Lumbago.

LADY SKIMPER. You said sciatica.

CHUGG. *This* is lumbago. Surely I am entitled to know.

LADY SKIMPER. Your father doesn't seem much inclined for conversation, Mary. Suppose we go and look at the skaters ? Mr. Avery, would it be too much trouble for you to get me my fur cloak which I left in the porch last night ? (RICHARD *brings cloak from porch, and assists* LADY SKIMPER *to put it on.* MARY *puts on a wrap.*) A thousand thanks. We are all going for a constitutional before lunch, Mr. Darracott. (*Aside as they go out.*) Mary, your father's nerves are terribly shaken : he has not yet got over our dreadful experience of Christmas Eve.

CHUGG (*alone*). I feel as if it would be a relief to tear my hair, but I mustn't do it. The head of a family, a justice of the peace, the lord of the manor, cannot be allowed to tear his hair. That is a luxury denied to greatness. What am I to do ? I have been gratified with a perusal of that fatal document—Pugsley holding on to it all the time—and there is no doubt as to its being genuine. Nor is there any doubt that the old Squire was in his right mind when he wrote that paper. Every word is rational and to the purpose. No, there is no escape from the fact that if that will were made known I must become again Tom Chugg, tenant farmer—and a pauper. I—Squire Darracott—I who have revelled in the possession of seven thousand a year, who have been courted and made much of by an impoverished landed gentry—I, the plighted husband of Lady Skimper, to descend from that proud elevation—to come down with a sudden slide from that giddy peak ! No, no, Darracott, thy motto must still be Excelsior ! And yet, how is the situation to be faced ? If I give Pugsley ten thousand pounds for that will and destroy it, am I not a cheat, a robber? am I not a felon, liable to the law's worst ignominy—penal servitude, hard labour on the breezy plains of Dartmoor? The picture is too horrible! I gave Pugsley a hundred pounds on Christmas day to keep him quiet—he has been placidly drunk ever since—and I told him I'd think about the ten thousand. He gave me till to-night for thought; and I have been cudgelling my brains ever since, without getting any nearer a decision. There is Mary, too, poor innocent child! I am bound to make some sacrifice of conscience, if it were only for her sake. Can I ask her to step out of the lap of luxury into the stony path of self-denial? No! I am a father; and a father's devotion to his child must rise superior to abstract morality.

Enter MARY.

MARY. Dear father, I wish you would come and look at the skaters; it is such a gay, pretty scene. The Vicar's family have joined us, and I am going to arrange a kind of picnic-luncheon in the Dutch summer-house. You don't mind, do you?

CHUGG. Mind, my dear? No. Be hospitable, Mary. Let everybody in the parish understand that the Darracotts of the maternal branch have princely souls. Race, my dear, race. Excelsior! Let us be benefactors in our neighbourhood. Are there any little charities you would like to bestow upon the poor?

MARY. Dear father, Richard and I wanted you to give blankets, and coals, and beef on Christmas Eve, but you refused.

CHUGG. Did I? It was absence of mind, Mary—mere absence of mind. To-morrow will be New Year's Day; we'll distribute a dozen waggon-loads of best Wallsend; we'll cut up half a dozen fat bullocks.

MARY. Ah! now you are my own dear, kind-hearted father once again—just what you used to be at the Farm.

CHUGG. Don't mention the Farm, Mary. We were paupers at the Farm—beings unworthy of mention in the county papers, which now chronicle our every movement. I wonder we took the liberty to exist in those humiliating days. Is there any other little kindness which you would like me to bestow upon my fellow-creatures, Mary? I feel in an expansive mood. I feel as if I could embrace the whole human species.

MARY. Dear father, you are so good. If you really wish

to make two people happy, I think you might do so very easily.

CHUGG. How so, Mary?

MARY. Richard has been wishing to speak to you ever so long. He wants me to marry him, early in the New Year. His father will settle the farm upon us—it is Mr. Avery's own freehold, you know—and will go and live at Torquay for his health.

CHUGG.—Oh, old Avery will go and live at Torquay for his health, and my daughter—Miss Chugg Darracott, sole daughter and heiress of the Lord of the Manor—is to sink into a farmer's wife—to milk cows, to feed pigs, to administer peppercorns to dyspeptic chickens. Never, Mary, never. On this point I am adamant—yes, child, adamant.

MARY. Then you are very unkind, father, and I can hardly help calling you unjust. *You* are going to be married—*you* have chosen for yourself.

CHUGG. But what a choice—a choice which the proudest in the realm might point to with a swelling breast. A title, too! Ah, Mary, did you ever expect to see your father the husband of a title? "Mr. Chugg and Lady Skimper." How do you like that style of announcement?

MARY. I don't like anything connected with Lady Skimper—an artificial, selfish, scheming person, who only cares for you because you are rich, and can make her the mistress of Darracott Manor.

CHUGG. Mary, you are an impertinent minx—I repeat, a minx! How dare you insinuate that your father is devoid of personal attractions, that he cannot be loved for his own sake——

MARY. Indeed, father, I do not mean that. I know of one person who loved you truly, and for yourself alone—who loved you long before you were owner of Darracott Manor.

CHUGG. Eh, Mary? Who was that individual?

MARY. I would not betray the secret for the world.

CHUGG. No matter, child. I am Lady Skimper's affianced husband. It were an idle dream to think of another attachment. I am bound, Mary—bound by the sacred ties of honour and loyalty to lovely woman. (*Imitating a servant's announcement*) "Mr. Darracott and Lady Skimper."

MARY. Oh, papa, I hope not. I hope your engagement is not irrevocable. I can't bear to think of your marrying such a meretricious person.

CHUGG. Meretricious is a long word, Mary. It ought to mean a good deal.

MARY. It means more than I should like to say. I can't think what attraction you can see in a woman whose hair is every bit of it false.

CHUGG. No, Mary, not all false—a plait or two, perhaps, a wandering tress here and there—an artistic touch introduced to give effect to the whole picture; but some of those luxuriant locks must be grown on the premises.

MARY. A woman who paints her face.

CHUGG. Paints! No, Mary, no, she does *not* paint.

MARY. My dear father, have you eyes?

CHUGG. Well, I flatter myself that I have.

MARY. Then surely you must see that Lady Skimper's complexion is a work of art—that those cherry-coloured lips of hers are painted.

CHUGG. No, Mary, not her lips. (*Wiping his own, with a wry face.*) Say not that those lips are painted.

MARY. But I do say it, and I can prove it. Mrs. Hammick saw stains of carmine on her ladyship's dinner-napkin.

CHUGG. Mrs. Hammick is a prying female—a household spy : she shall leave us to-morrow.

MARY. But, dear father——

CHUGG. No remonstrance ! Mrs. Hammick goes.

MARY. Oh, father, how can you be so blind as to throw away the purest gold for the sake of tinsel ?

CHUGG (*repeating announcement*). "Mr. Darracott and Lady Skimper—Lady Skimper and the Lord of the Manor."

MARY. In common justice, as you have made your choice, I must be free to make mine. I cannot live in the same house with Lady Skimper ; so, even at the hazard of being called disobedient and undutiful, the day which sees you married to Sir Paul Skimper's widow will see me the wife of Richard Avery.

CHUGG. Mary, take care that I don't disinherit you. Take care that I don't alter my will. (*At the word "will" he gives a convulsive leap.*)

MARY. Father, what is the matter ?

CHUGG. Neuralgia.

MARY Last time you said lumbago.

CHUGG. This time I say neuralgia—acute neuralgia, a sudden convulsion of the motor muscles, a something approaching tetanus—tetanus, Mary ; perhaps you have never heard of tetanus. Go, girl ; go and disport yourself among those giddy revellers on the ice. Leave me. Abandon me to my own gloomy thoughts.

MARY. Dearest father, I would not leave you for the world if you are in pain, or unhappy.

CHUGG. No, Mary, don't leave me. Don't abandon your poor father. Why should wealth and splendour part us— we who were all the world to each other when your dear mother died. You were a little toddling child at that sad time, Mary ; and you crept up to me, in the midst of my grief, and you put your soft little arms round my neck. "Don't be so sorry, father," you lisped, in your little childish voice ; and though my tears flowed all the faster, Mary, at those words of yours, they were tears that brought comfort somehow to my troubled heart. And now you talk of leaving me.

MARY. Not if you are in trouble of any kind, father ?

CHUGG. In trouble, child ? My whole system is an instrument of torture—a boot, a thumbscrew. Unhappy child, you behold in me the embodiment of an unparalleled despair.

MARY. But, dear father, there must be some reason for these dreadful feelings. Is it true that your nerves received a shock—on Christmas Eve ?

CHUGG (*aside*). Does she know ? Can she suspect ? (*Aloud*) Christmas Eve—who spoke of Christmas Eve ?—the jolliest night in all the jolly year. The night on which I joined in "Sir Roger de Coverley" with my child and my friends.

MARY. But since that night, papa, there has been something wrong with you. You have not been yourself. If it is your engagement to Lady Skimper that is making you unhappy, pray break it off.

CHUGG. That would not be easily done.

MARY. Oh, yes, it would, if you would stoop to a little ruse, a quite harmless deception. Lady Skimper has known you less than a fortnight. It is not possible that she can have a disinterested affection for you. Let us make believe that there was some flaw in the old Squire's will—that a discovery has been made which reduces you to your old position of Thomas Chugg, tenant farmer.

CHUGG (*laughing hysterically*). A brilliant notion, Mary, a splendid joke.

MARY. And you will carry out the idea ?

CHUGG. No, my dear, I think not. The sacred rights of property should not be tampered with. I cannot afford to make sport of my position. It is beneath my dignity as Lord of the Manor. Mary, if by some sudden turn of Fortune's wheel, you and I were to become once again the obscure occupants of Hazle Farm, how would you bear the blow?

MARY. My dear father, I was happier at the Farm than ever I have been at the Manor. Our life here is very fine; but I always feel as if everybody, even our own servants, must be laughing at us. At the Farm we had everything that could make life pleasant. We were not rich, but we had ample means for comfort and content; we had the means of helping those who were poorer than ourselves. We were obliged to be industrious; but the work we had to do suited us, and the days were never too long. Here the hours sometimes hang wearily for want of occupation; and we have so many grand visitors that we can seldom feel at home.

CHUGG. Mary, I am astounded by your low ideas. There is not a drop of the Darracott blood in your veins. You are a Chugg—an unadulterated Chugg. Go and skate, girl, go and skate. [*Exit* MARY.

CHUGG. What humbugs women are! She pretends that she was happier in the days of obscurity. Betsy Hammick pretends that *she* was happier. If those two foolish women could have their own way they'd make me believe that I was happier when I was Farmer Chugg than I am now. But it won't do. Excelsior, Darracott, Excelsior! Does Lady Skimper paint? I'll not believe it! I'll put her in a strong north light the next time I get hold of her, and if that complexion is bismuth — if those lips are rose-madder— I'll——

Enter TREMAINE.

TREMAINE. I am very glad to catch you alone, my dear Darracott, because I've something rather particular to say.

CHUGG (*alarmed*). Eh—what?

TREMAINE. It's about that fellow Pugsley.

CHUGG. You—you have made some discovery?

TREMAINE. Yes, I discovered that scoundrel in the saddle-room this morning helplessly drunk, while one of your finest hunters was given over to the tender mercies of a lad of thirteen, who was riding him round the strawyard in a way which threatened speedy destruction to boy and beast. You really ought not to keep such a man. When I tried to shake some sense into him just now he talked in a most extraordinary way.

CHUGG. Oh, he talked did he?

TREMAINE. He muttered something about a secret—said he had you under his thumb. Take my advice, and sack him.

CHUGG (*with dignity*). 1 thank you, Tremaine. I am always glad to receive advice, even from my juniors. I have for some time intended to dismiss Pugsley; but as the man is an old retainer—a favourite of the Squire's, too—I shall assist him to emigrate. The man would do well in San Francisco. (*Aside.*) He'd drink himself to death in a twelvemonth. I shall give him ten thousand pounds——

TREMAINE. Ten thousand!

CHUGG. Did I say ten thousand? I meant five hundred.

TREMAINE. Very liberal on your part, but hardly deserved. The fellow is such a thorough-paced scoundrel. And now, as I am off by the evening mail, I'll take this opportunity of thanking you for your kind hospitality.

CHUGG. Don't mention it. Come again as often as you like—make yourself at home here.

TREMAINE. You are very good. The next time I come I hope it will be to claim Sylvia. We have decided that we can manage to live upon a very modest income—two hundred and fifty a year to begin with—and we shall trust to industry and good fortune for a gradual improvement of our position. *Festina lente.*

CHUGG. Who is she?

TREMAINE. I mean that we shall not be too eager to get rich. No doubt there are many people who would call such a pittance beggary—you among them, perhaps.

CHUGG. No, my dear boy, no. I am not one of those snobbish persons. I consider two fifty a very snug little income—snug and compact, easily reckoned, no ragged edges to it, no delusive margin. But as Sylvia will marry from my house, I feel bound to give her a dowry. What do you say to twenty thousand pounds?

TREMAINE. My dear sir, you are joking.

CHUGG. I was never more serious. The Squire left a nice little lump of money—thirty thousand pounds—in consols. Consols are now at par, so I can sell without loss. I have a use for ten thousand pounds, the remaining twenty shall be Sylvia's dower.

TREMAINE. My dear Darracott, this generosity overpowers me. I am utterly unable to express my gratitude. I, who thought my grandfather's wealth had corrupted you—I cannot forgive myself for having so little understood your noble nature.

CHUGG. Don't mention it. I always gloried in doing good.

TREMAINE. May I go and tell Sylvia? Dear girl, how rejoiced she will be! [*Exit.*

CHUGG. Now, nobody would suppose that after performing such an action as that a man could feel small—that after giving away such a sum of money a man could feel mean. And yet I do feel both small and mean. What an anomaly is human nature!

Enter MRS. HAMMICK.

MRS. HAMMICK. Mr. Darracott, I am sorry to be troublesome, but in spite of your kind wish that I should retain my situation as housekeeper in your establishment, I am constrained to leave you this day. I am going to pack my boxes.

CHUGG. You have been crying again, Mrs. Hammick. What's the matter?

MRS. HAMMICK. I have been insulted, Mr. Darracott—my feelings have been wounded, my womanly pride outraged by one of your guests.

CHUGG. By which of them, Mrs. Hammick? That guest shall receive notice to quit.

MRS. HAMMICK. Lady Skimper has been most rude to me.

CHUGG. Lady Skimper! That is awkward.

MRS. HAMMICK. She has insinuated that I am a spy—an interloper. She called me fat and vulgar.

CHUGG. A little burst of feminine petulance—meant in mere playfulness, perhaps. Let it not rankle in your memory.

MRS. HAMMICK (*crying*). I shall never forget it. I could not stay in your house another hour with that—— painted female. I hate her.

CHUGG. Betsy, don't be vehement. Lady Skimper is my affianced bride. (*As before.*)—" Mr. Darracott and Lady Skimper."

MRS. HAMMICK. More shame for you both. She doesn't care a straw for you, and you don't care a straw for her. I call such a marriage wicked.

CHUGG. Betsy, you are expressing yourself with a vigour which does not become you.

MRS. HAMMICK. I can't help it, when I see you throwing

yourself away on a brewer's widow, just because she has a twopenny-halfpenny title.

CHUGG. It is not a twopenny-halfpenny title, Mrs. Hammick : many a true-born Briton has given as much as five thousand pounds, indirectly, for such a handle to his name. Lady Skimper—her ladyship—my lady. If she were a countess—nay, even if she were a marchioness, she could be called by no loftier name. And, apart from this proud distinction, she has other claims to my respect, my admiration. She is a woman of the world.

MRS. HAMMICK. Yes, so much so, that if you were not the master of this house she would never dream of marrying you. However, it is no business of mine. You must know your own mind. Good-bye, Mr. Darracott.

CHUGG. Call me Tom. Let us part friends, Betsy. You and I have known each other a good many years.

MRS. HAMMICK. It is just seven years since poor James died and you offered me a home ; and for six and a half years out of those seven your house was a happy home for me.

CHUGG. Well, yes, we contrived to be happy in those days. We had never ascended society's giddy peaks. We were nobodies, but we were—yes, I admit it—we were happy.

MRS. HAMMICK. Do you remember the Harvest Home, and the speech you used to make after supper—you were always such a good speaker—and the comic songs you used to sing ?

CHUGG. I haven't forgotten anything, Betsy, even to the flavour of the bacon and beans.

MRS. HAMMICK. And do you remember our winter evenings round the fire, when Mary and I used to sit at needlework, and you were so cheerful and so talkative ? And do you remember how you and I used to take a hand at cribbage now and then, and how you always used to beat me ?

CHUGG. And our cosy little hot supper, and my tumbler of gin-and-water afterwards. Betsy, I have not tasted gin-and-water since I became a Darracott. Yes, those were happy days.

MRS. HAMMICK. Indeed, they were. But there's no use in dwelling upon the past. Good-bye, Tom.

CHUGG. Good-bye, Betsy. One kiss before we part. (*She shakes her head.*) No, Betsy, don't deny one parting kiss to an old friend. (*He kisses her.*) There was a time, Betsy, when I thought that you and I might be something nearer and dearer than friends. But those days are past. I am the betrothed of another.

Enter LADY SKIMPER.

LADY SKIMPER. Can I believe my eyes ? Mr. Darracott, is this possible ?

CHUGG. Lady Skimper, I was only bidding farewell to an old friend.   Mrs. Hammick is about to leave me.

LADY SKIMPER. I am glad to hear that; for after what I have just beheld, it would not be possible for me to dwell under the same roof with Mrs. Hammick.

MRS. HAMMICK. Don't alarm yourself, madam. I am going.

Enter TREMAINE, RICHARD, MARY, *and* SYLVIA.

CHUGG. Stay, Betsy ; not yet.   I have a few words to say before you depart. (*Aside*) By heavens, I'll do it ! I'll test Lady Skimper's sincerity— I'll discover whether she is as false as her complexion. (*Aside to* MARY) Mary, I am about to put your future stepmother through a terrific ordeal. (*Aloud*) Tremaine Darracott, I have something of vital importance to communicate to you (*Aside*) I can't exist any longer with the sword of what's-his-name dangling over my head. I'll cut the hair. (*Aloud*) Lady Skimper, while you have been watching the skaters a strange discovery has been made—a discovery which will sternly try your metal as a woman and an affianced wife.   Look me in the face, Penelope.   Let me peruse your countenance (*turning her to the light*). (*Aside*) It *is* bismuth.

LADY SKIMPER. Is this madness, Mr. Darracott ?

CHUGG. No, Lady Skimper, it is the voice of reason—it is the voice of conscience.   I am no Darracott.

LADY SKIMPER. No Darracott !

CHUGG. No, Lady Skimper ; that proud name is not mine, or has only become mine by a fluke.   The will under which I inherited this mansion and its surrounding lands is made null and void by the discovery of a later will leaving everything to my young friend Tremaine Darracott, the Squire's grandson, and sole lineal descendant.

TREMAINE. Is this possible ?

MARY (*aside to him*).   It is only a trick to test Lady Skimper's sincerity.

CHUGG. Richard, send for Pugsley.   I want him instantly.

[*Exit* RICHARD, *who returns almost immediately.*

TREMAINE. I don't think you'll find him in a very suitable condition for the society of ladies.

CHUGG. We must risk that. I have business with Pugsley in the presence of you all ; drunk or sober that man must stand forth among you, and answer my interrogations.

Enter PUGSLEY, *intoxicated, but not helpless.*

PUGSLEY. Here I am, Tom Chugg. What do you mean by sending for me in such a plague of a hurry ? Are you going to settle with me ?

CHUGG. I am going to settle—for you.

PUGSLEY. There's rather too large an audience for a transaction of a delicate nature. Don't you think me and you had better square up in private ?

CHUGG. No, Pugsley, I do not. Whatever business has to be transacted between you and me must be done in the broad light of day—before the face of my fellow-man. Pugsley, I'll trouble you for that document for which you wanted to extort from me the modest price of ten thousand pounds.

PUGSLEY. What document ? You're a lunatic.

CHUGG. No, I'm not. I'm much nearer my right senses than I was a week ago, when I was half disposed to stifle the voice of conscience and to become your accomplice in a felony. Tremaine, that man has either about his person or somewhere on these premises, the last will and testament of old Squire Darracott, executed within a fortnight of his death. There ! The murder is out ! I've made myself a pauper, but I never felt happier in my life.

TREMAINE (*aside to* CHUGG). I understand it all—a trick to test the widow.

CHUGG. No, Tremaine, it is no trick. *You* are the rightful heir. I am an impostor : but I've only known the truth since Christmas eve. I've tried to be a rascal, Mary, but it wasn't in me. The character didn't fit. Tremaine, my generosity just now was all bosh. The estate is yours—yours, my boy—never was mine for an hour. That villain yonder (*pointing to* PUGSLEY) stole your grandfather's last will—a will made months later than that under which I inherited. Lady Skimper, you accepted the addresses of T. Chugg Darracott, Esq., J.P., Lord of the Manor, Custos Rotulorum, &c., &c. Will you allow plain Tom Chugg, tenant farmer, to stand in his shoes ?

LADY SKIMPER. My dear Mr.—Chugg, my feelings are unchanged, but I am no longer in the bloom of youth. I have a daughter. By the by, where is my daughter ? She left the ice two hours ago with Captain Vandean.

TREMAINE. And they were seen to leave the village by the Exeter express just half an hour afterwards.

Enter SERVANT.

SERVANT. A telegram for Lady Skimper. Eighteenpence to pay the messenger.

LADY SKIMPER (*snatching telegram*). Some one kindly settle, my purse is upstairs. (*Reads*) "From Leonora Vandean, Queen's Hotel, Exeter, to Lady Skimper. Have just married Captain Vandean before the Registrar. Kindly forward luggage." This *is* a blow. Mr. Chugg, I regret your reverse of fortune, but what are your feelings compared with those of a mother? I must leave by the Exeter express. Please let some of your people get me a carriage. [*Exit* LADY SKIMPER.

TREMAINE. Mr. Pugsley, you will be good enough to give up a document of which you are feloniously possessed, or it will be my painful duty to introduce a police-constable into this peaceful abode.

PUGSLEY (*unbuttoning his coat and taking out the will*). Tom Chugg, you're a lunatic! Tom Chugg, you're an idiot! I made you a gentleman, but you hadn't the pluck to keep the position. Yah, I'm ashamed of you! I'll emigrate, and forget that I ever knew such a mean cur.

CHUGG. Stop! What has become of the hundred pounds I gave you on Christmas morning in hard cash—eight ten-pound notes and twenty sovereigns out of my cash box. You can't have spent it *all* on beer.

PUGSLEY. No; I spent some of it on brandy.

TREMAINE. A hundred pounds, had he? Then by heaven he shall disgorge! Not a sixpence of Darracott money shall go to enrich such a thorough-paced scoundrel. Come, sir; you've got the cash about you, I'll swear. Turn out your pockets—turn them out, I say, unless you want me to break another hunting whip over your bones.

[PUGSLEY *reluctantly turns out his pockets and disgorges cash —some in necktie, some in boots, and some in hat lining.*

TREMAINE. Is that all?

PUGSLEY. Yes—all, except three pun' seventeen and six, as I spent at the publics. You've got it all, Muster Tremaine. You was always a mark on me from a boy.

TREMAINE. Because I always knew you were a scoundrel. And now, Mr. Pugsley, you'd better emigrate at your earliest convenience, or you may find yourself provided with airy lodgings on Dartmoor. (*Looks at will.*) Yes, this is a holograph will duly executed, leaving the Squire's whole estate, real and personal, to his grandson Tremaine. Mr. Chugg, I am very sorry for you. This document deprives you of everything.

CHUGG. I am perfectly aware of the fact. Society is no more my glittering bride. I am no longer Lord of the Manor, Justice of the Peace, Custos Rotulorum : but I am an honest man. I can bear the shock.

MARY (*embracing him*). Father, dear father, is it all true, then ?

CHUGG. Stern fact, my dear. I am sorry for you, Mary.

MARY. And I am glad, very glad. I never wanted to be rich ; and now I suppose you won't mind my marrying Dick ?

CHUGG. No, my dear, you have descended to Richard's level—your father is only a tenant farmer.

TREMAINE. Stop a bit, there is a second sheet of foolscap here, a codicil, dated three days later, in which the old Squire bequeaths to his good friend Thomas Chugg all that freehold land, with homestead and all farm buildings belonging thereunto, known as Hazle Farm ; and the codicil is every bit as sound an instrument as the will. Mr. Chugg, I no longer condole with you, I congratulate you. You are owner of some of the best agricultural land in Devonshire, with building frontages which must be a mine of wealth to your descendants.

CHUGG. And you mean to say that Hazle Farm—three hundred and seventy acres of pasture and arable—is my freehold ?

TREMAINE. Every rood, every perch.

CHUGG. This is the reward of honourable dealing. Betsy, I am a free man—Lady Skimper has renounced me. Will you be mine—mine and the proud mistress of Hazle Farm ?

MRS. HAMMICK. Oh, Tom, this is too much happiness. Can it be real ?

CHUGG. I have loved you all along. I made the discovery just now when we were going to part. Tremaine, may you be happy in the halls of your ancestors. Sylvia, God bless you ! As for me, I don't think there is a happier man in Devonshire than plain Tom Chugg. Chugg Darracott was an impostor, but Tom Chugg is true metal ; and as for the wealth which I renounced—why, money without content, money without a clear conscience, is only—DROSS.

Tableau and Curtain.

SIR PHILIP'S WOOING

'WELL, sirrah, what is your news of the house to which I
directed you?' asked Sir Philip Stanmore of his servant, as
that worthy entered the baronet's lodging, flushed and breathless as if with hurried walking. 'Is the lady I saw at the
play last night maid, wife, or widow?'

'She is the lady of a wealthy gentleman from the country,
Sir Philip,' answered the valet, 'Master Humphrey Mardyke.'

'My cousin Mardyke, as I live!' exclaimed the baronet.

'Your cousin, sir?'

'Yes, fellow, a cousin I never met, but whose father I knew
well enough twenty years ago. I have little cause to love
this Humphrey Mardyke, for he inherited a fine old place in
Warwickshire, which, but for his existence, might have come
to me. And so that lovely girl is my cousin Humphrey's
wife! I saw her but a few minutes, when she removed her
mask for coolness; but I swear I am over head and ears in love
with her. Never did I look upon a fairer face. Did you ask
all the questions I bade you?'

'Yes, Sir Philip; I contrived to scrape acquaintance with
Master Mardyke's servant, a country fellow. The house is
only a lodging-house, but the gentleman is rich. They see
few visitors, and have been only six months married.'

'Good; I will call upon my cousin this afternoon.'

In all the libertine court of Charles Stuart there were few
men more deeply dyed in sin than Philip Stanmore. He had
begun life with every advantage, but had wasted his substance
amongst the most profligate men of the day, and now lived
chiefly by his profits at the gaming-table, and by the victimi-
sation of younger men fresh from the provinces, who, in their
ignorance of court and town, regarded the accomplished
baronet as the arbiter of taste and fashion. He had spent a

handsome fortune, and had yet the reputation of the wealth that he had wasted. At thirty-seven years of age he had learned the sharper's wisdom, and contrived to hoodwink his friends and creditors as to the real state of his purse. Sir Philip had never married ; but the time had now come in which he felt the necessity of some happy stroke iu the matrimonial market. He was still an emineutly handsome man, aud on the strength of an occasional epigram and a few graceful love-songs modelled upon the verses of Dorset aud Rochester, and popular among the beauties of the court, he enjoyed the reputation of a very pretty wit and poet. Trading upon these gifts, it must go hard with him if he failed to fascinate some wealthy maid or widow. But in the meantime Sir Philip was so ardent an admirer of beauty as to be won by the first glance of a lovely face, and so firm a believer iu his own powers of conquest that he fancied he had only to secure access to the fair stranger whose charms had attracted his bold roving gaze iu the crowded play-house in order to obtain her good graces. His surprise on finding the name of the lady was very great, and not altogether unpleasant.

'Humphrey Mardyke,' he muttered, as he paced the room to and fro when his servant had left him, 'Humphrey Mardyke, that smooth favourite of fortune, whom my rich uncle chose for his heir for love of a woman who had jilted him to marry the lad's father ! Was there ever such a reason for favouritism ? And so that lovely creature is the wife of my country cousin, —a woman born to adorn a court. I will call upou these newly-found relations without an hour's delay.'

The baronet put on his plumed hat, and then paused to contemplate himself thoughtfully in the glass before leaving his lodgings.

'The crow's-feet begin to show, Phil,' he said to himself ; ' 'tis time thou wert promoted to the holy state of matrimony, couldst thou but find an object worthy so great a sacrifice.'

He strolled slowly down the staircase and out into the street, where he gave many a careless greeting to acquaintauce as he made his way to the neighbourhood of Covent-garden, in which locality his kinsman's lodging was situated.

Master Mardyke was out, the servant told him, but his lady was within, and alone.

Sir Philip was in nowise displeased to avail himself of this opportunity. He bade the man announce his name, and followed so swiftly on the lacquey's heels that Mistress Mardyke had no time to decline his visit.

He introduced himself with a perfect grace that went far to set the lady at her ease. The lovely face that had caught his attention in the playhouse appeared to him still more enchanting in the broad light of day, and the girlish timidity of manner, which testified to the young wife's provincial rearing, seemed to him only to enhance the charm of her youthful beauty. He set to work at once to ingratiate himself into her favour by his lively description of town life and town pleasures, of which she was completely ignorant.

'I cannot get my husband to take any interest in London,' she said. 'He is always sighing for Holmwood and his rural occupations.'

'He is an ardent sportsman, I presume?'

'Yes,' replied the lady with a sigh; 'he hunts from October to April, and in summer-time is occupied wholly with the care of his farms.'

'A dull life for you, madam.'

To this proposition Constance Mardyke was fain to assent; but she hastened to declare that Humphrey was the most indulgent of husbands, and that it ill became her to be discontented.

Master Mardyke came in while his wife was praising him, and on Sir Philip introducing himself as a kinsman, gave that gentleman a hearty welcome to his lodgings.

'It is vastly kind in you to seek us out, cousin, all things considered,' he said. 'I feared my Uncle Antony's will might have set you against me; but I see you are too generous to grudge me the favour which habits and neighbourhood won for me from the old man, while you were following his majesty's fortunes abroad.'

On this they shook hands a second time, and the baronet offered to introduce his kinsman to society which would make London pleasant to him during his sojourn.

' 'Tis but a desert at best, unless one knows the right people,' said Sir Philip. 'You must dine with me at half past twelve, cousin Mardyke—a mere bachelor's dinner; and in the evening we will escort your lady to some pleasure-gardens, where she will see the beauties of the court. She will find their graces but faded and artificial beside her own fresh loveliness,' he added with a low bow.

After some slight hesitation, Humphrey Mardyke accepted his cousin's invitation; and from this time the baronet scarce allowed a day to pass without showing some attention to the country gentleman and his wife. He con-

trived to make himself equally agreeable to both. Before
a month had passed, Humphrey had learned to take pleasure
in all the dissipations of his cousin's profligate existence ;
while Constance had fallen into a fatal habit of making comparisons between her husband's country-bred plainness of
speech and manner, and the subtle charm of Sir Philip Stanmore's discourse, which flattered without seeming to flatter.
She would have recoiled with horror from the idea that this
man was more to her than any acquaintance should be to a
married woman, yet she found the hours between his visits
long and heavy ; and as the time drew near for the return to
Warwickshire, she looked forward with supreme dislike to
the dulness of her country home.

The time came at last, however, when the return journey
could no longer be delayed. The London visit had cost
Humphrey a year's income ; for he had lost considerable
sums to Sir Philip at cards, and had paid heavy scores for
tavern suppers given to that gentleman and his boisterous,
hard-drinking friends. Nor was this the only objection to
London dissipation. Constance Mardyke was beginning to
lose the freshness of her beauty in the feverish atmosphere
of pleasure-gardens and playhouses. Her spirits were fitful,
her nights sleepless, and her manner was altogether changed
from its girlish gaiety to the weary, languid listlessness of a
woman of fashion.

It was in vain that Sir Philip entreated his cousin to remain longer in London. The hunting season was close at
hand, and Humphrey was obstinate.

'You must spend your Christmas at Holmwood, Philip,'
he said, cordially ; but Constance did not second the invitation. She stood a little way apart, yet the baronet saw she
waited anxiously for his reply.

He made the answer a doubtful one. He had so many
invitations for Christmas ; but, if possible, would spend a
few nights at his cousin's house.

'I should like to see Holmwood once more,' he said. 'I
was there when a boy, and well remember the fine old place,
which my father was foolish enough to tell me might be my
own some day. Do not think I envy your ownership,
Humphrey. You make a better squire than I should have
done.'

With this they parted : with much cordiality between the
two men—with a reserve that was almost coldness on the
part of Constance. Her hand trembled faintly as she gave

it to Sir Philip, and the one piercing glance which he shot into her eyes as she raised them timidly to his face told him that his tactics had been successful. He had played his cards with supreme caution, taking care that no word of his should offend the wife's modesty, or give her an excuse for banishing him from her presence. By every assiduous attention he had made his friendship valuable to her, and he trusted to the future to recompense him for the trouble he had taken.

Christmas drew near, after an interval that had seemed long and dreary to Constance Mardyke, fair as was the home to which she and her husband returned when they left London. To Humphrey the autumn months had brought pleasant occupation; and he fancied the simple course of their country life must needs be as agreeable to Constance as it was to himself; especially as she made no complaint of the dulness of her existence, and indeed contrived to assume an air of gaiety in his presence which beguiled him into a complete belief in her happiness. She was no skilled hypocrite, but a secret consciousness of her own sinful folly had taught her artifice. The pain of parting with Philip Stanmore had awakened her to the shameful truth. It was not as a common acquaintance that she had learned to take pleasure in his society. Unconsciously she had allowed his influence to become paramount in her mind, to the utter destruction of her happiness.

As Christmas approached, she was tortured by suspense; now hoping for his coming, now praying that he might not come.

'What good can arise from his visit?' she asked herself; 'the place will seem only drearier when he is gone.'

But however she might argue with herself, the secret feeling of her heart was an ardent desire to see Philip Stanmore again; and when his horse trotted up to the gothic porch of Holmwood House one fine December afternoon, it seemed to her as if dulness and sorrow vanished before the coming of that expected guest.

He came quite alone, unattended by his servant, who knew a little too much of his master's life to be safely trusted in a country house, where his tongue might have been fatally busy to the baronet's detriment.

Sir Philip was not a hunting man, and his mornings were given wholly to the society of his hostess. Humphrey had a perfect confidence in his wife, and knew no thought of jealousy. The baronet was, moreover, ten years his senior, and the simple country gentleman had no idea of the insidious power that lurks in the conversation of an accomplished courtier and diplomatist.

Left thus to their own resources, it was not long before the acquaintance between Sir Philip Stanmore and Constance Mardyke ripened into something more than friendship. Sir Philip knew himself to be beloved, and after a prudential delay ventured to reveal his passion. The avowal came when his victim's entanglement made her too weak even to assume indignation, and she could only implore him to be silent and to leave her.

'It was an evil hour in which we met,' she said. 'You know not how much I owe my husband for his disinterested affection. I was a penniless girl when he chose me for his wife, and from that hour to this have known nothing but the most indulgent kindness at his hands.'

Sir Philip responded to this speech by a lamentation of his own unworthiness, and an expression of his warm regard for Humphrey. He pretended that his avowal had escaped him against his own will, talked of a hopeless love which asked no reward from its object, and promised to offend no more.

'Forget what I have told you,' he said, imploringly. 'Your friendship is more to me than the love of other women. Trust me, Constance, and I will try to prove myself worthy of that friendship.'

Reassured by this declaration, Constance no longer urged the curtailment of Sir Philip's visit ; nor did he again offend her by any allusion to his guilty passion. The days passed rapidly in the dangerous pleasure of his society, while the evenings were rendered profitable to him by games at cards, in which his superior skill generally made him a winner. Humphrey could afford to lose, and lost with a good grace, little knowing how welcome his coin was to the empty pockets of his elegant kinsman. The simple-minded country gentleman had a perfect belief in his cousin's friendship, and gave him his entire confidence upon every subject.

'Yes,' he said once, when Sir Philip had been congratulating him on his good fortune, 'there are few finer estates than Holmwood ; and should anything happen to me in the hunting-field, my widow will be one of the richest women in the county.'

'What, are you so prudent as to have made your will already, cousin ?'

'I made it a month after my marriage. A hunting-man had need be prepared for the worst. In default of a son, my wife will inherit every acre and every sixpence I possess.'

Sir Philip had been artfully leading the conversation to this very point. Much as he admired, nay, after his own fashion, loved Constance Mardyke, it was far from his thoughts to encumber himself with a runaway wife, a penniless woman, whose dishonoured career would be a burden to himself in the future. Very different would be his prospects should some accident remove the owner of Holmwood from his path.

Once assured that the estate was secure to Constance in the event of her husband's death, Sir Philip gave himself up to guilty dreams and guilty wishes ; and if a wish could have killed Humphrey Mardyke, that gentleman would not have had long to live.

With Christmas came other guests to Holmwood : Constance Mardyke's father, a gray-haired country parson, a squire and his wife with a couple of pretty daughters, from their home at some twenty miles distance, and a young man called Basil Hungerford, a bachelor cousin of Humphrey's. To these guests Sir Philip contrived to make himself infinitely agreeable ; and the festival season passed with much mirth and joviality on the part of all except the hostess, whose guilty conscience weighed heavily upon her amidst these simple domestic pleasures. On New Year's-day there was to be a great meet and hunting-breakfast at a Ducal mansion house thirty miles from Holmwood, and Humphrey Mardyke had given his promise to be present at the breakfast as well as in the hunting-field. This would oblige him to leave home on the previous day ; and on hearing this Sir Philip declared his intention to depart at the same time.

'I came here from Lord Scarsdale's,' he said. 'His place is but fifteen miles distant, as you know, and my road will be with yours for ten miles of the way. We can go together, cousin. I promised Scarsdale to return long before this ; but you have made my visit so agreeable, it is hard to tear myself away.'

Sir Philip and his host set out together on the appointed morning, accompanied by Basil Hungerford. Constance came to the porch to bid her husband and guests good-bye. She was looking paler than usual, and strangely careworn, as it seemed to her husband, who looked at her anxiously as he bent down from his saddle to give her his farewell kiss.

'Why, you are as pale as a ghost, mistress,' he said; 'what is amiss?'

She assured him, in hurried accents, that there was nothing amiss; she was only a little tired.

Sir Philip Stanmore was the last to bid her good-bye, and as he did so he contrived to slip a letter secretly into her hand. Had she been inclined to reject the missive, she could not have done so without at once betraying herself and her lover; but she had indeed little inclination to decline this first letter which she had ever received from him. As the horses trotted gaily down the avenue leading to the park gates, she hurried to her room to read the baronet's communication at her leisure.

It was a passionate love-letter, in which the writer dwelt despairingly on the agony of this parting, deploring in eloquent words the fate that severed him from the only woman he had ever truly loved. Weakly, fondly, Constance dwelt upon these passionate words, and her tears fell fast upon the letter before she folded it and hid it in the bosom of her dress. For two days she was to be alone; ample leisure in which to brood upon a missive that seemed to her like a first love-letter. Humphrey had written to her but seldom before their marriage, and his epistles were very poor and schoolboy-like when compared with the composition of the courtly wit and rhymester.

Throughout those two long days of solitude Constance Mardyke was haunted by thoughts of the man who had won her heart from the path of duty. Vainly did she endeavour to banish his image from her mind. He had taken too complete a possession of her soft yielding nature, and happiness in a life-long separation from him seemed impossible to her.

The day appointed for the hunt was wet and stormy, and she roamed listlessly through the empty rooms, listening to the rain beating against the windows, and towards evening trying to distinguish the sound of horses hoofs in the avenue. But night closed in, and her husband did not return. She sat up late waiting for him, but at midnight he had not arrived.

'He will come to-morrow, no doubt,' she said, as she dismissed the servants and retired to her own room. Strange dreams haunted her that night—dreams with which the sound of the falling rain mingled dismally. She fancied that she was walking with her husband through the rain and darkness upon the road by which he must needs return; but although they seemed to walk rapidly, they could make no progress.

One particular turn of the road, with three gaunt poplars growing on one side, and on the other some pollard willows shading a stagnant pool, a spot she remembered well, was always before her in that weary, nightmare-like dream.

She woke in the morning, unrefreshed and low-spirited, to drag through another day. It was growing towards dusk, when she rose with a sense of weariness from her tapestry-frame, and opened the cabinet in which she had hidden Sir Philip's letter. An idle fancy had seized her to read it once more before her husband's return ; and then she might perhaps bring herself to destroy the precious document. She opened the door of the cabinet, took out the letter, and began to re-peruse the lines that were already but too familiar to her. As she read the first words, a faint sound near at hand, like a half-suppressed sigh, startled her. She looked up suddenly, clutching the guilty letter to her breast, and in a mirror opposite the open door she saw the reflection of her husband's face. He was standing on the threshold. She turned, in supreme confusion, to meet him. He stood within the door-way, his countenance, as it seemed to her, gravely reproachful; but before she could utter a word, the familiar figure melted into thin air. She hurried to the landing place outside the door, but there was no living creature there. The thing which she had seen was a shadow. She fell at the foot of the great staircase in a dead swoon, and it was not till an hour after-wards that her maid found her there, with Sir Philip's letter clasped in her hand. Her first thought on recovering con-sciousness was a fear lest this letter should have been seen : but throughout her swoon she had clutched the crumpled paper in the palm of her clasped hand.

' Has my husband come home ? ' she asked.

' No, madam.'

' You are quite sure ? '

' Yes, indeed, madam,' the girl answered, with surprise.

That night passed, and there were no tidings of Humphrey Mardyke, although his groom, who brought home the horse on which his master had hunted, said he had expected to find him at home.

' He left Wetherby before I did,' said the man, ' but I believe he had some notion of breaking the journey at Scars-dale Castle. I heard Sir Philip Stanmore give him the invitation to lie there for a night as they parted company at the cross-roads on Monday last.'

This seemed likely enough, and the prolonged absence of

the master gave no uneasiness to the household at Holmwood,
though Constance could not banish the memory of that pale,
shadowy figure, so like and yet so different from life, which
she had seen in the twilight. To the servants she had not
dared to mention this figure, believing it an emanation of her
own guilty mind, and fearing their ridicule of Ler folly, or
possibly their suspicion of her sin. She waited anxiously for
her husband's return, resolved to welcome him with affection,
and to struggle with all her might against her fatal regard
for Sir Philip. Unhappily, the opportunity to fulfil this
penitent resolve was not to be afforded to her. Next day
passed without any tidings of the absent ; and on the following
evening there came the news of her husband's murder. He
had been found, shot through the heart, lying on the brink
of the stagnant pool, at that very spot which she had seen in
her dream.

The country was up in arms to discover the doer of this
evil deed. Humphrey Mardyke had been as popular as he
was wealthy, and people were eager to see his assassin brought
to justice. Lord Scarsdale was one of the witnesses at the
inquest. He described how his guest had left him at noon,
intending to ride straight home. He had another guest, who
left him at the same hour ; but the roads of the two men lay
in opposite directions, for Sir Philip Stanmore was to ride to
a town twenty miles distant from Scarsdale on the London
road, there to join a coach that plied to and fro the metropolis.

This was all Lord Scarsdale could tell. He had seen the
two gentlemen part company at the lodge-gates, and had
then returned to his house.

The inquest was brief, and threw little light upon the
circumstances under which Humphrey Mardyke had met his
death. His pockets had been emptied of their contents by
hasty hands, for they were found turned inside out. His
horse was discovered loose in a field some distance from the
scene of the murder, and the state of his mud-stained
garments gave evidence to the fact that the fatal shot had
been fired while he was still in the saddle. Who could doubt
that the deed was the work of some highway robber ?
Humphrey Mardyke had not an enemy in the world ; and
what personal motive could prompt so vile an assassination
except the vulgar greed of grain? A large reward was
offered for the apprehension of the murderer ; but days and
weeks went by, and no information was brought to Holmwood, or to the little country town where the inquest had

been held. News was slow to travel in those days, and three weeks elapsed before Constance received a letter of condolence from Sir Philip Stanmore—a letter in which he dwelt with generous warmth upon the merits of the deceased, and delicately forbore from any allusion to his passion for her who was now free to return his affection. Weak and wicked as she had been, Constance Mardyke lamented her husband's untimely fate with genuine grief. The thought of her own guilty preference for another man filled her with self-reproach, and now that it was too late to atone for her error, that error seemed doubly base. She was not, however, suffered to mourn long in her country solitude. Within two months of her husband's death Sir Philip paid another visit to Holmwood, riding over from his friend Lord Scarsdale's as on the previous occasion, in order to give a kind of accidental appearance to his coming.

He had not been many hours at Holmwood before he assumed the speech and bearing of a lover, nor did he fail to win the widowed girl from her penitential grief. In the presence of the observant old butler he was, however, carefully ceremonious. It was too early yet to show his cards, except to the weak girl, of whose heart and mind he had long ago made himself master. A faint flash of triumph brightened his eyes every time he glanced round the noble rooms, or towards the wide expanse of park and wood before the old Tudor windows. The only obstacle to his possession of this place and all its belongings had been removed from his pathway. He knew that he had but to wait a fitting time in which to claim the widow and her fortune, nor did he leave Holmwood until he had made Constance promise two things : first, that she would come shortly to London, where change of air and scene would help to banish the haunting memory of the dead ; and secondly, that she would become Lady Stanmore as soon as a decent period of mourning had elapsed. While talking of her dead husband she had told Sir Philip, somewhat reluctantly, of the strange vision she had seen on the threshold of her bed-chamber. But this apparition he ridiculed as the work of a distempered fancy.

'It is little wonder for you to see ghosts in the solitude of this dull old house,' he said ; and it was upon this that he persuaded her to consent to a sojourn in town.

Once in London, remote from village gossips, he knew that it would be easy for him to hasten the marriage which would make him master of Humphrey's noble estate ; and he had pressing need that this change should take place speedily, as his finances were at the lowest ebb.

His hopes were not disappointed. Constance Mardyke came to London accompanied only by her faithful serving woman. She occupied the lodgings in which she had lived with her husband during the previous year, and being utterly ignorant of all business matters, and without friends in the metropolis, she very soon allowed Sir Philip to assume the management and to obtain the complete control of her affairs. No suspicion of mercenary motives on his side had ever entered her mind; she supposed him to be as wealthy as he was fashionable, a delusion which he took good care to sustain. He thus became, even before his marriage with the widow, absolute master of Humphrey Mardyke's fortune.

Sir Philip was not, however, less eager for the celebration of the marriage, and at the close of the summer Constance consented to become his wife. They started for Holmwood almost immediately after the marriage ceremony, the bride-groom secretly eager to inspect the estate which was now his own. He found it even wider in extent than he had hoped, and was much gratified by the reception he met with among the tenantry, who were fascinated by his easy, affable manners, and somewhat inclined to prefer him to the late lord of the soil, as a more friendly and familiar personage from whom greater favours might be expected.

For some months the novel duties and occupations of his position made life tolerably agreeable to the baronet; but he was a man of restless nature and long habits of dissipation. The time came when he grew weary of Holmwood; weary too of his wife's society, as it seemed to Constance, who kept a close watch on the changes of her husband's countenance. The accomplished courtier, who had been so devoted as a lover, was now often moody and absent-minded, and when his wife questioned him with tender anxiety, was sorely puzzled to account for his gloom.

'Nay, Constance, few men who think at all are without some subject for dark thoughts,' he said impatiently. 'You must not watch me so closely by day and night. The truth of the matter is, Holmwood is too dull a residence for a man who has spent his life in the society of a court. We must live in London if you would see me cheerful. There is a funereal atmosphere in this place, as if it were haunted by the shadows of every master who ever inhabited it in the past.'

'What, Philip, have you seen a ghost?'

'No, Constance, I am too much a man of the world for that; but the dulness of the place gives me bad dreams.'

'Yes, I have heard you cry out in your sleep,' answered his wife thoughtfully.

'Indeed! Have I uttered words that you could distinguish?'

'Not often. Once you spoke of the place where they found my husband. "Under the willows by that black stagnant pool!" you cried. Strange, is it not, that the place should haunt you in your dreams, as it haunted me on the night before the murder?'

Sir Philip's brow darkened in gloomy thought, but he made no reply to his wife's speech. He left her presently to ride alone, and an idle fancy took him to the spot of which she had spoken—the bend in the road where three tall poplars stood out black against the winter sky, and where the pollard willows bent their weird trunks across a shallow stagnant pool. He looked at the place for some minutes, lost in thought, and then turned and galloped home again, as if the foul fiend had been behind him.

From this time he daily became more restless in his habits and more gloomy in his temper. The wealth that he had won for himself could not give him happiness. His wife's beauty had no longer power to charm the fickle mind that had ever sought new conquests; nor was her gentle, yielding nature calculated to maintain ascendency over his fitful soul. He had determined to go to London soon after the beginning of the new year, and if possible to go there alone.

On the anniversary of the night on which the shadow of Humphrey Mardyke had appeared to his wife, it came again, but this time to the new master of Holmwood, who met the ghostly form of his dead rival in the corridor upon which his bedchamber opened. Again it was in the early twilight that the vision appeared, pale, grave, reproachful of aspect, with fixed eyes and solemn motion; and again Sir Philip tried to convince himself, as he had tried to convince Constance, that the figure was but the emanation of a disordered brain. He did not succeed in this attempt, however. Men were prone to superstition in those days; and the baronet was inclined to regard this spectral visit as an omen of his own untimely death.

He was on the point of starting for London next day, after declaring that he would not spend another night in that accursed house, when a couple of messengers came from the nearest town to request his immediate presence there. Something had transpired which promised to throw light upon the circumstances of Humphrey Mardyke's assassination, and the county magistrate wanted the attendance of Sir Philip and Lady Stanmore—the latter to identify some property which was supposed to have belonged to her first husband.

The baronet's face grew ghastly pale as one of the men stated their errand. He was at first inclined to resist the summons on the plea of his journey to London ; but the elder of the two men declared the magistrate's orders to be imperative. They were not to leave Holmwood without Sir Philip ; and Lady Stanmore was to follow immediately, in her coach or on horseback, as might be most convenient to herself.

'It is not a four miles' ride,' said the man, with grim politeness, as Sir Philip and he rode abreast along the avenue. The baronet said nothing. This species of summons was strangely like an arrest ; but any attempt at resistance would have been worse than useless. He saw that both men were fully armed, and that their horses were as good as his own.

Arrived at the town, he was conducted at once to the chief inn, where he found one of the county magistrates, Lord Scarsdale, and some other gentlemen seated in the principal room awaiting his coming.

The magistrate received him with stately politeness ; but his familiar friend, Lord Scarsdale, saluted him coldly, and scarce touched the hand which he offered.

'You were not present at the inquest held on the remains of Mr. Humphrey Mardyke, I believe, Sir Philip Stanmore ?' said the magistrate.

'I was not. I was in London at the time, and did not even know of my friend's unhappy fate. Nor should I have been able to offer any evidence had I been present at the inquest.'

'Indeed ! You were in London at the time. Can you swear to having reached London on the fourth of January in last year ?'

'Certainly, if there is any occasion for my taking an oath on the subject, which I cannot myself apprehend. Lord Scarsdale is aware that I left his house at noon on the third of the mouth, with the avowed intention of riding to Gorsham, on the London road, there to join the mailcoach.'

"And you never saw Mr. Mardyke after bidding him good-bye at Scarsdale gates ?'

'Never. Our ways lay separate from the moment of leaving the gates.'

'And how about your horse, Sir Philip—what became of him when you joined the coach?'

'I left him at the inn at Gorsham, to be brought up to London by a packhorse driver next day.'

'Will you swear that you were not in Haverfield village on the night of the third of January, several hours after the mail coach left Gorsham, and that you did not there exchange a broken-knee'd horse and a gold watch for a sound animal?'

Sir Philip started and grew deadly pale.

"I was never in any place called Haverfield in my life, that I am aware of,' he said, 'nor did I ever make such a bargain as that you speak of.'

"Indeed!' replied the magistrate. 'Then, Lord Scarsdale's groom must be mistaken as to the identity of a horse which was offered for sale here in yesterday's market, and which he swore to be yours—a bay gelding, with a white streak on one side of the face. Did you ever own such a horse, Sir Philip?'

'Nay,' interposed Lord Scarsdale, while the baronet hesitated, 'he cannot deny that the horse was once his. I remember the animal perfectly, and will swear to the watch as Humphrey Mardyke's.'

'The watch?' gasped Sir Philip.

'Yes,' replied the magistrate, producing a massive gold watch. 'On being questioned, the man who offered the horse for sale declared himself to be an innkeeper at Haverfield. He received this watch and a broken-knee'd horse from a traveller who took shelter at his house on the night of the third of January, after having broken his horse's knees in the attempt to jump a fivebarred gate that divided a short cut across fields from the main road. The man exchanged a good horse of his own for the injured animal and this watch, which he was wearing yesterday. His account of the circumstance seemed thoroughly honest, and his voluntary description of the traveller tallies in every respect with your appearance. You will scarcely be surprised, therefore, Sir Philip, that I considered it my duty to order your arrest, under the suspicion of being a party to the death of Lady Stanmore's first husband.'

'The story is a tissue of lies,' cried the baronet, 'a conspiracy.'

'In that case you can have no objection to see the man who offered the horse for sale, and whom we found wearing this watch,' answered the magistrate ; and at a nod from him a respectable-looking countryman was brought into the room.

He swore immediately to the identity of Sir Philip Stanmore with the traveller who had taken shelter at his house, drenched to the skin, and worn out with a cross-country ride on the night of the third of January. His evidence was perfectly clear and straightforward, and no questioning of Sir Philip's could shake his statements. Lady Stanmore had now arrived, and on being shown the watch, at once recognised it as her late husband's property. She had yet to learn the awful inference to be drawn from the manner of its recovery.

'If you are indeed unconcerned in this business, it will be easy for you to prove an alibi, Sir Philip,' said the magistrate ; 'but in the meantime you must consider yourself under arrest, and I shall be compelled to order your removal to the town gaol, there to await your trial at the next assizes.'

Constance uttered a cry of horror on hearing this, and sank, half-fainting, into the chair that had been placed for her. Sir Philip had by this time recovered his usual self-possession. He protested against his arrest as an infamous and preposterous proceeding.

'In all probability this man is himself the assassin,' he said.

'We have the evidence of Lord Scarsdale and his groom as to the identity of the horse, Sir Philip. It is that which justifies your arrest.'

'And I have twenty people at command who will swear that I was at home at Haverfield all through the day of the murder,' said the innkeeper.

Sir Philip Stanmore was removed to the town gaol, after having been compelled to surrender his sword and travelling pistols. He parted tenderly from his wife, who believed him the victim of some fatal error, and who would fain have accompanied him to his prison. This he forbade, and departed between his gaolers in haughty silence, after giving his wife the address of a London lawyer whom she was to summon immediately to his aid. A month would elapse before the assizes, and if the baronet were indeed as innocent as he protested himself to be, there could be no great difficulty in proving the fact of his journey to London. It was impossible for him to have reached London on the fourth, if he had been at Haverfield at the time sworn to by the innkeeper.

He was not destined again to face his accusers. His health,

which had been in a declining state ever since his coming to Holmwood, broke down completely under the misery of his position, and an attack of gaol-fever brought him to a grave at least less shameful than that which would have awaited him as a condemned murderer. On the night before his death he sent for his wife, and to her ears alone confessed his crime. He had turned his horse's head about immediately after leaving Scarsdale gates, had ridden across a common that skirted Humphrey's road home, and had overtaken him by the three poplars, where he shot him through the heart without a moment's parley. He stopped to rifle his victim's pockets, in order that the act might seem that of a highway robber, and had then ridden off across country, reckless which way he went in the great horror and agony that came upon him after the commission of the crime. At Haverfield, finding his horse completely lame, and having very little money, he had been compelled to offer the dead man's watch as a temptation to the landlord, who, seeing the traveller's distress, drove a hard bargain for his own animal.

'It was for your sake I did the deed, Constance,' he said ; and the unhappy woman believed him. 'There was only his life between us. I knew that you loved me, and in the last half-hour before I left Scarsdale, I came to the desperate resolve that resulted in your husband's death. The act was as mad as it was wicked, and I can truly swear that I have never known an hour's peace of mind since it was done.'

He died at daybreak ; and Constance returned broken-hearted to Holmwood, there to lead a life of solitude and repentant sorrow for a few years, at the end of which time she fell into a decline and died, leaving the fine old place to fall into the hands of her first husband's distant relations, who came from a northern shire to take possession of the estate, and who were never troubled in their occupancy by the shadow of Humphrey Mardyke.

DOROTHY'S RIVAL

'I am more and more convinced that none escape being evil spoken of but those who deserve not to escape it.'—*Charles Wesley.*

In the days when the thunder of Whitfield's voice had but newly resounded above the crowd at Moorfields, Mr. William Bolton, a simple country parson of the Established Church, lived very happily with his only daughter, Dorothy, on the outskirts of Hammersley.

The parsonage was a comfortable red-brick house, very square and very uninteresting from a picturesque point of view. It stood a little way back from the high coach road to London, with an orchard on one side, and on the other a common cottage garden, with two long flower-beds and a broad gravel-path, and vegetables growing in the middle distance, and espaliers in the background. All the roads were London roads in those days ; and people lived and died on the London road without ever seeing the metropolis, which figured, glorious and radiant, in their day-dreams : an enchanted city—not actually paved with gold, but altogether marvellous and beautiful.

To Dorothy Bolton the square red house, the orchard, and the garden were very pleasant and dear. What, indeed could be more beautiful than the parlour, with its two prim bookcases, the needlework pictures of a shepherd and shepherdess smirking from their oval frames ; the little room in which her father composed his sermons, with much aid from grim-looking black-leather-bound books, labelled Barrow and Tillotson ; the infallible eight-day clock in the hall, which groaned and rattled in such an awful manner before the striking of an hour, and above the dial of which there was something scientific in the way of a sun and moon that was never quite in working order. All these things to the eyes of Miss Dorothy were beautiful ; nor did she pine for any brighter or gayer existence than that which she enjoyed, or languish for any respite from the many duties of her simple life. She had no higher aspiration than to sit in the parlour wearing out her bright young eyes in the finestitching of her father's shirts, to help her mother at bread-making, or to trudge into Hammersley on a fine morning by the parson's side, to share in his round of visits among the poor folks, or to read that delightful story of 'Sir Charles Grandison' aloud to her father and mother in the long winter evenings. These things were at once her duties and her pleasures. In this peaceful home she had grown from childhood to womanhood, and was so innocent and childlike still, that she thought it was her gipsy-hat and scarlet ribbon that made such a picture of brightness and beauty in the little mirror that reflected her fair young face every Sunday morning while the bells were ringing for church. Yes, Miss Dorothy Bolton—or Mrs. Dorothy, as people were more apt to call a damsel in those days—had grown from a sunburnt, hoydenish girl into a very lovely young woman, without any consciousness of the transformation. The parson and his wife saw that their only child was now, indeed, a comely young person ; but these good people would have cut their tongues out rather than they would have confessed as much to the damsel herself.

'Handsome is who handsome does,' said Dorothy's mother; and the girl felt as if her good looks were in some manner dependent on the neatness of her stitching and the lightness of her last batch of bread.

By-and-by, however, there came to Hammersley Parsonage some one who, although by no means prone to dilate upon Dorothy's personal attractions, permitted the young lady to discover her power to charm. This new-comer was a certain Matthew Wall, a young clergyman, who came to share the burden of the vicar's duty, and who had so far proved himself a very worthy and efficient member of the Church.

Indeed, in sober truth, efficiency and energy were much needed for the cure of souls in Hammersley. The town was large and crowded, the population was rough and disorderly ; and an awakening voice was needed to arouse a people who had long been dead to the spirit and careless as to the letter of the faith.

William Bolton, the vicar, had a simple mind and a kindly nature ; but something more than these are required for the salvation of such a town as Hammersley ; and this something more seemed to have been given to the poor benighted creatures in the person of Matthew Wall.

The vicar preached a very orthodox sermon of the soporific school, and had a heart and hand ever open to the appeal of the poor; but, as his means were small and his judgment very fallible, he effected, with the best intentions, very little real good. He was getting old; and he liked his after-dinner pipe in the orchard in summer, and by the chimney-corner in winter. He liked to take his nap in the long winter evenings, while Dorothy read 'The Life and Surprising Adventures of Robinson Crusoe,' or 'Religious Courtship,' or an odd number of the *Rambler*. He visited his poor from time to time, and he was not unwelcome to them even when he came empty-handed; but it seemed as if his visits did very little good. Hammersley was, in truth, too big a place for this simple pastor, and the people of Hammersley too rugged a race for his mild rule.

Matthew Wall was a very different kind of pastor. Fatigue and discouragement were alike unknown to him. He had the energy of a Whitfield or a Wesley; and, in that day, Whitfields and Wesleys were needed in the Established Church as well as out of it.

William Bolton invited his curate to dinner on Sundays; a dinner served directly after morning service—plain and substantial, after the old English fashion. But Mr. Wall would eat very little between the services; he did better justice to the nine o'clock supper. The vicar, who exhibited a hearty appetite both at dinner and supper, called Matthew a poor trencherman. It is possible that Matthew's chief delight at the parsonage was not to be found in his trencher. He sat by Dorothy at supper, and seemed to derive much satisfaction from her society. He found her sweet-tempered and modest as Pamela, pious as Dorcas; and before he had been six months at Hammersley he made a formal demand for her hand.

The vicar hummed and hawed, and consulted his wife.

'Sure 'twould be but a poor match for the wench,' he said. 'Matt Wall has but his cure of seventy pounds a year, and a few hundreds to come from his father by-and-by. The rogue has good parts, I daresay, and has done good service amongst Hammersley folks with his fiery talk and hunting them out in their dens; which is pushing a parson's trade farther than I should care to push it. I doubt but he's touched with the Wesley and Whitfield madness; and we shall have him deserting the Church some day, as the two Wesleys did—to the shame of family and friends.'

Happily for Matthew Wall, the vicar, after consulting his wife, thought fit to say a few words to his daughter.

The girl reddened and cast down her eyes, and when hard pushed by her father's questions, confessed with tears that she loved Matthew very dearly, and would go to her grave unmarried sooner than she would give her hand to any but him. The vicar was no Squire Western. He expressed his astonishment by a long whistle, and reproved his daughter for a sly puss; after which feeble protest he consented to receive Matthew Wall as his future son-in-law. But there was to be no marriage for three good years to come. Matthew was but five-and-twenty, Dorothy just turned eighteen. The young people pledged themselves very readily. They met on Sundays, walked to and fro together between the parsonage and the church, dined and supped together; and whenever Matthew's business happened to bring him near the garden-gate on week-days, he would step in to say a few words to his Dorothy.

The three years passed very pleasantly. Matthew Wall had become a power in Hammersley before his period of probation was ended. There was some who called him wild and fanatic,—for to be earnest in those luke-warm days seemed a kind of fanaticism; but since, in many instances, the drunken became sober, and the reprobate became decent beneath his sway, folks were fain to admire his earnestness. The bishop of the diocese complimented the young man on the change he had brought about in Hammersley.

'I'm pleased you should show these Methodist folk that 'tis possible to do good without forsaking the Church we have sworn to hold by, sir, and that 'tis as easy to bring the stray sheep back to the true fold as to lure them into a strange one,' said the bishop, at a grand ceremonial dinner of which he deigned to partake on a certain occasion.

Parson Bolton was gratified that his curate and future son-in-law should win this meed of praise from the episcopal lips.

But there's more of the Methody about our Matt than I quite relish, for all that, my wench,' he said to his wife in the confidence of connubial discourse.

It is not given to mortal man—least of all to a religious reformer—to please everyone. There were people in Hammersley who did not like Matthew Wall. His long, earnest, even fervid, discourses displeased a few. He had refused invitations to tea and supper-parties,—solemn and yet boisterous festivities given by the richer tradesfolk of Hammersley—and had thus offended many. There were Wallites and anti-Wallites in Hammersley; and the anti-Wallites were strong. Amongst them the most notable people were a certain Mr. Jorboys, grocer and cheesemonger, his wife and daughters. The Misses Jorboys—Sally and Letty—were accounted beauties. They wore hats and muffs and gowns which their father brought from London when he went thither for colonial produce; and they took it ill of Mr. Wall that he had been so prompt to devote himself to the parson's dowdy daughter, who had never known what it was to powder her hair, or sail along the High Street prim and stately in pannier-hoops.

It was nigh upon Christmas, and there was to be much joviality at the parsonage, for this must be Dorothy's last Christmas at home. A neat little house in Hammersley had been hired by the curate, and comfortably furnished out of funds provided by his father, with certain additions in the way of a dragon-china tea-service, a brass-handled bureau, and liberal store of home-spun linen, provided by Mrs. Bolton, who with her own hands prepared the nest for these young turtle-doves.

'I could have wished my Dorothy had fancied Squire Hever of Hever Farm, who was like to die for her last winter,' the parson's wife said to her gossips; 'but she's been like one bewitched since Matthew courted her. "Sure, would you have me break my faith with a saint, dear madam?" she cried, when I told her how young Hever would have made a lady of her, with her own coach and a black footboy. And I do think the simpleton's right in that,' Mrs. Bolton would add with an air of conviction. 'I've seen young men more mannerly in turning a compliment, and softer spoken; but if there ever was a saint on earth since St. Paul, I think Matthew Wall is one.'

Of late the lady's gossips had been somewhat slow to respond to this observation; and she was not a little vexed on one occasion by the conduct of her particular friend Mrs. Jorboys, who went so far as to shake her head and groan audibly at this point in the conversation.

'I hope you have nothing to say against my daughter's sweetheart, ma'am?' the parson's wife observed with some acidity.

'Oh no, ma'am,' Mrs. Jorboys replied with a sigh more dismal than the last; 'I have nothing to *say* against him.'

There was an unpleasant emphasis on the word *say* that went nigh to freeze Mrs. Bolton's marrow.

'I don't quite take your meaning, ma'am,' she said stiffly. 'Matthew Wall may not be a rich husband for our Dorothy, but he don't need to be groaned over as if he was a beggar.'

'You wasn't talking of beggars, as I know of, ma'am,' Mrs. Jarboys answered with acrimony. 'You was talking of saints.'

'And what then, ma'am?'

'I have my thoughts, ma'am. I should be vastly sorry to hurt your feelings, Mrs. Bolton, but my thoughts are not my own making, and I can't help it if they are of a nature to lead to what you was so civil as to call groaning;' and hereupon Mrs. Jorboys sighed again, while Miss Letty and Miss Sally sighed in chorus. This occurred at a Hammersley tea-party, from which Dorothy chanced to be absent.

The parson's wife went home perplexed and miserable. The next batch of bread was heavy, and by no fault of Dorothy's, though her simple head was a little distraught by thinking of the great change so near at hand. It was the chief bread-maker whose mind was most troubled, whose hand was most uncertain. Those groanings and head-shakings of Mrs. Jorboys haunted the good soul by day and night, and Dorothy could but wonder what made her mother so thoughtful.

'I fear there's something troubles you, ma'am,' the girl said, after the respectful manner of those days.

'Nay, my dear, I have no trouble but the thought of losing thee,' answered the mother; 'and if it's for thy good, I'm content we should part.'

'But it's not parting, dear madam; 'tis but living in separate houses. Do you think there's a week will pass without my paying my duty to you? And I'll come to help with the bread-making, if you'll suffer me.'

This was on Christmas-eve. There was to be fine fun at the parsonage that evening, ending with the compounding of a beverage, made of eggs and spices and ale, that had been so compounded at the same hour on every Christmas-eve since the vicar had kept house. The beverage was always compounded in the parlour, and partaken of with all solemnity out of a great silver tankard that was said to have belonged to Oliver Cromwell. Dorothy vowed that it was but a battered old thing, and she had seen finer, spick-and-span new, at a silversmith's in the High Street.

The curate was to drink tea at the parsonage, and assist, not only in the compounding of the beverage, but in the composition of that much more sacred mixture, the Christmas pudding. To these simple diversions Dorothy looked forward with extreme pleasure. She thought of her betrothed with unmeasured tenderness, with reverence and devotion, amounting almost to fanaticism. She believed in him as a being almost too saintly for earth.

Mrs. Bolton had ample occupation for her hands on this eve of the great Christian festival ; but her mind was not free to devote itself to her labours. The image of Mrs. Jorboys pursued her through all her duties.

'I'm very like to want more raisins and spices for the puddings between this and the New Year,' she said to herself ; 'I'll walk to Hammersley this afternoon, and have it out with Mrs. Jorboys.'

Having once resolved on this course, the matron was more at ease. She set out on her expedition directly after dinner, leaving the vicar smoking his pipe by the chimney-corner, and Dorothy busy with her plain sewing. The girl had offered to accompany her mother, but the offer had been refused. The dame departed in very good spirits, promising to return by tea-time. Dorothy sat sewing while her father smoked and dozed, and dozed and smoked ; and at five o'clock in came the curate, tired with a day's hard work, but cheered by his Dorothy's welcome, and well pleased to find himself seated by her side.

'I've come all the way from Liscott Common,' he said, as he seated himself in the old-fashioned arm-chair which Dorothy had set ready to receive him ; 'and it's a long trudge.'

It was five o'clock, and Dorothy had brewed the tea, which was an infusion to be partaken of with a certain ceremony in those days as an expensive luxury implying refined taste and much gentility on the part of the consumer. Parson Bolton took no tea—but the curate liked all that Dorothy liked.

The pretty little china teacups—fragile things, without handles, like a child's toy cups and saucers—and the quaint little teapot were set out on the polished mahogany board, but there were no signs of Mrs. Bolton's return. So the lovers sat talking together in undertones while the father dozed, for one brief happy hour ; and then, after the usually preliminary groaning, the infallible eight-day clock struck six.

'I should be quite frightened about mother,' said Dorothy, 'if I didn't know that Jorboys' man is to come home behind her with the parcels.'

She had scarcely spoken when the door was opened, and shut again with a slamming noise, and Mrs. Bolton stalked into the room.

The matron's cheeks were crimson, and the matron's eyes flashed fire. Never before had Dorothy seen such a look in her mother's face.

'You're late home, madam,' she said, trembling, she scarce knew why, unless it were because of the strange look in her mother's face.

'Thanks be to God that I'm not too late,' the parson's wife answered solemnly.

The unfamiliar tone of her voice startled her husband from his comfortable doze, and he looked up alarmed, crying, 'What, what?' like his revered sovereign King George in after-days.

'Sit down, and drink thy tea, mistress,' said the good-natured parson, as his wife stood tugging at the string of her cloak, hindered by Dorothy, who made believe to assist with trembling fingers.

'Never, while that bad man is under this roof,' answered the dame, pointing to Matthew Wall, who had risen to receive her.

'Bad man!' cried the parson; 'art thou dreaming, wife? There's no one here but Matthew Wall, thy son-in-law that is to be.'

'My son-in-law that never shall be; I would see my daughter in her winding-sheet first.'

'Why, what maggot has bitten thee, wife?'

'May I ask the meaning of this strange talk, madam?' asked the curate, with that awful calmness peculiar to a proud man who feels himself outraged.

'Thou mayst ask, and shalt be told too, as plain as I can speak before this simple tender soul that loves thee,' answered the matron. 'I wonder thou art not ashamed to come to an honest man's house and steal his daughter's heart—you, that play saint on Sundays, and sinner on Mondays, and hypocrite all the week round.'

'Mother!' cried the girl—indignation, astonishment, anguish, reproach, all expressed in that piteous cry.

'I must ask for the second time what you are pleased to mean, madam?' said Matthew Wall with unshaken calmness.

‘I’ll answer that question with another, sir,’ returned the matron. ‘Will you be so good as to tell me here—before my husband and daughter—whether you know Liscott Common?’

There was nothing very awful in the question itself, but Mrs. Bolton’s tone made it awful, and it went like a pistol-shot through Dorothy’s heart, as she remembered how her lover had talked of his walk from Liscott Common that very afternoon.

‘Yes, Mrs. Bolton, I know Liscott Common.’

‘So, sir, you don’t deny your wickedness?’ cried the dame; ‘but perhaps you will deny your knowledge of Jane Gurd’s cottage, on the other side of the common, where you’ve been seen to go twice, three times, four times a week for this last six months; and where you’ve been known to stay two hours at a spell, times and often—you, that complain of wanting leisure for good works! You could find leisure for bad works, and to spare, I reckon. What, you start and change colour at last, my fine master! I doubt you did not think Hammersley folks were sharp enough to find out your doings.’

‘I did not think Hammersley folks were so wicked as to impute evil to a man who, when most unworthy, is at least urgent in his duty.’

‘Upon my word, sir,’ exclaimed the infuriate matron, pushing aside the trembling girl, who would fain have restrained her wrath, ‘you carry matters with a bold front; and I must needs speak plainer than I care to speak before this simple child here, who was too quick to love and trust you against her parents’ will, that had higher hopes for her. Nay, dry thy tears, Dolly; I’ll see thee mistress of Hever Grange, belike, instead of drudge and draggletail for love of that dirt yonder.’

And the matron pointed at Matthew Wall with a trembling finger—at Matthew, whose calmness was not yet shaken.

‘Will it please you to speak quietly and civilly, madam?’ he said. ‘You ask me if I know Liscott Common, and I answer yes; if I know Jane Gurd’s cottage, and I answer yes again. I came straight from there to this house an hour ago.’

‘You came from there to my child?’ shrieked Mrs. Bolton; ‘then, indeed, you are a shameless villain!’

‘Come, come, dame,’ expostulated the parson; ‘civil words, civil words.’

"'Tis easy talking for you, William ; but am I to pick and choose my words, when my heart is like to burst for grief and shame ? That wretch yonder, that was to be married to our Dorothy a fortnight come Saturday—him that pretends to be a saint—must needs have his fancy, like a London rake-hell. He keeps a fine madam hid away in Jane Gurd's cottage, and there's scarce a day passes that he does not waste a couple hours in paying his duty to the lady ; and he comes straight from that woman to my daughter ; and you ask me to keep my patience, William Bolton !'

'I'll not believe it !' cried Dorothy suddenly, flinging herself away from her mother, and standing bolt upright, looking at the dame with flaming eyes. 'I'll not believe it, mother, if all the people in Hammersley were to swear it on their Bibles.'

'There is no need for so much warmth, Dorothy,' the curate said gently. 'I do not fear thou wilt believe ill of thy chosen husband. And you, madam, will soon be sorry for having done me so much wrong. Pray, who was it told you this pretty story ?'

'I heard it from Mrs. Jorboys ; but 'tis the common talk of Hammersley.'

'I am sorry Hammersley should choose such vile discourse.'

'Can you deny this story ?'

'I will not trouble myself to deny it.'

'Oh, indeed, Mr. Brazenface ! You won't deny, then, that there is a young woman living in Jane Gurd's cottage, and that you took her there ?'

'That is quite true.'

'And is it true that you have paid for the vermin's board and lodging ?'

'Vermin is a very hard word, Mrs. Bolton, and the girl at Jane Gurd's cottage deserves no such bad name. I have paid for her meat and drink hitherto ; Jane is kind enough to give her shelter without recompense.'

'And you took her there ?'

'Yes, I took her there.'

'You are a bad man, Matthew Wall.'

'I thought you were too good a woman to be so ready to think ill, or to listen to gossip that is as idle as it is wicked,' answered the curate with the gentle gravity that had distinguished his manner throughout this interview.

'If there is no harm in your doings, why have you kept

them secret ?' asked the dame with no less anger, but with a certain admixture of uncertainty.

'I can but answer you with Shylock, it has been "my humour." There are things a man does not care to talk about. I have had my fancy about that poor wench at the cottage on Liscott Common. The fancy might have proved a foolish one, and I might have been laughed at for my pains.'

'And this is all you have to say ?'

'Yes; I will say no more to-night. If you want to know more, Mrs. Bolton, or if you would know more, Dorothy dear, you have but to walk to Liscott Common with me after service to-morrow, and you may find out more of poor Betty than you can learn of Hammersley gossip.'

'Betty !' exclaimed the matron, 'Betty what, pray, sir ?'

'She has no other name,' replied Matthew ; 'she had one when I first met with her ; but I have done my best to rid her of it. And now I will wish you good-night, madam, and a heart less prone to give heed to slander. Sure I know 'tis a kind one.'

He took Dorothy's hand as he passed her, and pressed it tenderly to his lips.

'Thou art too pure to doubt me, dear creature,' he murmured. 'I will show thy kinsfolk to-morrow that thy purity is wiser than their experience.'

In the next moment he was gone. The parson's wife sent Dorothy to bed—for in the days of Pamela and Clarissa it was within the scope of maternal authority to send a daughter of twenty-one years of age to bed—and immediately sat down and began to cry. She had her cry out, and then consented to answer her bewildered husband's inquiries. She told him how her suspicions had been aroused by certain hints and head-shakings on the part of Mrs. Jorboys ; and how she had gone that afternoon to Hammersley determined to have it out with that lady ; and how Mrs. Jorboys had told her with due solemnity that Matthew Wall's wickedness was the common talk of Hammersley, since he was known to have a mistress, some low common rubbish picked out of Hammersley gutter, hidden away in Jane Gurd's cottage ; and how his frequent visits to Mrs. Gurd's abode had in the first place aroused suspicion, after which he had been watched by good and zealous Christians anxious for the repute of their holy Church.

'But how do these spies and watchers know that the girl is Matthew's mistress ?' asked the parson.

'What else should she be, William?' exclaimed the dame, with an awful shake of the head.

There was no compounding of spiced drink on this Christmas-eve. The parson and his wife sat by the fire, sad, angry, bewildered, altogether ill at ease. Dorothy lay awake very unhappy. It was not that she suspected her lover of any wrong-doing. That was impossible. She wept over the breach between those two whom she loved so dearly, and fell asleep at last in the midst of a prayer that all might be made right again to-morrow.

The Misses Jorboys and their mother nodded and smirked at Dorothy as they passed her pew in their Christmas finery before morning service. They marvelled to see the girl's peaceful face, after the revelation at which they had assisted on the previous afternoon. It was the curate's turn to preach, and he chose for his Christmas discourse a very familiar text about the charity that thinketh no evil. Matthew Wall was a powerful preacher at all times; but to-day he seemed as one inspired, and the hearts of Mrs. Jorboys and her daughters quailed beneath their ribbon-bedizened stomachers as they heard him.

'It was but the common talk I repeated,' thought the grocer's dame; 'and 'twas for the good of yonder silly child I spoke so plain to her mother.'

The parsonage dinner had been put off till half-past two o'clock, much to the parson's discontent, in order that there might be time for the visit to Liscott Common.

'It goes against me to go near the place where the creature lives,' said Mrs. Bolton, when the matter was discussed; 'but it's best to hear the truth from Jane Gurd.'

Mrs. Gurd was the widow of a Hammersley tradesman who had died in extreme poverty. She lived partly by her own labour, partly on charity, and was supposed to be a decent sort of person.

The day was clear and bright. Mr. Wall and the vicar met Mrs. Bolton and her daughter at the gates of the churchyard; Matthew offered his arm to Dorothy, and the mother did not interfere to prevent the girl taking it. In sober truth the dame was somewhat shaken by the young man's firmness, and she had been not a little melted by that eloquent discourse on the charity that thinketh no evil.

The walk was not unpleasant to Dorothy, in spite of the cloud that darkened her horizon. Matthew Wall, with a rare delicacy, avoided all allusion to the business of the last evening. He talked of his parish work, in which Dorothy was deeply interested. The parson and his wife trudged after the young people, both silent.

'He could never take us to that house if he was the wicked wretch Mrs. Jorboys would have me think him,' the dame thought with some sense of remorse. Her confidence in her informant was beginning to falter. She had always liked Matthew, even when most ill-pleased that her daughter should make so poor a match.

They came to the humble little cottage. Matthew lifted the latch and entered, followed by his three companions. Jane Gurd was nodding in a roomy old chair by the chimney-corner ; a girl was sitting by a window staring out at the common. Such a girl ! If this was Matthew Wall's fancy, it was a passing strange caprice. The girl was the ugliest specimen of womankind on which Mrs. Bolton had ever looked. There was indeed something more than common ugliness in the dull vacant face, the heavy lower jaw, the low narrow forehead, scant sandy hair, and thick-set lumpish figure. The girl escaped by very little from being a monster.

'I have brought the vicar and his lady to see Betty, Mrs. Gurd,' said the curate, as the widow stood up and curtsied to the quality.

The girl neither rose nor turned her head at the entrance of strangers. A figure of stone could not have been more still than this clumsy peasant girl.

'You have not taught the creature manners, Matthew Wall,' said the outraged matron, 'or she'd be quicker to show her reverence for her betters.'

The curate smiled, and turned with a gentle compassionate look to the monster by the window.

'Bless your dear heart, ma'am,' cried the widow Gurd, 'Betty knows no more of your honour's coming in at that door than the Emperor of Chaney.'

'What !' cried the dame ; 'can't the creature see us ?'

'Lord, no, ma'am ; she's stone blind.'

'But she can hear us, at any rate ?'

'Not she, ma'am ; the postes isn't deafer.'

'But—but she can speak, I suppose ?'

'Four words, ma'am, as Mr. Wall has taught her in this last six weeks. The Lord knows how he found the patience and the cleverness to do it.'

'Blind, deaf, and dumb !' cried the vicar's wife, aghast. 'Oh, Matthew Wall, can you forgive me ?'

'With all my heart, dear madam. It was but a foolish mistake of the Hammersley folk;' and the curate held out his honest hand to the woman who had wronged him. 'Yes, poor Betty yonder is blind and deaf and dumb. I found her in one of the back slums of the town, worse treated than a dog ; for the sorriest cur has some ragamuffin that will stand by him ; and Betty had no friend. She was beaten, starved, kept in a hole like a rat—a horror to look at, a horror to think of. I told those she belonged to that it was a sinful piece of work, and they only laughed at me. I told them it was against the law ; but the law is a slow business, and they snapped their fingers at my talk of constables and justices of the peace. What could I do to help the poor wretch ? They called her Idiot Betty, and said she wasn't worth the bite and sup they gave her. I asked if I was free to take her away. They said yes, and welcome too. So I brought her to Dame Gurd. The good soul was willing to take the charge of her and give her a comfortable shelter for nothing, and her bit of victuals costs but a few shillings a week. She was a little strange and difficult to manage at first, from never having known kindness since her wretched cradle : but she soon got to understand that we meant well by her, and between us we have taught her a good deal.'

'Between us !' cried the widow ; ''twas all your doing, first and last, Muster Wall.'

'No one need call her Idiot Betty, now,' continued the curate ; 'she has learnt to make baskets and rush mats, and can ask by signs for what she wants.'

As he said this, the curate went softly towards the place where the girl sat, with the winter light shining on her dull sightless face. As he came close behind her chair the face changed all at once, and when he laid his hand gently upon her head, it was the face of a creature with a soul. The dull common clay—the mindless lump of ill-used humanity—brightened into life beneath that pitying hand. Here was a new Pygmalion who might well be proud of his work.

' I have been teaching her to talk,' said Matthew, 'and I have hopes that she will do something in that way by-and-by. She can say four words—God, bread, mother (meaning the kind hearted widow there), and parson (meaning me).'

He put his hand upon the girl's clumsy fingers. She understood the sign, and obeyed it. Her mouth opened like a box, and a sound came out of it—a loud, harsh, snapping, disagreeable sound, which was meant for the word 'parson.' It was more startling than pleasant, but to Matthew Wall it was sweeter than music.

'You'd never guess the trouble he had to bring her to that, your honours,' said Mrs. Gurd, proud of this successful performance.

Mrs. Bolton took a seven-shilling piece from her capacious pocket, and bestowed it upon the widow.

'She shall want for nothing while I am alive,' cried the mollified matron ; and then she turned to Matthew and kissed him. It was an audible smack that resounded in the cottage chamber.

'God bless you, Matthew Wall !' she said ; 'I'd rather see my Dolly the wife of so good a man than riding in the squire's chariot.'

AT DAGGERS DRAWN

BUSINESS had been rather dull at the Royal Terence Theatre when Mr. Lorrain, the lessee and manager, went on a starring tour in the provinces. It was in the course of this tour he met with a man who had attained some distinction as a local favourite in the large manufacturing town of Brazenam. The man was a low comedian, and played certain characters, which he had made his own, better than Mr. Lorrain, the London manager, had ever seen them played before.

Mr. Lorrain happened to say as much in the green room one evening, and the friends of Mr. Joseph Munford, the low comedian, took care to tell him what the London manager had said—the lips of a London manager being as the lips of the young person in a fairy tale, and every word that falls therefrom a jewel of purest water.

'You mind what you're about, Joey,' said the friends of Mr. Munford, 'and you'll get an opening at the Terence. Lorrain was standing in the prompt entrance the other night when you were on in " Dingleton's Little Dinner," and I know he was pleased.'

'Did he laugh?' asked Mr. Munford anxiously.

'Not a bit of it. A manager never laughs when he means business. He was watching you, my boy. I had my eye upon him while you were doing that by-play with the mustard-pot; and I wouldn't mind laying a fiver that he'll offer you an engagement before he leaves the place.'

Mr. Munford shook his head despondently. He had acted at more than one London theatre, and the London managers had beguiled him by delusive laughter. They had applauded his business with the mustard-pot ; and had straightway gone away and forgotten him. The fact that the manager of the Terence had not laughed was perhaps a favourable symptom ; but Joseph Munford steeled his heart against the flatteries of that false charmer, Hope. He found himself watching the prompt entrance, neverthe-

less, during the remainder of the London manager's engagement ; and on several occasions he perceived that gentleman
ostensibly engaged in conversation with the prompter, but
obviously interested in the business of the stage.

'I wonder whether he does mean anything ?' Joseph
Munford asked himself anxiously.

Life was a somewhat difficult business for the local favourite, who had given hostages to Fortune in the shape of a wife
and six children, and who found the healthy appetites of the
hostages press rather heavily upon him now and then. The
salary of a provincial favourite, be he never so beloved of pit
and gallery, does not afford a very liberal income for a family
of eight ; and actors are such imprudent people, that a man
with a wife and six children rarely manages to secure a
provision for his old age out of a weekly stipend of three
guineas. Mr. Munford was wont to remark with doleful
facetiousness that he found three pound three an uncommonly tight fit. These things happened many years ago,
before the days of big salaries and touring companies.

While Joseph Munford steeled himself against the insidious flatteries of the enchantress Hope, Mr. Lorrain of the
Terence deliberated with himself after the following fashion :

'The fellow is certainly funny—rather broad, perhaps ;
but he'd tone that down a little, I daresay, for a London
audience. I really think he might draw. But then there's
Tayte. Wouldn't it make Tayte angry if I engaged anyone
likely to interfere with him? However, I can't help that.
Business has been very flat for a long time ; and I really
think people are beginning to get tired of Tayte—*toujours
perdrix*, and all that kind of thing. I fancy the public
would like Tayte all the better if they saw rather less of
him. At any rate, I can but make the experiment.'

The result of this deliberation was the engagement of Mr.
Munford for the Royal Terence Theatre, at a salary of six
guineas a week. He would gladly have accepted four ; but
Mr. Lorrain was a liberal man, willing to give twelve honest
pence for an honest shilling's-worth, and above trying to
obtain his shilling's-worth for elevenpence halfpenny.

If an unknown uncle had suddenly revealed his existence
by dying and leaving Joseph Munford half a million of
money, the low comedian could scarcely have been more
elated than he was by the engagement for the Terence. His
wildest ambition was realised. He was going to play Dingleton before a London audience ; he was going to tread the

boards made slippery by the soles of the great Tayte—the favourite of favourites—the man on whom the mantle of Liston had descended.

Mr. Munford had a considerable opinion of his own merits, and he had battened on the praises of local admirers; but there were times when his soul sank within him as he thought that he was to enter the lists against the mighty Tayte; and he said as much to his friends and comrades at the snug little tavern next door to the theatre.

His friends bade him be of good cheer. They laughed to scorn his apprehension of failure.

'Let Tayte look to his laurels,' they exclaimed, 'when you make your first appearance as Dingleton. Tayte is a very good actor; but the London public have never seen anything like your by-play with the mustard-pot.'

Joseph Munford gave his friends a farewell supper at the snug little tavern and departed, carrying with him the seven hostages and all those eccentric wigs, dropsical gingham umbrellas, impossible swallow-tailed coats, preposterous plaid trousers, outrageous satin waistcoats, and fluffy beaver hats, which had long been the delight of his local admirers, and the pride of his own heart

He took lodgings for himself and his hostages in the neighbourhood of the Terence Theatre. The consciousness of his improved circumstances made him just a little extravagant: and his prudent wife looked around her with awe-stricken glances when she beheld the splendours of her new abode.

'Oh, Joseph,' she cried, 'the carpet is Brussels, and quite new: and look at those green-glass candlesticks on the mantelpiece; I'm afraid the rent must be *enormous*.'

As a sudden thunderclap that startles a drowsy traveller amidst the sultry calm of a summer day came the intelligence of Joseph Munford's engagement on the illustrious Tayte. He saw the new farce, 'Dingleton's Little Dinner,' underlined in the bills of the theatre, and shrugged his shoulders.

'More study for me,' he grumbled. 'I wonder what the consciences of managers are made of. When shall I have a little rest, I should like to know? I haven't been out of the bill since Christmas; and I don't think it does a man any good to be so much before the public.'

It is the speciality of popular low comedians to grumble; but those who best knew Mr. Tayte knew that he was very fond of acting, and would ill have brooked a rival near the throne. When it did transpire that 'Dingleton's Little Dinner' was intended to introduce a provincial favourite to the London public, the countenance of Tayte was terrible to behold. The fact burst upon him when he read the cast, which had been put up over the green-room mantelpiece. He stood upon the hearth-rug for five minutes by the green-room clock, staring at the document with a fixity of gaze that was almost apopletic, and breathing stertorously.

'And who is MR. MUNFORD?' he demanded presently, in an awful voice, pointing to the obnoxious name on the little slip of paper.

Nobody in the green-room professed to know anything about Mr. Munford. Perhaps anyone who had known the particulars of the new engagement would have shrunk from imparting his knowledge to the outraged Tayte.

'I'll ask Lorrain what it all means,' he said presently, and in due course Mr. Tayte had an interview with his manager —an interview at which no third person was present. It was rumoured that Tayte had been seen to issue from the Treasury pale of visage, and clutching the slim silk umbrella of private life with a convulsive grasp ; and that was all. It was observed that during the fortnight preceding the first appearance of Munford, Tayte played with a feverish energy ; that he, the past master in the art of 'gagging,' indulged in even wilder gags than were usual to him ; that he surpassed himself in the science of ' mugging,' and that he contrived thereby to keep the audience in a continuous roar of laughter from his entrance to his exit. He seemed to derive a grim kind of satisfaction from this fact; but his countenance as he stood at the wings waiting for his cue was very dark and repellent, and his oldest friends were afraid to speak to him. Two or three toadies and sycophants ventured to hint that this obscure provincial person, Munford, was foredoomed to be a failure ; but Mr. Tayte turned upon these flatterers with unwonted ferocity.

'Who told you I was afraid of Mr. Munford ?' he said, 'I have held my own in this house for nine years and a half, and I daresay I shall manage to hold my own a year or two longer.'

There was not much in the words : but with such men as Tayte the tone is everything ; and there was a crushing irony in the tone.

' Dingleton's Little Dinner ' was performed, and the new comedian's *debut* was eminently successful. All the papers

concurred in the opinion that Mr. Munford was an acquisition
to the company at the Terence ; and all the papers concurred
in praising the by-play with the mustard pot. Mr. Tayte
studiously avoided seeing the new comedian, but he heard
the laughter of the audience as he dressed to go home after
the first piece ; and the dresser who attended upon him beheld
his flexible lips shape themselves into the monosyllable
'Fools!' as the loudest of those peals of laughter reached
him. He made a point of reading the papers the next morning, and his lips shaped themselves into the same form as he
read of the business with the mustard-pot.

'Dingleton's Little Dinner' had a triumphant run ; and
Joseph Munford's success became an established fact. It was not
to be supposed, however, that the audience of the Terence were
in any way inconstant to their old favourite. The great Tayte
was playing one of his most uproariously funny characters
in the piece which formed the chief feature of the evening's
entertainment. Roars of laughter greeted his entrances and
followed his exits. He went up in a balloon ; he was caught
in the rain attired in dancing-pumps and a swallow-tailed
coat ; he hid himself in a cupboard where there were jam-pots
and pickle-jars, and emerged therefrom bedabbled with
treacle ; he had his head jammed between area-railings when
in the act of listening to a conversation between two
servant-maids, and kept the audience enraptured for five
consecutive minutes by means of his facial contortions while
in that attitude ; and what more could the heart of a low
comedian desire ?

The desires of a low comedian are not easily satisfied. The
great Tayte hankered after that business with the mustard-
pot, and grudged those peals of laughter which he heard every
night while he was exchanging a suit of scarlet and green
tartan and a red scratch-wig for the sombre attire of everyday
life.

Although he took very good care not to see Mr. Munford
in the part of Dingleton, he could not avoid occasional
encounters with the comedian at the wings or in the green-
room. The two men looked at each other with that stony
ferocity of expression to be seen in the countenances of rival
cats, who stand a few paces apart, glaring at each other, stiff
and statue-like, on the steps of an area.

'Morning,' said Munford. 'Cold, ain't it?'

'Yes,' replied Tayte, 'almost as cold as the audience last
night when you were playing Dingleton.'

'Ah,' answered Munford, 'you see I don't go in for area-rails and tartan trousers.'

'No,' cried Tayte; 'you go in for mustard-pots.'

And then the rivals turned upon their heels, each man thinking he had been witty. Mr. Lorrain, the manager, did his best to soften the feelings of the old favourite.

'You can't suppose I want to put anyone over your head, Tayte,' he said; and again Mr. Tayte's breathing became stertorous. 'I thought this fellow would be useful to pull up the half-price; and I'm sure you get the lion's share. Do be civil to him, Tayte. He's not a bad fellow, when you come to know him. We've been such a snug little family party in this house, that it goes against me to see two of my company at daggers drawn.'

'At daggers drawn!' cried Tayte ferociously. 'Daggers be ——! Do you suppose I'm afraid of such a fellow as that? Why, I pity him.'

'Pity him, Tayte! What for?' asked the manager innocently.

'Because you've done him the worst injury you could possibly do him by bringing him up to London,' said Tayte. 'That business with the mustard-pot *goes* because it's new. Wait till he plays in another piece. Mark my words, Lorrain—and I speak without prejudice—when he does, the audience will drop him like a hot potato.'

'Very likely you're right, Tayte,' Mr. Lorrain answered meekly. And this was mean of him, for he fully believed that Tayte was wrong.

The event proved that the manager had judged wisely. Joseph Munford played in other pieces, and the half-price approved of him. A drama was produced by-and-by, in which there were parts for the two low comedians. Each man thought his rival's part better than his own; each man watched his rival, and counted the peals of laughter extorted from the unconscious audience. Tayte still held his ground as leading favourite of the Terence; and there was neither wavering nor inconstancy in the minds of his audience. But there are monarchs who will endure no second power in the state; and a popular low comedian is of the same arbitrary temper.

Tayte was compelled to witness the performance of Munford now that the two men played in the same piece and were on the stage together; but on no occasion had the greater man been beguiled to smile at the buffooneries of the lesser man. The audience might be convulsed with laughter, the rest of the actors might abandon themselves freely to mirth; but let the drolleries of Munford be never so humorous, the countenance of Tayte was as a visage hewn out of stone.

The rival comedians met in the green-room every night during the run of the new drama ; and as a London green-room is a grand place for talk, it is not to be supposed that either of the two could keep perpetual silence. Then arose those arguments and disputations which fully justified the general idea that Tayte and Munford were at daggers drawn. On no possible point would these two men agree. In politics, in theology, in literature, their ideas appeared wide as the poles asunder. If Munford gave expression to sentiments of a Radical character, Tayte became on the instant a staunch Conservative. If Munford showed himself an orthodox Christian, Tayte boldly propounded doctrines which would have been too much for Voltaire or Tom Paine. If Munford spoke with enthusiasm of Garrick, Tayte proclaimed his conviction that the only decent actor of that period was Barry. If Munford recited a verse of Moore or Byron, Tayte planted himself beneath the banner of Wordsworth, and loudly averredthat no poet had ever produced a more thrilling composition than the history of Peter Bell, the waggoner.

The audience of the green-room looked on and listened, and enjoyed the fray. The antagonism between the two men gave a zest to every-day life in the Terence ; and on Saturday morning, when there was a good deal of lounging and idleness outside the treasury-door, the fun was almost riotous.

Munford held his own bravely, but he complained bitterly to his own particular friends. 'That man would crush me if he had the power,' he said ; 'I really think he would like to cut my throat.'

And indeed there were times when Mr. Tayte felt as if he might have derived a grisly satisfaction from the act of hacking asunder his rival's jugular vein with a blunt razor.

Things went on in this fashion for nearly a year, when all of a sudden Munford fell ill, and the farce in which he had been playing was withdrawn. A farce of Tayte's was reproduced, and once more Tayte had the burden of the half-price on his shoulders.

Did this state of affairs afford satisfaction to the mind of Tayte ? He little knows the soul of a popular low comedian who would suppose so. When Tayte heard for the first time of Munford's illness, he drew his shoulders up to his ears, and indulged in one of those facial contortions for which he was renowned.

'Ill, is he?' said he; 'I think I can guess the nature of his indisposition. The new farce, "Coals and Potatoes"—a literal translation from the last Palais-Royal absurdity, "Un Marchand de Charbon," by the way—was a failure, sir; a frost bitter and bleak as the February of 1814, when there were live oxen roasted on the Thames; and Munford is shamming ill in order to get out of the part. He's an artful card, my child, and knows the audience are tired of him. When the houses pick up again, Munford will pick up again; mark my words.'

This was the second occasion on which Mr. Tayte had requested that his statements in reference to Mr. Munford might be noted; and again the event proved that he had been wrong.

Joseph Munford's illness was not an affair of a few days or of a few weeks. He languished and drooped week after week and month after month. Again and again there was talk about his returning to the theatre, and one of his pieces was announced for performance; but again and again the doctor interfered at the last moment, and declared that it must not be. Poor Munford was wont to sigh wearily when people talked of his reappearance.

'I begin to think I shall never play Dingleton again,' he said.

His wife did her uttermost to console him, though very sad at heart herself. She reminded him how great he had been in the by-play with the mustard-pot, and how on one never-to-be-forgotten occasion in the provinces—his benefit—the mustard-pot business had been encored by an uproarious audience.

For four months Joseph Munford had been an invalid; for four months Mr. Lorrain the manager had sent him his salary every Saturday without question, as ungrudgingly as if the sick man had been working his hardest at the theatre. At the end of the fourth month, however, Mr. Lorrain called on the invalid, and told him, as kindly as it was possible to impart unpleasant tidings, that at the end of one more month the salary must cease, unless the actor should be well enough to return to his duties.

'If the season had been a good one, God knows I wouldn't grudge your screw, Joe,' said the manager; 'but you know yourself I have been losing money. After next month you must see what your friends can do for you.'

Unhappily Joseph Munford had no friends, or none capable of giving him substantial assistance in the hour of need. He did not tell the manager this ; for he knew that he had been generously treated, and to sponge on generosity is no attribute of the Thespian mind.

'You've been very good to me, Lorrain,' he said ; 'and I shall never forget your goodness. If I am ever to act again, I ought to be able to act before the month is out.'

Mr. Lorrain looked mournfully at the wasted figure and haggard pinched face. Alas, it seemed very improbable that the weak creature propped up by pillows and sustained by doctor's stuff would ever again make mirth for a delighted pit !

And were the two low comedians still at daggers drawn now that one of them lay on a sick-bed ? Ah, he little knows the heart of a comedian who fancies that Tayte's hatred endured when the object of it had such need of tenderness and compassion. For the man who had made a hit in 'Dingleton's Little Dinner,' the favourite of the Terence had no feeling but aversion ; for poor Joey Munford languishing in a London lodging James Tayte had nothing but pity and love. There were many who were kind to the sick man ; but the old port which warmed his poor sad heart, the hothouse grapes which cooled his poor parched lips, the comic periodicals which beguiled him into feeble laughter, were paid for out of the coffers of James Tayte.

Nor did Tayte confine his benevolent offices to such small gifts. He gave that which is grudged by many who will bestow hothouse grapes or rare old wines with liberal hands. He gave his sometime rival time and trouble. The atmosphere of a sick-room is apt to be stifling, the society of a sick man is apt to be depressing ; but when Tayte had a leisure hour before a late piece, or after an early piece, or in the pauses of a long rehearsal, it was his habit to run round to the invalid's lodgings for an hour's chat, or a hand at cribbage, as the case might be ; and nothing so revived the spirits of Joseph Munford as one of these visits from his mighty rival.

'I used to hate you like poison when you played Dingleton,' said Tayte frankly ; 'and I shall hate you like poison again when you come back to the *slum*. Two men who play the same line of business are bound to hate each other. It's human nature. But in the meantime let's be friends, old fellow, and take life pleasantly.'

And then Tayte showed his big white teeth in a grin which would have extorted a laugh from Socrates after he had swallowed the hemlock.

It was in the dark and dispiriting month of November that the manager of the Terence gave notice that in four more weeks he must needs stop the sick man's salary. The four weeks went by on the wings of the wind, and Joseph Munford was no better fitted for a return to his duties. He knew and felt that he was weaker and worse than when Mr. Lorrain had last called upon him. He appealed piteously to the doctor for comfort, and the doctor murmured something hopeful about next summer. Next summer! And it was December. There were five or six weary months to be lived through somehow or other, with seven hostages given to Fortune, and no visible means of subsistence. Christmas was near at hand too ; and that seemed to make it worse, poor Mrs. Munford said pathetically. Indeed the rich do well to be open-handed and pitiful at Christmas time ; for many a dole in the way of beef and blankets, and wine and tea, and coals and flannel, are needed to compensate the poor hungry ones for the bitter thoughts that *must* arise when the haggard eyes peer wonderingly in on the Christmas fruits and Christmas dainties, the toys and trinkets, the holiday food and holiday raiment, glittering and twinkling in the light behind the plate-glass shop windows.

As that time drew near, and the last shilling of his last sovereign melted away, Joseph Munford's fortitude abandoned him. His poor aching head fell upon his wife's shoulder, and he wept aloud.

'I know it's weak and childish, Mary Anne,' he said ; 'but I can't help it. I'm a mean hound ; but there's only one hope : I must appeal to Lorrain, and ask him to let the salary go on a few weeks longer. It won't be more than a few weeks, I'm afraid, Polly.'

And then the two poor creatures wept together ; while the muffin-bell went tinkling cheerily down the street, and the twinkling lights shot up in the December dusk, like so many flaming daggers piercing a blanket of fog.

If it had rested with Joseph Munford to entreat the manager's charity with his own lips, he could never have shaped them into the prayer. He relied on the influence of Tayte, the established favourite, who was known to be a power in the theatre.

'Tayte is a noble fellow, and I know he'll plead for me,' said Munford.

But when Tayte heard what was required of him he shook his head dejectedly.

'I'll ask if you like, Joe,' he said ; 'but upon my word, I

don't think it's any use. Lorrain has behaved very handsomely to you, old boy, you see ; and business has been so confoundedly bad, you know, since——'

'I know I oughtn't to ask it,' replied the other piteously ; 'but I must die of starvation if the salary stops. I'm in debt as it is, and everything is so dear, and the children eat so. By heavens, Tayte, you can't conceive the amount six children can devour! If it were likely to be for long, I wouldn't ask it ; but it won't be for long.'

Tayte murmured something to the effect that so far as an occasional pound or so would go, Munford might rely upon him ; and then departed, compelled, despite his better reason, to assume some show of hope, so heart-piercing was the despair of his friend.

The interview with the manager was a painful one, though no manager could have shown more feeling than Mr. Lorrain.

'I put it to you, Tayte,' he said, 'whether I am bound to continue the salary. You know how bad business has been since Easter, and you know I've been paying that poor fellow six guineas a week for the last five months, during which time he hasn't set his foot inside the theatre. He ought to have saved a little—he really ought, you know.'

Tayte dropped a word or two about 'six children' and 'doctor's bills.' But Mr. Lorrain shook his head.

'Munford had only three guineas a week at Brazenam,' he said, 'and he might have saved something since he has been with me. I'm very sorry for the poor fellow ; and so far as a sovereign now and then will go, I—' And he unconsciously echoed the words of Tayte.

Very heavy was the heart of the comedian as he went to the street near the Strand that evening after the first piece. He knew how bitter the interval of suspense must have been to the actor's penniless household ; he knew how much more bitter would be the tidings which he had to impart.

He was obliged to walk up and down the street once or twice before he had courage to knock at the door. But at last he did knock, and was admitted by the London slavey He went softly upstairs, unannounced. Mrs. Munford came out to meet him on the landing, and her look went to his heart.

'He's very low to-night,' she said, as she opened the door of the sick-room. 'Oh, dear Mr. Tayte, I hope you bring us good news !'

Tayte could not answer her. He made a little choking

noise—which might have been a fortune to him, if he could have done it in serio-comedy—and went into the sick-chamber. Munford was lying back upon the pillows pale as ashes: but he started up as his friend entered, as if galvanized into life.

'Poor lad!' thought Tayte, sadly: 'I think he's about right. Lorrain might have let the salary go on; it wouldn't have been for long.'

'Well?' gasped Munford hoarsely. And then he cried in a faint voice: 'Oh, Tayte, there's good news in your face! It's all right, isn't it? Ah, Tayte, dear old fellow, say it's all right!'

Tayte looked fixedly at that white wan face, in which the agony of suspense was so painfully visible.

'Yes,' he said at last, drawing a long breath; 'it's all right, dear boy. You're to have the salary.'

'God bless him for it!' cried Munford; 'and you too.'

He could say no more, but covered his face with the bed-clothes, and wept aloud.

It was a grand sight to see Tayte seated by the bed, and patting the counterpane as if his late rival had been a wakeful baby.

'Cheer up, old fellow,' he said; 'you'll play Dingleton again, and I shall hate you again, depend upon it.'

Joseph Munford did not live to reappear as Dingleton; but he lingered for many months, now better, now worse; and on every Saturday during those months Tayte took him six guineas, neatly packed in white paper and sealed with a business-like seal. This was rather a hard pull upon Tayte, who had himself given hostages to Fortune. He was observed to wear a shabby overcoat during that spring, and to ride in omnibuses when a nobler-minded man would have ridden in cabs—whereupon his intimate enemies were very sarcastic on the subject of his meanness.

'Don't say anything to Lorrain about the salary when he calls upon you,' the arch-hypocrite said once; 'he told me he'd rather you didn't mention it to him. It's a false delicacy of his, you know; but you may as well give way to it.'

So when Mr. Lorrain called at Munford's lodgings, bringing the sick man wine, or fruit, or flowers, no mention was made of the salary. There were only vague protestations of affection and gratitude on the part of the actor, which the manager had fairly won by liberality in the past and kindly sympathy in the present.

At last the day came when the Farce was to be finished and the curtain to be dropped. The doctor told Munford that the end was very near ; and the dying comedian bade good-bye to the poor faithful wife who had hoped such bright things for him.

'I think your sister Susan will be kind to you and the little ones, Polly, when I'm gone,' he said. 'She set her face against my profession ; but I believe she's a good Christian, though she does come it just a little too strong about the wickedness of her fellow-creatures. She can't set her face against a poor friendless widow and six fatherless children. And then there's Lorrain, we know *he's* a trump ; and I'm sure he'll do what he can for you ; and Tayte is a good fellow, too, in his way, and he'll stand your friend.'

This the comedian said in faint gasps, with a wan smile upon his lips, and tears in his eyes, while his wife sat by his bedside with her hand locked in his.

'I think they'd give you a benefit at Brazenam, Mary,' he said after a pause ; 'and it would be a bumper. Do you remember my reception the last time I played Dingleton down there ? '

On this bitter day Tayte boldly turned his back upon an important rehearsal. The poor wife was worse than useless, and in this sad extremity Tayte was the nurse as well as the comforter of his fading friend. The manager of the Terence heard how matters were, and came without delay to the sick-chamber.

He found Joseph Munford lying asleep with his head on Tayte's arm, while the popular favourite sat by the bed like patience on a monument.

'This is a change indeed, Tayte,' said Mr. Lorrain in a whisper ; 'you and he used to be at daggers drawn.'

'I only wish there were any chance of our being at daggers drawn again,' Tayte answered with a stifled sob.

The sound woke the sick man. He looked up with a start, and recognised the manager.

'Give me your hand, Lorrain,' he said ; 'thank God you've come in time to hear me say it. I thank and bless you with all my heart for your goodness to me and mine in the last six months.'

'Don't say that, my dear Munford,' said the manager, taking the wasted hand in his very tenderly ; 'I've done little enough, but God knows how it went against me to refuse you the salary last Christmas.'

'Refuse !　You refused ? '

'Business had been so bad, you see, my dear boy,' murmured the manager.

Joseph Munford turned his dying eyes on Tayte, down whose cheeks big tears were rolling thick and fast.

'James Tayte,' he cried, ' I did not think there was so good a man upon this earth !'

He groped feebly for the hand of his benefactor, found it, pressed it to his lips, and, kissing it, died.

A GREAT BALL AND A GREAT BEAR

A Story of Two Birthdays.

BIRTHDAY THE FIRST.

ON a certain Christmas-eve, some eight or nine years ago, there was a very noisy gathering on the third floor of a house in Hyde-park-gardens. The party had assembled very early in the afternoon, and the great bare branches of the trees, tossed savagely by bleak December winds, and groaning as in mortal agony, were still visible in the winter dusk. Below, in the Bayswater-road, the lights were twinkling; and the bell of the muffin-man, plying his plebeian trade even in that patrician district, made merry music. Upstairs, in the spacious, cheery third-floor school room, the Christmas firelight shone brightly upon the happy faces of a circle of young people, who were seated on the carpet for the performance of the mystic rites of that favourite Christmas game called 'hunt the slipper.'

The ages of the revellers ranged from five to fifteen. One of the eldest among them was the damsel in whose honour the festival was held—Miss Laura de Courcy, who had made her first appearance on the stage of life on a Christmas-eve fifteen years before, and who was entertaining her cousins of all degrees with certain mild dissipations appropriate to the occasion. They were to drink tea in these third-floor regions, which were sacred to Miss de Courcy, her younger brother, her reliable English governess, her accomplished Parisian governess, and the patient maid who brushed the damsel's silken curls some sixteen times in the day, after those hoydenish skirmishings with her younger brother, in which the vivacious young person was wont to indulge.

Miss de Courcy was an only daughter, and an heiress to boot. A grandmamma of unspeakable descent and incalculable wealth had bequeathed all her possessions to this favoured damsel; and the damsel carried the sense of her wealth and her dignity as lightly as if it had been one of the commonest attributes of girlhood.

It was her own pretty little black-satin slipper for which the disputants were now struggling. The door was opened suddenly while the noise was loudest, and a young man put his head into the room.

'Our bear-fights at Maudlin are nothing to this,' he said.

Laura de Courey sprang to her feet as he spoke.

'How dare you come here, sir? This is my room, sir, and my party. You are to be downstairs, with papa and mamma. I won't have grown-up people intruding on my friends.'

'Not if grown-up people bring you a pair of bullfinches?'

'Bullfinches! Oh, Abberdale, that is quite a different thing! I have never had bullfinches. Oh, what a pretty cage!'

The cage was a Chinese pagoda, in delicate wirework, with little bells that rang merrily as the intruder carried the cage to a table. There was a diversion among the slipper-hunters, and the children all clustered round the new-comer. This new-comer was Viscount Abberdale, a dark-eyed handsome young fellow, with a kind pleasant face, and one amongst Miss de Courcy's numerous cousins.

'So you remembered that to-day is my birthday, George?' said Laura, when the bullfinches had been rapturously admired.

'My dear Laura, you know how kind your cousin always is,' remonstrated Miss Vicker, the reliable English governess.

'Ah, *mon Dieu!* is it not that he is good?' exclaimed the irrepressible Parisienne in her native tongue.

'As if I could forget your birthday, Laura! Who was that unfortunate person who had Calais written on her heart? I have your name, and the date of your birthday, and ever so many memoranda respecting you, written on my heart, Laura. I don't think there can be room for any more writing.'

'We all know that Lord Abberdale possesses a talent for talking nonsense,' said the reliable one, as a hint that this kind of nonsense was inappropriate to the third floor.

'But I have disturbed all the fun, Lorry,' cried his lordship. 'Get away, Leo,' he added unceremoniously to the heir of the De Courcys, who was dragging at his coat tails; 'it isn't your birthday; and if you're looking out for anything from Siraudin or Boissier, you won't find it in my dress-coat. I left a great coat in the hall, and I shouldn't be surprised if there were a few thousand boxes of goodies in the pockets of that.'

Off sped the heir, swift as a lapwing.

'And now we'll have "hunt the slipper,"' said Abberdale.

'Ah, that is a droll of a young man!' shrieked the irrepressible.

'Laura, my love, I think the little ones will be anxious for their tea,' said the Reliable; 'suppose we adjourn to the next room. Lord Abberdale, may we give you a cup of tea?'

'Thanks—yes. But why not more "hunt the slipper'?"

'Miss de Courcy's little friends will be leaving her very early, and tea is ready. If you would *really* like a cup, you can go into the next room with us, Lord Abberdale."

'O, yes, if you please, Miss Vicker; I want to drink tea with my cousin on her birthday.'

They went into the next room, another sitting-room, brightly but plainly furnished, like the first; and here was a table spread with all that is prettiest and most tempting in the way of tea.

'Oh, what pretty-looking cakes!' cried the undergraduate of Maudlin; 'a dinner-table isn't half so pretty as a tea-table; and there's something so social and pleasant about tea. We always have coffee at our "wines" you know, but they don't allow us such cakes as those when we are training.'

Lord Abberdale insisted upon staying all tea-time, and further insisted upon making himself very busy with the dealing out of cups and saucers, and the nice admeasurement of cream and sugar.

Lionel de Courcy came shouting up the staircase, laden with bonbon boxes; and the tea-table was thrown into confusion presently by the appearance of these treasures, and the excitement caused thereby.

All quiet Miss Vicker's excellent arrangements for her pupil's youthful guests were thrown out of gear by this wild Oxonian. The two white-aproned waiting-maids could scarcely make head against the confusion; and that Babel and riot arose which is common to all juvenile communities, unless kept down by the iron hand of despotism. Little ones clambered from their chairs, and bigger ones stretched out eager arms across the table to clutch at a satin bag of *pralines* or a daintily painted box of *violettes glacées*. Cups of tea were spilt over æsthetic or fantastic frocks, devised by fond mothers and clever maids for this special occasion;

pyramids of cake were overthrown, a glass preserve dish was broken,—all was chaos; and across the 'wrack' which she surveyed from her seat at the head of the table, Miss Vicker beheld, as in a vision, Lord Abberdale and Laura de Courcy seated calmly side by side, engaged in that kind of discourse which, had the damsel been 'out,' would have been called flirtation.

'How very wrong of Mrs. De Courcy to allow him to come upstairs!' she said to herself.

And then she sank back in her chair, and abandoned herself, with a sigh of resignation, to the inevitable.

'What an awfully rigid individual your Miss Vicker is!' said the young man; 'she will hardly allow me to look at you: as if we were not cousins, and as if we are not going to be something more than cousins one of these days."

'And pray what more than cousins shall we ever be, sir?' asked Laura, who was quite able to hold her own against this impertinent young nobleman.

'Never mind now, you will find out by and by. Do you know, I have secured a talisman which I shall keep as long as I live?'

'What kind of talisman?'

'The magic slipper,—*la pianella magica!* The slipper you were playing with just now. Was it made for Titania?'

'It was made for me, sir; and it is too large.'

'You won't be troubled with it any more: I hope you have one on.'

'Of course. That slipper was fetched from my room. Do you think I would hop about with one shoe on this cold winter's night? O dear, I hope there are no poor people without any shoes!'

'I'm afraid there are, my dear. But don't think of them now; it makes you look so sorrowful. I mean to keep this slipper.'

'You are a most presuming person; and I shall tell Miss Vicker.'

'Oh, no, you won't! Poor Miss Vicker! She is watching us now. How awful she looks, doesn't she? Quite a genteel Medusa.'

'And pray what are you going to do with my slipper?'

'Keep it to be thrown after you on your wedding-day.'

'You will throw it?'

'O dear, no!'

'And why not?'

'For the best possible reason : I shall be with you in the carriage.'

Miss de Courcy blushed and laughed. For a beauty of three lustres she was tolerably advanced in the art of coquetry.

Tea was finished by this time. The younger guests were cloaked and shawled, and hooded and muffled, for departure. The elders were to go down to the drawing-room after dinner for a quadrille or two. There were visitors to the heads of the house expected, but not many. Town was empty ; and only urgent parliamentary business had induced Mr. de Courcy to spend his Christmas in Hyde-park-gardens. Far away on the Scottish border there was a noble old castle where the family were wont to pass this pleasant season, with much festivity, and great advantage to the poor of the district. Of course arrangements had been made whereby the poor should be no losers because of the family's absence ; but their absence was regretted in that Border district nevertheless ; and blankets and flannel cloaks and comfortable winter gowns scarcely seemed of as good a quality when received from the hands of a grim old housekeeper, instead of the ladies of the mansion.

The party in the drawing-room assembled between nine and ten. Miss de Courcy and her three or four chosen friends came down at nine, and met her cousin ascending from the dining-room. She sat down to the piano and played to him, while her mamma dozed in the further drawingroom ; and then the grown-up company arrived, and there was a great deal of music and a little impromptu dancing. It was altogether a delightful evening, Laura thought.

'I shall keep my next birthday at Courcy,' she said. 'Shall you be with us, Abberdale ?'

'I think not. I am going in for travelling when I leave Oxford.'

'You will go to Switzerland and Italy ? How delightful !'

'I shall do nothing so slow. I shall go to Africa, or the Caucasus. I mean to do the Caucasus completely.'

' Is the Caucasus a nice place ?'

'Oh, it's perfectly sweet ! And the Amoor, and the Himalayas. When one considers the encroachments of Russia upon our Indian empire, you see, Lorry, it's a kind of duty every man owes his country to get himself coached-up in the Amoor and the Himalayas.'

'Shall you be long away ?' asked Laura, with a disappointed face.

'Oh, no; only half-a-dozen years or so. Of course I shall go in for the North Pole. A man who isn't well up in his Arctic regions gets snubbed by somebody every time he goes out to dinner. In fact, the Arctic regions are getting almost as common as the Matterhorn.'

'Then if you're going to all these places, I'm sure you won't be at home when I come of age. And papa has promised me all sorts of grand doings then. A fancy ball at Courcy. And I have so longed for a fancy ball: but I shall be dreadfully disappointed if you are not at my ball. I have always thought what fun it would all be, and what an absurd dress you would wear—a dress that no one would know you in, you know—a chimney-sweep or a baker's man.'

'I should like amazingly to come as a chimney-sweep. You will be something magnificent, of course—a princess of the Middle Ages, in that dim period of shadowy kings and queens, and Princes of Wales trying on their father's crowns before the cheval-glass in the royal bed-chamber, when there were sumptuary laws to regulate the height of the women's head-gear. I can fancy you in one of those high-peaked head-dresses, with a cloth-of-gold gown. You would look very jolly.'

'Jolly!' repeated Miss de Courcy; 'I shall not spend poor dear grandmother's money on a cloth-of-gold gown in order to look jolly.'

'You will look an angel; and I shall dance the first quadrille with you—chimney-sweep and princess. The contrast will be sweet.'

'Very sweet. You will be at the Caucasus, or on the North Pole, I daresay, when I come of age.'

'From the heights of Caucasus, from the remotest depths of Polar regions, from the snow-drifts where the bleached bones of perished wanderers gleam ghastly white against the ghastly snow, from the Ganges, from the Chinese Wall, I shall come.'

'Very well, sir. I shall remember your rash promise when my ball begins without a chimney-sweep. However, the loss will be yours if you forget the occasion.'

'I shall not forget.'

'Mother is beckoning to me,' said Miss de Courcy, and thereupon slipped away to take shelter beneath the maternal wing. Miss Vicker, the reliable, had just drawn Mrs. de Courcy's attention to the fact that his lordship's attentions to his cousin were rather more pronounced than was consonant with the damsel's tender years.

'You are not paying any attention to your friends, Lorry,' said mamma; 'there is Bella Hargrave turning over a book of photographs in the dreariest manner. I shall not give you birthday-parties unless you behave better. You are always laughing with your cousin.'

' Abberdale is so funny. What do you think, mamma? He has actually pledged himself to appear at my birthday ball when I come of age. It is to be a fancy ball, you know—that is an old promise of father's; and Abberdale declares he will dance the first quadrille with me dressed as a chimney-sweep.

'D.V.,' murmured the Reliable One piously.

After this, Laura de Courcy danced more than one dance with her cousin Abberdale. When eleven o'clock chimed from the clock on the chimney-piece, Miss Vicker came in search of her charge. The young friends had all departed within the last half-hour : only grown-up company remained. A young lady was singing an Italian canzonette in the second drawing-room. Abberdale and his cousin were almost alone in the large southward-looking room where they had danced. The birthday was over. Miss de Courcy was no longer queen of the occasion : she was there on sufferance, and was liable to be sent to bed at any moment. Miss Vicker and the moment came.

'I was just coming, Carry,' cried Miss Laura. She called her monitress by her Christian name on occasions.—'Good-night, Abberdale.'

'Good-night and good-bye, Lorry ; I'm off to Norfolk for the shooting to-morrow, and then back to Oxford, and then——'

'What then ? '

'Two fellows and I have planned a trip to Africa in the pring.'

'To Africa ! You really mean it ? But there are tigers and crocodiles, and dreadful things like that, are there not ? '

· Oh dear, no : not the genuine Bengal animal ; not the splendid striped monster of India. The African tiger is only a paltry spotted thing. There's no credit in shooting such an impostor.'

'But that kind of impostor might eat you,' cried Laura, in terror.

'Oh dear, no. The genuine man-eater is only to be found in the jungle. Besides, we shall have a tutor with us, to take care of the luggage and coach us in our classical geography, and all that kind of thing ; and, as a conscientious person, it will be his duty to be eaten first. Good-bye, Lorry, until this night six years.'

'Until this night six years!' repeated the young lady, almost crying. 'I think you might kiss me, Abberdale, if you are going to stay away as long as *that*.'

His lordship obeyed this hint, heedless of Miss Vicker's murmured protest. He blushed like a girl as he set his lips on the innocent upturned face, bade the governess a hurried good-night, and was gone.

BIRTHDAY THE SECOND.

Miss DE COURCY at twenty-one was a lady of vast accomplishments and considerable experience. She could converse very agreeably, within ballroom limits, in three or four continental languages—could give her opinion of the arrangements of a court-ball in Italian ; decline refreshments in Danish ; accept a partner for the next waltz in German ; and chatter all the evening through in very pure French. She was musical, and performed with effect upon the violin and piano : and beyond all this, in the eyes of that, unhappily, shallow-minded section of humanity in which her lot was cast, she was undeniably beautiful. The cold-hearted worldling who, when first introduced to her, remembered that she had forty thousand pounds in her own right, had not been half-an-hour in her society before he forgot everything except that she was one of the loveliest and most charming of women.

More than one advantageous opportunity of settlement in life had offered itself to Miss de Courcy before her one-and-twentieth birthday : but she had refused the most brilliant of these opportunities without a moment's hesitation. She had been something of a flirt, but had given no man the right to consider himself ill-used by her. She was eminently popular. Men called her a jolly girl, a lovely girl, no end of a nice girl, according to their lights—or their darkness ; but all agreed in the broad fact, that she was a good girl—good in the widest sense of the word ; a girl to whom the simulation of demi-mondain audacities and the lying arts of Rachael and enamel were ' hateful as the gates of hell '—a genuine, true-hearted Englishwoman, worthy to become the mother of brave and noble Englishmen in the time to come.

In the middle of December in that year, a British yacht, built for honest work, and bearing traces of hard usage, lay at anchor off the coast of Norway. This yacht was the ' Lorley,' commanded by George Lord Abberdale; and that young nobleman, with three chosen friends, was roughing it in a Norwegian hostelry while the 'Lorley' was refitted for her homeward voyage. Lord Abberdale and his companions had spent their summer in the neighbourhood of Baffin's Bay, and, having been very fortunate in the matter of sport, were returning to their native shores in excellent spirits and temper. Vasco di Gama or Marco Polo, Columbus or Raleigh, would have been struck with amazement on perusing the notebook of Lord Abberdale, in which was recorded the extent of country over which that young nobleman had travelled. But the heir of all the ages has the advantage of mediæval explorers, and the day may come when, in the handsome squares and crescents, streets and terraces of Baffin's Town or Behringville, lighted by electricity, and warmed by mineral oil from the Caucasus, the dwellers of a northern world may marvel to hear how English travellers once perished, forlorn and hopeless, in the regions of untrodden snow.

Lord Abberdale had 'gone in' for Arctic exploration, and the last few years of his life had been given entirely to the cultivation of the explorer's renown. He had not even had time to regret his long separation from that favourite cousin who, he had long ago promised himself, should some day be something nearer and dearer than cousinship, pleasant as that tie between them had been to him. He told his love-story to his companions to-night in the Norwegian hostelry. He had no idea that reticence as to the liege lady of his love was a point of honour.

'I shall call that love-story of yours the thousand-and-one nights, George,' said one of his friends. 'I'm sure we've heard it a thousand-and-one times. It seems to me rather a spoony notion of yours, falling in love with a chit of fifteen.'

'Fifteen!' cried George, 'I've been over head and ears in love with my cousin Laura ever since she was seven. Not having any people of my own, you know, and De Courcy being my guardian, I used to spend my holidays at Courcy; and sometimes in the summer months they used to have a house at Maidenhead, or Old Windsor, or somewhere thereabouts, while I was at Eaton, and, of course, I was always hanging about the place—boating and fishing—and, in a general way, playing Old Gooseberry. I was within an inch of drowning Lorry half-a-dozen times or so: but she didn't seem to mind it. And her brother Lionel has no end of pluck, and used to take his duckings sweetly.

And then Lord Abberdale told the story of the birthday ball, and produced the treasured slipper, which he carried in a pocket of his log-book, the log and the slipper being about equally sacred in his eyes.

'And you mean to be home in time for the fancy ball?' asked one of his companions.

' I should think I do, indeed ! Why, I'd smash the "Lorley" and every man aboard her sooner than break my word to that dear girl !'

'Then I fancy you'll have a tight squeeze of it,' replied his friend. "We haven't been paying much attention to the operations of the enemy since we've left off keeping the log. This is the 15th of December, and the "Lorley" won't be ready for sea in less than a week.'

'She shall be ready in three days, Hal,' roared Abberdale; 'I'd sooner miss a pot of money on next year's Derby than that ball.'

'You may do it, with luck.'

'I'll do it with luck or without luck,' replied his lordship, unmindful of that 'D.V.' piously interjected by Miss Vicker on a previous occasion.

'How about your dress?'

'What dress?'

'Your costume for the fancy ball?'

'I've got that safe enough with the rest of my traps on board the "Lorley," answered Abberdale with a laugh ; 'I had it from a costumier in the neighbourhood of Baffin's Bay.'

Late in the afternoon of December 24th a gentleman might have been observed—if travellers generally were not too much occupied by their own affairs to observe anyone— journeying by express, northward to Kelton, the nearest station to Courcy Castle. When the train stopped at this small station, for the special accommodation of this traveller, there was some little difficulty about the luggage, and a certain black case was missing, the temporary loss of which threw the traveller into a fever of rage and impatience.

Happily, it was fished out of some darksome cavern of a luggage-van before the express—snorting defiant and angry snorts all the time of the delay—had snorted itself out of the station, with a farewell shriek of rage at having been detained at so insignificant a halting-place. The traveller glared at the porter who ultimately produced the case with a most appalling glare.

'It's very lucky for you it turned up,' he said, ' or I should have been very much tempted to break every bone in your body.'

' Do you know who that is ? ' asked the porter of the station-master, when the furious traveller and his black packing-case had been driven away in a fly.

' No—do you ? '

' Yes ; it's Lord Abberdale, nephew to Mr. de Courcy. He's going to the ball. That's his fancy-dress as he's got in that box, I'll be bound.'

The eventful night had arrived. Lights shone from all the windows of Courcy Castle, and the poor of the district rejoiced and made merry, inasmuch as their dole of this year was double the customary bounty, and that was a royal one. Scarlet cloaks and comfortable blankets, packets of grocery and baskets of wine, had been dealt out with liberal hands. Miss de Courcy had been driving about the neighbourhood all the week in her pretty basket-carriage ; and if there were sad hearts or cheerless hearths within twenty miles of Courcy on this cold Christmas-eve, it was because of no shortcoming or stint on the part of the Castle that there was sadness and cheerlessness.

In Miss de Courcy's dressing-room there was much excite-ment as the hands of the little timepiece drew near ten o'clock. At ten o'clock the guests had been bidden ; and the guests bidden to this birthday ball included some very important people. It was to be altogether a most brilliant affair ; and everybody in the Castle seemed in the highest possible spirits —except Laura, the one person who ought naturally to have been the most joyous of all. The faithful Miss Vicker—still retained as monitor and friend, though for some time super-seded as instructress—watched her late pupil with mingled anxiety and wonder, as the young lady sat before the cheval-glass, while her maid was occupied with the solemn task of adjusting her head-dress.

The head-dress was a difficult one, demanding great skill and nicety in the adjustment thereof. It was one of those lofty sugar-loaf head-gears affected by the women of the Middle Ages. Mrs. de Courcy had suggested the powder and patches of the Watteau period for her daughter's adorn-ment ; but the young lady had her own whims, and adhered obstinately to her own fancy.

'I will be a mediæval princess and nothing else, mother,' she said ; 'and my dress must be cloth-of-gold. I have found the costume in father's illustrated edition of Planché.'

Mrs. de Courcy turned up her nose at the conical head-gear.

'Why, the hideous thing must be a foot and a half high,' she said. 'I'm sure I don't know what you'll look like, child, —you, who are rather too tall at the best of times.'

The conical head-gear was ordered, nevertheless ; and the trailing robe of cloth-of-gold, with lions and leopards in black velvet laid thereupon, with broideries in spangles and bullion of unutterable splendour. The petticoat was of cherry-coloured brocade ; the shoes were long and pointed ; the ruff was a marvel of historical research ; the sugar-loaf head-piece an epitome of the old chroniclers ; and the result was an embodiment of the grotesquely beautiful. The quaint *moyen-age* dress imparted something uncanny and fantastic to the damsel's loveliness. So might appear the vision of long-buried beauty, if we could conjure it from its chilly resting-place ; and so might shine, in all the glamour of unreal loveliness, the ideal princess of a dreaming Chaucer.

All the best people within a reasonable distance of Courcy, together with distinguished visitors staying at the Castle, were assembled in the great drawing-room at eleven o'clock. The costumes were good ; many of them had figured at the court balls of forty years ago. The people were agreeable, the arrangements seemed perfection, except to one person, and that person was the mediæval princess.

Mr. de Courcy had several times suggested that the signal should be given to the band in the gallery for the first quadrille, but the princess made some objection on every occasion.

'The bishop has not come yet, father,' she said; 'it would be the worst possible taste to begin dancing before he comes. I consider it so very liberal of him to come at all, especially as he is rather low.'

It must be remembered that Miss de Courcy used this last obnoxious word in the ecclesiastical, and not the vulgar sense.

The bishop came presently, attired as William Penn, in a cheap, and not especially compromising costume. But his daughters were all that there is of the most Pompadour, and his son was attired as Lord Dundreary, and came prepared to afflict the company with weak imitations of Mr. Sothern. Mr. de Courcy again suggested the signal for the first quadrille, but again Laura resisted.

'There is Lady Louisa Sparkleham, father. Dobbins walked home from church with her maid last Sunday, and she is coming as Queen Elizabeth, in the costume she wore at Buckingham Palace forty years ago ; and I am sure she is just the sort of person to be offended if her appearance produces no effect ; and of course it won't if we're all jogging about in a quadrille.'

'I don't see why you need be jogging about,' grumbled Mr. de Courcy. 'It's eleven o'clock. People expect to be earlier, you know, in the country.'

At last the time came when excuses would be no longer accepted. The inevitable signal was given. The band in the gallery began one of D'Albert's Introductions with a great crash, then a series of smaller crashes—slow, quick, crescendo, tremulo ; a plaintive little pianissimo bit for the cornet, rallentando—and off we go into Pantalon.

The mediæval princess and Lord Dundreary are partners. William Penn smiles benignly on his son from the circle of lookers-on, in spite of his lowness. Is it not written in the dowager Mrs. de Courcy's will that the mediæval princess shall have forty thousand pounds ?

'Eleven o'clock,' says the inward voice of the princess, ' and no chimney-sweep. His promise is quite broken now.'

The thought has scarcely shaped itself in her mind when there is a sudden confusion among the lookers-on. The evangelical bishop is pushed irreverently on one side, Lord Dundreary recoils horror-stricken, the ladies scream in their usual charming manner, as an appalling form plunges clumsily in among the dancers.

A Polar bear—white as the icebergs of his native land, shaggy as the ragged drifts of snow that fringe those icebergs, awful as the dangers of those trackless regions—displaces the bishop's son, and seizes the shrinking hand of the princess in his ponderous paw.

No word spoke this hideous brute ; no heed took he of Dundreary's remonstrances, the bishop's indignation, the titters and little screams of the company ; but through the mazy figures of the dance—in the solemn settings of L'Eté, the see-saw movements of La Poule, the graceful advancings and retirings of Pastourelle, the whirl and riot of the final gallopade—did the monster drag the mediæval princess, to the surprise and admiration of the assembled multitude.

When the quadrille was finished he led the damsel to her parents, and lifting the grim jaw and throwing back the shaggy head as if it had been a knightly visor, the uncouth visitor revealed the countenance of Lord Abberdale.

' I'm afraid I've been very rude to a lot of people,' he said ; ' but you must introduce me to them presently, aunt Sophia, and I must make my peace somehow. I didn't reach the Castle till five minutes before I came into the room. Six years ago, in Hyde-park-gardens, I promised Lorry I'd dance the first dance with her on this night, and I've done it. And, by Jove, I don't much care whom I have offended !'

' But you were to come as a chimney-sweep,' said Laura.

' Well, you see, I hadn't time to think of the elegances of costume. I shot this poor beggar—I beg your pardon, Lorry—this unfortunate animal—in Baffin's Bay ; and very sorry I was to do it, considering how tame the poor creatures are when they haven't the honour of *our* acquaintance.'

' You see *I* remembered the dress you said you'd like me to wear,' Miss de Courcy said later, when a compact of peace, or at least armed neutrality, had been made between Lord Abberdale and the bishop, and these two cousins had danced more than one dance together.

' Yes, darling, and very lovely you look in it. And now there is only one other dress that I languish to see you in.'

' Indeed ! and what may that be ? '

' White satin and orange blossoms.'

And to oblige this audacious young nobleman, Miss de Courcy made her appearance in this costume at St. George's, Hanover-square, early in the ensuing April.

THE LITTLE WOMAN IN BLACK

THERE was hardly anything talked about in the clubs and the coffee-houses that November of 1753, but the approaching marriage of Miss Sarah Pawlett and Lord Bellenden. My lord was one of the finest gentlemen in England, a statesman and a diplomatist, a man of great learning, eight-and-thirty years of age, honoured and favoured at Court, on terms of friendly intimacy at Strawberry Hill and Marble Hill, where Lady Suffolk swore he was the one honest man in his Majesty's dominions. He was owner of a splendid estate in Hertfordshire, and a fine house in St. James's Park ; he had a castle in Ireland, and a deer forest in North Britain. In a word, he was the best match in all London.

Had the beautiful Sarah been about to marry some lordling of the fribble and fop tribe, instead of this splendid gentleman, the town would doubtless have had a good deal to say about her promotion ; for it is not an every-day incident for an actress to be raised to the peerage, albeit Polly Peacham, after more than twenty years of probation, had lately been made Duchess of Bolton ; but for the Covent Garden actress to carry off the finest gentleman in London was another matter, and folks were greatly amazed at her high fortune. She herself bore her success calmly, was said, indeed, to have a somewhat melancholy air when she showed herself in her coach in the park, or attended a fashionable auction to bid for some old delft jar or Indian monster. But a pensive air best became that statuesque loveliness of hers, and rollicking and blithsome as she was in a comedy part, she had ever in society the look of a tearless Niobe, pale as marble, and with large violet eyes full of a strange pathos.

'She had not always that doleful air,' said little Tom Squatt, the critic, an early admirer of Sarah's ; 'I remember the time when she was as gay as a bird—ready to jump over the moon—and that was when she was not always sure of her dinner.'

'Ah, that was before she took the town,' said another literary gentleman at the Little Hell Fire Club, a room over a tavern in Covent Garden, where a choice circle of garretteers and hireling wits met every night after the play. 'Success sobers 'em all. They begin to think of saving money, and turn religious. Besides, that was before she fell in love with Ned Langley.'

At this there was much head-shaking and elevation of eyebrows in the little assembly, and divers pinches of snuff were taken with an air and a shoulder-shrug, as who should say, 'We could, an' if we would,' and so on. Yet scandal had hardly breathed its venom over the young actress's fair fame. She had never left the wing of the old half-pay Major, her father, who had fought with King George at Dettingen, and who was punctiliousness itself upon all points of honour; and she was known to have supported a brood of younger sisters, down-at-heel slatterns, with pretty faces and towzled heads, out of her earnings as an actress.

True! But she was also known to have been for at least one brief season—the girl's dream-land time—over head and ears in love with handsome Ned Langley. Langley the irresistible, the beau-ideal lover and reprobate of the dear old reprobate-drama, the Wildair, the Lovelace, the Mirabel, the Ranger of fashionable comedy; polished, elegant, supple, villainous, bewitching.

Ned could hardly help carrying some of his comedy characteristics into real life. The town would not have had him otherwise. Society began by giving him his diabolical reputation, and poor Ned had to live up to it. He must be Don Juan or nothing. His fashion would have waned in a season had it been hinted that he lived soberly and had ceased to intrigue with women of quality. In dress, and manner, and morals, he must needs be as the heroes of Wycherley and Vanburgh, if he would keep his vogue. And Ned was vain, and loved to be the fashion; and he deemed it his first duty to himself and society to ruin the peace of any beautiful woman who came within his ken.

Sarah Pawlett came into Covent Garden Theatre innocent, fresh, warm-hearted, pure-minded, pious even, in an age when unbelief was the last fashion. She came from her humble training in booths and barns, and queer little provincial theatres, and took the town by storm. Her beauty, her youth, her buoyancy came upon the jaded London playgoer as a surprise. It was long since so bright and spontaneous a being had flashed and sparkled on those boards. She seemed the very spirit of comedy; and to see her act a love scene—half sentiment, half mockery—with Ned Langley, was to see the very perfection of acting.

The town flocked to hear these two interchange the joyous banter of Wycherley or Congreve, charmed with their sparkle and fire, their dash and exuberance.

Of course, stage-lovers so delightful must be lovers off the stage and in earnest. The tumultuous love scenes of that broad, bright comedy must find their counterpart off the stage in a deeper and more fatal love. This is the universal belief of the playgoer.

For once in a way the audience were right in their guess-work. Those stage-lovers had not wooed and bantered each other in the shine of the oil lamps for half a year before they had fallen deeper in love than ever Wycherley or Congreve dreamed of in their gamut of passion. She gave up heart and soul to the gallant lover, surrendered her young fresh lips to his stage-kisses, melted in his arms, heart beating against heart, sweetest eyes lifted confidingly to his, while the audience applauded and cried, ' How exquisite, how natural!'

She was to be his wife. No shadow of any other thought had ever crossed the unsullied surface of her mind. As yet there had been no word spoken of their marriage. They two had been but seldom alone together. The old Major was at his post behind the scenes every night, and carried his daughter off to their lodgings in Holborn directly after the performance. He attended rehearsals, took snuff with the actors and actresses, and bored them exceedingly with his prosy old stories of Dettingen, or the forty-five. He had been stationed at Derby when the young Pretender turned back with his rabble army. He was Hanoverian to the marrow.

No, there had been no word of marriage. The wooing had been all stage-wooing—tender embraces, eyes entangling themselves in eyes, swooning sighs, impassioned kisses, hearts beating to suffocation, but all stage-play. If the Major complained that these love scenes were too natural, the town was enraptured, and greeted those two young lovers as if the pair had made but one perfect whole. Applause given to her was sweetest laudation for him. He looked down at her fondly, proudly, as they stood hand in hand at the fall of the curtain. He was much more experienced in stage-craft than she ; and it may be that he fancied he had taught her to act. Those who know genius when they see it, knew that with her acting was as the gift of song to the bird, God-given, spontaneous.

After that first half-year of stage courtship there came a time when little hints and faint breathings of venom began to be heard in the side-scenes and green-room : shrugs, innuendoes, a suggestion that the prosy old Major was being hoodwinked by those fiery spirits ; that the lovely girl who walked off to her dingy lodgings so meekly every midnight, muffled and hooded, and clinging to the father's arm, had begun to be experienced in the ruses by which ladies of quality overreach a tyrannical parent or a jealous husband ; that the frank smile and the sparkling eye now served to mask a secret.

'Why don't they marry?' asked the comic old man.

'The old Major would never consent to throw away his clever, beautiful daughter upon an extravagant wretch like Langley,' answered the lady who played the heavy mothers. 'Why, her salary has to keep the whole family—yes, feed and clothe all those hulking sisters, and find the old man in grog. She is the milch-cow; and if she were to marry Langley they must all starve.'

'If Ned were a man of spirit he would run away with her,' said the actor ; 'or get himself spliced by one of your May Fair parsons.'

'Ned has too many strings to his bow,' answered the lady, with her tragic air ; 'half the women of quality in London are in love with him. He has the *ton* at his beck and call. Ned would be a fool to marry.'

'Not to marry Sarah Pawlett, my good soul. That girl is a fortune in herself. She is a genius, madam, a genius. Ned must be a man of snow if he can resist such charms, such graces. When she comes on the stage it is like the sun breaking through a cloud. The whole scene—nay, the whole theatre brightens.'

But time went on, and there was no hint of marriage between those ideal lovers. The old Major was laid up with gout, and unable to haunt the side-scenes as of old ; but he was represented by a duenna of Irish extraction—an old servant who had nursed all the towzle-haired girls, including Sarah herself. This dragon was of a mild nature, and the lovers enjoyed each other's society very freely while the demon Podagra laid the old soldier by the heels. They seemed to move in a paradise of their own, regardless of those around them, thoughtless of the morrow, forgetful of yesterday, infinitely happy in the present hour.

Their careless joy gave occasion for more shoulder-shrugging among their worldly-wise comrades. There were some who gave the lovely Sally over for lost, some who denounced the handsome Ned as an arrant scoundrel—behind his back, mark you ; but if this beautiful butterfly creature were hovering on the brink of a precipice, there was no hand stretched forth to hold her back from the abyss.

Suddenly the stream of gossip was turned into a new channel, and the only talk of wings and green-room, club and coffee-house, was of the wonderful conquest Sarah Pawlett had made in my Lord Bellenden—no light-minded haunter of play-houses and French taverns, but one of the magnates of the land, a gentleman of the purest water, a gem without a flaw, white and perfect as the Regent's diamond. While Ned Langley had trifled and fooled, this most estimable gentleman had stooped from his high estate to make the actress an honourable offer of marriage.

Old Major Pawlett was on his legs again by the time this happened. His gout had fled before the magic wand of supreme good luck. He proudly accepted his lordship's generous offer. The girl was but a child—not nineteen until next April—and she had all a child's waywardness. Yet she could not be otherwise than deeply grateful, moved and melted to her heart's core by his lordship's generosity.

The girl herself said nothing of gratitude, or any other feeling. She stood up in the midst of the shabby lodging-house parlour, thin and straight and pale, like a tall white lily, and allowed herself to be given away to this stately nobleman as if she had been a chattel.

He looked down at her with his grave, grand face, smiling calmly ; confident in his power to hold that which he won, strong in past triumphs over the hearts of women, strong in the consciousness of his own worth. He put a diamond hoop on the third finger of the cold, unresisting hand—so cold albeit so yielding.

'Let our wedding bells sound as soon as may be, dear one, he said ; 'we have nothing to wait for.'

'Oh, not too soon, not too soon,' she pleaded piteously ; 'your lordship is almost a stranger to me.'

'Never again lordship, and not long a stranger,' he answered gently.

He saw that look of anguish in the lovely face, and knew that her heart was not his ; but he saw the pure and candid soul shining out of the sorrowful eyes ; and he told himself that such a heart was worth winning.

There was a painful scene between Sally and her old father as soon as the nobleman's back was turned. The girl grovelled at the Major's feet, vowed with passionate sobs that she would do anything for her father and her sisters, except this one thing that was wanted of her. She would work like a pack-horse. She would bring them evey guinea she earned —she would wear one old grogram gown from year's end to year's end. She would live on bread and cheese. But the Major upbraided her with basest ingratitude to him and to Providence—to Providence for having given her such a lover as Lord Bellenden, to her father for his having been clever enough to bring such a lover to honourable proposals.

'Do you suppose if I had been anything else than an officer and a gentleman, and a man of the world to boot, his lordship would have offered you marriage?' he demanded indignantly.

'Nay,' answered the girl, with a touch of pride that ennobled her—pride in the man who loved her, albeit she could not return his love, 'his lordship is a man of honour, and would not have made dishonourable proposals to the lowliest orphan in the land. He is like King Cophetua in the old ballad.'

'I wonder you have the impudence to praise him after the fuss you have been making,' said the old man angrily, and he emphasised his speech with sundry forcible epithets common to the conversation of military men in those days.

He watched his daughter like a lynx that night at the theatre. Not a word could Ned Langley and she say to each other in the green-room or at the side-scenes ; but there was one opportunity on the stage when they two were standing together at the back of the scene, while the low comedian and the comic old woman were fooling in front of the foot-lights.

She told him what had happened, clasping his hands in hers, looking up at him with divine love and confidence.

'You must marry me, and quickly too,' she said. 'There is no other way out of it. If you don't I shall be married to Lord Bellenden, willy nilly. My father's heart is set upon it, and all the girls were in tears this afternoon beseeching me. If you love me, Ned, as you have sworn you do, ah, so often—so often, you must make me your wife without a day's delay.'

He looked at her with passionate earnestness, betwixt love and pain. 'My dearest, it can't be,' he said, 'it can't be.'

'But, why not ?'

'Don't ask me, love, it can't be—and only reflect, sweet one, what a chance you are throwing away. Such a match as Lord Bellenden is not offered to an actress twice in a century. You would be doing better than either of those Gunning girls about whom we have all heard so much—and indeed you are handsomer than either; and what,' he whispered in her ear, drawing close to her as the serpent to Eve, ' what is to prevent us loving each other till the end of the chapter, even if you *are* Lady Bellenden ? '

Her hands grew cold as death, and she wrenched them from his, as she would have snatched them out of a fiery furnace. She recoiled from him, stood apart from him for the rest of the scene, neither looked at him nor spoke to him, save when the business of the stage compelled her.

Three days afterwards Ned Langley went over to the enemy, accepted an engagement at the rival house, and the manager was left in despair.

' What the plague am I to do ? ' he asked piteously, with his wig pushed on one side, from sheer vexation. ' There is no comedian like him in London—not in the world, perhaps —in spite of their talk of those frog-eating jackanapeses in the Rue St. Honoré.'

' Play tragedy,' said Sarah, ' and then you won't miss him. You have Mr. Deloraine, who took the town in Romeo. I am dying to act tragedy.'

' What, you, Mrs. Madcap ? Do you think that you, who have kept the town laughing so long, will ever set them crying ? '

' Try me ! ' she answered, fixing him with those beautiful eyes of hers, so large, so limpid in their exquisite azure. ' I can cry myself, mark you, sir ; and that's half the battle.'

She stood a little way from him, threw her head slightly backward, and lifted up her eyes to heaven, in a Carlo Dolci attitude. Slowly, gradually, the beautiful eyes filled, and slowly overflowed. Pearly drops chased each other down the delicate cheeks ; not a contortion disfigured the chiselled features ; no flush disturbed the pure pallor of that ivory skin.

' Yes, you will do it,' cried the manager. ' What a face to prelude Juliet's potion scene, when mother and nurse have left her, and she stands alone, like Niobe, fixed in despair. Yes, you shall play Juliet next week. Deloraine is at his best in Romeo, and at forty looks an admirable twenty-five.'

The manager kept his word, and mistress Sarah's Juliet was the mode for a month. The town was all agog about her matrimonial engagement, and flocked to see her act with ever increasing fervour. She had refused to leave the stage till the eve of her wedding ; refused with a charming feminine

obstinacy which delighted her lover, though he would have
had it otherwise. A man so deep in love is all the more
smitten by having his every wish denied. Sarah was the
coyest, proudest, most tormenting of mistresses; and there was
that shadow of sadness, which came and went like the clouds
that drift across the moon on a windy autumn night, and
only made her more beautiful.

Mr. Deloraine was plain and pock-marked, and lacked all
the graces of handsome Ned Langley; but he contrived to
make himself handsome on the stage, by the aid of white
lead and ceruse, and he was a highly respectable gentleman,
who paid his way and went to church on Sundays. He had
a dull wife and eleven children, so Lord Bellenden had
no cause for jealousy about this Romeo, even when he saw
Juliet in his arms at the passionate hour of parting, what
time the lark carolled above the olive woods beyond Verona.

Little by little—by infinitesimal stages of days and hours—
Sarah learnt, first to honour, and then to love her noble wooer.
He was a man worthy to be loved—generous, chivalrous as
that lover in the old ballad which Sarah knew by heart—
nobler than the ideal of her girlish dreams. She surrendered
her heart to him almost unwillingly, deeming herself unworthy
to be loved by him, unworthy even to love him; but she could
not withhold her love. He commanded her affection, as he
had first commanded her respect.

She loved him, and in a few weeks she was to be married
to him. The most fashionable mantua-maker at the West
End was busy with her gowns and falballas : the Bellenden
diamonds were being remounted for her : a chariot of the
newest shape and style was being built for her : and ladies of
the highest *ton* stood up in their carriages to stare at her as
she drove through the Park in a hired Berlin with her father.

With all this she was not happy, and she had more than
one reason for her unhappiness. First, there was the thought
of Ned Langley's treachery, and the love she had wasted
upon him. This rankled like a green wound. Then there
was the stinging memory of certain girlish half-mad letters
she had written to him, when she had believed him noble as
a Greek god. Thirdly, there was the haunting presence of a
little woman in black, who dogged her in the street by day,
now following her, now lurking at corners to watch her, and
who sat on the same bench, in the same spot—the third seat
from the end near the door on the prompt side, in the
second row of the pit—every night.

At first, Sarah had been interested, amused, flattered by the lady's constant attendance. She had pointed her out to Ned Langley, solitary, silent, intent upon the play; evidently a friendless creature, alone in the desert of the town, with no amusement but the play-house.

'She looks a poor little shabby-genteel creature, but a lady all the same,' Sarah had said to Langley, 'and how she watches you and me, and hangs upon every word we utter. I am quite taken with the poor harmless soul. I wish you would find out who she is?'

'Impossible, child!' a stranger from the country, most likely. A waif thrown up by the ocean of change—a widow who has lost her fortune and her husband, and has come to London to seek new ones.'

On another occasion, when Sarah talked of the little woman in black, Ned had a vexed air.

'I believe she is a political spy,' he said ; 'the Government is still suspicious of dealings with the Pretender, and has all sorts of agents.'

And now, when she and Ned Langley were strangers for evermore, Sarah found herself watched more closely than ever by the little woman in shabby black—a pale, sharp-featured little woman, who might, perchance, have been pretty in girlhood, but who had lost all her beauty at five-and-thirty, which was about the age Sarah gave her. She had a restless, lynx-eyed look, as of one who had worn herself out with watching other people.

One night that the Major had stayed late at a convivial party, Sarah, walking home with her maid, was overtaken by a pair of lightly-tripping feet in Lincoln's Inn Fields, and was startled by the tap of a hand on her shoulder.

She turned and fronted the little woman in black, whose pale, pinched face seemed ghostly in the dim light of the oil-lamp overhead. They had just turned the corner by his Grace of Newcastle's big stone mansion.

'What do you want, woman?' asked Sarah haughtily.

'Five minutes' conversation with you, madam ; and it is for your welfare that you should grant me the interview.'

'You can fall a little in the rear, Margaret,' said Sarah to the old servant. 'This lady wishes to talk with me in private.'

The Irishwoman looked doubtful, and fell back only a few paces. The woman in black seemed too small a person to be dangerous. Her head hardly reached the queenly Sarah's shoulder.

'You are going to make a great match, madam,' said the stranger; 'all the town is full of your good fortune.'

'I hope you have not stopped me so solemnly in order to tell me that!' retorted the actress. 'I have noted you in the pit many an evening, madam, and as you seem an admirer of the drama I should be sorry to deem you crazy.'

'No, madam, I am not crazy, though I have had more than enough to make me so. A father's anger, aye, and the loss of every friend I had in youth, a fortune forfeited, and, for a crowning mercy, an unfaithful husband—yes, unfaithful—though it was for him I sacrificed father and fortune, friends and position. I was the only daughter of a bishop, madam, and kept the best company before I was married.'

'Those facts are interesting, madam, to yourself or your personal friends, but hardly so to me. I wish you good-night,' said Sarah hastily, assured that the lady was a lunatic. But the little woman pressed upon her steps.

'I shall find means to awaken your interest presently, madam,' she said. 'You are about to be married to the best match in London, as I was saying, and your fortune is to be envied by all your sex. I have heard wagers in the pit as to whether the marriage would or would not come off.'

'The people who made such wagers were monstrously insolent.'

'No doubt, madam; but insolence is the order of the day. Now, I myself would not mind wagering that your engagement with Lord Bellenden would be off to-morrow if he knew as much as I do; and if he were favoured with the perusal of certain letters which you wrote—and by the dozen—to handsome Ned Langley, your stage-lover, madam, and your very earnest lover off the stage.'

'My letters!' cried Sarah, aghast. 'What do you know of my letters?'

She was utterly unskilled in deceit, unpractised in denial, and admitted her folly as freely as a child would have done.

'What do I know of them? They are my daily reading; they are my morning service. I know them by heart, madam. Yes, and I know of your meetings, too; your stolen kisses in the old house by the river—among the rats and the spiders, and the ghosts, madam—yes, the ghosts. You were scared by a ghost once, I think, when you and Ned were standing side by side in the twilight in that empty house which you chose for your *rendezvous.*'

'Yes,' cried Sarah, 'there was a figure flitted by—noiseless

—shadowy. It turned my blood to ice—a figure in black.
It was *you!*'

She stood gazing at the little woman in the moonlight—so
pale, so attenuated. Yes, that was the form which had flitted
past on the shadowy landing by the open door of the room in
which she and Ned were standing, hand clasped in hand,
pouring out their tale of love.

She had taken the little black figure for a visitant from the
other world ; and now she knew that it was even worse than
a ghost—a woman, mad, or it might be, only jealous—a woman
with a bitter, unscrupulous tongue bent on doing her mischief.

This creature would betray her to her lord, whom she
reverenced, whom she loved. It was of Bellenden she thought
as she faced her foe in the corner of the square by the turn-
stile, the moon shining down upon them, the shadows of the
houses making great blots of darkness here and there.

She had done this foolish thing, she, Sarah Pawlett, whom
Lord Bellenden deemed the purest of women. She had com-
promised herself deeply for that false lover of hers, consenting
to stolen meetings in an old empty house by the river, between
the Temple and Blackfriars, a house that had been in Chancery
for fifty years, and which was supposed to be haunted. Ned
Langley had procured a key somehow ; and here they had
met with impunity between the morning rehearsal and the
evening performance. When Sally was late in returning to
the family dinner or the family tea, she had but to say that
the rehearsal had been longer than usual.

There had not been many such meetings, a dozen at most,
and the *rendezvous* had been of a perfectly innocent character ;
but the mere fact of such secret stolen interviews would have
been quite enough to compromise or to condemn Sarah in the
opinion of such a man as Lord Bellenden.

Her letters were full of allusions to these meetings ; she
had dwelt with all a girl's romantic fondness upon the delight
of being alone with her idol ; of touching his soft silken
locks, of looking up into his eyes. The letters were written
with all the self-abandonment of a young heart, written to
one who was to be the writer's husband, who was her all in
all, the beginning and end of her universe ; written to one
whom she would no more have suspected of falsehood or
meanness than she would have doubted the purity of the
blue ether far away above the common earth, in a region
where defilement cometh not. She had not asked for the return
of her letters, for, until that never-to-be-forgotten night when

she had told Ned Langley that the time had come for their
marriage, she had lived in the assurance that she was to be
his wife. He had not definitely spoken of their union, but
it had seemed to her a thing of course from the hour in which
they confessed their mutual love. What else had they to
live for, either of them, but to love and wed? they who
seemed made to be mated; like two flowers on one stem,
turning to each other naturally as the wind of fate blew them.

After that bitter moment in which her lover had revealed
his worthlessness, Sarah had been too proud in her deep anger
to approach him, or communicate with him in any form, even
for the sake of regaining her letters. She had hardly
thought of those letters, indeed; thinking of the whole
love story as a chapter in her life that was closed for ever;
a vault sealed and secret, in which lay the dead corpse of her
first passionate love.

And now she was learning that there might be a second
love, sweeter even than the first; graver, deeper, truer; less
romantic, but more ennobling; she was learning this and
forgetting everything else, when this new trouble came upon
her. Those letters, those foolish, wildly sentimental letters,
were in the keeping of this strange woman.

'How came you by my letters, madam?' she asked indignantly. 'Are you a thief?'

'No, madam. I am a much injured woman; and you
ought to take it kindly that I have borne my wrongs so
patiently, and not disgraced you in your theatre, where you
are like a queen. But stage queens have had mud thrown
in their faces before to-day.'

'*You* disgrace me! you?'

'Yes, I, madam; Ned Langley's wife.'

'Ned—Langley's—wife!'

Sarah repeated the words slowly, almost in a whisper.

'Oh! he did not tell you that he was a married man, did
he? he never does. You are not the first he has deluded.
He does worse than that, for he tells villainous lies about me;
he tells his fellow-actors that the poor little crack-brained
woman at his lodgings is not his wife, but his mistress—a
young lady of quality whom he ran away with, and who has
been a burden to him ever since. *That's* what he tells his
friends, madam; because that story leaves him at liberty to
make love to the last fashionable actress, and to promise her
marriage. And I am fool enough to stay with him and to
slave for him, knowing all this; to warm his slippers of a

night before he comes home, and mix his grog for him, and
bear with him when he staggers home drunk from his Hell
Fire Club, and hear his boasts of women of *ton* who are over
head and ears in love with him. It was one night when he
was in liquor that I found the first of your letters in his
pocket ; and after that I watched him, and picked them up
everywhere. You've no notion how careless he is of such
letters ; and, madam, the women all write alike, and lovers
get tired of so much honey. I've heard him say, "More of
their precious scribble." We wives have the best of it, perhaps, with such fellows ; for, at least, we are behind the
scenes, and we see them with their masks off.'

'And you have my letters—all of them ? '

'Three-and-twenty, madam. I doubt that's all, for I
ransack every corner in quest of such things. I know my
gentleman's ways !'

'Will you give them me back, to-night ?' asked Sarah,
eagerly.

'No, madam, neither to-night nor to-morrow. I will not
give them back to Sarah Pawlett ; I will only return them
to Lady Bellenden. When you are his lordship's wife,
madam, the letters shall be yours."

'I see,' said Sarah, gloomily, 'it is the old story. I have
heard of such things. You mean to keep the letters, and
hold them over me as a continual threat after I am married.
You will make me pay you to be silent about them.'

'Pay me ! No, madam, I am not so base as that. I have
no grudge against you. I cannot even blame your conduct,
though it was somewhat imprudent. You are but one of
many whom handsome Ned Langley has deluded. I am not
a double-dealer. The letters shall be yours when you are
Lady Bellenden. On your wedding-day, if you like.'

'Why wait till then ? Give me the letters to-morrow, and
I shall be your grateful debtor for life. There is nothing
in my power, as an honest woman, that I would not do for you.'

'You promise fair, madam, but I have my fancy. I will
only surrender those letters to Lord Bellenden's wife.'

'But you must have your price—you must want something
of me.'

'Well perhaps I do. Yes, every man has his price, and I
suppose every woman has hers too. I shall tell you mine
when I give you back your letters on your wedding-day.'

Sarah tried, even with tears, to argue Ned Langley's
wife out of this rigid determination. The three women—

Irish Margaret in the rear—walked round Lincoln's Inn Fields twice in the moonlight, Sarah pleading— the little woman as firm as a rock.

'On your wedding-day, madam, and no sooner,' she sad at parting ; 'I shall be in the church, with the letters in my pocket. I wish you a very good-night.'

She made a low curtsey as ceremoniously as if she had been at Ranelagh, and tripped lightly off towards Clare Market; leaving Sarah and the maid to go on to Holborn together.

After this midnight interview, came a period of keenest anxiety, nay, almost of mental torture for Sarah Pawlett. Three weeks had yet to pass before she would be my Lady Bellenden. How she regretted her own persistency in having postponed the wedding—her obstinacy in having insisted upon acting until the eve of her marriage. She acted now in fear and trembling, expectant of some demonstration from the little woman in black. The little woman never missed a night in her accustomed seat in the second row of the pit. She had acquired a prescriptive right to that seat by her constant attendance, and by being always one of the first to enter the theatre. Regular pit-goers knew her by sight, and gave way to her—a dramatic enthusiast, doubtless, a little distraught, but harmless.

Sarah's first look when she came on the stage was to that seat in the pit.

She acted the potion scene in Juliet with her eyes fixed on the little woman in black, fixed as if she had been face to face with Nemesis. It was a wonderful expression : people remembered it, and quoted it a quarter of a century afterwards as a marvel of finished art and high-wrought feeling.

Driving with Lord Bellenden in the park, or attending a fashionable auction with him, or at an afternoon water-party, Sarah was tortured by the expectation of the same haunting presence. The little woman seemed ubiquitous. Small, active, insignificant, neatly dressed, and with lady-like manners, she was able to push herself in anywhere. She tripped about auction-rooms and looked at china monsters. She had her seat in the park, as she had in the pit. She might even be seen on the river, alone with her waterman, shooting about among the crowded wherries and gaily-clad people—a creature of no more significance than a blot of ink on a gaudy flowered wall.

Sarah was always dreading an explosion ; and her future

husband was so devoted to her, so chivalrous, so true. His love lifted her to a calm heaven of proud contentment. To be beloved by him was to enter into a state of tranquil blessedness ; just as she had pictured to herself the condition of the elect in the world to come.

Sometimes she had a mind to fall at his feet and confess everything : her romantic passion for Ned Langley, and the way she had been fooled by him—even their secret meetings in the deserted house—yes, she would have confessed all that, she would have endured the shame of it ; but the idea that those letters of hers, written in all the intoxication of a first love, should be read in cold blood, read by a man of cultivated mind—those foolish, rambling sentences and reiterations, the poor little stock of words so repeated and misused, and, worst of all, the bad spelling. Yes ; Sarah had been educating herself severely since her engagement to Lord Bellenden, and in the course of her studies had discovered how sorely she had erred in that matter of orthography. To think that throughout those fatal letters she had spelt affection with one f, and rapture with sh, instead of t. Orthography is such an arbitrary thing ; has neither rhyme nor reason in it, Sarah thought, submitting her old lax notions to the rigid schooling of the dictionary.

And now came the wedding-day. She was to be married at St. Martin's-in-the-Fields, his lordship's house being in that parish. The wedding was to be a very quiet ceremonial. His lordship's mother, a dowager of seventy years of age, and of great dignity, of whom Sarah lived in awe, was to be the only relative present on the bridegroom's side. His best man was an old friend. On Sarah's side there were the four sisters, and an oafish brother. The Major was to give his daughter away, and was to have a new coat for the occasion. The eldest of her sisters was to be bridesmaid.

After the wedding, bride and bridegroom were to step into a travelling carriage, and drive off as fast as six fine horses could take them to Tunbridge Wells, where they were to spend the honeymoon at the dowager's secluded villa near Leeds Castle. It was said to be one of the prettiest seats in Kent, on a small scale—gardens, fountains, shrubberies all perfection. It had been the lady's delight in her thirty years of widowhood to create and beautify the grounds and gardens.

' We shall be vastly quiet there, Sally,' said his lordship, when he was describing the beauties of the place. ' I hope you will not get tired of me.'

'Tired of you !' She looked up at him with worshipping eyes—how strangely different from that despairing look with which she had once entreated him to delay their marriage !

He felt ineffably proud of his conquest. He had told himself that he could win her, and sworn to himself to make her his in heart and soul before the law bound her to him.

'When we are very sick of each other we can go to the Rooms or the Pantiles to see the modish people,' he said, smiling at her.

'I would rather stay at home and hear you read to me,' she answered gravely. 'Think how much I have to learn before I shall be worthy to be your wife !'

'I think you have learnt the only lesson I shall ever care about teaching you,' he said.

'How do you mean ?'

'I think you have learnt to love me, Sarah. That's the only wisdom I ask of you.'

'Yes, I have learnt that with all my heart. Yet when you first came to this house I almost hated you.'

'That was because you loved another. Nay'—as Sarah tried to speak—'neither deny it nor confess it, my dear. I want to learn nothing about the past. I am happy in the present, and confident about the future.'

Sarah changed from red to pale and was silent.

How could she speak of those accursed letters after this ? How could she ever let him look into the depth of her past folly ?

She was as white as sculptured marble next morning—as white as her ostrich feathers, but a bride has a privileged pallor. Nobody wondered at Sarah's colourless cheeks.

'You look frightened, my dear,' said the out-spoken dowager as she kissed her in the church. 'I hope you don't repent what you are doing.'

'No, madam. I love your son with all my heart, and am proud with all my heart of his love.

Then the organ played a psalm, and the little procession went up to the altar rails, or the rails which defended that table which should have been an altar.

Very clear and firm and full were Sarah's accents as she gave the responses that made her George, Lord Bellenden's, wife.

'There is some advantage in having been taught to speak,' thought the dowager, as she heard those rich, round tones.

Anon came the business in the vestry. The old Major was weeping for very pride that his daughter was now one of the nobility. Sarah signed herself Sarah Pawlett for the last time in her life, kissed her husband, and went out of the church leaning on his arm, happy, since he was verily hers now, and yet painfully expectant.

So far there had been no sign of the little woman in black. Sarah had looked about the church expecting to see her in the corner of a pew, or lurking behind a pillar ; but she had descried the pinched little face nowhere. 'How could I suppose that she would keep her promise ?' thought Sarah despairingly ; 'she will treasure those letters as a weapon to use against me whenever the fit takes her.'

But in the church porch the little woman in black pressed forward to speak to the bride, with a small brown paper parcel, very neatly packed, in her hand.

'Mr. Jones, the glover, was anxious that you should have this ere you started, my lady,' she said. 'He could not execute your order sooner.'

'Give it to one of my servants, madam,' said his lordship, but Sarah snatched the parcel.

'I thank you, madam, from the bottom of my heart,' she murmured, with an earnest look, while her bridegroom was giving an order to one of the outriders who were to escort them to Tunbridge Wells.

Another minute and she was in the chariot, sitting by her husband's side, the brown paper parcel in her lap.

'Shall we open it and see what the gloves are like, which the man sends you at the eleventh hour ?' asked Lord Bellenden.

'No,' she said, 'I know all about them; I want to talk to you.'

So they talked, and the parcel was not opened, and the streets and the new bridge, and the long suburban road, which in those days so soon became rustic, fleeted by them like a dream that is dreamt, a happy vision of sunlight and glancing leaves, white houses, cottage gardens—now and then a carriage, now and then a cart—and on to the woods and pastures, orchards and hop-gardens of Kent.

Before the bride dressed for dinner she burnt every one of those foolish letters—burnt them without reading a line in any of them.

'If I were to read them I should hate myself too much for my silliness in ever having written such trash,' she said to herself, as she flung them into the fire, and thrust them down among the blazing coals, and held them there with the poker till not a vestige of that romantic bosh remained.

Three days afterwards Lady Bellenden received a prim little letter with the London postmark, written in a niggling hand, and beautifully spelt :

'Honoured Madam—

'When we were talking together that night you asked me if I had a price for your letters, and I said perhaps I had.

'You are now Lady Bellenden. You will be a leader of fashion before long, if you play your cards cleverly. Ask me to your parties. I have long languished for modish society. The loss of that is a greater deprivation to me than any of the troubles of my married life—wretched as that is. Ask me to all your parties. I shall not disgrace you. I know how to behave in company, and I shall always come in a chair.

'God bless you. I am very glad you are happily married, and have escaped that scoundrel, my husband. Be sure you send me a card for your first rout.'

Lady Bellenden readily complied with this request, and Mrs. Edward Langley, of Castle-street, Leicester-square, received a card for her ladyship's first reception, and with the card a parcel of black Genoa velvet for a gown, and Spanish lace to trim the same. The little woman looked to advantage in her velvet gown, and mingled in the throng of English and foreign nobility, men about town, wits and authors, without attracting any adverse criticism. But as the years went by the little woman in black became as familiar an object in Lady Bellenden's drawing-room as the looking-glasses which her ladyship had brought from Venice, or the statues which his lordship had brought from Rome. She was very harmless ; she listened to the music, and looked on at the dancing, and never obtruded herself upon anybody's attention. But it was observed that Lady Bellenden was always particularly kind to her, and by-and-by, when there came a bevy of sons and daughters, the little woman in black acquired the position of a maiden aunt or a godmother, among these young people, and spent the greater portion of her life with the Bellendens either in town or country.

Ned Langley had vanished from the stage of the world long ere this, after having dropped into disrepute as an actor in consequence of his intemperate habits.

He died in a sponging house, very suddenly, struck down by cerebral apoplexy, after a midnight drinking bout. Most people had heard the little woman in black spoken of as Mrs. Langley ; but very few people knew that she was the widow of handsome Ned Langley, the famous comedian.

ACROSS THE FOOTLIGHTS

PART I.

FIVE and twenty years ago, Helmstone-by-the-Sea was almost as gay and as fashionable a resort as it is now. It was the holiday ground—the lungs of London—just as it is now. Of course, it was not so big. The development of gay little Helmstone during the last quarter of a century is in some wise phenomenal. It has grown a new pier, a grand hotel, an aquarium, a colossal and splendid swimming bath in place of a small and shabby one. It has grown new churches, new streets, new terraces, crescents, club-houses, rinks, concert-rooms, gardens, promenades, winter-drives. All the good things that a sea-side resort can offer to resident or visitor are provided by Helmstone. It boasts the prettiest shops, the cleverest doctors and dentists, the keenest lawyers, the blandest riding-masters, the most accomplished professors of music and art that all England can show. Novelties and prettinesses come into being at Helmstone even before they are seen in Bond Street. It is as if they were wafted across the channel by some magical power. From the Palais Royal to the Queen's Parade is but a step.

Yes, Helmstone has doubled, trebled, quadrupled itself in wealth and splendour since the days when 'Pam' was a power and the Indian Mutiny was still fresh in the minds of men, when Macaulay's History and Tennyson's Idylls were the books of the hour. It has swollen and spread itself over the face of the surrounding country ; it has swallowed up its own suburbs and green spaces, like another Saturn devouring his children ; and elderly people look back upon that cosy little Helmstone of a quarter of a century ago with a touch of regret.

What a pleasant place it was in those days, with its sparkling parade, and narrowest of side streets, its shabby old baths and shabby old pier, and old-fashioned hotels—not a *table d'hôte* in the whole town—private sitting-rooms, stately little dinners, and wax candles, in the good old Georgian manner —expensive, exclusive, dull. Helmstone had its own duke, its own resident duke, in that corner mansion on the cliff at the east end of the town. Helmstone had its own single old-established club. Helmstone had still a royal flavour, as having been thirty or forty years before the chosen resort of princes.

To an old fogey it seems as if there were prettier girls marching up and down the Queen's Parade in those days; better favoured, grander-looking men. Every other man one met between four and five on a November afternoon had the air of Life Guards or Hussars. One seemed to hear the clink of spurs, and the jingle of sabretache as those tall moustached youths strode by, with golden lockets and fusee-boxes flashing on their waistcoats, clad in peg-top trousers and rough overcoats. All the girls had golden hair shining under porkpie hats, and dainty little seal-skin jackets, and flounced silk frocks,showing the neat little boot, and slender ankle, just revealing at windy corners that portion of the feminine anatomy which French novelists describe as ' the birth of a leg.'

It was at this lesser Helmstone, at the old Theatre Royal —a smaller, shabbier building than the theatre of to-day— that Miss Rosalie Morton appeared as fairy-queen in the pantomime of 'Gulliver and the Golden Goose,or Harlequin Little Boy Blue, and Mary, Mary, quite contrary, how does your garden grow ?'—in the new year of 1860.

Now the rôle of queen of the fairies in a Christmas pantomime is not the loftiest walk in the British drama. It does not rank among the Portias and Juliets and Lady Teazles, The fairy-queen is apt to be snubbed by the first singing chamber-maid who plays ' Mary, Mary, quite contrary,' and even to be looked down upon by the *première danseuse ;* but still there is a certain dignity about the part which is respected by the gallery, and regarded kindly by boxes and pit.

Above all, the fairy-queen should be young and pretty. A plain or an elderly queen would be a blot upon any pantomime. The first dancer may be as old as she likes, provided her legs are nimble and her petticoats well put on. It is for her steps she is valued. But the queen of the fairies must be young, and fair, and gracious looking.

So young, so fair, so gracious, was assuredly Miss Rosalie Morton, the queen of that particular Christmas entertainment of Gulliver and Mary. She was not quite eighteen years of age, and she had only been on the stage just six months. It had been considered great promotion for her when, after trying her young wings, as it were, and familiarising herself with the glare of the footlights at the little theatre in the Isle of Wight, she had been engaged—for the sake of her pretty face, *bien entendu*—by Mr. de Courtenay, of the Theatre Royal, Helmstone.

Mr. de Courtenay was the kindest of men and of managers. His actors and actresses adored him. He was so thoroughly good, so friendly, so honourable, so conscientious, that it was impossible to grumble at anything he did ; so as actors and actresses must grumble, they all found fault with the stage-manager, who was a good, honest soul, but not quite so cultivated a person as a stage-manager ought to be, and who cast the pieces in a rough-and-ready way which was intensely irritating to the artists whose talents and individual rights he so often disregarded.

For once in a way, however, Mr. Badger was right when he cast Rosalie Morton for the part of fairy-queen in the pantomime. She had only about a hundred lines of doggerel to pronounce, doggerel highly spiced with those local and topical allusions which enhance the charm of such dialogue : but she had to occupy the stage for a long time, and her beauty would be of value to the scenes in which she appeared.

'It is the prettiest face Courtenay has picked up for the last three years,' said the leader of the orchestra, who was a critic and connoisseur, and always gave his opinion freely. 'She ought to have played Mary, instead of Miss Bolderby, who is as old as the hills, and sings out of tune. I could have taught Miss Morton to sing her half-dozen songs in as many lessons. She has a pretty little voice, and a capital ear.'

'She can't act a bit," said Mr. Badger, 'and Bolderby is a roaring favourite with the gallery. Morton will do very well for fairy-queen.'

It was one of Mr. Badger's pleasing ways to call actresses by their surnames, *tout court*.

So Miss Morton played 'Cerulia, the queen of the azure fairies in the hyacinthine dell'—that is how she was described in the play-bill. The wardrobe-woman made her a short frock of palest blue tulle, starred with silver, and a silver tissue bodice, which fitted her willowy figure and girlish bust to perfection. She had the prettiest legs and feet in the theatre, and her satin shoes and sandals became her to admiration. She had magnificent chesnut hair, with flashes of gold in it, large hazel eyes, a Grecian nose, and a mouth of loveliest mould. She was delicately fashioned ; of middle height, graceful, refined; altogether charming. Mr. de Courtenay felt that he had secured a prize; and he raised her salary from thirty shillings a week to five-and-thirty without being asked. Theatrical salaries did not range quite so high in 1860 as they do nowadays. Under the present liberal management of the Helmstone theatre, so pretty a fairy as Rosalie Morton would count her salary by guineas, and not by shillings.

That extra five shillings weekly was a godsend to Miss Morton and Miss Morton's mamma. The mamma was a clergyman's widow, whose annual revenue was of the smallest. She had a married daughter among the professional classes in Bloomsbury; fairly, but not wealthily wedded. She had a son in Somerset House, and another son in the colonies, working for their daily bread. And she had this youngest of all her children—her rose of roses—who adored her, had never been separated from her for more than a week, and who had found even a week's visit to kindest friends a dreary exile from the beloved mother.

Rosalie had cherished a childish passion for play-acting from the days of short frocks and sky-blue sashes, when she had been taken to the York theatre by an uncle and aunt who lived in that cathedral city, and with whom she occasionally spent a day and a night. The father's vicarage was in the rural village between York and Beverley. Rosie had been to the theatre about three times in all; but those three nights of enchantment had made the strongest impression on her youthful intelligence. She and her brothers acted plays in the old vicarage parlour, the shabbiest room in the house, given over to the children, but a delightful room for play-acting, since there were two closets and two doors, besides a half-glass door opening into the garden. What tragedies and melodramas Rosalie and her brothers acted in the long winter evenings! The elder sister was too sensible and too busy to waste her time with them. She had an idea of going out as a governess, and had her nose always in an Ollendorf.

Poor little Rosie fancied herself a genius in those days. She mistook her love of dramatic art for capacity, and thought she had only to walk on to a stage in order to become a great actress, like the star she had seen at York. She did not know that the star was five-and-thirty, and had worked laboriously for ten years before audiences began to bow down to her. The vicar had been dead nearly three years when Rosalie was seventeen, and the mother and daughter were existing on a pittance in a dreary second floor in Guildford Street.

Mrs. Melford—the girl's real name was Melford—was a lady by birth and education, and had no more power of earning money than if she had been a humming-bird.

Rosalie was panting to do something for the beloved mother ; to bring home money and shower it into the maternal lap. She had read of Edmund Kean's London *début*, the startling success, the morning before his first benefit, the child playing upon the floor of the actor's lodging, wallowing in gold, the guineas having rolled in so fast from aristocratic patrons and an enthusiastic public that there was no one to pick them up ; and she, poor child, thought that she too was a genius, and could delight the town as Portia, just as Kean had done as Shylock. She did not recall that other tradition about the great actor which told how as a lad he had strutted and ranted in a booth, learning the rudiments of his art in the rough-and-ready school of Richardson's show, delighting the yokels at country fairs before he thrilled the *cognoscenti* at Drury Lane.

Much pleading and many long discussions were needed before the mother would consent to her child's appearance on the boards. The vicar's widow had heard terrible stories of theatres ; and she had to be reminded again and again of the glorious examples of feminine virtue to be seen on the metropolitan stage ; and that if there were some shadows on the dramatic profession, there are also spots upon the sun. And then they were very poor, those two, in their shabby London lodging. They had drunk deep of the cup of genteel penury. And the mother could but own that it would be a nice thing if her darling were earning from twenty to thirty pounds a week at the Haymarket or the Lyceum. That dear Mr. Buckstone would doubtless be delighted to secure this lovely young Rosalie for his leading lady, in place of the somewhat mature personage who now filled that position.

So one morning Mrs. Melford gave her consent, and Rosalie tripped off at once to the dramatic agent in Bow Street, and paid him five shillings by way of entrance fee to the mysteries of the drama, and opened her heart to him. The agent smiled at her blandly, with his eyes half shut, looking down at the toes of his varnished boots : and then he swept away all her illusions in a sentence or two. He told her that she would be lucky if she played Portia to a metropolitan audience before she was forty ; lucky if she got an engagement of any kind in a London theatre within the next ten years. What she had to do was to go to some country theatre and work hard. She would have to play small parts for the first year or so; anything, everything, general utility; nay, perhaps, at the first, she would have to *walk on.*

Rosalie had not the least idea what the agent meant by 'walking on,' but his manner implied that it was something humiliating. All her high hopes had evaporated by this time; but she was not the less eager to secure an engagement—yea, even *walk on.*

'You have a nice appearance,' said the agent, who was too superior a person to be rapturous about anything, 'and I daresay I can get you an engagement in the country.'

Rosalie had to tramp backwards and forwards between the Bloomsbury lodgings and Bow Street a good many times before even this modest opening was achieved; but, after some heart-sickening delays, the agent engaged her for the Theatre Royal, Ryde, at a salary of a pound a week. Oh, how happy poor little Rosie was when she carried home the first pound after a week's drudgery! She had played a round of the most humiliating parts in the British drama : Lady Capulet; a black girl in 'Uncle Tom's Cabin ;' Maria, in the 'School for Scandal ;' and she had *walked on* in a cluster of five or six ballet-girls, supposed to represent either a seething populace or a dazzling assembly in high life. But she had seen the footlights ; she had heard the sound of her own voice— which was more than the gallery had done—and she had earned a golden sovereign.

It must be owned that Rosalie in this stage of her being was something of a stick : but she spoke like a lady, and she was so pretty and graceful that the audience were always pleased to see her. The good old manageress favoured her, and cast her for parts that were beyond her capacity ; and then came Mr. de Courtenay, of the Helmstone Theatre, which ranked next best in fashion to a London house, and Rosie was speedily transferred from the Isle of Wight to the full blaze of Helmstone-by-the-Sea.

And now all the Helmstone papers had praised the fairy Cerulia's beauty, and Miss Rosalie Morton had a reception every night. It was not such a reception as greeted Miss Bolderby from her admirers, the gods, when she came dancing on to the stage as 'Mary, Mary, quite contrary,' with a very short red petticoat bedizened with silver bells, and a black velvet bodice garnished with cockle shells, and very *décolletée.* Rosalie was the favourite of the stalls and the boxes. It was the young military men from the barracks in the Brewis Road, or the cavalry barracks in the Castle, the Helmstone Bucks and Dandies of all professions, who used to applaud the fair girl with the brilliant hazel eyes, and gentle girlish voice. Miss Bolderby talked like a clown and sang like a nigger minstrel.

There was one young cavalry officer who used to occupy a stall at the Helmstone theatre nigbt after night during the run of that eminently successful pantomime of 'Gulliver and the Golden Goose.' Miss Bolderby thought that he came expressly to hear her sing her topical song, and see her dance her break-down with Mr. Powter, the low comedian, who played Gulliver, afterwards clown—the clown being, of course, somebody else and not Mr. Powter. Powter thought it was his gagging and comic singing which attracted cavalry and infantry alike, and charmed and delighted the gallery. But Herr Hopenfeuer, the leader of the orchestra, knew better than Powter or Bolderby. He knew that it was Rosie's lovely face and sweet manner which held that nice, frank-looking young officer spellbound. A shrewd observer, Herr Hopenfeuer, behind those blue spectacles of his.

Yes, it was Rosie whom Randolph Bosworth came night after night to see. He abhorred Miss Bolderby and her nasal twang ; he detested the irrepressible Powter. He seemed only to live when that graceful form of the fairy-queen was before his eyes. He drank in her smiles as if they had been wine. How sweetly she looked as she waved her wand, with that graceful sweep of the round white arm—such a lovely curve of the slim wrist, the drooping hand with its tapering fingers ! When she invoked the fairies to come forth from their coral caves and disport upon the golden sands, she looked really the ethereal and immortal being she represented—something too delicate to be of the earth, earthy. What a stalwart, common herd the ballet-ladies looked as they came lumpily bounding from the furthest wing, shaking the stage at every bound !

He was only a lieutenant, very young, very simple-hearted, a thorough gentleman. He was the only son of a wealthy father, and could afford to choose a wife without reference to ways and means. He meant to marry Rosalie Morton, *alias* Melford, if she would accept him as her husband. No other thought had ever entered his mind in relation to that stage divinity. His mother and father would hardly like the idea of his choosing a wife from the theatre. His father was a Devonshire squire, and had all the usual rustic prejudices, and would have liked him to marry a county heiress, some

Miss Sticktorights, whose land was conterminous with his own future estate.

"If she is a good girl they will be easily reconciled to her,' Randolph told himself, and he contrived very soon to find out that Miss Morton was a good girl, living with her widowed mother, as secluded as a cloistered nun.

Mother and daughter went for afternoon walks in almost all weathers, but they never appeared on the Queen's Parade, for the girl to be stared at or followed. They always turned their faces to the country, and went roaming over the downs ; capital walkers both of them.

All through that first month of the new year Randolph was pining to get himself introduced to his divinity, and knew not how to bring the matter about. If he had been more of a man of the world he would have asked Mr. de Courtenay to dinner, and would have made an ally of the manager, who would have been glad to help him, once assured that his views were strictly honourable. But Randolph was only twenty-one, and was overpowered with shyness when he tried to speak of his love. At last a happy accident seemed to favour him. He made the acquaintance of a Major in the line regiment then stationed in the Brewis Road ; a mere casual acquaintance initiated across a billiard table. Major Disney was a man of the world ; had seen a good deal of foreign service ; was nearer forty than thirty ; quite an old fogey Randolph thought him. But he was a tall, handsome fellow, broad shouldered, dashing, with a good manner, and a fine sonorous voice ; altogether a very agreeable man. Mr. Bosworth asked him to dinner at the Old Yacht Hotel, and they swore eternal friendship over a bottle of *Mouton*.

Soon after eight o'clock the younger man began to grow fidgety, looked at his watch, played with his wine-glass, glanced uneasily at the door.

'I generally drop in at the little theatre of an evening,' he faltered. 'They're doing a pantomime ; not half a bad thing—almost up to a London pantomime,' and then with a sudden fervour, blushing like a girl, he asked, 'Would you care to go ?'

'Certainly, if you like,' answered the major cheerily. 'Provincial pantomimes are rather slow ; in fact, I consider the whole breed of pantomimes ineffably stupid ; but one hears the children laugh, and one sees the jolly grinning shop-boys in the pit, and that sort of thing is always refreshing. Let's go by all means.'

'How kind of you!' cried Randolph. 'I shouldn't have liked to miss to-night.' He hurried on his coat, helped his friend into a heavy Inverness, and they went off to the theatre.

It was a cold snowy night, and the audience was thin. There were plenty of vacant stalls when Randolph took his accustomed seat, just behind Herr Hopenfeuer.

The major and he had not been seated five minutes before the band played the melody to which the azure dell opened. 'Ever of thee, of thee I'm fondly dreaming,' and then Rosalie came on with her pretty gliding step, and her waving arms, like a syren's.

'A devilish pretty girl,' muttered the major, and the tone and the words sounded like blasphemy in the ears of Randolph the devotee.

Later on in the evening he spoke again of the fairy queen's beauty.

'She is like Heine's Lorelei,' he said, and then, looking at Randolph, he saw the adoring expression in the frank blue eyes, and knew that this fisher's barque was in danger.

'She speaks like a lady, too,' he went on presently. 'Do you know who she is, and where she comes from? She is not the common stamp of stage fairies.'

Randolph imparted that information which he had gained laboriously from the stage-doorkeeper at the cost of many half-crowns, and more than one half-sovereign.

'Her mother is a Mrs. Melford, you say, a Yorkshire parson's widow?' exclaimed Major Disney. 'Why, what a narrow little world this is in which we live. My eldest sister went to school with that girl's mother. Mrs. Melford was Rosa Vincent, the daughter of old General Vincent, who died at Bath just ten years ago; a splendid old fellow, all through the Peninsula with Wellesley, Burgoyne, and the rest of them.'

'You know her mother?' gasped Randolph, breathless with emotion; 'then you can introduce me to them; you can take me to see them. I am dying to know them.'

'But to what end?' asked the major, looking at him severely, with penetrating gray eyes. 'She is a very pretty girl, and we both admire her. But do you think it would be wise to carry the thing any further?'

'I adore her, and I mean to marry her—if she will have me,' answered Randolph, all in the same agitated whisper. 'If you won't introduce me to her I must find some one else who will.'

'And you are sure that you mean all fair and square?' asked the Major very seriously. 'You won't make love to her and propose to her, and then let your people talk you over and persuade you to jilt her? That kind of thing has been done, you know.'

'Jilt her! not for worlds! If she will have me, I shall consider myself the luckiest young man in England. I am an only son, you know, ånd I have some money of my own, from an old aunt, that nobody can touch. I can afford to marry to-morrow, with or without my father's leave. But I shall try to make things pleasant at home; and as Miss Melford is a vicar's daughter——'

'Well, I'll call upon Mrs. Melford to-morrow afternoon, and ask leave to present you next day.'

'Can't I go with you to-morrow?' pleaded Randolph.

'Certainly not. Remember it's altogether a critical business. I have to introduce myself to the widow, whom I last saw seven and twenty years ago, when she was just going to marry her parson, and when I was a mischievous young imp of eleven.'

'You'll take her some hot-house flowers, some new book from me?' entreated Randolph.

'Take them to the widow?'

'No, no—to Rosalie.'

'Not a fragment,' said the stern Major.

Poor Randolph would have sent a truckload of presents if he had been allowed. He was pining to know the size of his darling's hand, that he might load her with Jouvin's gloves. How he would have liked to buy her a sealskin jacket, instead of the poor little cloth garment he had seen her wear as she walked beside her mother on the windy Downs!

Mr. Bosworth had to languish for three dreary winter days before he was allowed to cross the syren's threshold. Then, to his infinite delight, he was invited to take tea with the widow and her daughter on Sunday evening. There was no such institution as afternoon tea in that benighted age. Mrs. Melford invited the two gentlemen to repair to her lodgings after their seven o'clock dinner, and she regaled them with tea and thin bread-and-butter, and sweet biscuits, at half-past eight, in a neat little drawing-room within a stone's throw of the Castle, where the Enniskillings were stationed. Mr. Bosworth had not asked permission of the severe major this time. He carried a large bouquet of camelias and other hot-house flowers, such as those dark ages afforded, and he offered them blushingly to the syren, so soon as he had been introduced to her. He had the satisfaction of seeing the blossoms arranged in an old china bowl by the fair hands of his beloved, but of speech he had but little from her : she, like himself, was overpowered by shyness.

But, on the other hand, Mrs. Melford and Major Disney found plenty to say to each other. The widow was delighted to talk of those unforgotten girlish days, before the shadow of care had crossed her horizon ; her dearest friend Lucy Disney ; the finishing school in Lansdown Crescent ; the rapturous gaiety of Bath—so superior to any place she had ever known since her courtship ; her last visit to the Disney's fine old house in Wiltshire, when the Major was a lively boy of eleven.

'What ages ago ! ' exclaimed the widow ; 'and yet when I look back it seems as if it had all happened yesterday.'

And then with womanly tact, Mrs. Melford led the Major on to talk of himself and of his own career. He had not married ! How strange ! said the widow. He had been through the Crimean War, and he had fought and marched under Havelock in India the other day. In such a career there had been much that was striking, heroic even ; and without one word of self-laudation, the Major told of many thrilling adventures in which he had been concerned, while the others all hung on his words and encouraged him by their evident interest.

It was a cosy little party round the winter fire in the lodging-house drawing-room. Rosalie sat in a corner by the fireplace, sheltered and shadowed by her mother's portlier form ; and from his seat on the opposite side of the hearth, Randolph Bosworth was able to gaze at her unobserved, as she listened almost breathlessly to the Major's stories.

No, there was no disenchantment in that nearer acquaintance with the 'Queen of the azure dell.' Rosalie was as lovely in this little room, between the glow of the fire and the light of the candles, as ever she had seemed to him on the stage, in the glare of the gas, and the glamour of the magnesium lamp. She was such a perfect lady, too, he told himself with delight. No rouge or pearl powder tainted the purity of her complexion. Her dark brown merino frock and little linen collar were exquisitely neat ; her lovely tapering hands were as beautiful as the hands in an old Italian picture. How proud he would be of her, by-and-by, in the time to come ! how delicious to present her to his people, to his friends, and to say, 'This is the pearl I found unawares on the beach at Helmstone !'

His heart beat high with joyous pride. He had no fear of failing in his suit, now that he had once obtained an entrance to the syren's cave. He had hardly exchanged half-a-dozen sentences with Miss Melford to-night, but he told himself that he could come again to-morrow, and again and again, till he had won her. And in the meantime he was pleased to see her hang upon Disney's words : it was sweet to see a girl of nineteen so keenly interested in the adventures of a battered old warrior.

He called in Blenheim Place the next day, and the next, finding some fresh excuse for each visit ; a basket of hot-house grapes for the widow, at a season when grapes were fourteen shillings a pound ; flowers, books, music for Rosie. Mrs. Melford protested against such lavish generosity.

'If you only knew how happy it makes me to come here— to be allowed to drop in now and then,' faltered the young man ; and the widow did know, and hoped that her Rosie would smile upon the young soldier's suit.

The Major had told her all about his young friend's pro-spects, and they were both agreed as to his goodness of heart, his high moral character, and that he would be a splendid match for Rosie. The widow's heart thrilled at the thought that her youngest and best beloved child might secure to herself such a happy future. In her day-dreams she ruth-lessly made away with old Squire Bosworth, who had never done her any harm. She brushed him out of existence as if he had been a withered leaf, so that Rosie should reign sole mistress of Bosworth Manor.

Mrs. Melford and the Major put their heads together like a couple of hardened old match-makers, and planned the marriage of the young people—the Major with a somewhat mournful air, as of a man who had known heart-wounds, whose part in life was renunciation. Mrs. Melford thought him very kind, but regretted that he was not more cheerful.

When the time came for the mother to talk to her daughter, there was bitter disappointment. Rosalie was as cold as ice at the mention of her lover's name. She declared that she meant never to marry ; at least she thought not. She was quite happy with her mother ; she liked her profession; in a word, she did not care a straw for Randolph Bosworth. She admitted his manifold virtues, his kindness, his chivalry. The widow put forward his claims, item by item : those

grapes at fourteen shillings a pound ; that lovely copy of the
'Idylls,' bound in vellum ; the flowers that transformed
their shabby lodging.

'And you would have such things all your life, Rosie.
You would have a grand old country house, with twenty-two
bedrooms—he admitted that there are twenty-two bedrooms
at the Manor, without counting servants' rooms—and you
would have carriages and horses. I used to dream of such a
life for my darling, but I never thought to see my dream
realised ; so quickly too, while my pet is in the first bloom of
her beauty.'

'What nonsense you talk, mother dear !' said the girl.
'Captain Bosworth has never asked me to marry him.'

'No, love ; but he has asked me, and he means positively
to ask you, by-and-by, if you will only give him a little
encouragement. He adores you, Rosie, that dear young man.
He adored you at first sight. Don't make light of such a
love, dear. You are very pretty, and will have plenty of
admirers as you go through life ; but true love is not a
flower that grows in every hedge.'

'Dear mother, it's no use talking,' pleaded Rosie, half
crying. 'I know how good Captain Bosworth is, but—but I
don't care for him ; and you wouldn't have me marry a man
I don't love.'

'Try to love him, Rosie,' urged the mother. 'Only try, dear,
and the love will come.'

Rosalie shook her head, and gave a low, long sigh ; a sigh
which might have told a great deal to a shrewder woman than
the widow ; but Mrs. Melford had not a penetrating mind.

To please the match-making mother Rosalie was very
polite and agreeable to the young officer when he called at
Blenheim Place. She was particularly grateful for the lovely
copy of the 'Idylls.'

'She is reading it day and night,' said Mrs. Melford. 'I
never knew a girl so devoted to a book of poems. I'm sure
Mr. Tennyson ought to be flattered.'

'He would be if he knew,' murmured Randolph fatuously,
gazing at Rosalie as if she had been a saint.

He asked her which character she most admired in the
'Idylls.'

'Oh, Launcelot,' she answered, clasping her hands, and
looking up at an imaginary knight, with just the same
radiant enthusiasm as might have shone upon the face of the
Lily-maid when she worshipped the real Launcelot.

Major Disney was announced at this moment, and the girl flushed crimson ; no doubt because he had broken the spell.

The pantomime season was waning fast, and the Theatre Royal, Helmstone, would shortly close. There was a talk of Charles Mathews on a starring engagement after the pantomime, and then the theatre must inevitably be shut ; and Rosalie would have to earn her bread elsewhere. Lovely as she was, no eager London manager had offered to engage her. Perhaps the London managers saw that Rosalie's *gamut* hardly went beyond the fairy-queen line of business ; and fairies are 'only wanted at Christmastide. Rosalie's brightest prospect was an engagement at Coketown, in the north, to play first walking ladies ; and that line of business includes some of the most intolerable parts in the British drama—ay, even Lady Capulet and Sheridan's Maria.

Mrs. Melford began to be very anxious. Captain Bosworth had been all patience and devotion. He had endured Rosalie's coldness ; he had waited for the dawn of hope. But patience cannot last for ever, and the widow felt that this splendid chance must soon be lost, unless Rosie relented. She had all manner of little schemes for bringing about *têtes-à-têtes* between the lovers, but so far nothing had come of the *têtes-à-têtes* so planned. She had come back to the little drawing-room after a quarter of an hour's seemingly enforced absence, to find Rosalie and the soldier sitting on opposite sides of the hearth, as prim and as cold as two china figures. There are some young men who cannot propose in cold blood.

One afternoon—a bleak February afternoon, the earth ironbound with a black frost, the sky leaden, the sea livid —Mrs. Melford proposed a long walk on the Downs. Rosie had been complaining of a headache, she said : nothing so good as a walk to cure a headache. Perhaps Captain Bosworth would like to join them.

Captain Bosworth would have liked to go to Siberia under the same conditions. He snapped at the offer.

'I adore those Downs,' he said.

But Rosalie did not want to walk. She was tired ; she had the third volume of a novel that she was dying to finish. She made at least half-a-dozen excuses. Major Disney was announced just at that moment, and the mother appealed to him.

'Is not a long walk the very best thing for Rosie's head-ache ?' she asked.

'Of course it is,' answered the Major, 'and Miss Melford must obey her mother. We will all go. I have been writing letters all the morning, and am sadly in want of oxygen.'

Rosie went off to put on her hat and jacket as meekly as a lamb. It was nearly three o'clock when they started, two and two, Randolph and Rosie in the van, Mrs. Melford and the Major in the rear. Just on the opposite side of the gardens in front of Blenheim Place there is a narrow little street almost as steep as the side of a house ; a shabby raggamuffin of a street, but it leads straight up to the purity and freshness of the Downs, just as Jacob's ladder led to heaven.

Randolph and Rose tripped lightly up that Mont Blanc of Helmstone, but they found very little to say to each other on the way. The Major and the widow followed at a good pace, she lamenting Rosalie's folly, and pouring her maternal griefs into the bosom of her friend.

'It is certainly very strange that she should not care for him,' admitted the Major, 'for he really is a capital fellow— handsome too.'

'And young, and rich,' urged the widow. 'It is absolute perversity.'

'Do you think there is anyone else she cares for ?' inquired the Major after a pause.

He spoke with some hesitation, almost falteringly, as if he hardly dared to shape the question.

'My dear Major, who else should there be ? Think what a child Rosalie is ! We were buried alive for the three years after her father's death, and she never saw a mortal except my son-in-law, Mr. Bignell, who is about as plain a young man as I ever met. And since she went on the stage, the only gentlemen who have crossed our threshold are yourself and Captain Bosworth. I call it sheer perversity,' concluded the widow, with an aggrieved air.

The Downs were delightful on that keen winter afternoon. Such bracing air, bracing yet not too bitter ; the breath of the sea seemed to temper the north-easter. And how glorious the sea looked from that airy height ; and how white and clean and glittering that dear old Helmstone, which everybody loves—ay, even those who pretend to loathe it.

Rosie's spirits rose as she tripped over the turf, and let the wind buffet her. There was no more walking two and two. Major Disney was at her side now, and he and she were talking gaily enough. Her spirits grew almost wild with delight in the wind and the sea. 'Let us have a race,' she cried, and flew off like Atalanta, the two officers running on either side of her, careful to adjust their pace to hers, till she stopped breathless, and laughing at her own folly.

'How lovely it is up here!' she said.

'If we're not careful we may have to stay here all night!' cried the Major; 'there's a sea fog coming.'

He was right. Drifting across from the ocean there came a great white cloud, which began to wrap them round like a dense veil.

'We had better get back as quickly as we can,' said the Major. 'Take my arm, Miss Melford, and double quick march.'

And Rosalie took his arm without a word,

'Run on and look after Mrs. Melford,' said the Major; and Randolph obeyed, hastening to rejoin the distant figure in the midst of the white cloud. He thought it was not a little unkind of his friend to order him off upon outpost duty, when he might have turned the sea-fog and the lonely height to such good account with his divinity. He felt that he should have had pluck enough to propose to her under cover of that sea-fog. He was still very far from understanding how the land really lay.

He steered Mrs. Melford homewards very skilfully; but Rosie and her guide were an hour later in their return, and Mrs. Melford was devoured by two several apprehensions. First, that her darling should be lost altogether, frozen to death on those windy Downs, or crushed at the bottom of a chalk-pit; secondly, that she should not be home in time to play her part in Harlequin Gulliver, and the Goose with the Golden Eggs. She and Captain Bosworth sat staring at the little clock on the chimney-piece and counting the minutes, till a cab dashed up to the door, and she heard her child's voice, silver-sweet, in the hall below.

Yes, Rosie and the Major had lost themselves upon the misty Downs; they had lost themselves, and had found bliss unspeakable, the beginning of a new life, the threshold of an earthly paradise, as it seemed to both. They had wandered ever so far from Helmstone in that dream of bliss, and had found their way back to the furthest end of East Cliff, where they luckily encountered a strolling fly, which rattled them gaily to Blenheim Place.

Rosie threw herself into her mother's arms in the little passage, and sobbed out her bliss:

'Oh, mother, I am so proud, so happy.'

And a new light dawned upon Mrs. Melford as she saw the Major's radiant smile. She gave him her hand without a word. It was a very poor match for Rosie, compared with that other marriage which the girl might have made. But George Disney was a soldier and a gentleman—almost a hero, and Mrs. Melford liked him.

Randolph Bosworth accepted his defeat nobly, although he was very hard hit, as near broken-hearted as a man well can be. He bade Rosie and her mother good-bye next morning, and in his brief interview with the girl he told her how he had loved her from the first moment in which her beauty shone upon him across the Helmstone footlights ; how he should cherish her image until the end of his life ; how he never could care for any one else. And then tenderly, gently, bravely, he bade her good-bye.

'Let me kiss you once,' he said ; 'let me have something to remember when I am far away.'

She turned her face to him without a word, as simply as a child to a father, and he kissed the pure young brow. It was the kiss of chivalry and high-feeling, the pledge of a life-long devotion.

'If ever you need a friend in the days to come, remember me,' he said ; 'to the last coin in my purse, to the last drop of my blood, I am your servant— your slave.'

And so they parted, Rosalie deeply moved by his devotion. He contrived to get away on leave a few days afterwards, and went to Ireland to shoot wild duck, and before Rosalie's wedding-day he and the Enniskillings had sailed for India, one of the first regiments to be ordered there under the new dispensation.

PART II.

It was the Christmastide of 1880, and dear old Helmstone had become Helmstone the new, Helmstone the smart, Helmstone in a state of daily and hourly development. The new pier, the aquarium, the tramway, the monster hotel, the colossal club-house, the new theatre, were all established facts. The Helmstone of fifty-eight and fifty-nine, the Helmstone which Thackeray praised and Leech and Doyle drew, was a place to be remembered by old fogies, and regretted by middle-aged matrons, who had spent the gayest, brightest hours of their girlhood prancing up and down the Queen's Parade.

Amongst those fogies who regretted the days that were gone was a military-looking man who sat at his solitary meal in one of the bow windows of the Old Yacht Hotel, there where the wind-lashed surges seemed almost to break against the door-step, so high rose the waves above the sea-wall. It was a blusterous evening just after Christmas, and the soldierly person yonder had only arrived at Helmstone by the four o'clock express from Victoria.

He was bronzed by tropical skies, and he had the look of a man who had been long upon foreign service. He was about forty, tall, broad-shouldered, good-looking, with frank blue eyes, and a kindly smile when he spoke. But the expression of his face in repose was grave almost to sadness. He sighed as he glanced round the old-fashioned coffee-room, where three or four solitary diners, like himself, were dotted about at the neat little tables.

'This house is very little changed within the last twenty years,' he said to the waiter, presently.

'No, sir; we are an old-fashioned house, sir. I don't think any of our friends would like to see anything altered here. Our house is about the only thing in Helmstone that has not changed during the last twenty years.'

'Indeed. I thought, as I drove from the station, that the town looked much larger. But you seem to have increased most of all in a perpendicular direction. All your houses and streets have gone up into the skies.'

'Where we are limited in space, sir, we mount,' said the head waiter, who was a superior personage, quite equal to any discussion ; 'but when you go westward to-morrow, you will see how we can spread. You will find a city of palaces where there used to be a cricket field.'

'Indeed,' said the soldier, with an absent air.

His eyes had wandered to a play-bill hanging against the wall by the mantelpiece.

'You have your theatre still, I see,' he said ; 'the same old theatre, I suppose ?'

'Oh dear no, sir ; we have had a new theatre for the last ten years. Very fine theatre, sir. Very well patronised. Pantomime just out. Very good pantomime. Harlequin Robinson Crusoe, Old Mother Shipton, and the Little Old Woman who Lived in a Shoe.'

The soldier sighed, as if at some sad memory.

'The usual kind of thing, no doubt,' he said ; 'and there are fairies, I suppose, and dances, and a fairy queen ?'

'Oh yes, sir, there is a first-class fairy scene. The Ruby Glade in the Sunset Glen, and there is a fairy queen, and a very pretty girl she is too. I don't remember ever seeing a prettier girl on the stage.'

'Ah !' sighed the officer, 'perhaps you were not in Helmstone twenty years ago ?'

'No, sir,' replied the waiter, with a superior smile which implied that he was hardly out of his mother's arms at that period.

The waiter whisked the last crumb off the tablecloth and left the soldier in silent contemplation of a dish of walnuts and a claret jug.

So there was a pantomime being acted in these latter days, thought Colonel Bosworth, and there were fairies, and dances, and tinselled groves, and sham waterfalls, and the glamour of coloured lights, and gay music, just as there had been twenty years ago, when he was a young man, and lost his heart in that little theatre at Helmstone—a youngster, an untried soldier, almost a boy—and yet very steadfast, very certain of himself in that first real passion of his life.

He had not over-estimated his constancy in those days. When he told Rosalie Melford that he could never care for any other woman, he had made an assertion which after events had warranted. He had seen much of life since that time. He had seen hard service in India, had marched with Napier in Abyssinia, and had fought with Wolseley in Ashantee. He had been courted and made much of in London society during his brief intervals of foreign service ; hunted by match-making mothers, who knew the number of his acres and the excellence of his moral character : but not once during those twenty years had Randolph Bosworth yielded to the fascinations of the fair sex. The one beautiful face which had been the star of his youth was his only ideal of womanly loveliness. He had never met any woman who resembled Rosalie Melford ; and he told himself that until he should meet such an one he was secure from all the pains and perils which spring from womankind. He was like a man under a spell.

And in all those years he had heard hardly anything of his lost love. The Major had married her directly after Easter, and had carried her off to Canada, with his regiment. Six years afterwards Disney was stationed at the Cape, and no doubt Rosalie was with him there ; and then Randolph heard that he had retired on half-pay, and that he was living with his wife and family in some out-of-the-way Welsh village, a rustic nook hidden among the hills. Randolph would have given much to know more about his darling's fate —whether she was happy ; whether the Major was comfortably off—but he had a delicacy in intruding himself upon them in any manner ; and then so much of his own life was spent far away. He thought that if Rosalie were in need of a friend's help she would be sure to appeal to him.

He sat and sipped his claret for half-an-hour or so, in a dreamy mood, the very sound of the surges recalling old thoughts, old fancies, the old hopes which had been so cruelly disappointed, and then he got up and put on his hat and overcoat, and went to the theatre.

He was courting the tender, half sweet, half painful memories which beset him in this familiar place. Yes, he would go to the theatre. It was not the same theatre, but it stood on the same spot : and the lights, and the music, and the girlish faces would help to recall those old feelings which were to him as a cherished dream.

The new theatre was much larger and handsomer than the funny old house with its stage doors, and its old-fashioned proscenium, and its suggestions of Mr. Vincent Crummles and Miss Snevellicci. It had a more metropolitan air, and was better filled than the old house. The pantomime had begun when the bronzed and bearded soldier took his seat in a corner of the stalls. There had been a dark scene in which Mother Shipton and a congress of witches had been interviewed by Crusoe ; and now that bold mariner was tossing on the southern ocean in imminent danger of shipwreck from the huge canvas waves which were flapping against his wicker keel, and raising more dust than one would expect to meet with in mid-ocean ; and the next scene, as per bill, would be the Ruby Glade in the Sunset Glen, and Diaphanosia, the queen of the water nymphs, would appear with her fairy court : and Senora Niña Niñez, of the Theatre Royal, Covent Garden, would dance her renowned *cachuca*.

Colonel Bosworth wondered what kind of prettiness that would be which the head waiter at the Yacht had praised. A vulgar, trivial beauty, no doubt ; as different from Rosalie Melford's poetic loveliness as a double dahlia from a wild rose.

The scene representing a dark, storm-tossed ocean was rolled slowly upward, revealing the sunset glen, a glow of rosy light and sparkling coral, and golden sand, and a background of ultramarine wavelets. The band played a tender melody—not that old, old ballad, 'Ever of thee,' which the soldier remembered so well. It was a newer strain, by Sullivan, a song with a waltz refrain, 'Sweethearts.' And to the rhythm of the waltz some fifteen or twenty water-nymphs came gliding on to the stage, and after the water-nymphs their queen, with a single star shining on her fair young brow.

Was he mad or dreaming? Was his trip to Helmstone, this scene in the theatre, all a foolish dream; and would he awake presently in his bedroom at the British Hotel, and hear the London cabs and 'buses grinding over the stones of Cockspur Street? This was what Randolph Bosworth asked himself as Diaphanosia came slowly forward in the rosy glow, waving her wand with a slim, round arm, whose graceful curve he remembered so well.

Surely it must be a dream; or time in Helmstone had been standing still for the last twenty years. The fairy of to-night was the fairy of twenty years ago. Rosalie Melford, unchanged, as it seemed to him, since the hour in which his boyish heart first went out to her. And now he was a grave, middle-aged man : yet, as he gazed at the sweet face, with its classic outline and alabaster purity of. tint, his heart beat as passionately as it had beaten twenty years ago.

He looked at his programme, tried to collect his senses, to convince himself that he was not dreaming.

'Diaphanosia : Miss R. Morton.'

Yes ; it was the old name even. And it was she herself, the woman he had loved for twenty years of his life—for half his lifetime. He knew every tone of that voice, which had been as music in the days gone by. He remembered every movement of the graceful figure, the carriage of the head—every turn, every look.

He sat gazing at her, breathless almost, with all his soul in his eyes. But she gave no sign of having seen or recognised him. She went through her part graciously, with a refined elegance which was altogether charming, and which just suited the colourless, passionless character. So might Titania herself have looked and moved, an ethereal being, free from all taint and stain of human nature. He stayed till the transformation scene, patiently enduring the buffooneries of Crusoe, and the street-boy twang of the lady who played Crusoe's young woman, and who was evidently the idol of the gallery, just as Miss Bolderby had been twenty years before.

X

He waited and watched, greedily expectant of Diaphanosia's reappearances, which were of the briefest, and it was not until she had changed Crusoe into clown, and condemned a villainous sailor to the expiatory infamy of pantaloon ; it was not until the golden temple and the peacock throne of dazzling gems had been abruptly extinguished by a pork-butcher's shop in the front grooves, that the Colonel rose from his seat and left the auditorium.

He did not go back to the Old Yacht, but he groped his way along a dark passage which he had known of old, and planted himself close beside the stage door. There was a little stone yard of about ten feet square at the end of the passage, and here he could lurk unobserved.

He had lurked on that spot many a night in that winter of 1860, and had waited patiently, just for the brief joy of seeing his beloved go swiftly past him by her mother's side, two dark figures, thickly shawled and closely veiled, obscure as phantoms in the sombre passage.

To-night he was bolder, and meant to accost his old love when she came out of the stage door, to claim the privilege of friendship, and to learn what sad reverses had brought her back to that stage. He did not for a moment believe that it was idle vanity which had impelled her to such a reappearance.

She came out of the door sooner than he had hoped, a tall, slim figure, neatly dressed in black. She wore a cloth jacket, such as he remembered her wearing twenty years before, and a small black straw hat, which fitted close to her head, and left the delicate profile unshadowed.

He came forward bareheaded to greet her.

'I hope you have not forgotten me in all these years, Mrs. Disney,' he said. 'My name is Bosworth—Randolph Bosworth.'

'Forgotten you ; no, indeed ! How could I forget anyone who was so kind to my mother and me ?' she faltered ; and he knew from the tone in which she spoke her mother's name that Mrs. Melford was dead. 'I have never forgotten you. Only I should hardly have known you just at first, and in this dark passage, if you had not told me your name. You are much altered.'

'And you not at all,' he answered tenderly. 'It seems miraculous to me to find you after twenty years as young, as beautiful, as when I saw you first.'

'You do not know what you are talking about,' she answered, laughing a little at his enthusiasm. 'You have only seen me across the footlights. I shall be nine-and-thirty next week, and I am very old for my age. I have seen so much trouble in the last six years.'

'You have had trouble, and you never told me. Then you forgot my parting prayer,' said Randolph, reproachfully.

'No, I did not forget those kind words of yours. But my chief sorrow was beyond human aid. My dear husband's health broke down ; mental and bodily health both gave way. I nursed him for three years, and in all that time he only knew me once—for the last few minutes before he died. Till just that last ray of light his mind had been a blank. It was a sunstroke which he got at the Cape. We brought him home an invalid, and settled in a little out-of-the-way nook in Wales. He was fitful and strange in those days, but we hoped that he was gradually recovering. But he grew worse as time went on, and the doctors discovered that the brain was fatally injured. The last three years were terrible.'

She gave a stifled sob at the recollection, and Colonel Bosworth could find no word of comfort for such a grief.

'Good night,' she said, offering him her hand.

'Let me see you home,' he pleaded ; 'I want to know more. Let me walk as far as your lodgings. Are they in the old place ?'

'No, we are not in such a nice neighbourhood as Blenheim Place ; and it is further from the theatre. I am afraid I shall be taking you too far out of your way.'

'You know that I would walk with you to the end of the world,' he said quietly ; and she made no further objection.

It was such a new thing to her to hear a friend's voice, and this was a voice out of the old time, when she had been young and happy.

They had walked away from the theatre, and the cabs, and lights, and the crowd by this time ; and they were in a wide dark street leading to Prince's Square, and the sea, and the old-fashioned hotels ; stately old houses still extant in this older part of Helmstone.

'You spoke just now as if you were not alone here,' hazarded Colonel Bosworth presently ; 'have you any of—of —your family with you ?'

He spoke in fear and trembling. He had seen the announcement of a child's birth long ago in the *Times*, but the child might have died an infant for all he knew. Mrs. Disney might be a childless widow.

'I have them both with me. My boy and girl are both

here,' she answered frankly. 'It is a dull life for them, poor children, but they are such a comfort to me.'

'Would you mind telling me what train of circumstances led to your coming back to Helmstone to act?' he asked presently.

'That is easily told,' she answered. 'When my dear husband died we were left very poor. His terrible illness had swallowed up all our money. There was nothing but my small pension, and I had my two children to provide for. People advised me to go out as a governess, but I am not accomplished enough to earn a large salary in these days when everybody is so clever; and I could not bear the idea of parting from my children. I tried to get employment as a morning governess, and after waiting a long time, and spending two or three pounds upon advertisements, a lady at Kensington was kind enough to engage me to teach her five children, from half-past nine to half-past one, for a guinea a week. I believe she considered it a rather handsome salary, as I could only teach English, French, Italian, music, singing, and drawing, while what she most wanted for her children was German, the only thing I could not teach them. So I was only a *pis aller*, you see. It was very hard work, and I was getting dreadfully tired of it last November, when I happened to meet Mrs. de Courtenay, the widow of my former manager. She recognised me directly—I believe I have altered rather less in twenty years than people usually do—and she asked me what I was doing. She is the kindest woman in the world, and when she heard how I had toiled for a guinea a week, she declared she must find me something better than that, and a few days afterwards I received a letter from her asking me to play my old part of fairy queen at a salary of four guineas a week. My darlings and I were so rejoiced at this good fortune. It seemed like finding a gold-mine. We hurried down here directly my Kensington lady set me free : and my children and I have been as happy as birds in this dear old place.'

'I am deeply wounded to find how slight a value you put upon friendship, Mrs. Disney,' said Colonel Bosworth, gravely. 'If you had ever considered me your friend, surely you would have let me come to your aid when your natural protector was taken from you. You knew that I was rich, alone in the world.'

'What would you have thought of a woman who could take advantage of a boyish fancy—a dream of twenty years old ?' murmured Rosalie. 'I had my own battle to fight, my children to work for. I was not afraid of poverty.'

'It was ungenerous to deprive me of the happiness I should have felt in being useful to you—and to your children,' replied Bosworth earnestly.

His tones faltered a little when he came to speak of her children. He could not picture her to himself as a widow and a mother. To him she was still the fairy of his youth— his 'phantom of delight'—the ethereal vision, the ideal of his boyish dream. They had crossed Prince's Square, and they were on the broad parade that ascends the East Cliff. A full moon was shining on the sea and the town, steeping all things in a clear and silvery light, and in this soft light Rosalie's beauty seemed to have lost none of its youthful charm. There were lines perhaps; the gazelle-like eyes were hollower: the oval of the cheek was pinched a little towards the delicately-rounded chin. There must needs have been some markings of advancing years in the face of this woman whose nine-and-thirtieth birthday was so near. But to Randolph Bosworth the face was as beautiful as of old, the woman was no less dear than of old.

'It is not a dream of twenty years old,' he said, after a long pause, repeating her own words. 'My love for you was a reality then, and it is a reality now. It has been the one great reality of my life. Give me some reward for my stead-fastness, Rosalie. I claim no other merit; but I have at least been steadfast.'

'You cannot be in earnest,' she said. 'I am an old woman. The last ten years of my life count double, they have been so full of sorrow. All my hopes of happiness are centred in my children. I live for them, and for them alone.'

'No, Rosalie, you are too young for all womanly feeling, all personal ambition to be extinguished in you. Twenty years ago I was at your feet, young, prosperous, devoted to you. I thought then that I could have made your life happy; your mother thought so too. But it was not to be. You chose an older and a poorer man. Granted that he was worthy of your love——'

'He was more than worthy,' interjected Rosalie. 'I am proud of having loved him—I was his fond and happy wife, till calamity came upon us. I was his loving wife till death parted us. I have never regretted my choice, Colonel Bosworth. If I had to live my life over again I would be George Disney's wife.'

'I will not be jealous of his shade,' said Bosworth. 'Providence has dealt strangely with us both, Rosalie. Fate has parted us for twenty years, only to bring us together again, both free, both lonely. Why should I not win the prize now which I lost then? I could make your fate, and the fate of your children, happier than it is. I could indeed, Rosalie. Houses and lands are gross and sordid things perhaps, but some part of man's happiness depends upon them. Bosworth Manor is still waiting for its mistress. It shall wait until you go there. Do you remember that picture of the old house which I brought you one day, and which your mother admired so much?'

'My poor mother, yes, she was so fond of you. No, Colonel Bosworth, no, it cannot be. I should be the weakest of women if I were to accept your generous offer. I honour you for having made such an offer; I feel myself honoured by it. But I am an old woman. It is all very well for me to play fairy queen, and to pretend to be a girl again, in order to earn four guineas a week. That means bread for my children : and if there is anything ridiculous in the business I can afford to ignore it for their sakes. But I cannot forget that I am twenty years older than when you first knew me.'

'And am I not twenty years older, Rosalie?' asked her lover eagerly. 'Do you suppose that time has been kinder to me than it has to you?'

'Age does not count with a man. You may find a girl of nineteen who will worship you, just as I worshipped George Disney, loving him for his heroic acts, for the charm of his conversation, for so many qualities which had nothing to do with his age. Why should you choose an old and faded woman, a widow, the mother of grown-up children?'

'Only because she is the one woman upon earth whom I love,' answered Bosworth. 'Come, Rosalie, I will not be too importunate. I will not ask you to accept me to-night. I come back to you after twenty years, almost as a stranger. Let me be your friend, let me come and see you now and then, as I used in Blenheim Place ; and by the time the pantomime season is over you will have discovered whether I am worthy to be loved, whether I am an impostor when I pretend that I can make your life happier than it is.'

'With all my heart,' said Rosalie, with a sigh of relief ; ' Heaven knows we have need of a friend, my children and I, We are quite alone in the world.'

'Anxious though he was to please her, Colonel Bosworth could not bring himself to speak of her children yet awhile. Struggle as he might against a feeling which he deemed unworthy, the idea jarred upon him ; there was an instinctive repugnance to the thought of Rosalie's love for George Disney's children.

They had arrived at the street in which Mrs. Disney lived. It was the narrowest street on the East Cliff, an old, old street built in those remote ages when Helmstone began to develop from a fishing village to a fashionable watering-place. The old bow-fronted houses were very small, and rather shabby ; but that in which Mrs. Disney had taken up her abode was neat and clean-looking, and there were some tamarisk plants in front of the parlour window by way of decoration.

Colonel Bosworth and the widow shook hands on the doorstep. The door was opened before Mrs. Disney had time to knock or ring, and a bright, frank-faced lad welcomed the mother's return. The Colonel walked slowly away as the door closed upon mother and son.

'A nice gentleman-like boy,' he thought, beginning to reconcile himself to his future position as this bright-eyed lad's step-father ; and then, after five minutes' musing, he said to himself, 'No doubt I could get him an Indian appointment through General So-and-so. I wonder if he has any taste for forestry ?'

Colonel Bosworth spent a sleepless night in his cosy bedchamber at the Old Yacht. He lay broad awake, listening to the sad sea waves, which had nothing better to do all that night than to talk about Rosalie. Yes, it was a strange fatality which had brought him back to that place to find his old love there. How beautiful she had looked in the moonlight ! Her countenance was more pensive ; but it was even lovelier than of yore—spiritualised ; the expression more thoughtful, more intense.

He counted the hours next day until it would be decent to call, and at three o'clock he turned the corner of the narrow street, and knocked at Mrs. Disney's door. He had employed part of his morning in choosing new books and hothouse flowers to send to his divinity. When the door was opened, the house smelt of hyacinths and jonquils. A neat little slavey admitted him and ushered him into the front parlour immediately, feebly murmuring her own particular reading of his name—Colonel Gosswith.

'Rosalie!' he exclaimed, bending over the girlish figure that rose hastily from a seat in front of the window; 'No, the moonlight did not deceive me. You are lovelier, younger-looking than when we first met.'

A sweet face—Rosalie's face, and yet not quite Rosalie's—looked at him with a bewildered air; fair girlish cheeks crimsoned beneath his ardent gaze.

'I think you mistake me for my mother, Colonel Bosworth,' faltered those lovely lips.

'You are——

'I am Rosa; mother is Rosalie. She looks so wonderfully young that we are often mistaken for sisters.'

'And was it you whom I saw at the theatre last night?' exclaimed the Colonel, beginning to lose his balance altogether, feeling that he *must* be going mad.

'No; that was mother,' answered the girl simply. 'She will be here directly. She has been helping my brother with his French. He is capital for Greek and Latin, you know,' which the Colonel did not, 'but he is not so good at French, and mother helps him. How kind of you to send us those exquisite flowers!'

'It was a great pleasure to me to send them. I knew your mother twenty years ago, Miss Disney.'

'Oh yes; we feel as if you were quite an old friend. Mother has so often talked about you.'

'If she had cared a jot for me, she would never have breathed my name,' thought the Colonel.

He felt humiliated by the idea that he had been trotted out for the amusement of these children, in the character of a rejected swain. And then he looked at Rosa Disney, and tried to reconcile himself with the idea of her as his step-daughter. Surely there could be nothing nicer in the way of step-daughters.

Yes, it was a lovely face, lovelier even than Rosalie's in her bloom of youth, if there could be lovelier than the loveliest. Colonel Bosworth wanted a new form of super-lative to express this younger beauty.

There was a higher intellectuality in the face, he thought —a touch, too, of patrician loftiness, which came from the larger mind, the older lineage of the father. A most interesting girl, and so sweetly unconscious of her own charms.

One of the new books was lying open on the table, Browning's last poem: Rosa had been devouring it, and she and the Colonel were discussing it in a very animated way, unconscious that they had been talking nearly half an hour, when Mrs. Disney came into the room.

'That silly servant has only just told me you were here,' said the widow. 'I see you have made friends with Rosa already.'

'I had need make friends with her if she is to be my step-daughter,' thought Colonel Bosworth ruefully.

He looked at his old love gently, tenderly, in the cold prosaic light of a December afternoon. Yes, time had been lenient, very lenient, to that fair and classic beauty. The delicate Grecian nose, the perfect modelling of mouth and chin, these were as lovely as of old. But, ah! how wide was the gulf between Rosa in the bloom of her girlish freshness, and Rosalie after her twenty years of changes and chances, joys and sorrows.

'She was right,' thought Randolph: 'time and sorrow must always tell their tale.'

His visit was a long one, for he stayed to take tea with the little household. He made friends with his future step-son—talked about India and forestry, and he escorted Mrs. Disney to the stage-door, before he went to his dinner. He asked permission to see her home after the performance; but this was refused.

He did not go to the theatre that night. He told himself that he did not want to vulgarise his impressions of the Fairy Diaphanosia. He wished to cherish her image as it had flashed upon him last night, a sweet surprise.

He sat by the cosy fire at the Old Yacht, reading Browning and thinking of Rosa. He wanted to accustom himself to the idea of a step-daughter.

Next day was bright and sunny, and Colonel Bosworth went for a walk on the new pier, where he met George and Rosa, his future step-children. They did the pier thoroughly together, and at George's instigation, went to see a Pink Tortoiseshell Cat, the Industrious Fleas, and a cockle-shell boat which had brought some adventurous souls across the Atlantic, each of these wonders being severally on view at threepence a head. The Colonel vowed that it was the pleasantest morning he had spent for years. He was charmed with the pink cat, though its pinkness was only in the proportion of about five per cent of its normal hue.

Although Colonel Bosworth only parted from his future step-children at the corner of the narrow street on the East Cliff at half-past one, he was at Mrs. Disney's door soon after three, and again he spent the afternoon in the little bow-windowed parlour, talking with Rosa and her brother, while the widow sat by the fire working a grand design in crewels on a sage green curtain.

'Is that to be hung up at Bosworth Manor by-and-by?' asked Randolph.

'If you like,' she answered sweetly; and it seemed to him that in those simple words there was an acceptance of his offer. The threads of their two lives were to be inter-woven, like the woof and warp of that curtain.

He was not so elated at his victory as he would have felt the night before last, when he pleaded his cause on the Cliff in the glamour of the moonlight. He was sober, as became a man with new responsibilities, a man who was so soon to be a step-father. He stayed to tea as before, and escorted the fairy to the theatre. Their talk on the way there was hardly lovers' talk. It was serious and friendly rather. Mrs. Disney told him of her married life, and how she had brought up her children. He seemed to have a greedy ear for all early traits of character in his future step-daughter. 'And had she really shown such an ear for music at two and a half? And did she really rescue a puppy from drowning, at the risk of spoiling her pinafore? Heroic child!'

The next day he bought a splendid half-hoop of diamonds in Prince's Square, and offered it to his affianced wife by way of engagement ring; but to his surprise she declined it.

'I have an idea that engagement rings are unlucky,' she said. 'You shall give me nothing but flowers and books till after your marriage.'

'I—I—wish you would let me buy a sealskin jacket for Rosa,' he said. 'She is to be my step-daughter so soon that it can't matter. I thought she looked cold yesterday morning on the pier.'

Mrs. Disney thanked him for his thoughtfulness, and consented to this fatherly gift. So the next day they all went to Bannington's, and Colonel Bosworth bought the handsomest sealskin coat which that establishment could produce. He would be satisfied with nothing less than the very finest. It clothed Rosa from her chin to her ankles, and she looked lovely in it.

'I shall feel so wicked every time I pass a poor little beggar girl shivering in her ragged frock,' said Rosa.

'Never mind how you feel,' said her brother George; 'you look like an Esquimaux princess,'

Colonel Bosworth suggested that his betrothed should close her engagement at the Theatre Royal before the pantomime was withdrawn from the bills.

'What, break faith with Mrs. de Courtenay, who was so kind to me!' cried Rosalie. 'Not for worlds!'

The Colonel had urged her to name the day for their wedding. The sooner it should take place the happier he would be. He was getting restless and out of spirits. He had left off walking on the pier of a morning, and had lost all interest in pink cats.

Mrs. Disney hung back a little about the wedding. It could not be until after Lent, she said. It was to be a very quiet wedding. They could decide upon the date at any time.

'Don't you think it would be an advantage to Rosa to spend a year or two at a first-rate finishing school in Paris, or even with a private family?' said the Colonel, rather abruptly, one evening, as he was escorting his betrothed to the theatre.

'But why?' asked Mrs. Disney.

'Why—oh, only for improvement. She told me she wanted to improve herself in French.'

'And you would exile my child at the very outset,' exclaimed Rosalie, with deepest reproach. 'What a cruel stepfather you are going to make!'

A week after this the pantomime came to an end, and Lent began. The widow and her old lover were walking on the East Cliff together after the last performance. The moon was at the full again, just as it had been on that first night they two had walked together. The tall white houses, the wide dark sea were shining in that silvery light.

'And now, Rosalie,' said Randolph gently, with a gravity of manner that had been growing upon him of late, 'it is time that you and I should come to some definite arrangement about our wedding. When is it to be?'

'Never,' she answered, sweetly, sadly, proudly; looking at him with a steadfast gaze, the lovely eyes dim with tears. 'You have been good and true, Randolph—true to the shadow of an old dream. You have offered me a fair and happy future—yes, I feel that the life you offer would be full of brightness and delight, for me who have tasted very few of the joys of life. But I am not base enough to take advantage of the generous impulse which prompted you to offer to a widow of nine-and-thirty the love you once gave to a girl of nineteen. It cannot be, dear friend. In years we may be fairly equal, but in heart and mind I am ages older than you ; my cares and sorrows should all count for years. You have asked me for bread, and I must not give you a stone. You are still a young man. Your heart is as fresh as when you asked me to be your wife twenty years ago : and only a young fresh heart can give you such love as you deserve. Randolph, I know of one young heart, pure, innocent, and childlike in its simple trust, and I think that heart has gone out to you unawares. Can you reciprocate that innocent half unconscious love ? Will you accept the daughter instead of the mother ?'

Would he ? His heart was beating so violently that he could not answer. He clutched the iron railing with his broad, strong hand ; he heard the roaring of the sea vaguely, as if it had been a tumultuous noise in his own overcharged brain.

'You have guessed my secret,' he said hoarsely, after a pause.

'Nearly a month ago. I saw how it would be from the beginning. Don't apologise, Randolph. I am so proud, so happy, for my darling's sake. I have nothing to regret. Good night. No, no, pray do not come any further.'

She snatched her hand from his, and walked swiftly to the little street, which was not far off. Randolph Bosworth went back to the Old Yacht like a man walking upon air. Oh, what an earthly paradise the world seemed ! The mother had not been deceived. Yes, Rosa loved him—this soldier of forty years old—loved him just as fondly as Rosalie had loved her hero in the days gone by. The Colonel met his darling on the pier in the breezy winter morning, and they had a happy talk together amidst the fresh wind and the briny spray. And in Easter week there was a quiet wedding in one of the smaller churches of Helmstone, and Randolph Bosworth carried his fair young bride to Rome to see the eternal city in its Easter glory, while Mrs. Disney repaired to the Manor, provided with full authority to set the house in order for her daughter's home coming.

MY WIFE'S PROMISE

It was my fate at an early period of my life to abandon myself to the perilous delights of a career which of all others exercises the most potent fascination over the mind of him who pursues it. As a youth I joined a band of brave adventurers in an Arctic expedition, and from the hour in which I first saw the deep cold blue of the northern sea, and felt the subtle influence of the rarefied polar air, I was for all common purposes and objects of life a lost man. The expedition was unfortunate, though its leader was a wise and scientific navigator—his subordinates picked men. The result was bitter disappointment and more bitter loss—loss of valuable lives as well as of considerable funds. I came back from my cruise in the 'Weatherwise,' to the western world, rejoiced beyond measure at the idea of being once more at home, and determined never again to face the horrors of that perilous region which had lost me so many dear companions.

I, Richard Dunrayne, was the elder son of a wealthy house, my father, a man of some influence in the political world, and there were few positions which need have been impossible for me had I aspired to the ordinary career affected by British youth. I had been indulged in my early passion for the sea, in my later rage for Arctic exploration; and it was hoped that, having satisfied these boyish fancies, I should now settle down to a pursuit more consonant with the views and wishes of my people. My mother wept over her restored treasure, and confessed how terrible had been her fears during my absence; my father congratulated me upon having ridden my hobby, and alighted therefrom without a broken neck; and my family anxiously awaited my choice of a profession.

Such a choice I found impossible. If I had bartered myself body and soul, by the most explicit formula, to some demon of the icebergs, or incarnate spirit of the frozen sea, I could not have been more completely bound than I was. From the

Christmas hearth round which dear friends were gathered, from my low seat at my mother's knee, from worldly wealth and worldly pleasure, the genius of the polar ocean beckoned me away, and all the blessings of my life, all the natural affections of my heart, were too weak to hold me. In my dreams, again and again, with maddening repetition, I trod the old paths, and saw, ghastly white against the intense purple of that northern sky, the walls of ice that had blocked our passage. It seemed to me that if I could but find myself again in that dread solitude, success would be a certainty. It seemed to me as if we had held the magic clue to that awful labyrinth between our fingers, and had, in very folly, suffered it to escape us. 'A new expedition, aided by the knowledge of the past, *must* succeed,' I said to myself ; and when I could no longer fight against the prepossession that held me, I consulted the survivors of our unfortunate voyage, and found in their opinions the actual echo of my own convictions.

We met many times, and our meetings resulted in the organization of a new expedition. Money was poured into our little treasury like water, so poor a dross did it seem to us compared with the jewel we went to seek. Our preparations had begun before I dared tell those who loved me that I had pledged myself to a second expedition. But at last, one bright spring evening, I went home and announced my decision. I look back now and wonder at my own heartlessness, and yet I was *not* indifferent to their grief. The cry that my mother gave when she knew the truth rings in my ears as I write this. No ; I was not indifferent. I was possessed.

My second voyage resulted in little actual success, but was to me one prolonged scene of enjoyment. I was a skilled seaman and navigator, no indifferent sportsman, and having acquired some slight reputation during the previous voyage, now ranked high among the junior officers on board the 'Ptarmigan.' We wintered at Repulse Bay, with a short stock of fuel, and a shorter supply of provisions ; but we managed with a minimum of the former luxury, and supplied all deficiency of the latter by the aid of our guns. Never was a merrier banquet eaten than our Christmas dinner of reindeer steaks and currant dumplings, though the thermometer had sunk 79° below freezing-point, and our jerseys and trousers sparkled with hoar-frost.

The brief summer of that northern latitude brought us some small triumphs. We spent a second winter in snow houses, which resembled gigantic bee-hives, and were the snuggest possible habitations, and in the second summer turned our course homeward, in excellent health and spirits, but my gladness was to be sorely dashed on landing in England.

I returned to find my mother's grave bright with familiar autumnal flowers in a suburban cemetery, and to know that the tender arms which had clung about me in the hour of parting would never encircle me again. The blow was a severe one, and for some time to come I thought with aversion of that strange northern world which had cost me, and which was yet to cost me, so much.

Time passed, and I remained in England, at twenty-five years of age a broken man. With the men I met I had no point of sympathy. Their pursuits bored me, their paltry ambitions disgusted me. The pleasures of civilized life had not the faintest charm for me. A polar bear would have been as much at home as I was in a West-end ball-room, and would have been as interested in the conversation of a genteel dinner-table. Away from my old comrades of the 'Weatherwise' and the 'Ptarmigan,' I had not a friend for whom I really cared ; and as the civilized world grew day by day more distasteful to me, the old longing revived—the old dreams haunted my sleep. In my father's handsome drawing-rooms I yearned for the rough stone cabin of Repulse Bay, or the snow-hives of Cape Crozier. Another expedition was afloat, and letters from my old messmates announced anticipated triumphs, and warned me of the remorse which I should suffer when the hardy victors returned to reproach the idler who preferred to live at home at ease, while old friends were drifting among the ice-floes, and bearding the grisly tyrant of the north.

I let them go without me, at what sacrifice was only known to myself. My father's health had been declining from the hour of my mother's death, and I was determined not to leave him. *This* duty at least I would not abnegate. This last sad privilege of attending a father's death-bed I would not barter to the all-exacting demon of the frozen seas. For three empty, patient years I remained at home. My hands reverently closed the eyes that had never looked upon me but with affection, and I alone watched the last quiet sleep. This being done, I was free once more, and the old infatuation held me close as ever. My father's death left me wealthy, and to my mind wealth had but one use. All the old yearnings were intensified by tenfold, for the saddest reason. The 'Ptarmigan' had never been heard of since the hour she left Baffin's Bay, and the fate of those familiar comrades with whom I had lived in the closest communion for two happy years was a dark enigma, only to be solved by patient labour. The expedition had not been of sufficient importance to attract much attention from the scientific world ; there had been too much of a volunteer and amateur character in the business ; but when the fact of the 'Ptarmigan's' disappearance became known, a meeting of the Royal Society gave all due consideration to the case, and promised help to a party of investigation.

My ample fortune enabled me to contribute largely to the expenses of the new voyage, while volunteers and voluntary contributions poured in from every quarter. I had difficulty in selecting officers and crew from so large a number of hardy adventurers ; but I was prudent enough to engage the crew of a battered old whaler for the staple of my men. We were away in all six years, wintering sometimes in South America —once in New York, and getting our supplies as best we might. We made some discoveries, which the Royal Society received with civil approval ; but of those we went to seek we found no trace ; and I began to think that the fate of my old friends was a mystery never to be solved below the stars.

I came back to England at thirty-four years of age, a hardy wanderer, with a long brown beard that seemed lightly powdered with the northern snow, and with the strength of a sea-lion. For the best years of my life I had lived in snow-hives and stone-cabins, or slept at night amidst the wilderness of ice, in a boat which my stalwart shoulders had helped to carry during the day. Heavens ! what a rough, unlicked cub, what a grim sea-monster I must have been ; and yet Isabel Lawson loved me ! Yes, I came back to England to find a fairer enchantress than the spirit of the frozen deep, and to barter my liberty to a new mistress. One of my sisters had married during my absence, and it was at her country house I took up my abode. The young sister of her husband, Captain Lawson, was here on a visit, and thus I met my fate.

I will not attempt to describe her ; the innocent face, so lovely to my eyes, was perhaps less perfect than I thought it ; but if perfection wears another shape, it is one that has no charm for me. Isabel was my junior by sixteen years, and for a considerable period of our acquaintance regarded me as a newly-acquired elder brother, whose age gave something

of a paternal character to the relationship. For a long time
I looked upon her as a beautiful picture, an incarnate pre-
sentment of all that is tender and divine in womanhood, and
as far away from me as the stars which I pointed out to her
in our summer evening rambles by the seashore near our
country home.

How I grew to love her I will not ask myself. She was a
creature whom to know was to love. How she grew to love
me is a mystery I have often tried to solve ; and when I have
asked her, with fear and wondering, why I was so blessed,
she told me it was because I was brave and frank and true,
and worthy of a woman's love. God help my darling, the
glamour of the frozen north was upon me, and the mere story
of the wondrous world I knew had magic enough to win me
the heart of this angel. She was never tired of hearing me
describe that wild region I loved so well. Again and again
I told her the histories of my several voyages, and the record
seemed always to have a new charm for her.

' I think I know every channel in Davis's Strait and Baffin's
Bay,' she said to me a day or two before our wedding ; ' and
the icebound coast, from Repulse Bay to Cape Crozier, and
the ice-packs over which you carried your boats, and the
shoals of seals and clouds of ducks, and the colony of white
whales, and the dear little snow-houses in which you lived so
snugly. Don't you think we ought to spend our honeymoon
at Cape Crozier, Richard ? '

' My precious one, God forbid that I should ever see you
in that wild place.'

' Be sure, Richard, if you went there, I should follow you.
And she kept her word.

Dreamlike, and oh, how mournful, seems the bright scene
of my bridal day, as I recall it to-night beside a lonely hearth
in the house of a stranger. My Isabel looked like a spirit in
her white gown and veil ; and I, to whom the memories of the
North were ever present, could well-nigh have fancied she
was clad in a snow-cloud. I asked her if she were content
to have given her young beauty to a battered veteran like
me ; and she told me yes, a thousand times more than content
—inexpressibly happy.

' But you will never leave me, Richard ? ' she said, looking
up at me with divine love in her deep-blue eyes ; and I promised again, as I had promised many times before, that the
North should never draw me away from my beloved.

'You shall be my pole-star, dearest, and I will forget that earth has any wilder region than the woods and hills around our happy home.'

My darling loved the country, and I loved all that was dear to her : so I bought a small estate in North Devon—a grange and park in the heart of such a landscape as can only be found in that western shire. I was rich, and it was my pride and delight to make our home as beautiful as money and care could make it. The restoration of the house, which was as old as the Tudors, and the improvement of the park, employed me for more than a year,—a happy year of home joys with as sweet a wife as Heaven ever gave to man since Adam saw Eve smiling on him among the flowers of Paradise,—and during the whole of that time I had scarcely thought of the North. With the beginning of our second year of happy union, I had even less inclination to think of my old life ; for God had blessed us with a son, pure and blooming and beautiful as the region in which he was born.

Upon this period of my life I dare not linger. For nearly two years we held our treasure ; and if anything could have drawn us nearer to each other than our love had made us long ago, it would have been our affection for this child. He was taken from us. 'The Lord gave, and the Lord taketh away ; blessed be the name of the Lord.' We repeated the holy sentences of resignation ; but it was not resignation, it was despair that subdued the violence of our grief. I laid my darling in his grave under the midsummer sky, while a sky-lark was singing high up in the heaven, where I tried to picture him, among the band of such child-angels ; and I knew that life could never again be to me what it had been. People told me I should perhaps have other children as dear as this.

'If God would give this one back to me, He could not blot from my memory his suffering and his death,' I answered impiously.

For some time my sorrow was a kind of stupor—a dull dead heaviness of the soul, from which nothing could raise me. Isabel's grief was no less intense, no less bitter ; but it was more natural and more unselfish. She grew alarmed by my state of mind, and entreated me to try change of scene.

'Let us go to London, Richard,' she said ; 'I shall be glad to leave this place, beautiful and dear as it is.'

Her pale face warned me that she had sad need of change ; and for her sake, rather than my own, I took her to London, where we hired a furnished house in a western square.

Being in town, and an idle man, with no London tastes and no friends, it is scarcely strange that I should attend the meetings of the Royal Society. The fate of Franklin was yet unknown, and the debates upon this subject were at fever-heat. A new expedition was just being fitted out by the Government, and there could be no better opportunity for a volunteer band, which might follow in the track of the Government vessel.

In the rooms of the Society I encountered an old comrade who had served with me in my first voyage on board the ' Weatherwise,' and he exerted his utmost powers of persuasion to induce me to join himself and others in a northward cruise, to search for Franklin and for our lost companions of the ' Ptarmigan.' I was known to be an old hand, well provided with the sinews of war, adventurous and patient, hardened by many a polar winter; and my friend and his party wanted me for their leader. The proposal flattered me more than I can describe, and caused me the first thrill of pleasure I had known since my son's death. But I remembered my promise.

' No, Martyn,' I answered; ' the thing is impossible. I am a married man, and have given my word to the dearest wife in Christendom that I will never go out yonder again.'

Frank Martyn took no pains to conceal his disappointment at my decision, nor his contempt for my motives.

It was my habit to tell my wife everything; and I told her of the debates of the Royal Society, and of this meeting with an old comrade.

' But you will keep your promise, Richard ? ' she asked, with a sudden look of fear.

' Until the end of life, my darling, unless you should release me from it.'

' Oh, Richard, that is not likely; I am not capable of such a sacrifice.'

I went again and again to the Royal Society : and I dined at a club, with my friend Martyn, who made me known to his friends, those eager volunteers who panted for the icy winds of the Arctic zone, and languished to tread the frozen labyrinth of polar seas. I listened to them, I talked with them, and the demon of the North resumed his hold upon me. My wife saw that some new influence was at work, that my home life was no longer all in all to me.

One day, after much anxious questioning, she beguiled me of my secret. The old yearning was upon me. I told her

how every impulse of my mind—every longing of my heart—
urged me to join the new enterprise; and how, for her dear
sake, I was determined to forego the certainty of pleasure,
and the chances of distinction. She thanked me with a sigh.

'I stand between you and the purpose of your life,
Richard,' she said; 'how selfish I must seem to you !'

'No, darling, only tender and womanly.'

Upon my persistent refusal to command the expedition,
my friend Martyn was unanimously elected captain. A
wealthy brewer of an adventurous turn provided the larger
part of the funds, to which I gladly contributed my quota.

'I know Dunrayne will go with us,' said Frank Martyn.
'He'll turn up at the last moment, and beg leave to join. But
remember, Dick,' he added, turning to me, 'if it is the last
moment you'll be welcome, and I shall be proud to resign the
command to a fellow who knows the Arctic zone as well as a
Cockney knows the Strand.

The preparations for the voyage lasted longer than had been
anticipated. Months went by, and I still lingered in town,
though I knew that Isabel would have preferred to return
to Devonshire. I could not tear myself away while the ' Forlorn Hope,' the vessel chartered by the brewer, was still in
dock. I saw the adventurers almost daily, assisted in their
preparations, pored over the chart with them, and travelled
over every inch of the old ground with a pencil for their
edification.

It was within a week of the departure, and the fever and
excitement of preparation was stronger upon me than on any
one of the intending voyagers, when my wife came to me
suddenly one morning, and threw herself, sobbing, into my
arms.

'My dear Isabel, what is this ?' I asked in alarm.

'O Richard, you must go,' she sobbed; 'I cannot hold you
from your destiny. My selfish fears are killing you. I can
see it in your face. You *must* go to that wild, awful world,
where Heaven has guided you in safety before, and will
guard and guide you again. Yes, darling, I release you
from your promise. Is God less powerful to protect you
yonder than here ? He made that world of eternal ice and
snow; and where He is there is safety. No, Richard ; I will
not despair. I will not stand between you and fame. I
heard you talking in your sleep last night, as you have
talked many nights, of that distant solitude : and I know
that your heart is there. Shall I keep my husband prisoner

when his heart has fled from me? No, Richard, you shall go.'

She kissed me, and fell fainting at my feet. I was blinded by my own selfish folly, and did not perceive how much of her fortitude was the courage of despair. I thought only of her generosity, and my release. It was not too late for me to accept the command of the 'Forlorn Hope.' I thanked my wife with a hundred kisses as her sweet eyes opened upon me once more.

'My darling, I shall never forget this,' I cried ; 'and it shall be the last journey, the very last. I swear it, by all that is most sacred to me. There is no danger, believe me, none, for a man who has learned prudence as I have done— in the school of hardship.'

There was only a week for leave-taking.

'I can bear it better so,' said my wife: 'such a blow cannot be too sudden.'

'But, my darling, it is no more than any other absence ; and, remember, it is to be the last time.'

'No, Richard, do not tell me that. I think I know you better than you know yourself. A man cannot serve two masters. Your master is *there*. He beckons you away from me.

'But for the last time, Isabel.'

'Well, yes,' she answered, with a profound sigh, 'I think that when you and I say good-bye next week, we shall part for the last time.'

The sadness of her tone seemed natural to the occasion ; nor did I remark the melancholy significance of her words, though they often recurred to my mind in the time to come.

'I will make you a flag, Richard,' she said to me next day. 'If you should discover any new spot of land out yonder, you will like to raise the British standard there, and I should like to think that my hands are to be associated with your triumph.'

She set to work upon the fabrication of a Union Jack. I remembered a melancholy incident in the life of Sir John Franklin, and I hardly cared to see her thus employed ; but I could not sadden her with the story, and she worked on, with a happier air than I could have believed possible to her. Alas ! I little knew that this gaiety was but an heroic assumption sustained to save me pain.

My darling insisted upon examining my charts, and made me show her every step of our projected journey—the point where we hoped to winter—the land which we intended to explore on sledges—the spots where we should erect cairns to mark our progress. She dwelt on every detail of the journey with an interest intense as my own.

'I think I know that distant world as well as you, Richard,' she said to me on the last day of all. 'In my dreams I shall follow you—yes, I *know* that I shall dream of you every night, and that my dreams will be true. There must be some magnetic chain between two beings so closely united as we are, and I am sure that sleep will show you to me as you are —safe or in danger, triumphant or despondent. And in my waking dreams, too, dear, I shall be on your track. My life will be a double one—the dull, commonplace existence at home, where my body must needs be, and the mystic life yonder, where my spirit will follow you. And, dear husband,' she continued, clinging to me and looking up with a new light in her eyes, 'if I should die before you return——'

'Isabel!'

'Of course that is not likely, you know; but if I should be taken from you, dearest, you will know it directly. Yes, dear, at the death-hour my spirit will fly to you for the last fond parting look upon earth, as surely as I hope it will await you in heaven!'

I tried to chide her for her old-world Scottish superstition; but this speech of hers, and the looks that accompanied it, shook me more than I cared to confess to myself; and if it had been possible to recede with honour, I think I should have resigned the command of the Forlorn Hope and stayed with my wife. O God, that I had done so, at any cost of honour, at any sacrifice of friendship!

But my fate drew me northward, and I went. We started in July, and reached the point that we had chosen for our winter harbour at the end of August. Here we walled our vessel round with snow, and roofed her over; and in this grim solitude prepared to await the opening seas of summer. To me the winter seemed unutterably long and dreary. I was no longer the careless bachelor who found amusement in the rough sports of the sailors, and delight in an occasional raid upon the reindeer of the ice-bound coast. I had indeed tried to serve two masters; and the memory of her I had left behind was ever with me, a reproachful shadow. If, now, I could have recalled the past, and found myself once more by that hearth beside which I had languished for the old life of adventure, how gladly would I have made the exchange!

The long, inactive winter that was so dreary to me seemed

pleasant enough to my companions. We had plenty of stores, and all were hopeful as to the exploits of the coming summer. We should find the crew of the 'Ptarmigan,' perhaps, hardy dwellers in some inaccessible region, patiently awaiting succour and release. With such hopeful dreams my comrades beguiled the wasted days ; but I had lost my old power of dreaming, and a sense of duty alone sustained my spirits. My friend Frank told me that I was a changed man —cold and stern as the veriest martinet.

' But all the better man for your post,' he added; ' the sailors love you as much as they fear you, for they know that they would find you as steadfast as a rock in the hour of peril.'

The summer came, the massive ice-packs were loosened with sounds as of thunder, aud drifted away before a southern breeze. But our freedom brought us nothing save disappointment. No traces of our friends of the 'Ptarmigan' gladdened our eyes : no discovery rewarded our patience. Scurvy had cost us four of our best men, and the crew was short-handed. Before the summer was ended we had more deaths, and when the next winter began, Martyn and I faced it drearily, with the prospect of scant stores and scanter fuel, and with a sickly and disheartened crew. We had reason to thank God that the poor fellows were faithful to us under conditions so hopeless.

Before the coldest season set in, we left our vessel in tolerably safe harbour, and started on a land expedition, still bent on our search for traces of the missing Ptarmigan. We had a couple of sledges and a pack of Esquimaux dogs, faithful, hardy creatures, who thrived on the roughest fare, and were invaluable to us iu this toilsome journey. No words can paint the desolation of this wild region—no mind can imagine that horror of perpetual snow, illimitable as eternal.

Martyn and I worked hard to keep up the flagging spirits of our men. One poor fellow had lost his foot from a frostbite, and but for our surgeon's clever amputation of the disabled member, must have surely perished. He was of course no small drag upon us in this time of trial, but his own patient endurance taught us fortitude. We had hoped to fall in with a tribe of Esquimaux, but saw none after those from whom we bought our dogs.

So we toiled on, appalled by the grim change in each other's forms and faces, as short rations and fatigue did their work. The dead winter found us again reduced in number.

We built ourselves a roomy snow-house, with a cabin for the dogs ; and here my friend Frank Martyn lay sick with three other invalids throughout our hopeless Christmas. My own health held out wonderfully. My spirits rose with the extremity of trial, and I faced the darkening future boldly, beguiling myself with dream-pictures of my return home, and my wife's glad face when she looked up from her lonely hearth and saw me standing on the threshold of the door.

It was Christmas-day. We had dined on pemmican—a peculiar kind of preserved meat—biscuit, and rice. Spirit we had none, save a little carefully stored in case of urgent need. After our scant repast the able men went out in a body in search of sport for their guns, but with little hope of finding anything. The invalids slept, and I sat by the fire of dried moss which served to light our hut, with the aid of a glimmer of cold, dull daylight that came to us through a window of transparent ice in the roof.

I was thinking of England and my wife—what else did I ever think of now ?—when one of the men rushed suddenly into the hut, and fell on the snow-bank that served for a bench. He was white to the lips, and shivering as no man shivers from cold alone.

'Good God, Hanley, what is the matter ?" I cried, alarmed by the man's terror.

' I went away from the others, Captain,' he began, in rapid, gasping accents, ' thinking I saw the traces of a bear upon the snow ; and I had parted from them about half-an-hour when I saw——'

His voice died away suddenly, and he sat before me, with lips that moved but made no sound.

' What ? For pity's sake speak out, man.'

' A woman ! '

' Yes ; and of an Esquimaux tribe, no doubt. Why didn't you hail her, and bring her back to us ? Why, you must be mad, Hanley. You know how we have been wishing to fall in with some of those people, and you see one, and let her slip through your fingers, and come back scared, as if you'd seen a ghost.'

' That's it, your honour,' the man answered hoarsely. ' What I saw was a ghost.'

' Nonsense, man ! '

' But I say yes, Captain, and will stand by my word. She was before me, moving slowly over the snow ; you could scarce call it walking, 'twas such a smooth gliding motion.

She was dressed in white—no common dress—but one that turns the heart cold only to think of. While I stood, too scared to move hand or foot, she turned and beckoned to me, and I saw her face as plain as I see yours at this moment, a sweet face, with blue eyes, and long fair hair falling loosely round it.'

I was on my feet in a moment, and rushing towards the door. 'Great God of Heaven!' I cried, 'my wife!'

The conviction that possessed me was supreme. From the moment in which the sailor described the figure he had seen, there was no shadow of doubt in my mind. It was Isabel, and she only. The wife who had promised that her spirit should follow me step by step upon my desolate journey was near me now. For one moment only I considered the possibility or impossibility of her presence, and pondered whether some northern-bound vessel might have brought her to an Esquimaux station near at hand that we knew not of; for one instant only, and then I was hurrying across the snow in the direction to which the sailor pointed as he stood at the door of our hut.

The brief winter day was closing in, and there was only a long line of faint yellow light in the west. Eastwards the moon was rising, pale and cold like that region of eternal snow. I had left our hut some two hundred yards behind me, when I saw a white-robed figure moving towards the low western light; a figure at once so dear, so familiar, and yet in that place so awful, that an icy shiver shook me from head to heel as I looked upon it.

The figure turned and beckoned. The sweet face looked at me, awfully distinct in that clear cold light. I followed, and it drew me on, far across a patch of snowy waste that I had left unexplored, or had no memory of traversing until now. I tried to overtake the familiar form, but though its strange gliding movement seemed slow, it eluded my pursuit, follow swiftly as I might. In this manner we crossed the wide bleak waste, and as the last glimmer of the western light died out, and the moon shone brighter on the frozen plain, we came to a spot where the snow lay in mounds—seven separate mounds ranged in the form of a cross beneath that wild northern sky.

A glance told me that civilized hands had done this work. The Christian emblem told me more. But though I saw the snow-mounds at my feet, my eyes seemed never to leave the face of my wife—O God, how pale in the moonlight!

She pointed with extended finger to one of the mounds, and I saw that it was headed by a rough wooden board, almost buried in snow. To snatch a knife from my belt, and throw myself on my knees, and begin to scrape the coating of mingled ice and snow from this board, was the work of a few moments. Though it was of *her* I thought only, yet it was as if an irresistible force compelled me to stop, and to obey the command of that pointing hand. When I looked up I was alone beneath the wintry sky. My wife was gone. I *knew* then what I had *felt* from the first—that it was her shadow I had followed over that wintry waste, and that on earth she and I would never look upon each other again.

She had kept her promise as truly as I had broken mine. The gentle spirit had followed me to that desolate world in the very moment it was liberated from its earthly prison.

It was late that night when Hanley and his messmates found me lying senseless on the snow-mound, with the open knife beside my stiffening hand.

They brought me back to life somehow, and by the light of the lanterns they carried, we examined the board at the head of the mound. An inscription roughly cut upon it told us we had found the lost crew of the Ptarmigan.

'Here lies the body of Morris Haynes, commander of the Ptarmigan, who died in this unknown region, Jan. 30th, 1829, aged 35.'

The other mounds also had headboards bearing inscriptions, which we dug out from the snow on the following day, and carefully transcribed. After this we found a cairn containing empty provision-tins, in one of which was a book that had evidently been used for a journal ; but rust and snow had done their work, and of this journal nothing was decipherable but the name of the writer, Morris Haynes.

These investigations were not made by me. The new year found me laid low with rheumatic fever, and Frank Martyn had to take his turn as sick-nurse beside the snow-bank where I lay. Our provisions held out better than we had expected, thanks to the game our men shot, and the patience with which they endured privation. The spring came, and with it release. We contrived to make our way to Baffin's Bay,—a consummation I scarcely thought possible in my dreary reveries of mid-winter,—and a Greenland whaler brought us safely home.

I went straight to my brother-in-law's house at the West end of London. He was at home, and came without delay to the library where I had been ushered, and where I sat awaiting him with a gloomy face.

Yes ; as I expected : he was in mourning : and behind him came my sister, with a pale face, on which there was no smile of greeting.

Lawson held out both his hands to me.

'Richard,' he began in a faltering voice, 'God knows I never thought it possible I could be otherwise than glad of your coming home—but——'

'That will do,' I said ; 'you need tell me no more. My wife is dead.'

He bent his head solemnly.

'She died on the twenty-fifth of last December, at four o'clock in the afternoon.'

'You have been told, then,' cried my sister ; 'you have seen someone ?'

'Yes,' I answered, 'I have seen *her !*

MARJORIE DAW

A Household Idyl

IN TWO ACTS.

[Suggested by a Story written by T. B. ALDRICH.]

DRAMATIS PERSONÆ.

FRANK HEATHCOTE, *a painter*; JAMES LUTTRELL, *a surgeon*; MATILDA GRESLEY (otherwise MATTIE), *Frank's cousin*, MARY, *a servant*.

ACT I.

SCENE.—-*Heathcote's lodgings.   A room furnished as painting-room and sitting-room.   Easel, and all the belongings of an artist ; books ; a low easy-chair near the fire-place ; a window on the opposite side of stage.*

Enter LUTTRELL from adjoining bedroom.

LUTTRELL. He's horribly fretful and discontented this morning. Why is it, I wonder, that our superior sex is so very inferior to the weaker sex in its capacity for enduring bodily affliction ? My experience as a medical practitioner has convinced me that women beat us hollow in their power to suffer and be strong. If Job had been a woman I don't suppose we should have heard anything about him. Ah, here comes Mattie—dear little soul—a living instance of womanly patience and long-suffering. I'm sure her care of my old friend Frank is above all praise.

Enter MATTIE, plainly but prettily dressed.   She carries a neat little basket, a bunch of spring flowers, and a book.

LUTTRELL. Well, little woman, how are you this morning ?
MATTIE. How is *he* this morning ? That's the question. Did you ever hear of me being ill ? I've no time for any such expensive luxuries. I never remember being ill in my life since mother used to give me brimstone and treacle on spring mornings. *That* nearly did it. And that's my only experience of the healing art, Æscu—what's his name ?
LUTTRELL. You can call him Æsculapius if you like,

Robust little party! What would become of the medical profession if all women were like you?

MATTIE. I rather fancy the medical profession would die a natural death, and people in general would get better. But please tell me about *him*. How is he this morning?

LUTTRELL. About as irritable and low-spirited as a human being can be, short of lunacy or suicide. If I were not his old friend and schoolfellow I think I should resign my post of medical attendant.

MATTIE. No you wouldn't, you dear thing. You are much too kind-hearted.

LUTTRELL. Well, if *you* can bear with his airs and his tempers——

MATTIE. Neither airs nor tempers, poor dear—only low spirits.

LUTTRELL. That's a kinder way of putting it. If you can endure his low spirits for four or five hours at a stretch every day, I ought to put up with him placidly for twenty minutes.

MATTIE. Bear with him! put up with him! Am I not his own flesh and blood—his only surviving relation?

LUTTRELL. Something in the way of second cousins, aren't you?

MATTIE. Well, I know it's not a near relationship; and it's rather difficult to explain. My mother's first cousin married his father's sister, so I suppose Frank and I must be second cousins. But we were brought up together, don't you know? We are almost brother and sister.

LUTTRELL. Precisely—almost. But in that kind of connection there's a good deal of difference between "almost" and "quite."

MATTIE. He used to spend all his holidays at my mother's cottage, near Dorking, don't you know? Such a sweet little place, all over roses and honeysuckle—such a dear old garden, fruit and flowers all mixed up anyhow, where Frank and I used to make ourselves dreadfully ill with unripe gooseberries. Such a delicious little farm—two cows and a calf, and four pigs, and any number of Dorkings and Spaniards.

LUTTRELL. Dorkings and Spaniards?

MATTIE. Fowls, don't you know? While Frank was at Rugby he delighted in coming to us—drank gallons of new milk—revelled in fresh eggs—enjoyed haymaking—taught me to ride—learnt to milk the cows—declared there was nothing so delicious as a rustic life. But when he settled in London as a student at the Royal Academy, and boarded

with a very fashionable family in Gower Street, he seemed
somehow to outgrow mother's cottage. He was ever so much
too tall for our spare bedroom—sloping roof and window in
the gable, don't you know?—the last time he came to us.
And then—mother died—and I came to London to study
music at the Royal Academy, and to give lessons as soon as
I was able to teach; and I boarded with a—not at all
fashionable family, who didn't mind taking me cheap—and
I saw no more of Frank, till one day he and I ran against
each another in the Bayswater Road, and I found he was
living only two streets off my street, and that he had just begun
to be successful as a painter, and to be praised in the newspapers, when his sight began to fail him.

LUTTRELL. Very sad case. Cataract. But if next week's
operation results successfully, and we can keep him quiet
after it is over, he will be able to see as well as you or I.
The greatest difficulty we have to contend with is his mental
condition. If his present state of depression continue, I can't
answer for his health or his senses. Now, you're a bright,
clever little woman, Mattie. You really must try to amuse
him.

MATTIE. But, good gracious, I have been trying my very
hardest for the last ten days. I read to him the newest
books I can get hold of. Here's the last fashionable novel—
"She only said my life is dreary!" I skimmed it over as I
came from the library—heroine sixteen and a half—madly
in love with an ugly hero, aged forty-seven. Heroine has
run wild from infancy, never brushes her hair nor buttons her
boots. Hero hunts, shoots, swears a good deal, plays polo,
and makes love to heroine. Intensely interesting; but I
don't suppose Frank will care about it. I'm afraid I must
read rather badly, for he generally begins to yawn before I
get through a chapter.

LUTTRELL. How can you expect a man to enjoy boshy
novels all about girls who don't brush their hair?

MATTIE. Ought I to read him a story about men—Rob
Roy, Jack Sheppard, Paul Clifford?

LUTTRELL. My dear child, novels are no good in his case,
You must try and interest him in actualities—you must
divert his mind—take him out of himself—prevent his
brooding on his affliction.

MATTIE (*half crying*). Yes, but how am I to do it? I'm
sure I tell him every scrap of news I can think of. All about
the family I board with, the mother and daughters, and

aunts, and cousins. They are not a very interesting family, but they do quarrel now and then, and that makes them almost amusing. But they don't seem to interest Frank.

LUTTRELL. Of course not. How could he be interested in a shabby-genteel family, who eke out their income by taking boarders?

MATTIE. It's for the sake of the society. That was expressly stated in the advertisement. "A widow and her daughters. being desirous of cheerful and musical society, are willing——"

LUTTRELL. Of course, that's the style. But how long do you think they'd keep you for the sake of your cheerfulness and your music if you didn't pay for your board?

MATTIE. I'm afraid it wouldn't be very long.

LUTTRELL. Now, what you have to do is to amuse your cousin. Tell him about some one or something that will rouse his curiosity—awaken his interest.

MATTIE. I understand. But then you see I don't know any one of that kind.

LUTTRELL. What does that matter? You must draw on your imagination.

MATTIE. What, tell fibs?

LUTTRELL. Anything is better than to let Frank fret himself to death with gloomy anticipations about the operation and its result. I assure you I never saw any fellow in a worse state of mind.

MATTIE. I'll do it. I'd do anything for his good. And if I am led into doing anything very dreadful while he's ill, I can be a model of penitence when he gets better.

LUTTRELL. Of course you can. Here he comes. Good-bye.

[Exit LUTTRELL.

Enter HEATHCOTE, *feeling his way with a stick.* MATTIE *runs to meet him and guides him to easy-chair.*

MATTIE. Poor darling! I do hope you feel just a little better this morning.

HEATHCOTE. You oughtn't to hope anything so foolish. How can I be better till this wretched business is over? How can I take life easily when I don't know how this operation may result? Perhaps in total failure—life-long blindness! And just as I was beginning to make some way in my profession—just as I was beginning to make a name!

MATTIE. (*standing behind his chair, and looking over him.*)

It is very hard, dear, very hard.   But other people have had
to go through the same trial.

HEATHCOTE. Do you think that makes it a jot easier for
me? Other people! What do I care about other people?
What a plaintive little sigh! (*Taking her hand.*) I do care
about you, Mattie, and I do appreciate all your goodness to
me, my little sister of charity. What should I do without
you?

MATTIE. It might be just a little worse, mightn't it, if I
were not living close by, and able to run in and sit with you
for an hour or two. I've brought you a few spring flowers ;
primroses, violets. Don't they smell delicious? (*Offering
them.*)

HEATHCOTE. Rather sickly (*putting them aside*).   If I
could only see them! Ah, Mattie, if you could understand
what it is to a painter to lose the one sense which is the
source of all the happiness of his life--to hunger for light
and colour—to feel his occupation gone—his ambition
baulked—his existence reduced to a dismal, purposeless,
hopeless life in death, you would pity me, and forgive me
for my fretfulness.

MATTIE. I do pity you, dear, without understanding anything. And yet, though I am a poor ignorant little thing,
and never painted so much as a primrose, I think I can understand your feelings, in some small measure. I know how
hard it must be to have all this beautiful world of ours
darkened—not to see the sun, or the spring flowers—the
florist's in Westbourne Grove was a picture as I came by this
morning—or the clouds, or Whiteley's, or the Bayswater
Road. I feel quite sorry, too, that you can't see the big
house over the way.

HEATHCOTE. What, that great barrack of a house that has
been to let so long? I can endure that deprivation.

MATTIE. The house that was to let, you mean.

HEATHCOTE. You don't mean to say that it's let?

MATTIE. Yes, it was let a week ago.

HEATHCOTE. Why didn't you tell me?

MATTIE. I forgot—at least, if I didn't exactly forget, I
didn't think the news would be interesting to you.

HEATHCOTE. You're not generally so reticent. You tell
me all sorts of twaddle about those old maids you live with,
and their harridan of a mother, and when an actual event
takes place on the other side of the street you haven't a word
to say about it. When are the family coming in?

MATTIE. They are in.

HEATHCOTE. Impossible. Why the house was in an abominable state of dilapidation. It would want renovating from cellar to garret.

MATTIE. It has been done. Painted, and papered, and whitewashed, and dadoed, and everything.

HEATHCOTE. Dadoed ?

MATTIE. Yes, don't you know ? Beautiful dadoes of unpolished oak, and walnut, and cedar, in all the rooms. Nobody with any pretence to good taste can live in a room without a dado. So the house has been dadoed since the day before yesterday.

HEATHCOTE. Why, Aladdin's palace is nothing to this. Have these people the genius of the lamp at their command ?

MATTIE. No, but they have a silver mine in Mexico, and an account at Coutts's. And now it's time for your lunch. You must have your natives. (*Rings bell.*)

HEATHCOTE. I say, little woman, are not oysters rather an expensive luxury for a man in my circumstances ? There wasn't a very large amount in the exchequer when I made you chancellor. I'm afraid it must be running dry by this time.

MATTIE. Oh, no, there's plenty left. We shall get on very comfortably till your dividends come in ; or till you sell that lovely picture that is going to be in the Academy.

Maid brings in tray with luncheon.

HEATHCOTE. If the lovely picture is lucky enough to get hung. Oh, here are the oysters. Do have a few.

> [MATTIE *arranges tray, makes him comfortable, and then retires to extreme corner of stage, where she seats herself on a low hassock, takes out sock, and begins to knit.*]

MATTIE. No, thanks, I detest oysters. (*Aside*). I adore them, but I always feel as if I were swallowing threepenny pieces when I eat them. Poor fellow, if he only knew that I spent his last sixpence a week ago, and that we have nothing but my poor little purse to depend upon ! (*He takes an oyster.*) There goes threepence.

HEATHCOTE. Please tell me about the family over the way. I feel faintly interested. (*Eats an oyster, and another.*)

MATTIE. Sixpence—ninepence. You would be more than faintly interested if you could see them. Fifteenpence.

HEATHCOTE. Are they so very interesting?

MATTIE. Eighteenpence. She is.

HEATHCOTE. She? Who?

MATTIE. The daughter—an only daughter. The father is rather a commonplace person, don't you know? the sort of man who begins life with half-a-crown, and dies the owner of millions. Bought a silver mine for a barrel of whisky, a pug dog and a waterproof coat. Silver mine supposed to be worthless till he took it in hand, when he found the silver lying in slabs, like slices of bread and butter.

HEATHCOTE. And you say the girl is pretty?

MATTIE. Pretty is no word for her. She is absolutely lovely.

HEATHCOTE. I never think much of a woman's taste in beauty. Please describe her. Fair or dark?

MATTIE. Complexion fair—exquisitely fair, something between alabaster and ivory, with a faint rose tint. Eyes liquid blue, dark, like dewy violets, or sapphires—in short, the loveliest shade of blue you can imagine.

HEATHCOTE. Why not say ultramarine at once? Well, go on.

MATTIE. Features strictly classic, forehead low, nose delicately Greek, hair gently waving—dark chestnut in shadow, pure gold where the sun touches it.

HEATHCOTE. Very sweet, but those Greek beauties are apt to be namby-pamby.

MATTIE. Not with her expression—such a speaking countenance—such variety—even emotion reflected in her face.

HEATHCOTE. I see—face perfect, but figure quisby.

MATTIE. Figure as perfect as her face—about the middle height, slender, yet plump—dignified, yet full of graceful movement — waist willowy — shoulders a poem—arms a sculptor's dream.

HEATHCOTE. If you are not exaggerating——

MATTIE (*with a virtuous air*). Exaggerate! Did you ever know me exaggerate?

HEATHCOTE. No, little woman. You are the very essence of truth. And if your enthusiasm has not run away with you in this particular instance, Miss Whatshername must be a very sweet creature. By-the-way, what is her name?

MATTIE (*puzzled*). Name? Her name?

HEATHCOTE. Yes. She has a name, I suppose.

MATTIE, *swaying backwards and forwards on the hassock, and softly singing to herself, "See-saw, Marjorie Daw."*

HEATHCOTE. Do you mean to say your womanly curiosity has not found out the name of these silver mine people?

MATTIE. Why, yes, of course. My mind was wandering a little. (*Jerkily*) Her name is—Daw.

HEATHCOTE. Daw?

MATTIE. Daw. D A W, Daw

HEATHCOTE. Daw, spelt with a D A W! Miss Daw. What a queer name!

MATTIE. Very uncommon, isn't it?

HEATHCOTE. I should have preferred something more patrician —Vavasour, or Ponsonby, or something of that kind.

MATTIE. But, don't you see, Frank, her father rose from the ranks. Bought the silver mine for a pair of waterproof boots, a pony, and a barrel of oysters.

HEATHCOTE. You said coat, pug dog, and whisky.

MATTIE (*innocently*). Did I? Then I've no doubt it was whisky. (*Aside*) I'm afraid his interest is flagging.

HEATHCOTE. What is Miss Daw's Christian name?

MATTIE. Christian name?

HEATHCOTE. Yes. I suppose they christen girls, even in San Francisco.

MATTIE. Of course. Her name is Marjorie. Poetical, isn't it?

HEATHCOTE. Rather Arcadian; but I should have preferred Isabel, or Gwendoline, Mildred, Violet. Marjorie! Yes, it is pretty! But Daw—I cannot admire Daw. Marjorie Daw. I have a vague idea that I have heard that name before.

MATTIE. Perhaps you have met with it in poetry.

HEATHCOTE. Possibly. It sounds familiar. (*With languid interest.*) And now tell me all you know about this Californian goddess. You women have a marvellous knack of picking up waifs and strays of information from butchers. and bakers, and candlestick makers. Is she what girls call nice?

MATTIE. She is simply perfect. And (*with dignity*) I am happy to say my knowledge of her character has *not* been derived from butchers, makers, or candlestick bakers, but from personal experience. Miss Daw and I are acquainted.

HEATHCOTE. What, she has only been in the neighbourhood two days, and you and she are acquainted ? Did you call upon her ? I should never have thought you so pushing.

MATTIE. I am not pushing, and I did not what you call *call* on her, though I had the right to do so, as the older inhabitant (*softly*). Accident made us friends. You remember that violent shower yesterday afternoon.

HEATHCOTE. Yes, I heard the rain rattling against the windows, and I could not help thinking how exquisite the spring foliage in the lanes beyond Croydon would look after such a shower.

MATTIE. I was out in that very shower.

HEATHCOTE. Poor little woman !

MATTIE. And, what's more, I had on my best bonnet. I had been giving a lesson in Pembridge Square—very stylish pupil—nothing less than a best bonnet would do for *her* ; and just as I was turning the corner to come to you, I was caught in that dreadful shower. It came upon me like an avalanche. I looked round wildly, with a vague hope of an omnibus in a street where omnibuses never come, as you know. I had no umbrella. I suppose my distress was visible in my attitude and countenance, for the door of the big house suddenly opened, and a powdered footman ran across the road carrying an immense umbrella—almost as big as a marquee—and most politely requested me to step indoors.

HEATHCOTE. But, good gracious, child, why didn't you come here ? You must have been as near this house as that one. Why stand in the street and make a spectacle of yourself for powdered footmen ?

MATTIE (*laughing faintly*). Do you know that never occurred to me. It was rather absent-minded of me, was it not ? but you know I *am* absent-minded. It was the shock of the avalanche—the shower—I suppose. Well, the footman was so crushingly polite that I could not say a word. I went across the street like a lamb, and allowed myself to be ushered up into Miss Daw's morning-room, on the first floor, exactly opposite this. Such a room, I feel myself powerless to describe it.

HEATHCOTE. Skip the description of the room—I don't care much for still-life, except in one of my own pictures—and come to the lady.

MATTIE. Oh, but the lady and the room made one harmonious whole. I could not possibly divide them. Picture to yourself a lovely dark-haired girl against a background of creamy satin.

HEATHCOTE. Dark-haired. Why, you said she was fair.

MATTIE. Did I? Yes, of course, *she* is fair, complexion alabaster, but hair chestnut—I think I said dark chestnut.

HEATHCOTE. Well, perhaps you did. Women have so little feeling for colour. But I know there was something about sunshine, and golden lights, and I have pictured *my* Miss Daw with golden hair.

MATTIE. Imagine a girl with a profusion of golden hair, against a background of sage-green velvet.

HEATHCOTE. You said creamy satin.

MATTIE. Certainly. The room is upholstered in panels— alternate panels of sage-green velvet and cream-coloured satin

HEATHCOTE. Wasn't that rather a spotty effect?

MATTIE. Not in the least. I tell you the room is an ideal room. I don't believe there is such another in London. And she so sweet, so caressing! She received me like a sister.

HEATHCOTE. Very bad form. I detest gush.

MATTIE. Oh, but you would like it in *her*. She is so natural, so confiding!

HEATHCOTE. And she lives in the room just opposite this —like a beautiful bird in a golden cage. I am positively beginning to be interested in her. I have made a picture of her in my mind. I love that creamy complexion—those liquid grey eyes—I think you said liquid grey.

MATTIE (*aside*). Haven't the least idea. (*Aloud, eagerly*) Yes, that's her colour. (*Aside*) And now I must stick to it.

HEATHCOTE. Pretty bird! What does it do with itself all day long in its cage?

MATTIE. Sings—and plays.

HEATHCOTE. Sings?

MATTIE. Divinely. A rich mezzo-soprano—old English ballads—Shakespeare, Bishop.

HEATHCOTE. Cruel! Why doesn't she leave her window open?

MATTIE. Too east-windy. But she will leave it open, no doubt, when the weather gets a little warmer.

HEATHCOTE. And then I shall hear her. "Where the Bee Sucks," "A Little Western Flower," and that kind of thing, eh?

MATTIE. Precisely. (*Aside*) How delightful to arouse his interest!

HEATHCOTE. And what other amusements has Miss Daw?

MATTIE. Why don't you call her Marjorie? it's so much

HEATHCOTE. So it is. (*Fatuously*) Marjorie! My Marjorie —what a pretty alliteration.

MATTIE. As for her amusements—well—she paints.

HEATHCOTE. Not her complexion, I hope.

MATTIE. Her complexion—the untrodden snow—alabaster —ivory.   No; she paints flowers, almost equal to Mrs. Angel's.   She paints plums, and birds' nests, and primroses, and blue china.

HEATHCOTE. That is to say, she is strikingly original in her choice of subjects.   What else?

MATTIE. She reads—she works.

HEATHCOTE. What kind of work?

MATTIE. Crewel.

HEATHCOTE. Cruel!   Surely not vivisection?

MATTIE. Good   gracious,   no.   Crewel—C R E W E L. High art, wool work, don't you know? Storks and sunflowers.

HEATHCOTE. What else?

MATTIE. Sunflowers and storks.

HEATHCOTE. Isn't that rather monotonous?

MATTIE. Perhaps, but it's the highest style of art.   I think she occasionally makes a new departure, and goes in for a flamingo.

HEATHCOTE. Well, and after being received like a sister, and given tea (of course you had tea)——

MATTIE. Yes, *the* most delicious tea, in *the* most adorable tea-pot, and *the* loveliest egg-shell cups and saucers.

HEATHCOTE. After having sworn eternal friendship (of course you swore eternal friendship)——

MATTIE. We kissed each other, and I promised to take her to Whiteley's.

HEATHCOTE. That means   eternal friendship — till you quarrel.   After having plunged into this delightful intimacy, pray, what did you talk about?

MATTIE. I'm almost afraid to tell you.   It might make you angry.

HEATHCOTE. Angry?   No.   I am so intensely interested in your Daw, that——

MATTIE. Please don't call her my Daw.

HEATHCOTE. Well, then, in my Marjorie.   I have made such a vivid picture of the little puss, that I shall enjoy hearing what you talked about, if it were ever such twaddle.

MATTIE (*with dignity*). It was not twaddle.   We talked about you.

HEATHCOTE. About me!   Come, that's too much of a good thing.

MATTIE. I was afraid you'd be angry. But you know, Frank, when one is continually thinking of a person it's almost impossible to avoid talking about that person (*leaning over the back of his chair, coaxingly*) ; and since you have been a sufferer, dear, I have never had you out of my thoughts.

HEATHCOTE. Dear tender-hearted little Mattie ! (*Kissing the hand which hangs over his chair.*) How shall I ever be grateful enough to you for all your goodness to me ? And so you spoke of me to Marjorie ?

MATTIE. Yes, dear. I told her how clever you are, and how splendidly you were getting on in your profession before this unfortunate business about your eyes, and she was so intensely interested—so sympathetic. " Poor—dear—fellow !" she said ; and the tears stood in her eyes—those lovely dark-grey eyes—-as she said it. She is *so* tender-hearted.

HEATHCOTE. " Poor, dear fellow." How nice it sounds.

MATTIE. I told her about your lovely picture—Launcelot and Guinevere riding through the wood—and she is going to the Academy on the opening day to see it. I told her there would be a dreadful crush, but she said she would risk any-thing to see your Launcelot and Guinevere.

HEATHCOTE. How do you know the picture will not be rejected ?

MATTIE. I have an instinct which tells me it will be hung, and on the line. I should not wonder if they were obliged to have a railing round it, and a couple of policemen to keep off the crowd, before the season is over.

HEATHCOTE. Mattie, you are a silly little thing ; but your foolishness is much more comforting than other people's wisdom in the hour of trouble. And so Marjorie was really interested in—my picture ?

MATTIE. Your picture and you—especially you. She likes your eyes, and she rather admires your forehead. If she has a fault to find, it is with your chin.

HEATHCOTE. What are you talking about ?

MATTIE. Oh, I forgot to mention that I showed her your photograph.

HEATHCOTE (*pleased*). How absurd ! Which attitude ?

MATTIE. The dreamy one. (*Throws herself into an exag-gerated attitude across the back of a chair.*) The one in which you are gazing into space, with that lovely far-away look I am so fond of.

HEATHCOTE. Mattie, you are too ridiculous ! And she liked the photo ?

MATTIE. She thought it simply lovely.

HEATHCOTE. Except the chin. She did not approve of my chin ?

MATTIE. She fancied there was a faint indication of weakness—that you might falter in the pursuit of a purpose.

HEATHCOTE. Not if it were worth pursuing—not if it were the winning of a lovely, innocent, fresh young creature like Marjorie.

MATTIE. And with a million of money. Don't forget the money.

HEATHCOTE. I wish to forget it. Why do you remind me of it ? Don't you know that it must create an impassable barrier between us ?

MATTIE. Not a bit of it. You don't know what a liberal-minded man her father is—a man who began life with half-a-crown. He is passionately devoted to Art. I believe he would be very proud if his daughter were to marry a famous painter.

HEATHCOTE. Then I must make myself famous—if—the light of day ever dawn again in my miserable life. I must work as man never worked—strive as man never strove—to win so sweet a reward. Mattie, you are sure she really was interested in me. It was not sham ? You are not fooling me ?

MATTIE. (*guiltily*). Fooling you ! Oh, Frank how *can* you suspect me of such a thing ?

HEATHCOTE. There is a quaver in your voice. If I could only see your face I should know. That frank, bright little face could never look a falsehood. Forgive me, darling. I know how true you are—true as steel. And she does really sympathise with me in my trouble—she did really rather admire my photo ?

MATTIE. Really—really—really. (*Aside*) Oh, I hope I am not going too far.

HEATHCOTE. Mattie, you are my good angel. You have filled me with hope. I will give way to despondency no more. I feel that my sight *will* be restored—that I shall once more be able to work at the art I love—that I shall win wealth and reputation—and that Marjorie will be mine. And to think that she is there—so near me—in all her beauty and sweetness, and that I cannot see her. (*Walking about the room.*)

MATTIE. Oh, pray be careful. You'll hurt yourself against the furniture.

HEATHCOTE. (*Throwing open the window.*) Oh, for the blessed sense of sight—if it were but for a moment—just for one glimpse of the fair young face. Is she at the window now?

MATTIE. No. She has gone for a drive.

Enter LUTTRELL.

LUTTRELL. Well, Frank. (HEATHCOTE *takes no notice of him.*) Well, little woman, how is he? Why, what have you been doing to him? He looks a new man—radiant—positively transfigured.

MATTIE. Yes, it's all my doing. He has fallen violently in love with Miss Daw.

LUTTRELL. Miss Daw? What Daw? I never heard of a Daw.

MATTIE. The young lady over the way.

LUTTRELL. Which young lady?

MATTIE. Hush! It's all right. I've been drawing on my imagination.

ACT II.

SCENE *as in* ACT I., *but the window is open, and there are brighter flowers, as with advancing spring.*

MATTIE (*discovered dusting the furniture*). I never met with a housemaid who knew how to dust a room properly. Their only notion is to drive the dust into corners and leave it there. And I want all the furniture to look its brightest and its best to-day, when my poor Frank is to see it all again, after living so long in sorrow and darkness, uncertainty, and fear. I want the very chairs and tables to smile a welcome at him, when he comes out of his prison-house into the glad light of day. I'm very glad it's a fine day. I should have felt angry with the weather if it had been rainy, and dull, and unsympathetic. (*Folds up her duster, and seats herself by the little wicker table.*) Oh, dear, dear! I don't think I ever felt so unhappy in the whole course of my life—just when I ought to feel so intensely happy.

Enter LUTTRELL.

LUTTRELL. Well, little woman, I congratulate you.

MATTIE. About the result of the operation? (*Dolefully.*) Yes, it's a great blessing that it turned out so successfully.

LUTTRELL. Of course it is; but you don't seem altogether cheerful about it.

MATTIE. Cheerful! I am positively miserable! I feel the guiltiest creatures in the universe. It's all your fault, Mr. Luttrell. You told me to draw upon my imagination, and I drew. I never knew that I had any imagination : but when once I began to draw it came with such a flow that it quite took my breath away. And now what am I to do ? For the last six days poor Frank has been living upon thoughts of Marjorie Daw. She has been his all-absorbing idea by day, his dream by night ; and to-day he is to come out of his darkened room into the sunshine, and he is to see *her*. That is his only thought. His friends—his profession are as nothing to him. He is full of gratitude to Providence for his restored sight ; but it is because he is to see Majorie Daw. And when he discovers——

LUTTRELL. That you have been romancing——

MATTIE. Romancing? That I have been wading up to my neck in falsehood—that I have hardly ever opened my lips within the last week except to tell him some stupendous fib, what will he think of me? But it is all your fault. You set me going, and I have been obliged to go on. The conversations that I have invented between Miss Daw and myself, all about Frank—the afternoon teas that I have described, to the very flavour of the bread and butter—the messages that I have given him—the flowers she has sent him—the books she has lent me to read to him—the favourite passages in her favourite poets that she has marked for him—the delicate attentions of every kind that she has paid him—through me. All these wicked falsehoods have been the occupation of his mind—the delight of his life. The blow will be absolutely crushing.

LUTTRELL. Pooh! pooh? He can't be so much the slave of a fancy.

MATTIE. Perhaps you have no idea how poetical I am when I give full play to my imagination. No young man of ardent temperament could help falling in love with my Marjorie Daw.

LUTTRELL. If I were Frank I would much rather fall in love with you. Yes, Mattie, I would rather have one honest-hearted, self-sacrificing little woman like you than a whole ship-load of Marjorie Daws. And I think if Frank had a spark of gratitude——

MATTIE. Oh, don't, please don't! I hate the word. I would not have his gratitude for all the world.

LUTTRELL. Because you would so much rather have his love.

MATTIE. (*drawing herself up indignantly.*) Mr. Luttrell, you are extremely impertinent.

LUTTRELL. I think I am very pertinent. What more natural than that you two should love each other ? Are there not all the tender associations of childhood and youth to unite you—all those sweet, half-mournful memories of the past which make the strongest bond between two souls ? Do you think a young lady over the way—were she the loveliest girl in creation—could ever be so dear to Frank as the little girl he played with in the woods and meadows in life's cloudless morning ? His fancy might be caught by the beautiful stranger, but his heart would be faithful to the little sweetheart of his boyhood. I'll wager you were sweethearts once upon a time, and that you swore you would marry no one else.

MATTIE. There might have been something of that kind— but we were such babies. It is all forgotten now. I am much too homely a person for Frank to think about, except as a humble friend. He wants something beautiful—stately— "a daughter of the gods, divinely fair, and as divinely tall." He wants just such a perfect creature as my fancy has depicted for him in Marjorie Daw. And when twelve o'clock strikes he is to come out of that dark room, and he has made me promise that Marjorie shall be at her window—and, oh, Mr. Luttrell, what am I to do ? (*Looking at her watch.*) Ten minutes to twelve ! In ten minutes he will know what a vile impostor I am, and he will detest me.

LUTTRELL. Nonsense ! He may be just a little vexed, but it will soon blow over.

MATTIE. Ten minutes ! I wish some good fairy would stop all the church clocks in Bayswater—or that there would be an earthquake—or that the very worst of Mother Shipton's prophecies about the ending of the world were going to be realised this very minute. He will hear the clock strike, and there will be no possibility of getting a moment's delay. You won't go away, will you ?

LUTTRELL. No, no. I'll back you up.

MATTIE. How I wish *something* would happen ! (*Loud knock and ring at street door.*) Good gracious, what's that ?

LUTTRELL. Miss Daw, perhaps. (MATTIE *runs out.*) Poor little thing, how fond she is of him, and how innocently unconscious of her feelings ! His heart must be as hard as the nether millstone if he can remain unresponsive to such affection. But if he should, perhaps someone else might profit by his folly.

MATTIE (*rushing back*). Such good news ! Such delightful

news! Young Green, the water-colour painter, has just called to say that Frank's picture has been accepted and will be hung on the line. He heard it from a benevolent old R.A., who is on the Hanging Committee, and who has so long forgotten how to paint, that he has left off being spiteful to rising talent. Isn't that lovely?

LUTTRELL. Very much so. This will put Miss Daw out of Frank's head. (*Clock strikes twelve.*)

HEATHCOTE (*calling*). Luttrell. Mattie.

> [LUTTRELL *goes into adjoining room and returns immediately, leading* HEATHCOTE, *with a silk handkerchief tied across his eyes.*

HEATHCOTE. But I tell you the bandage is quite unnecessary. Critchett said I might leave my dark room to-day—he didn't say anything about a bandage.

LUTTRELL. Ah, but I'm sure he meant it. To bring you into the glare of day all at once would never do. We must let you down gently.

MATTIE (*leading him on the other side*). Yes, we must let you down gently. There you are, in your favourite arm-chair (*forcing him to sit down*), and there at your elbow is a too-lovely Marshal Niel, in a specimen glass.

HEATHCOTE. A hothouse flower. Did *she* send it?

MATTIE. Ye—es. *She* sent it. (*Aside*) *She* gave her very last shilling for it, half an hour ago.

HEATHCOTE. God bless her! (*Trying to remove bandage.* MATTIE *lays her hands gently upon it, restraining him.*)

LUTTRELL. I say, old fellow, we have such glorious news for you!

MATTIE. Such glorious news!

HEATHCOTE (*starting up*). She is coming! She is on the stairs! Let me go to meet her.

LUTTRELL. No, no, ever so much better than that.

MATTIE. He and she—Launcelot and Guinevere—are to be on the line. In less than six weeks all London will be raving about your picture. Mr. Green called just now to say that the Hanging Committee accepted it with rapture, and that you are looked upon as *the* painter of the future.

HEATHCOTE. And she will see my picture! Does she know? Have you told her?

LUTTRELL. Told whom?

HEATHCOTE. Marjorie.

MATTIE. No, there hasn't been time enough. Mr. Green only called a few minutes ago.

HEATHCOTE. But she *will* know. Mattie, you did not forget your promise? You asked her to be at the window when twelve o'clock struck? She is there now—waiting—and I sit here like a log. Let me go, Luttrell. (*They both restrain him.*)

MATTIE (*falteringly*). The fact is—we have a kind of a surprise for you.

HEATHCOTE. I hope it is a pleasant one.

MATTIE. Well, I am sorry to say it is rather in the nature of a disappointment   Miss Daw——

HEATHCOTE. Mattie, you are trembling—your voice falters —some calamity—is she dead?

MATTIE (*quickly*). Oh, dear no! Not the least little bit.

HEATHCOTE. She is ill?

MATTIE. She never was better.

HEATHCOTE (*breaking loose from them, and throwing off the bandage*). Then why do you try to humbug me? I tell you I will see her—and at once. If she is not at her window—if you have broken faith with me—I will go across to her house and call upon her. She has given me the right, by her sympathy, by her interest in me and my affliction. (MATTIE *interposes herself between him and the window.*) Why do you try to stop me?

MATTIE. Because you haven't heard my little surprise. Oh, please, please don't be quite too awfully angry with me —but—you know the big house over the way?

HEATHCOTE. Yes.

MATTIE. Which was to let so long?

HEATHCOTE (*impatiently*). Of course.

MATTIE. It is still empty.

HEATHCOTE. And the Californian millionaire—the dadoes —the sage-green satin—the peacocks' feather—the blue china?

MATTIE. All my imagination—invented to keep you amused, when you were so dreadfully low-spirited, and when Mr. Luttrell said you must have your mind occupied somehow.

HEATHCOTE. And Marjorie—my Marjorie—the girl with the liquid grey eyes——

MATTIE. Never had any existence, except in the old nursery rhyme.

(*Sings.*)   See Saw, Marjorie Daw,
         Sold her bed to lie upon straw.
         Wasn't she a dirty slut
         To sell her bed, and lie upon dirt?

HEATHCOTE (*terribly overcome*). And I have fallen in love with a shadow——

LUTTRELL. While you neglected the substance.

HEATHCOTE. Mattie, you have broken my heart. (*Goes to window and looks across street.*) A blank. Windows darkened by the dirt of years—stucco dilapidated—all emptiness and ruin where I had filled my mind with images of light and colour—a fairy palace with a fairy queen to reign over it—flowers, brightness, sweetness, and love—love unutterable—born of divine compassion—nourished by a fond belief in my genius. Nothing in this life was ever more real or more vivid for me than this girl's image—and it is a mockery—a lie. Mattie, I can never forgive you.

MATTIE (*making faces at* LUTTRELL). See what you have done.

LUTTRELL. My dear Heathcote, I am the chief offender. I urged upon Mattie the necessity of interesting and amusing you somehow—at any sacrifice of truth.

MATTIE (*despondently*). He told me to draw upon my imagination, and I drew. Very strict people might call it story-telling, but it wasn't meant in that way.

HEATHCOTE. But when you saw that my heart was becoming engaged why did you not then tell me the truth? Why lead me from folly to folly—playing upon my vanity—fostering my self-love—giving me sweetest messages—describing her lovely looks—her smiles—her tears—smiles and tears for me—giving me flowers which her lips had kissed—flowers that I have worn next my heart, and kissed and cried over in the dead of the night. And my tears—my dreams—my passionate longing, have been wasted on a shadow—a creature who never existed.

MATTIE. I'm dreadfully sorry, Frank; but I hope I haven't done you any serious wrong. This fancy of yours for an imaginary being can't be any worse than falling in love with the hero of a novel. I'm sure when I was twelve and a-half I was in love with Guy Livingstone to such a degree that I left off taking any interest in dinner.

HEATHCOTE (*leaning on the back of a chair and looking across the street*). She never lived! The fair young face—

the heart that was almost mine. All lies—lies—lies ! Mattie, I never will—I never can forgive you.

MATTIE (*half crying with gentle seriousness*). I am sorry for that, Frank, because I don't think I have quite deserved your anger. In all the long dreary time while the light of day was turned to darkness for you—when your thoughts, having no pleasant objects to dwell upon, turned inwards on yourself and your own troubles, I did my best to comfort and amuse you. And when Mr. Luttrell told me that your mind was getting into a bad way—that your thoughts must be diverted at any price—I invented Marjorie Daw. I did not think your feelings were so easily engaged : you and I have known each other a long time, and you have never fallen in love with me—and I thought when your sight came back you and I would have a hearty laugh over Miss Daw and her perfections. But I see now how wrong I have been, and I am very—very sorry. Good-bye, Frank (*Going.*)

LUTTRELL. Nonsense, little woman ; you are not going away.

MATTIE. Yes, I am ; and, what is more, I am never coming back again. He says he can never forgive me, and no doubt the very sight of me is disagreeable to him, as I must remind him of Marjorie Daw. He has regained his sight—he can resume his profession—and he doesn't want me any more. There are plenty of real Marjorie Daws in this world. He has only to go and look for one of them. Good-bye, Frank.

LUTTRELL (*seizing her by the hand as she is leaving the room*) Stop, Mattie, you must, you shall stay till he has asked you to forgive him, on his knees. Heathcote, are you a fool as well as an ingrate ? Are you so young in the experience of life that you don't know the difference between reality and romance—that you are a slave to the vision of a beautiful face, and have no eyes for the real worth at your elbow—no heart for the truthful, unselfish girl who has watched over your hours of trouble and lightened all your cares by her devoted attention, her unfailing good] temper, her inexhaustible patience? No, Mattie (*as she tries to break from him*), you shall not go till you have heard me testify to the worth of the noblest heart I ever met with in woman. You have been blind for the last month, Heathcote, but I have been able to see, and I have seen this little woman's devotion ; and if you do not reward it by the tribute of a faithful heart, I at least have given her mine. Yes, Mattie, it is yours—my heart and hand are both at your disposal if you will have them. You will make me the proudest and happiest man in Bayswater if you say yes. Oh, Mattie, why do you turn from me so coldly? Don't look at Frank in that appealing way. He does not want you. He only wants Marjorie Daw.

HEATHCOTE. But I do want her—I should be utterly miserable without her. Luttrell, I am beholden to you for showing me what an ass I have been—a most egregious ass. But you are not going to steal Mattie away from me. You can have Marjorie Daw. She was your invention—or at any rate your suggestion, you know.

MATTIE. Oh, yes, she really was your suggestion.

HEATHCOTE. Mattie, can you ever bring yourself to forgive me?

MATTIE. You said you would never—could never—forgive me.

HEATHCOTE. That was in the first paroxysm of disappointment. But—I am resigned to the loss of Marjorie.

MATTIE. And the Californian silver mine?

HEATHCOTE. Come, Mattie, do me the justice to own that I never cared for the silver mine. My passion was disinterested. I am resigned to the loss of that fair vision—if—if the dear reality will be kind and forgiving.

LUTTRELL. And I suppose I am to be left out in the cold.

MATTIE. Oh, I am very sorry, for you are so good and so nice, but you know Frank and I were engaged when we were babies.

HEATHCOTE. Never mind, old fellow. So long as you are a solitary bachelor you shall always have a chair by our fireside, and shall always be made much of by us both, in remembrance of your goodness during the time of trouble. Mattie, dear, do you really and truly love me, or are you only pretending? You know you are very good at make-believe.

MATTIE. I have loved you all my life!

HEATHCOTE. And one such constant and faithful love is worth all the visions of loveliness that were ever invented. Mattie, if Providence ever blesses us with a daughter she shall be christened MARJORIE DAW.

———

London: J. & R. MAXWELL, 35, St. Bride Street, E.C.

| Rt 211 | 5/86 | G 78 |